The Travelling City

Adrienne Miller

Copyright © 2023 Adrienne Miller

All rights reserved.

ISBN: 9798396937192

DEDICATION

For Anna and Rory. I'm sure you already know what I'd say.

CONTENTS

1   Chapter 1: Reihan   9

2   Chapter 2: Reihan   25

3   Chapter 3: Reihan   42

4   Chapter 4: Phillippe   55

5   Chapter 5: Ellis   71

6   Chapter 6: Reihan   83

7   Chapter 7: Phillippe   110

8   Chapter 8: Reihan   119

9   Chapter 9: Phillippe   144

10   Chapter 10: Ellis   157

11   Chapter 11: Reihan   166

12   Chapter 12: Reihan   181

13   Chapter 13: Phillippe   196

14   Chapter 14: Reihan   210

15   Chapter 15: Ellis   220

16   Chapter 16: Phillippe   233

17	Chapter 17: Reihan	247
18	Chapter 18: Reihan	260
19	Chapter 19: Reihan	279
20	Chapter 20: Ellis	292
21	Chapter 21: Reihan	308
22	Chapter 22: Phillippe	320
23	Chapter 23: Reihan	337
24	Chapter 24: Ellis	350
25	Chapter 25: Reihan	362
26	Chapter 26: Phillippe	376
27	Chapter 27: Reihan	388
28	Chapter 28: Reihan	400
29	Chapter 29: Reihan	416
	Author Bio	429

CHAPTER 1: REIHAN

The Travelling City was a closely monitored paradise of euphoria. A place where every thought could be turned into reality, and every new reality spread like the most seductive sickness. Much of the city's history had been washed over by ever-renewing fantasies of what life could be like. And most of its inhabitants did not care which version they lived in as long as life continued in a way that suited them.

Growing up in the Travelling City was dangerous, and its inhabitants did not value children. Every new person posed the risk of tipping over the precarious balance the colony had carved out, where humans could use their manifestation abilities to cause life-ending catastrophes. Often unattended and wild amidst the chaos of everyday life, many children fell to their deaths, tumbling over the cliff edges of the Travelling City's rock face and descending deep into the cloud sea. Some turned each other to stone and could not turn back in time. Some disappeared, wandering the lightless streets at night, never to be found again.

Most parents knew and accepted this. It was the way things

had always been. But some were eaten up by grief and begged the dead gods and the universe to return their children for a second chance. The most reckless and desperate amongst them created manifested copies of their lost offspring, their longing and love shaping reality until it gave them what they thought they wanted. Those false children, first celebrated and coddled upon their arrival, inevitably failed to live up to their parents' memories. Soon, they became unwanted shadows haunting the Travelling City's streets, feral and confused, banded together like dogs to survive. They stole and killed and could not understand why their bodies turned this way or that as their parents' impression of them changed.

Some parents had enough good sense to put their creations to rest before they caused too much harm. For the others, Reihan and the Enforcers were called.

One of the visitors to the Asylum had spotted a small colony of shadows in one of the abandoned settlements just below the Weeping Stairs. There had long been talk that the streets of the abandoned district were haunted, and now the rumours had been proven correct. A troop of Enforcers from the Artisans' Quarters was asked to investigate, and given the location one of the Asylum seaver was obligated to accompany them. Reihan had volunteered for the job. She didn't relish the idea of returning to patrol, but she did not want one of her junior colleagues to be chosen for it.

That's just how it goes, she mused as she walked behind the Enforcers, who were nervously chattering amongst themselves. *The Asylum attracts bad energies. Unwanted, lost things feel at home here.* She felt her sword heavy by her side. It was too much to hope that today wouldn't end in death. One had to be realistic about these things.

The abandoned buildings grew on either side of their path like the ribcage of a giant beast, its edges uncaressed by light. The deeper they pushed into the quiet district, the more the Enforcers fell silent, their steps on stone-hewn streets a beat that matched their quickening hearts. Reihan pushed forward, guessing at the men's fears. As a seaver, manifestations did not affect her, rendering her safer than the humans surrounding her.

Nobody protested their change in formation. The skies were full of clouds, but down here they were protected from the madness. The rock face painted deep shadows onto the streets, a melancholic set of colours that dripped into the heavy air. Reihan hadn't been surprised when she'd heard that the district had been abandoned. Humans needed light to function. It was only the seaver who were able to traverse the darkness they left behind.

Finally, they found the shadow children. They were too tired to move, having lived on the energies of their parents' initial manifestations for too long. With dull eyes, they glanced upward, uncomprehending what they saw. Now they were little more than old pets who had to be laid to rest. Reihan heard silent groans and fluttering breaths behind her and, not for the first time, remembered how young this group of Enforcers was. Barely of age, they were already asked to cut down the helpless, crude human copies in front of them. Reihan glanced across the swarm of shadows. They had huddled into the space between two buildings, deeply nested in the darkness where their bodies had started to blur together. Pairs of dull eyes swimming in a sea of black.

"Mother?", a voice echoed from the chorus of beings, and she did not know who had spoken. One of the Enforcers cursed quietly. Reihan closed her eyes for a moment, then shook her head.

"I don't need you. Stay back."

"That isn't protocol, seaver", the leader of the Enforcers replied, a tall man whose name she had already forgotten. She could hear the hesitation in his voice, but he knew his place. Reihan gave him a small smile.

"You know you are not allowed to question my orders. I need you to watch the perimeter in case of any surprise attacks."

Both knew that there would not be any forthcoming attacks. The shades were too weak to move, let alone conjure a beast to ravage them. The Enforcers nonetheless formed a half-circle around Reihan, looking out towards the black tower-like buildings rather than down at the dying shades. Reihan pulled out her sword, hearing the blade sing in the open air.

"Mother", the shades repeated, all eyes looking up at her in a single motion. Reihan shook her head in distaste. The children had merged into one being now, and it was slowly becoming one with the darkness that surrounded them. *Why does it always have to be me?*

She brought down her sword, and the pleas turned to wailing. Sick, suffering copies though they were, the children cried as they died, as they felt each other die in the darkness. There was barely any weight beneath her blade as Reihan cut through bodies, arms, and legs, but somehow the children's voices rang within her head all the same.

When she was done, she panted, leaning against her sword. The troops turned around. Reihan couldn't read their emotions at first, but she hoped for gratitude or at least for pity.

"Do you declare the mission complete?", their leader asked in a strained voice.

"She's killed them all", one of the men whispered to his comrade.

"Thank god", muttered a third, "Only a machine could do this."

"Let's go", Reihan said with a heavy voice, "I have to return to the Asylum."

They always wanted to trade. No matter who came to the Asylum, whether it was a parent, a sibling, a friend, or a concerned neighbour, they all thought there was a bargain to be made. As if Reihan and the other seaver could be convinced to do the right thing with enough honey-dripping words or sweet-laced tears. Maybe the humans thought that the seaver wanted to keep them all here.

The man in front of her was no exception.

"What can I do?", he repeated. Reihan shook her head, more an implication than a response, then pulled the registration sheet closer.

"Tell me your name", she asked, in the same tone she used

for everyone. There was no real benefit to modulating her approach to accommodate the different visitors' emotions. She just didn't understand humans well enough.

"Phillippe. And this is Alexander", he replied, gesturing at the man beside him. They shared the same skin and the same eyes, but Alexander's were unfocused, blankly moving with the random sways of his body. They had tied him around the chair for convenience, even at Phillippe's repeated protestations.

"That's fine", she said, taking note of both their names, "And you said you are brothers?"

"Yes", Phillippe responded quickly, as if the speed of his answers would have an effect on the outcome. Another common, yet pointless thing humans did.

"All right, Phillippe. How did this happen?"

"Well, we –"

Phillippe's eyes grew almost as glossy as his brother's, and for a moment, Reihan wondered if he had also been infected by the madness that lurked beneath the rock face, seeping up from the sea of clouds.

"We went past the Undercity", he explained, "Down to the *World's End*."

"The pub?", Reihan clarified.

Phillippe nodded.

"You know that's past the recommended borderline, right?"

"Well, yes. We did – we do."

"And so why would you go there?"

Phillippe's eyes narrowed.

"Does it matter? Can you help us or not?"

Reihan sighed internally. There was really nothing she could do, and Phillippe should know better than to ask. Still, she had to fill out this form.

"I need to know how long you were exposed for", she replied, "It is important."

It was a mandatory box on the form, so she always filled it out. She reckoned some researchers wanted to correlate the length of exposure to the mind fog with the severity of the symptoms experienced by the victim. But no one in the Asylum had ever recovered from the Submergence, at least not while she had worked there. It seemed like a pointless dataset to collect, but Reihan didn't think it was worth arguing over.

"Half a day. Or something like that. It was hard to tell when we were immersed and when we weren't."

Phillippe's voice was shaking, and Reihan nodded, more to appease him than to agree. She wouldn't know. She would never head down there, even though she was supposedly immune.

"And were there other people at the pub?"

"Yes. That's why we thought it wouldn't be so bad. That we could go a little further even."

"How many people?"

"I'm not sure. Maybe five or six. They didn't really speak to us."

"What were they doing?"

"I don't know. They were mumbling amongst themselves."

"Right. Has it occurred to you that they might have been manifestations, not humans?"

Phillippe stared at her.

"That's possible?"

"Why wouldn't it be?"

He kept staring at her, and Reihan shook her head.

"All right. And then you proceeded?"

"We … just stepped outside. We didn't go any deeper or anything like that. There's a ledge outside the pub, and we went to look down into the clouds. We thought the closer we were –"

"The more powerful your ability to manifest would be once you returned to the city. Yes, I am familiar with the concept."

Reihan suppressed another sigh and completed her notes. If she had any power in this word, she would use it to tear down the *World's End*, that blasted pub at the edge of the cliff on which the Travelling City rode the cloud sea. Largely abandoned, drenched in madness, and absolutely forbidden, it drew in the foolhardy and desperate with the force of a mother's open arms.

"Can you do anything to help him?" Phillippe's voice was very small in the Asylum's registration hall. He did not look like a man who usually spoke quietly, Reihan thought. His hair was long and well-kempt, raining over his chest and adorned with tiny pearls and gold strands. His skin practically glowed whenever a bit of sunlight touched it. His eyes were large and rimmed with fading black coal, and his cheeks were just a little too red.

He refused to look at his brother. Reihan waited until he looked up at her, however.

"You know how this works, don't you?"

"I know that he was exposed."

"Exposed to the force of an entire city's collective unconscious. To the mind fog."

Reihan gestured around her.

"Every one of you humans produces manifestations from your conscious will. And that's nice because that's the way everything works around here."

Phillippe didn't know where to look. His gaze shifted from the space between her eyes to the corners of her eyebrows, landing somewhere in the landscape of her right ear.

"Now, manifestations aren't only caused by conscious thoughts. The products of your unconscious desires, fear, anguish, lust, and joy gather towards the bottom of the city, clinging to its cliff sides and crevices like vermin refusing to die. Humans look up – it is natural for them. So, we get to live on top while everything below gets succumbed in madness."

Phillippe opened his mouth, but she interrupted him.

"So, *don't go down into the madness*. It is the one rule you really, really have to follow."

Phillippe stared at her, clearly never having been spoken to like this, least of all by a seaver.

"Don't tell me what to do", he snapped back, half-heartedly.

"You're here asking for help. I can tell you whatever I want to."

"So, help him! Do something other than filling out that damned form."

"No."

A part of Reihan enjoyed watching Phillippe's face slip as if it had melted just a little, outstretched by a hot sun on a summer's day. Seeing small ripples appear on the young man's skin, she quickly shook her head, dispersing the thought. *Not now.*

"What do you mean, no?"

Reihan assumed he hadn't noticed the shifting and stretching on his skin.

"I mean that I can't help him", she clarified. She gestured to his brother, his eyes as empty as the light, his body limp and cold.

"We'll keep him here for caretaking and observation, but I'll not lie to you. None of that is going to help him. None of that is going to bring your brother back. You took a risk, and it didn't pay off. And that's really all there is."

"But you – at the Enforcer station, we were told you'd help us here. That you knew what to do."

"This *is* what we do. We take your problems and lock them away, so you don't have to look at them."

Reihan's eyes and voice remained cold. She'd had this conversation one too many times, she feared. Perhaps they shouldn't let her speak to visitors anymore.

"Why would you say that to me?"

Phillippe's voice was still shrill, but it assumed a layer of calm that Reihan found unusual. His eyes fixated on her, almost as if he was intrigued by the callousness lurking behind her words.

"Because I didn't cause this, Phillippe. Because I was created to solve a problem that you humans could so easily avoid if not for your petulant greed and insistence on breaking every rule, no matter how well-meaning."

"We had no choice", Phillippe replied, still with that eerily resigned tone of his.

"I don't believe that. All you people can manifest at least to a degree. You'll never truly go hungry, and you'll never truly go cold. Hells, if you get sick, you can make yourselves healthy, and when you get old, you can make yourselves young, at least for a little while. Everything else is a choice."

"You don't know – you wouldn't understand."

"No. I wouldn't. I will take your brother with me and wash him and feed him until he lives out his natural lifespan. And in doing so, I am the one who has no choice."

Phillippe stared at her.

"You seaver really don't feel any emotions, do you?"

"Does it matter?", Reihan asked, "You don't need me to get emotional. You need me to do my job. And you just wanted me to lie to you, so you'd feel better about fucking up."

"I don't want you to lie", Phillippe replied, and somehow, Reihan believed him. His eyes were almost as cold as hers, and his voice had lowered. It was always better if they were angry at the seaver caretakers rather than themselves. Reihan still remembered the instructions clear as day from her time at the Upside-Down Palace.

"Good. Because seaver don't lie. We weren't designed to."

She sighed, this time out loud.

"Your brother is in good hands here. You won't need to worry about him. He is the burden of the city now in exchange for past and future services you provide."

"Do any of them ever recover?"

"No."

"Ah."

Phillippe's gaze softened.

"And will I be able to visit him?"

"As often as you like. But everyone stops coming after a while."

She saw his expression, then added:

"But you may do as you please. That is your prerogative, human."

Phillippe fell silent for a while, and Reihan took that as her cue to wave over some of the other seaver. They pulled Alexander up, one on each arm, and led him down into the cell where he would be staying. The inmates barely ever reacted to stimulation, so they did not require much.

"Have you been doing this for long?", Phillippe asked, still fixating on her.

That part surprised Reihan. They usually left as quickly as they could once they realised their bargain had failed.

"Over a century", she admitted. She was technically one of

the higher-ranking seaver at the Asylum. Not that it mattered, as the rota of tasks remained cyclical, and few of them preferred one responsibility over another. And she did not look senior because seaver bodies did not age. They were created and would die at the peak level of physical fitness that was appropriate for their position. They were even given an instruction manual on how to best take care of their bodies. There were some places you could go to customise your exterior, but many seaver never did.

"And you've gotten sick of us by now."

It wasn't a question. Phillippe's hands interlinked, twisting and turning at the knuckles. Reihan considered the question carefully.

"I wish I understood you better. It's frustrating that I don't, because many of the things humans do end up being my mess to clean up. But I am not sick of you. I'm not even truly sick of the work I do."

"But it seems pointless to help us because our mistakes seem to serve no purpose."

"Yes. You always crave more power, and you always fail. Every time."

"Hm."

Phillippe rubbed his eyes and smeared a little coal across his cheekbones. *He is gorgeous*, Reihan thought, *and he's clearly enhanced his natural appearance, if not completely changed it.* She had been told that Phillippe was an escort. Nobody was born that good-looking, so a good deal of his mental prowess had to go into maintaining his looks.

"I see how you'd get frustrated with all this", Phillippe

mused. Reihan raised her eyebrows.

"You do?"

"Sure. Every time I got us into trouble, there was this moment when Alex looked like he was ready to throw me off the rock and watch me drown in the cloud sea. Because, as he never failed to tell me, none of the shit I put us through had to turn out quite as badly as it did."

"I take it he never did? Throw you into the cloud sea, that is."

Phillippe shook his head with a laugh.

"No. That's where the brotherly privilege comes in. We make mistakes, and we deal with the consequences together. Although I suppose I took advantage of that privilege far more than he ever did."

He smiled. Reihan did not think this would be a good time to mention that Phillippe would never speak with his brother again.

"So, are you telling me to cut you people some slack?", she asked instead. Phillippe winked.

"What if I am? Would that work?"

Reihan genuinely thought about it, something that seemed to amuse Phillippe. They held each other's gaze until she finally shrugged, feeling both awkward and intrigued.

"Sure. Let's say it worked."

"Great!", Phillippe replied, yet another smile blooming, "Then I shall look forward to a more pleasant conversation next time."

"Next time?", she asked, feigning surprise.

"You said I could visit as often as I like. So, you will find me a very constant presence in your life, seaver."

Reihan sighed.

"Reihan", she said.

"Reihan?"

"My name. It's Reihan. We're not all called seaver, you know?"

Phillippe blinked a few times.

"I guess that makes sense. It had never occurred to me to ask any of you for your name. How rude."

"Indeed."

"So, who names you? They grow you in tubes, don't they?"

Reihan scoffed.

"Great tube mother names us, of course. Glory be to her grace and wisdom."

"Really?"

"No. There's a book of names, and one of our instructors chooses one at random."

"Ah. And Reihan was one of those?"

"What's wrong with Reihan?"

"I don't know, it's just so –"

"It's so – what?"

Phillippe shook his head, the smile a ghost amidst his slowly returning despair.

"Nothing. Until next time, Reihan."

THE TRAVELLING CITY

CHAPTER 2: REIHAN

The man's eyes were glassy as a bauble. Reihan remembered playing with baubles when she was new, blue like the clouds that seeped into her bedroom through spider-thin cracks in the wall and through windows that had been left open. And play was good for cognitive development, according to the founders. All the newest research supported it. So, baubles it was.

"Respond", Reihan demanded. The man stared at her.

"It is your duty to respond if you are able to. You are now part of St. Leopold's Asylum for the Mentally Incapacitated, funded by the taxpayer", Reihan continued, taking a lecturing tone. The speech was easy to remember, even though nobody still called the Asylum by its full name. It was the only one of its kind that was left.

"It is your duty to respond if you are able to, lest you waste valuable researcher time and the resources of the facility."

She concluded, aware that she was essentially repeating herself. But it was fine. None of the other seaver on guard duty were paying attention to her patient, having deemed him a minimal risk to himself and those around him. Their focus lay across the admissions hall where five other inquiries were taking place. Someone else might need their help. Admissions were one of the riskiest times in the entire process.

Sunlight was awash as the day was barely beginning but already drawing colour from the place. Sometimes she forgot how long it had been between one day and another.

She focused on her charge once more and couldn't suppress a sigh. Completely unresponsive. They'd put him in a cell so they could have something to show to his family when guilt drove them to the Asylum on birthdays and the week after public holidays. It didn't matter how often she told them there was no cure for the Submergence. She even had a file that ran through all variants of those conversations. But people didn't seem to listen.

"Under the Thirteenth Government of the Travelling City, you are hereby committed to St. Leopold's Asylum for the Mentally Incapacitated",

Reihan concluded, then pricked the man's fingers with a sterilised needle. No pain found its way into the bauble-like blue of his eyes. It was strange how strong memories stirred within her this morning. She wondered if she had manifested the blue into her patient's eyes. How inappropriate if that were the case. She hoped nobody would notice, that no old pictures would show the man with brown or green eyes, some time in his prime, doing this or that impressive thing. Reihan sometimes forgot what humans did for fun. Her few reference points were less than reliable.

A soft knock towards the other side of the hall made her look up. A young seaver called Ember hurried over to Reihan and asked if she could do the rounds in the lowest level of the Asylum. Ember had only come to them two weeks ago, and she was still uncomfortable with the place. Most seaver hoped that after their time in the Upside-Down Palace, they would be called to a position in Government or at the Manifestation Mineshafts, where they never had to do anything. Some hoped to be called into a private individual's household, which could be as fun and exciting as it could be torturous. Nobody ever chose the Asylum, so a lottery decided who would be stationed there. Ember still held out the futile hope that she might be transferred one day.

"Is there no one on duty for level five?", Reihan asked. Ember shifted uncomfortably. The young seaver looked so unfinished, Reihan thought. No modifications to her skin, no alterations to her hair. But, then again, she would have looked exactly the same a century ago.

"Well, there is", Ember admitted. Reihan narrowed her eyes. They held one another's gaze for a moment, then Reihan sighed.

"I'll go with you, but I won't cover your shift. You need to get comfortable with them."

"I don't think that's possible", Ember complained, but she looked a little happier when Reihan got up. They left the admissions hall and found a small spiral staircase that led into the bowels of the asylum. As Reihan held on to its black iron railing, she felt the crumbling rust beneath her fingers. They had so few visitors that the seaver had not bothered expanding or updating the architecture. And it wasn't as though anyone had shown them how to.

Ember's footsteps trailed slowly, and Reihan threw a

disparaging glance towards the girl.

"You know, they don't require any more than our other patients. All you need to do is change the occasional bandage."

"I just don't want to do anything wrong", Ember murmured, but Reihan did not believe her. She might not be particularly good at reading humans, but she could predict every thought a young seaver had when they started working at the Asylum. Ember hated the patients. She was angry at their digressions, bored by the work, and frustrated that the rest of her life would be spent cleaning up after their mess.

"It's not like it matters if you fill out a form incorrectly", Reihan replied, "Who do you think will care? What matters is that you show up."

Ember responded only with pregnant silence. Their steps echoed against the white walls of the Asylum until they reached the lowest floor. Reihan opened the door to a long corridor of small cells, each with glass windows through which the inhabitants could be observed and with small clipboards that sat in a folder by the doors.

"Okay, let's start", Reihan said, steering towards the closest door on the left. Inside sat Eugene, who had once been a promising city official, working on developing youth initiatives in the lower parts of the city. He had been their patient for fifteen years after he had been exposed to a flood of cloud sea that had seeped in through his open window. He had been warned not to live so far down the rock face but insisted on staying close to the people he was trying to help.

"Dead gods", Ember whispered, "I can never get used to him."

"You will", Reihan promised.

The left side of Eugene's body had melted when he was exposed to the clouds. Just by a few centimetres, but it was enough to serve as a reminder of the grotesque impermanence of skin. The other half of his body was mercifully hidden beneath a heap of claws, scales and feathers that had grown into a twisted tower atop his shoulder.

A talented Enforcer could have reversed all this damage in an instant. But too much of the cloud sea still clung to Eugene from when he had first been Submerged, even after all these years. They couldn't do anything about it except clean up the stray manifestations Eugene's dreams sometimes conjured into reality, into his little cell at the end of the world.

Reihan checked the clipboard.

"He was given depressants for the pain five hours ago. He'll only need them again in the evening."

"How do we even know that he's in pain?", Ember asked, looking at Eugene's bauble-like eyes. They were empty like the moon, shining brightly in the dark.

"We don't. It's a precaution. We would not want him to suffer. Especially not while we collect skin and blood samples for the researchers."

"Why not – ?"

Ember paused, falling silent once more. Reihan turned around to see the young seaver restlessly moving about as if to escape her thoughts.

"Why not what?", Reihan asked, remembering every step of

this conversation. Seamus had talked her around the same corners a lifetime ago.

"Why not just let them die? These people are never going to get better, are they?"

Reihan shook her head.

"These won't. With enough time, perhaps one of the humans will find a cure. But honestly, I doubt it."

She sighed.

"And if they did, it'd be dangerous to use. It would encourage even more people to douse themselves in the clouds to gain godlike powers. And this rock is already overflowing with recklessness as it is."

"So, what are we doing this for?"

Ember's eyes were bright, and Reihan forced herself to remember that she was still very new.

"Because what we do gives hope to the families. Even if their loved ones might never recover, they will be taken care of."

"But what for?", Ember repeated, louder this time.

"Because hope is the most powerful weapon we wield. Drive the humans into despair, and they'll kill us all. Give them too much power, and they'll do likewise. But give them just a little hope, however fleeting, and most continue as normal. Content with the fantasy of things changing, even if they never do."

Seamus's words echoed through Reihan's mouth as if he was there to speak them with her. Ember gazed at her for a few moments longer, defiant of her lot in life, but then she finished the rest of the corridor alone.

Reihan liked to take her lunch at the same time in the same spot. She had discovered it on her seventeenth birthday, and roughly one hundred years later, it still held a similar appeal. A quiet, abandoned courtyard at the back end of the Asylum, whose quiet corners were full of nesting birds. The lush overhang of trees peaked just over the top of the high stone walls, and during afternoons the little square was flooded with pale sunlight.

No one really thought about this spot much, so it didn't change. Reihan liked that. She took her lunch to the only table left after all this time and placed her chair in the same spot, scraping the black steel against the stone underneath her feet. She leaned her head into the sun and filled her stomach with the same burning soup that she ate every day, kept hot by a speck of concentration.

It was fine. Seaver weren't supposed to use their manifestation abilities – people weren't supposed to know they had them – but she was just heating some soup.

The Asylum could be loud. Sometimes the Submerged screamed their hearts and lungs out, trying to escape the nightmares that were conjured up by the remnants of the mind fog. It never truly left you once you had bathed in the manifest subconscious that surrounded the lower overhangs and cliffsides of the Travelling City. Reihan thought she deserved the odd treat for spending every day of her life in this place.

It was fine. Taking care of humans was what the seaver had been created for, after all. At great expense to the Travelling City. It was only fair that she paid back her dues.

"Mind some company?"

Reihan sighed. Showing this spot to Phillippe had been a mistake. Or, well, she hadn't exactly shown him. On his twenty-third visit to the Asylum, Phillippe had demanded to observe everything she did, step by step. Whether it had been a futile attempt to help or to criticise, she wasn't sure. He had been in one of his most insufferable moods, jumping from tangent to tangent as he chattered away incessantly. She had considered skipping lunch that day, but seaver were made to require specific food intakes. If she hadn't eaten, she might not have made it back to her rooms on the top floor of the Asylum.

Although she should have just eaten in the canteen. Then Phillippe wouldn't know this place existed. Her little refuge from people like him.

"I do", she said slowly, taking a deliberately slow spoonful of her soup. Phillippe rolled his eyes and manifested another chair opposite her.

Or – no. Reihan paid closer attention to the human body facing her. Small but noticeable breasts, encased in a corseted dress. A heap of red curls floating down to the bodice. Skilfully applied make-up, but then again, Reihan didn't think she'd seen Phillippe without glittering lids on more than a handful of occasions. Only the eyes and some facial features had remained the same. Yellow irises, set in deep eye sockets, surrounded by rolling cheekbones and a long nose. There was a stigma against changing one's eye colour in the Travelling City.

"Well, that's just too bad", Phillippe replied, sat down, and sipped Reihan's coffee. She scrunched up her flawless face.

"Ugh. Do you have to put that much sugar in that?"

"Seaver require several nutritional additives to their diet."

Phillippe gave her an incredulous look, and Reihan had to resist the urge to smirk. Seaver could eat anything they wanted. That wasn't to say that it wasn't fun to confuse the humans every now and again.

"Are you okay?", Reihan asked after Phillippe stared into space for a few seconds too long. It wasn't as if Phillippe interrupted her lunch every day. Like everything about her, her routine was infuriatingly unpredictable.

"Feeling female?", she asked after Phillippe remained silent, "or was that a client request?"

She tried to phrase the question as carefully as she could. Phillippe did not tend to speak of her work at the Brothel of Transformative Curiosities. Or maybe she just didn't speak about it to Reihan. Like most humans, she probably assumed that the seaver did not get curious.

"Hm?", Phillippe said, her eyes slowly focusing back into the present. Reihan repeated herself, and Phillippe barked out a laugh.

"Can't it be both?"

She winked.

"Being female I've enjoyed for a few days now. The get-up? That's my client."

She groaned and tugged on her bodice.

"Do you have any idea how uncomfortable corsets are? They

really dig into every single rib known to the human body."

She made it disappear with a thought and replaced it with a flowing silk blouse.

"I wouldn't know", Reihan replied drily, looking down at the scratchy white uniform all seaver wore at the Asylum.

"Really? They don't make you dress you up all pretty every now and again? For a nice little dance or – ah, for some horrifying blood ritual?"

Phillippe's eyes sparkled with mad imagination.

"To keep up morale or to recharge your secret seaver powers?"

"Excuse me?"

Reihan's eyes narrowed.

"Contrary to what you might believe, we're not dolls that you humans get to dress up for your gratification."

"Dressing up for others hardly turns you into a doll", Phillippe scoffed, "We all play the roles we're given. Fulfilling other people's fantasies is an art form, and there's nothing wrong with being thorough."

Reihan felt irritated after her conversation with Ember and irritated at having her lunch interrupted. She knew she should be polite, but she just didn't have it in her. If Phillippe wanted to talk about herself, Reihan would oblige.

"Yes, and with the right justification, people will do just about anything for a bit of praise and a whole lot of privilege", she snapped.

Phillippe shrugged, but she could tell the comment had hit its target.

"Everyone wants to get ahead, Reihan."

"Not if it means hurting others."

"I didn't – I mean, I…."

Her eyes glazed over for a second, then she snarled.

"That's bloody rich coming from a seaver. Our very own glorified execution commando."

"I follow orders, Phillippe."

"And if you were willing to break a rule or two rather than mindlessly sticking to your precious orders, maybe you wouldn't be stuck down here."

"I was created to work at the Asylum. I don't have the luxury of choice."

Phillippe snorted.

"I've seen seaver in the Undercity. They don't keep you on as short a leash as you'd like to believe."

"Why would I like to believe anything?", Reihan snapped, her voice louder than she had intended.

Phillippe shrugged.

"Well, maybe you're just scared of the outside world. Maybe that's why you're trying to convince yourself that you have to stay here."

Reihan scoffed.

"Oh yes, I am positively terrified of the people out there. Especially the chatty ones, who think themselves so very wise after stumbling into fame and good fortune."

A twinkle of humour stole its way into Phillippe's eyes, and her tone became more reconciliatory.

"All I'm saying is that you could do other things in the city if you were unhappy here. Don't pretend that you have no choice."

Reihan felt another flash of anger rise in her throat.

"Sure, Phillippe. I could sew some little crafts and sell them to people in the Undercity. Or I could give you some competition at the Brothel and sell my body to some seaver fetishists. Or I could steal an airship and hope there really is a continent beneath the sea of clouds."

She shook her head.

"Or maybe you and I just see things differently. Maybe I think there's dignity in fulfilling your duty."

"Well, you could –"

Reihan cut her off.

"Now stop pretending like you've come here to talk about me. What do you want? If you're so desperate to start an argument, you probably already think I'm going to say no."

Phillippe's eyes darkened, a golden hue against her skin. It was good that she kept them, Reihan thought; she would be impossible to recognise otherwise. Phillippe loved shifting between one face and the next, growing bored of each exquisitely crafted body as quickly as the sun raced across the sky.

"I want to take Alex home."

Reihan sighed.

"Out of the question."

"See! I knew you'd say that."

Phillippe blew a strand of red hair out of her face. It looked like a streak of blood.

"I just… I just feel like things might be different if I –"

"They won't be. I monitor your brother every day. There has been no change. I would tell you if there was."

"Would you?"

The question came too quickly.

"I am legally obligated to. And I would even if I wasn't."

Phillippe closed her eyes for a moment, and the sun disappeared. Just for a flicker. Reihan shook her head, and the clouds dispersed again, and she suddenly felt rather foolish.

"I had a dream about him tonight. We were kids again in the Undercity. It was a game inside a story we were making up. You needed to collect all the marbles, and there was a rule to do with sticks. Alex let me win; I remember that. I wish he hadn't. Maybe I'd be better at the game if he hadn't."

"Phillippe, the last time I let you see your brother, you almost broke his head in two when you imagined the corruption shooting out of him like steam. I can't let you take him home. It would be unsafe."

Phillippe stayed quiet. The strand of red returned, hot and angry against her skin. She sucked on the tips of her fingers.

"One day, you'll have to say yes", she whispered.

Reihan's eyes turned cold.

"You could make me say yes right now. You're powerful enough that the rules don't truly apply to you, do they? Go on if you so wish. Make me march down to the cellars with you, and make me hand over your brother."

Phillippe's eyes flashed.

"Really?", she whispered, "Could I really do that?"

She said nothing else. She glanced down at the table, fixated on the nothing in front of her. Maybe Phillippe didn't believe her. The seaver were supposed to be immune to manifestations after all. Nonetheless, Reihan felt release expanding in her chest with each second that passed.

She waited out a few more minutes of silence, then pulled a cool drink of apple juice from underneath the table.

Phillippe blinked.

"Th-thank you?"

She took a sip.

"Thank you", she repeated, then sighed.

"Sorry. Today is a really bad day."

"I figured."

Phillippe finished the rest of her drink in one long sip, then cocked her head to the side as she glanced under the table.

"Where did you keep that?"

"What?"

"The juice – it…."

"I had it here the whole time. Where else would it have come from?", Reihan asked, her voice perfectly innocent. Phillippe stared at her for a few moments, then shook her head.

"I'm sorry. I didn't mean to sound like I was threatening you."

Reihan felt her composure, fine-tuned and trained over a hundred years, crack a little more. Phillippe was truly testing her today.

"You didn't. If I thought you truly posed a threat to the Travelling City, I could kill you on the spot. No human outranks a seaver, no matter what you'd all like to believe."

Her voice was quieter than before, impossibly soft.

"Reihan…", Phillippe replied, shifting in and out of her skin.

"What, it's uncomfortable for you when I say it out loud rather than just leave it implied?"

"I don't think I'm above you. I don't think I'm above anyone."

Reihan drummed her fingers on the table. She was being too soft on him, too relieved that the situation hadn't escalated.

"You say that. And as soon as I stop obeying you, you think you can threaten me. Just like all the other humans."

Phillippe's eyes narrowed.

"Listen, Reihan; I'm trying to apologise here –"

"No, you're not. You're the type of person who only apologises to make themselves feel better."

"You don't get to tell me who I am!"

Reihan rolled her eyes.

"Oh, will you get over yourself? Go, fuck your client, and stop wasting my time."

"Screw you, Reihan."

Phillippe got up, eyes blazing with tears. She stared at Reihan's white uniform, proudly displaying the symbol for seaver. She took a deep breath as if to spit out the words she was holding in, one more cutting than the next. But she didn't teleport away. She took another breath, then another. Reihan's heart slowed down again.

"I'm sorry if I'm wasting your time", Phillippe said quietly, "I like talking to you. Weirdly, even though I have all this new power to manifest, I feel completely powerless. I thought you might get what that's like."

"I do", Reihan said softly, although her gut twisted as she admitted to the feeling.

"I haven't told anyone else about what happened to Alex. So, that means you're the only person I can really talk to without pretence."

"Oh wow", Reihan laughed, "True friendship, born out of sparse options and convenience. Well, I suppose I should take what I can get."

"No, I didn't mean ... Sorry", Phillippe said with a long sigh, "Again. None of this is coming out right."

"Very well", Reihan replied, "I'll forgive you twice today. But I don't have the patience for a third time, so I think it's best you leave."

"Now you're mad at me", Phillippe whined, "That's not what I wanted."

"Yes, and I imagine living with yourself is so very hard, but you'll just have to manage for today."

Reihan waved her hand. Phillippe gave her a pleading look.

"I don't want to go back yet. Can't we have another argument?"

"No. My lunch is almost over."

"But I haven't even insulted your strange white face yet."

"Well, there's always next time."

"But, I –"

"Goodbye, Phillippe."

CHAPTER 3: REIHAN

The eyes of the Submerged followed the seaver when they entered the cells. Reihan had found it disconcerting during her first few years in the Asylum. She had been convinced that the patients were aware of their surroundings, cursed to sit as prisoners within their bodies as they silently screamed at their seaver caretakers. She had cried herself to sleep at night, feeling trapped in this role she'd been assigned, confined to the same rooms in the bowels of the Asylum day after day after day.

Everything in her world was faded. White walls, steel chairs and desks, and rust trickling down from the pipes that rattled when the seaver upstairs were heating water. And everything was so quiet, especially on the lower floors of the Asylum. Until she re-emerged to the surface where things were suddenly loud, where a patient might inadvertently create a manifestation, where a seaver might collapse from poor maintenance, or where family members might pointlessly demand the seaver caretakers cure their relatives.

She didn't think about it much these days, but when she entered one of the patients' rooms, she still felt a little uncomfortable for the first few moments and found herself searching for movements in her charges' eyes. She busied herself by flicking through the paper on her clipboard and dragging a chair over to Alexander.

Phillippe's brother stared at her, his eyes bauble-like and flickering with the light from the wall sconces. He had been sitting in his chair since being placed there in the morning, and he would probably sit there until the night shift put him to bed.

One time, thirty years ago, all the Submerged had moved in anticipation of an earthquake that had almost torn the city's rock face in two. They had risen in a single, horrifying motion and pressed their faces against the nearest exit. The earthquake had spared the Asylum but ripped many other houses into the depths beneath the cloud sea. Reihan had been so scared watching the patients suddenly move that she had cowered in the corner of the cell, content to die if only the squeezing in her chest came to rest.

But there was nothing unusual about Alexander, so Reihan relaxed after the moment it took for experience to become routine.

"I am your caretaker Reihan", she introduced herself, the same as she did every time. It was protocol.

"I am going to perform a standard observation on you. Please shake your head now if you do not consent to this."

No reaction, same as always.

"All right then."

Health checks first. She took Alexander's hand and felt for his pulse, feint but present.

She counted out a minute, then two. All within normal bounds.

She felt for fever, then felt for lumps. Nothing.

She filled out the relevant boxes on her clipboard and reached for her candle, normally strapped to her belt. She cursed when she realised that she had forgotten it, most likely in her room, half burned down after spending her allotted free time reading. She could walk up the four flights of stairs and get it. It would be no trouble at all and it wasn't as if she had many appointments to keep. But still.

She narrowed her eyes and raised her right hand. A small white flame appeared between her fingers, blinding in its brightness. Reihan allowed herself a small smile.

Seaver couldn't talk about their ability to manifest, not even to each other. The humans would almost certainly go on one of their famed killing sprees if they discovered that their peacekeepers, their carefully designed army of servants, had the same abilities they did. Even if their manifestations were a flicker in the dark compared to the inferno humans were capable of conjuring. And even if the seaver had lived in comfortable servitude for a long, long time, content to protect those that feared and hated them. Still, it wasn't safe to talk about. Seamus had told her that time and time again.

Alexander's pupils narrowed in response to the light, but the stimulus did not increase the rate at which he was blinking. He didn't even focus on the flame, looking straight past it, straight at Reihan's face.

"Are you dreaming in there?", the seaver asked, feeling self-indulgent.

No response. *Of course not.*

"Do you know that your brother comes here to ask about you? He's irregular, but he always returns, no matter how long it's been."

She smiled again.

"That's pretty rare. Most people forget as soon as they can. So, Phillippe must force himself to come back even if it pains him. Or maybe he does it because it pains him."

She shrugged.

"Maybe that's just a stupid human thing. But in a city where you can have anything you want, it means something that he chooses you, don't you think?"

She laughed.

"Look at me, talking to the walking dead."

Alexander smiled in turn, and Reihan's heart sank. It slid down her throat, dropped to the bottom of her stomach, then fell through the wood of the chair and shattered on the stone floor of the Asylum. Its ice-shaped pieces rose, light blue and sparkling, then fit themselves into the white crevices of the walls, now alight with new interest, twisting into a collage of smiling faces.

All were inhabitants of the asylum. Reihan recognised them from her daily rounds. Colours screamed in the in-between of eyes and mouths and noses, then the faces folded into paper dolls that began to encircle Reihan, edging closer with each step. She felt glued to her chair, spellbound by Alexander's suddenly expressionate eyes, her hands iron-gripped around her clipboard.

The paper army wore high-heeled, clicking shoes whose rhythm echoed in the small room as if it were a hall with tall columns and high ceilings. And just as Reihan held the thought, just for a moment, the walls yawned, creaking with effort as space and time crawled with a lust for expansion. Stain-glass windows appeared on both sides of the hall, alight with the shine of a cold moon, soft piano music, and the twittering of birds that filled the stone-graven air.

The paper people still encircled Reihan, edging closer as the hall continued to stretch outwards. She somehow knew what would happen if they touched her, so she cowered further into herself, shaking on her chair.

"Don't move."

The voice was disembodied, fluttering above her like a moth. Reihan recognised it as Phillippe's voice, and part of her relaxed, even as madness threatened to pull her under.

"No problem", she pressed out between gritted teeth, "Now what?"

"Let me handle it."

She turned her head just a little. An androgynous young man hung from the ceiling, suspended on a strip of moonlight. Straight, black hair grazed the tops of his shoulders, and his bright yellow eyes were coated in shimmering silver. He wore an open suit jacket that resembled peacock feathers, revealing skin that was coated in goosebumps. Something about his expression, both strained and vulnerable, was so familiar to Reihan that she wanted to jump up and run to him.

She didn't, of course. That would be idiotic.

A small flame started near the circle's edge, and the stink of burning paper shot into Reihan's nose. She inhaled sharply.

"Stop!", she called, "These might be the actual patients. Your fire could kill them."

The fire grew smaller, but it didn't entirely disappear.

"If they touch you, you'll die", Phillippe's voice said softly, and the sound felt so close to her ear that her skin prickled.

"Not necessarily. I'm immune to manifestations."

"It's not worth the risk. If they don't kill you, they'll kill my brother."

"You wouldn't say that if Alexander was one of them."

Alexander, who still sat opposite her, still with that strange smile on his face.

Phillippe cursed quietly, and the fire fell to embers. A few endless seconds stretched between them, and Reihan felt a breeze as the paper came closer and closer. One of the figures stretched his paper hand towards her and tried to bury itself inside her skin. The attack was repelled by her resistance to manifestations, and the dancer returned to the circle for now, but its touch left a streak of blood on her cheek. She whimpered and muttered words she later couldn't remember. Phillippe raced across the ceiling to get a different view of the paper army, and she could see his glass shoes reflecting the glowing mosaic dome growing above them.

"Try to contain them within something", she said, breathless, feeling unable to release any more air, any more loudness into this cursed hall.

She heard Phillippe mutter an affirmation, then a sudden gust of wind picked up and ripped the paper dolls upwards as if the hand of a resurrected god had commanded them to follow. One of them almost grazed her cheek once more, and she could feel her skin peel in response, threatening to slice itself open in mere anticipation.

The dolls were far above now, dancing beneath a chandelier that sparkled like the sun, each marvelling at their reflection and smiling so brightly that she almost believed they were real.

Then, a gigantic leather folder appeared and snatched the dolls up. As quickly as it had arisen, the paper became a memory of its dancing self.

The folder fell, fast and large, towards Reihan and Alexander, but before reaching either of them, it shifted into smallness and grew feathery, white wings. It fluttered, disoriented momentarily, then flew into Phillippe's arms, who lowered himself onto the stone floor.

"Close your eyes", Phillippe warned, and Reihan obeyed without question.

She felt him step closer, and his fingers almost came to rest on her cheek, where her skin felt irritated with the echo of the paper's touch. But the closer Phillippe's fingers came to her wound, the less painful were its remnants.

"Fascinating", he whispered and wiped away the blood.

"Can I open my eyes again?", Reihan snapped, despite the gratitude she felt.

"Hm? Oh, yes."

Reihan did so and found herself inside Alexander's cell once more. It was largely the same as before, bar some inconsistencies in the wall structure that she knew her own manifestations would soon rearrange.

Alexander's strange smile had disappeared. Reihan ran her hands through her thick, white braids and groaned.

"These visitors, I swear. We always tell them to get their emotions under control when they come here. All the psych evals we run before letting them into the cells, and still."

"Well, staying calm can be rather difficult when –"

"Yes, yes, yes, everything is *difficult* for you lot. If I catch whoever caused this bloody manifestation, I'll throw them from the city bannisters with my own two hands. That'll give them a reason to be scared of the seaver."

Phillippe chuckled at her outburst, but his eyes remained serious.

"Is that why the dolls were so focused on you? Because their manifester is scared of seaver?"

"Scared, obsessed, hateful… who knows. These things always go for us."

She narrowed her eyes.

"And it's a serious offence each and every time."

"What if it was my manifestation?", Phillippe asked, his voice extremely soft, "What if I lost control?"

His hair was even shinier than usual, Reihan thought, and the silver on his eyelids looked as beautiful as starlight. She wondered if he had teleported here from a job.

"It wasn't. Your freak-outs would be more imaginative, I reckon."

"Do you now? Do we know each other so very well?"

He winked.

"Go on, then, seaver. What would my despair manifestation look like?"

Reihan shrugged.

"It would be even more grand and striking than this, all colours and sparkles, and oh so terribly overwhelming. But its centre would be hollow because you're not angry at me or anyone else. You're angry at yourself. So, the manifestation would collapse in on itself, and every shining image would crumble into dust."

Her voice turned a little wistful.

"And, of course, even the dust you leave behind would be beautiful. Stardust that tears the world apart, and we'd all be too enraptured to notice."

She coughed, embarrassed, as Phillippe's eyes measured her intensely.

"Or something like that."

"That is horrifyingly astute. Well done", Phillippe responded, his voice strained.

"Don't take it personally. I don't really get people. It's just that you humans are all the same."

"Hard not to take that personally, Reihan."

"Well, try harder then."

She grumbled and finally made herself get up from her chair. Her legs shook, but she stayed upright by holding on to the backrest.

"Also, you came here to save your brother. You'd hardly be lucid enough to do that if you were the one to cause the despair manifestation."

"A compelling point", Phillippe replied, smoothing out the skin around his mouth.

"Speaking of, how did you know to come here? Not to appear ungrateful or anything."

"Of course not."

Phillippe's voice betrayed some amusement, and he winked.

"On the outside, this has been happening for the best part of a day. I was informed by the Enforcers, as were all the relatives of the other inmates. Given that, I'd say your shift is well and truly over, seaver."

"A day? Ugh, I hate it when they mess with time."

"Oh yes. Gives me the worst stomachache. One time a client of mine insisted that we spend the best part of a week –"

He interrupted himself.

"Never mind."

The seaver cleared her throat.

"So, you decided to swoop in here, the grand saviour?"

"Well, the Enforcers certainly weren't about to. They said the manifestations needed to quieten down before they were willing to step in."

"Ah. How reassuring."

The Enforcers had a division of experts at 'fixing' manifestations, that is, to scale them back to a level of perceived normality. If those guys hadn't wanted to enter the Asylum, Reihan shuddered to think of the chaos the manifestation had caused. She reckoned they'd be fishing winged tortoises out of the privies for weeks.

"What a bloody mess", she repeated instead of thanking Phillippe, then gestured at the folder that still sat on his shoulder, its winds flapping uselessly, "How the hell are we going to get our patients out of there?"

"I can try to restore them", Phillippe offered. He probably could, Reihan thought for a moment. The way he had entered and transformed the manifestation in Alexander's room was nothing short of brilliant, becoming one with the shifting realities as if he was a grain in a sandstorm. But instead of scaling back the manifestation, he had manipulated it from within, marking him as a creator and not a deconstructer. Reihan started to understand why he had been employed at the Brothel of Transformative Curiosities and not as an Enforcer or a Government official.

Reihan shook her head.

"No. If you get something wrong, we'll be in real trouble with the relatives, should they deign to show up here."

She sighed.

"I suppose we could try to get an Enforcer and show them old pictures. Or we could ask someone from the victims' families to counter the transformation and hope their manifestation abilities hold up to the test."

"And if they don't?"

"Then it'll be their fault, not ours."

He huffed.

"I have visited this place often enough to know the patients here by heart. I could restore them better than anyone else, Reihan, and you know that. Don't you think it would be good practice for –"

"Yes", she agreed, "I do."

Phillippe gave her a haughty look.

"Humour me then, seaver. Why should I not make use of the immense powers I obtained? Do you really think the patients need protection from me when they'd all be dead without my interference?"

Reihan sighed.

"This rule doesn't just exist to protect the patients. It exists to protect you."

"But –"

"No. I know you'd do a good job. You might even do a perfect job. But people invariably look for mistakes in restorations, and they might even subconsciously create flaws where they didn't exist before. And this is especially true with the restoration of someone they love. Now, if you were an Enforcer, they couldn't do anything to you, but with you volunteering –"

She sighed.

"Rules like these exist to save us from humanity's worst impulses. And believe me, you don't want to get caught up in those."

Phillippe opened his mouth to retort, but Reihan interrupted him.

"Phillippe, please. You just saved my life, and I don't want to see you punished for it."

Phillippe stared at her.

"I can take care of myself", he replied, his voice strained now.

Reihan nodded, and before he could flinch with surprise, she wrapped her arms around him in a quick embrace.

"Thank you for saving me", she whispered, "I won't forget it."

"I won't either", Phillippe said, equally quiet, then pressed his face into her shoulder, "Reihan."

CHAPTER 4: PHILLIPPE

Phillippe tried to lift his head out of the water until he remembered that no air was left in the room. Technically, there wasn't even a room. Just an eternity of lilac water, darkening on the edges so he couldn't see past the horizon. The regular pounding motions behind him started to feel frantic, although he couldn't hear any panting within the depths of the sea. He opened his mouth and tasted snowflakes of sugar on his tongue. *Lungs don't need air.* He just needed to keep repeating that, for his benefit and especially that of his client. His client, who insisted on fucking him in this godforsaken place every single time, turning himself into a sea creature come to ravish the foolish, gorgeous diver who had strolled into his domain.

Phillippe pushed the sugar around in his mouth and considered if he should at least try to enjoy this. Part of him always felt dirty doing that. Like he was taking the spider-thin fantasy of a stranger and pushing his fist into it whole and reshaping it into something perverse. It wasn't really what he was here for. He was here to keep the manifestations in place and to play the lead actor, the magical creature, the demure maiden, the tall, muscle-laden champion who had come to save the day. He was here to be whatever they wanted him to be.

Then again, he'd been doing that all day. He was tired and bored, and they were done with the interesting part of the appointment in which he was asked to construct an entire world around the stray fantasies of a stranger. And until the client's time was up, there wasn't anything else to do besides wait. So, he told himself that he could feel things again, that the numbness he'd enwrapped himself with didn't exist.

He instantly gasped at the sharpness of his client's touch, even amidst the warm lilac waters, and at the intensity, the desperation of his motions that threatened to sweep him away into the depths. But people enjoyed this, didn't they? He imagined what it must feel like. He felt his stomach coil, and heat spread into his thighs, his hands, his head. He sighed quietly and tried not to imagine where the feeling came from. Tried to picture anything else. Marianna, who worked downstairs, who looked like she was floating whenever she moved, or Tony's broad shoulders on which he lifted supplies into the Brothel's kitchens, always with a smile covering his entire face.

Phillippe groaned and gave himself over to the feeling. The motions from behind increased in line with his need, and soon enough, they washed over him as the waters turned into a sugar-sweet whirlpool. He felt disoriented and desperately out of control, which in no way culled the intensity of the feeling he had conjured up and now dropped as quickly as he could. More than ever, he felt as though the rest of the world did not exist at all.

Sometime later, the bell rang to indicate that time was up, and his client left. Phillippe was grateful for the lack of small talk. Maybe his client felt awkward that the appointment had gone differently than usual. Or maybe he just wanted to get going, and he wasn't thinking about Phillippe at all. Grateful as he was to be alone, he also felt an inexplicable tang of irritation nagging at his ribs that he couldn't quite place.

Phillippe huffed, then glanced in the mirror. He wanted to change. He made his hair grow long and his body androgynous, then manifested high stiletto boots, a long black skirt and a white shirt with an open chest. He laced his cheekbones with silver sparkles and made his eyes doe-shaped and innocent.

Then he spun around and found himself somewhere else.

Jesimin Kinnad, a teacher turned connoisseur of hallucination-inducing beverages, had recently created her magnum opus, a bar hanging onto the highest point of their little world. It floated on a thin slate of marvel, perpetually suspended in thin air by Jesimin's two daughters, both singularly talented manifesters. On certain days, the slate hung so high up that it could only be seen with binoculars and only from the Upper city, the Amusement Park, or certain parts of the Artisan's Quarters.

The bar itself was nothing special. A counter with five

wobbly stools behind which Jesimin stood. The hostess was an unassuming woman somewhere in her early forties. She had reportedly taught body augmentation manifestations at school and, as part of that, had lost all taste for the practice.

Only five guests were allowed on the marble slate at any one time. If a guest were talented enough to fly all the way to the bar or even to teleport directly onto the slate, they would be turned away if there was no space left. If one wanted to avoid expending the energy, it was usually worth catching Jesimin in the Undercity in the early mornings, where she hesitantly joined in her lover's religious rallies. Reportedly, you could trade for some of her cocktails there as long as you joined at least one resurrection cult.

Phillippe didn't care about the risk of being turned away. It barely caused him a twang of a headache to imagine himself on one of the barstools in front of Jesimin's counter, with only a hint of disorientation and dissociation from the world. And, just like he had imagined, the bar was largely empty at this time of day, with only one other guest occupying the barstool to the far left; a hooded figure who turned away as soon as they spotted Phillippe.

Jesimin, all stern darkness and flashing white teeth, clicked her tongue.

"You shouldn't manifest onto the chairs, you know", she told him in the tone of one who had never quite gotten over teaching, "You could manifest into one of my patrons. And that would be a whole mess."

"One I would untangle with grace", Phillippe retorted,

although he had no idea how he would go about doing that. He winked at her, "And you have to admit, this has far more style than that little landing platform over there."

He gestured dismissively towards a small, fenced-off area towards the right side of the marble platform, flanked by Jesimin's daughters, who stared at him with wonder and fright.

Jesimin rolled her eyes.

"On your conscience be it, pretty boy. Now, what will it be today? You may have three drinks from me this week."

Only manifesters who held the most prestigious positions in the Travelling City had the right to be served at Jesimin's bar. Perhaps the folks in Government were allowed unlimited access to her cocktails and potions; Phillippe didn't rightly know. Besides himself, none of the other escorts in the Wing of Romantic Fantasy were entitled to even a single beverage here. It was a fact that filled him with stubborn pride and made him return here again and again. They had given him the top room at the Brothel for a reason. He had earned all this. And paid dearly.

"Something against anger", Phillippe said, not caring if he exposed himself. The hooded figure at the end of the counter clicked their tongue in an irregular rhythm.

"I've got just the thing for you, sweet cheeks", Jesimin said with a wide grin. She pulled a long cocktail glass from underneath the counter, filled with a steaming green liquid and decorated with a complicated assortment of lemon and orange slices.

Phillippe took a deep breath and smelled sweet grass, its scent far more intense than the grass outside the Asylum or the Upside-down Palace. It danced around for a little, then was replaced by tangy notes of citrus, carried this way and that by a mild breeze. He took a large sip without hesitating, letting the liquid run down his throat and fill his chest.

He stared ahead at the marble platform, impatient for his new and improved emotions to take shape. This was one of the few places that hadn't lost their novelty once he could see how they worked from within.

After a few minutes, the view changed, and tall, sweet-smelling grass appeared atop the white stone. It moved with the wind, and small soft cats wove through the blades, bending their faces to fit perfectly around the dancing green. Then a powerful gust blew the grass apart, and Phillippe saw his brother riding towards him in a wheelchair, his eyes wide and awake, and the smile on his face so very real. Reihan was pushing him towards Phillippe, her expression mild yet challenging, and he knew what she was thinking; she was thinking, 'how did he possibly do it, how did he cure his brother when no one in the world had ever been able to?'

Soft piano and violin notes rose to a crescendo, and he felt himself floating towards Alex, who was just there on the platform, rolling ever closer towards him.

"Don't leave the chairs. It's a safety risk", Jesimin snapped, ripping him back into a reality in which he had never left the barstool and in which the marble platform was once again empty.

Phillippe made a gargled noise of frustration, then downed

the glass of water Jesimin had placed in front of him. The hooded figure on the end of the bar muttered 'about time', then directed their face towards the platform. Purple winds filled the air, dancing in the shapes of naked men and women, intertwining in various sexual acts. Phillippe felt sick to his stomach, and without another word, he teleported away.

Phillippe remembered walking through the market streets near the Watchtower before the Submergence. The houses grew like trees, touching each other at their windows and roofs and cutting off the streets in unpredictable ways. Within the shadows, between doors, windows and brittle, pastel-coloured walls, there were the artisan merchant stalls. Every third day of the week, they carried glimmering gold, soft fabrics, extravagant cuts, and wide-brimmed, lacy hats amidst the clattering of heels traversing the streets and the chatter floating down from doorways and open windows.

    Phillippe and Alexander had made it their ritual to walk through the stalls, subsumed in the all-present shadows of the Watchtower that loomed on the furthest Western point of the rock face. Their eyes gleaming, they took in all the things they wanted but could never afford; all the beautiful jewels and silks that had been painstakingly assembled, melted together in old, creaking forges, or had simply been imagined into reality by master manifesters. Many of the clothes and finery the brothers had thought to wear were only given to those who could prove that they had performed a magnificent deed for the city.

But the frustration hadn't been enough to ruin the experience. Their fantasies were never realistic enough to choose a deed they might attempt, one that might give them enough credit to spend at the stalls. It was enough to see the vision of an unobtainable life to feel as though their day was now a little less mundane, as though there was a little more beauty in their step.

Since working at the Brothel of Transformative Curiosities, Phillippe had never been turned away at any of the stalls. Having an escort wear their wares was both a point of pride as well as an effective method of advertisement for the merchants and many sent items to Phillippe as unasked-for presents.

But now he could manifest anything he'd ever envisioned or seen into existence. Even a stray thought sometimes changed his entire outfit or the shapes and curvatures of his body. And while the merchants perhaps had more original ideas or designs, the magic of pining after their wares had vanished.

Phillippe sat on an outstretched roof, glancing down at the stalls until his breath had calmed. It was mid-day, so the streets were fairly empty, although some families and friend groups took a casual stroll through the markets. Few bought anything, fewer still weren't turned away. Mercantile trade in the Travelling City was all about making a name for yourself. You wouldn't want to have no clientele, but worse still was being associated with the wrong people. Phillippe understood that implicitly. And yet, understanding didn't recolour his memories of being turned away at those same stalls. On his name day before the Submergence, when Alex had still been himself, Phillippe had impulsively thought to buy a golden bracelet with a scarab inlay for his brother, using a heap of trinkets and favours as currency. Alexander loved all animals, but beetles, insects, and lizards especially. It would have been perfect.

After the Submergence, Phillippe had been sent the bracelet for free. Either the merchant remembered him, or the universe had a funny sense of humour. Phillippe had shown it to Alexander, but by that point his brother hadn't reacted. Phillippe had tossed it against the wall and dowsed it in flames until he stood in the middle of the room, consumed by anger and shaken by tears. Sometimes he had no idea how he wasn't still standing there. What had pulled him out of it? Things hadn't changed. Alex was still gone. And yet, here he was.

He shook his head, trying to chase away the thoughts. He needed to move. He felt restless. Shopping was inane now, but there had to be somewhere he could go where he'd never been able to go before.

Perhaps dancing. He'd not done that much in the years before. After long days of appraising his skills on the Weeping Stairs or in the Undercity, he'd never felt like he had the energy for physical exertion. In contrast, now he sometimes felt like all he had to do was lie on his bed and hold onto his tongue lest it run away from him.

He summoned a jug of potent wine and imagined the taste to match the wine they had served at the last banquet at the Brothel. The whole place had been decked out in flowers, and everyone had been naked, their skin chubby and dewy, inviting their visitors' touch. Food, drink, small presents, and extravagant erotic toys had been hidden behind the petals of the flowers, and the day had soon turned into a treasure hunt. Some of the more diligent escorts had danced then, making their limbs soft and so bendable that it looked as though there was not a single bone left in their body.

Phillippe remembered the event quite fondly, mainly because staying near some of the other escorts and joking loudly with them kept most visitors at bay. But perhaps he would have enjoyed the dancing if it hadn't felt so much like an invitation for his more unsavoury clients.

He downed the wine in one long sip, then stood up. With a single thought, he turned his body into an unassuming shape, lean, with brown hair to his shoulders, and wearing an open vest. Some glitter on his eyelids and his chest. Nothing extravagant compared to what he usually wore in the Brothel or what he knew other escorts wore to high-society events.

He vaguely remembered where the clubs were located in the Travelling City. There was one above the Amusement Park on one of the small floating islands, from which people frequently fell, either to be rescued at the last second by the park workers or to ruin a small child's day.

But he did not fancy that one. It was out in the open, so it'd be far too sunny in the day's heat. He wanted to forget that he was in a body, that he had a past and a future, and that the world would continue to exist once he closed his eyes. He wanted darkness and warmth, and he wanted to drink until fullness was all he felt.

He teleported away again. He vaguely recalled the location of a club his fellow escorts had taken him to in his first week of starting at the Brothel. They still went back regularly and always asked him to come, but while he frequently joined them at pre-drinking in the Brothel's main hall, he rarely followed to the club, feeling too disoriented after attending to his clients to match the cheerfulness and ease of their demeanour.

But now that he was alone and did not need to appear as anything to anyone, he thought he might cope.

He found himself in complete darkness, only the thrumming heartbeats of other humans as a reminder that he was not completely alone. Then, after a moment and another, the music set back in. A deep bass pulled on his veins and lifted him on a wave, only to throw him back down a moment later. Drums rang across the cavern from deep below, and a dark cello played a melody that was melancholic and life-defying. He imagined himself drunker still, then surrendered his body to the motions the sound demanded. He could see no one, and no one could see him, and he moved with absolute certainty and extravagance in that knowledge. For a little while, he forgot himself, hoping the universe might forget him in turn, as sweat ran down his temples and chest, and he felt happy catching his breath between ear-shattering songs.

Then someone stumbled into him, taking them both down in a pile of interlocking limbs. He knew it was an accident. Whoever it was profoundly apologised immediately and laughed at their clumsiness in that overly affected way that betrayed profound embarrassment. Phillippe helped them up and reassured them that everything was fine, that there was no problem whatsoever.

His voice felt like it was being choked by his throat, and his heart raced against his temples and fingertips. He tried to dance again but felt that his movements were stiff and his breaths shallow, his body primed to escape whatever assault would come next.

No, he reminded himself. It wasn't an assault. People touched one another. It was normal. Life is the people that surround you.

But something within him screamed to leave, to flee this dark cave with the thrumming beats and the thrumming hearts and the sticky heat, and he could do nothing but obey. He teleported into an alley in the Artisan's Quarters and screamed with frustration until he was alone.

The cobblestones resonated with the sound and replied in their silly stone-language, breaking apart to let the air out. Flocks of snow rained from above to cool his burning skin, and Phillippe pressed his back against the side of a large tower block, wiping the tears from his face. Power was dancing around him, ripping at everything, and he didn't care. *Let it. Just make them all leave me alone.*

"Please identify yourself."

The voice was mercifully far away, but Phillippe knew it was talking to him. He blinked away the wetness and glanced up. A seaver stood at the end of the street, hesitant to approach. His hand rested on the long sword he carried on his hip, and his white eyes stared at the flurry of snow covering the street in a thin blanket.

"Phillippe. I work at the Brothel of Transformative Curiosities."

He knew he had to respond to the seaver. Everyone else he could chase away. But the seaver had to be obeyed. Every child knew that.

"Why are you manifesting in this manner, Phillippe from the Brothel of Transformative Curiosities?", the seaver asked.

"I felt hot and wanted to cool off", Phillippe replied, "Is there a problem?"

"You are disturbing the inhabitants of this street."

"Ah", Phillippe made. The snow still flurried about him, a halo in the darkening street. He was glad it covered up the broken stone below.

"Cease your manifestations and leave this place", the seaver commanded, taking a step towards Phillippe.

Phillippe nodded slowly. It shouldn't be a problem. All he had to do was focus his thoughts on the snow and have it stop raining down. Compared to the feats he had accomplished over the last year, this was nothing.

And still, his power refused to harden the way it needed to. He imagined the street back to its usual, warm self, but the image refused to stick. He was drowning in this water that slowly ran down his arms and legs and still drenched his cheeks in salt. The seaver stared at him. His heart continued to thrum so hard he thought it might stop at any second. The snow continued to sail, crossing seas of air until it melted into the ground.

He could choose to be difficult. If he didn't figure out a way to calm down, that might turn out to be his only option.

"Hello, Phillippe."

A voice appeared out of the dark from behind the seaver. It sounded familiar before he realised where he knew it from. All seaver voices sounded the same, it was the intonation that was different. And if you paid attention, Reihan's intonation was really quite unique.

"And hello, Piotr."

Piotr turned around to Reihan with a speed that seemed deferential. Reihan wore civilian clothes rather than the white uniform she wore at the Asylum. She smiled in a way he had seldom seen on her before. He forgot about the snow and the holes in the ground, and they disappeared with another breath.

"Reihan", the seaver said, giving her a long nod, "Pleasure or business?"

"Both, I suppose", Reihan said in a playful tone but did not elaborate further. She gave Phillippe a long look, noticing the drenched state of him and the remains of the water on the street.

"You all right?", she asked, and for a moment, he felt as though she could see right through him, could smell his racing heart and his elusive thoughts.

"Why, of course", he replied, "Just making my escape from work and general responsibilities."

"Sounds delightful", Reihan responded with a twinge of humour playing around her mouth. She turned around to Piotr.

"Did we have a problem here?"

She said it in an entirely neutral tone, clearly trusting the other seaver to tell her the truth without prompting. Piotr hesitated for a moment, then shook his head.

"No."

"Good", Reihan said, "In that case, I believe I noticed some teenagers are giving a new face to the Founder Statue up on Front Street."

Piotr did not waste a second to follow up on her lead. Phillippe waited a few moments, then leaned against the closest house and painted a wry smile on his face.

"Really? Blaming children? What a ruthless excuse to talk to me in private, seaver."

"Who says I need an excuse?", Reihan responded, slowly approaching.

"Well, I suppose I did recently tell you that you're my new favourite person."

He had said that after seeing the seaver take Alexander around the gardens for fresh air. Reihan had been visibly uncomfortable with his praise, reminding him several times that she was just doing her job. He had found her hard to read at that moment.

She reached his side, close enough that she could have touched the water that remained on his body. He wished he could manifest it away, but he still couldn't. She had to think him very strange, but then again, there were worse things she could think of him.

"Are you sure you're all right?", she asked in a low voice. Her tone was strangely soothing.

"No", he wanted to whisper. But she couldn't help him. Nobody had ever been able to help him until he had helped himself to far too much stolen power.

"Sure", he said instead.

CHAPTER 5: ELLIS

Morning rose, and Ellis rose with it. As soon as the first flecks of sunlight hit her windowpanes, she jumped out of bed. She had a mission today. In fact, most days, she had a mission. She didn't really care what the mission was, but she was excited to have it looming on the horizon like a storm sent to blow her ship off course.

She stepped in front of the mirror. Her fuzzy, bright-coloured pyjamas sucked the brightness out of her features, and she made them disappear with an annoyed glare.

"What do you think, sis? What has boss man got planned for us today? Another bureaucrat to intimidate so that he can get some motion or other approved?"

She summoned up a black, shining catsuit, hugging the straight lines of her body and found a dangerous glimmer deep within her eyes.

"Or, maybe I'll get to kill someone again. Those missions are always exciting, aren't they, sis?"

Her sister nodded mechanically. She always agreed with Ellis, never interrupted, never disturbed. She could just stand to be a little more enthusiastic at times, Ellis thought.

"Ugh. No. Not the catsuit."

She made it disappear and replaced it with loose-fitting brown trousers and a black shirt that showed a small part of her chest.

"Like that? Or is that boring? What do you think?"

She turned to her sister, who sat on the same shelf as usual amidst all the other dolls that looked like her. Beneath a picture of the cloud sea that Lukacz, her boss man, had commissioned for her. Next to two open windows because Ellis hated to sleep in unaired rooms. It took her a while to realise which doll she'd chosen for her sister today until the doll in question made a motion that sat somewhere between a nod and a shrug.

"Not sure, huh? Do we need to jazz it up a bit?", Ellis asked. Her sister nodded hesitantly. Her hair was curly but no longer blonde – Ellis had dyed it weeks ago. She was wearing a black, lacy dress covered mostly by a black velvet cloak. Ellis had tried to draw nail polish onto her plastic fingers, but it didn't look quite right.

"How shall we do that, hm? With a hat?"

Ellis summoned a black fedora hanging precariously off the left side of her head. She made her sister nod, tweaking the manifestation she'd spun into the doll. Then, a small knock sounded at the door. Ellis just hmm-ed, not bothering to ask who it was. Only one person knew where she lived, atop one of the abandoned towers of the Upside-Down Palace.

"Lose the hat", was the first thing Lukacz said when he entered her bedroom. Boss man was dressed in a simple suit today, and given how much he hated formal wear, he was probably meeting with someone important.

"Whyyy?", Ellis whined, "Sis helped me pick it out."

Lukacz threw an impassioned glance towards the family of dolls that stared at him with blank, glossy eyes.

"Because things might get rowdy later, and it would get in your way", he explained, without commenting any further on the presence of her 'sister'. Really, Ellis had first started to make the dolls move to frighten Lukacz, a mild form of protest after he had given her the room of a little girl to stay in. Now, she was just used to it. It gave her someone to talk to when the Government didn't have work for her.

"Rowdy, huh? I like where this is going, boss man", Ellis said, then made the hat disappear.

"Yes, you'll like this one. A thoroughly despicable man and very likely to blow."

Lukacz's gaze wandered to her bookshelf.

"Have you been reading the book I gave you?"

Ellis rolled her eyes. Lukacz loved murder mysteries, books about plants, and stories about children having a philosophical awakening through an encounter with a mystical being. This one featured all three.

"It's all right", she muttered. Lukacz forced out a small smile.

"Give it time. It really gets going in chapter twenty-five."

Ellis, who had just started chapter thirty-two, decided to leave that uncommented.

"Do you want to get breakfast?", Lukacz asked. Ellis snorted.

"You don't need to fuss over my eating habits, boss man. It's not like I'm human."

Lukacz narrowed his eyes.

"And do you believe that the seaver do not eat?"

"I'm not a seaver."

"No. And yet you eat."

Ellis could see she was starting to annoy him, so she stopped immediately, agreeing to a breakfast of sweet waffles and milk. It was only fun when Lukacz was in on the joke. She would never truly want to annoy her boss man. He had dragged her off the streets when she had been a stray thought away from death. He believed that she was real, and so she was. If Ellis thought she could love anyone in the world, it was Lukacz.

"Bladeti-bladi-bla."

"Blö-blö-bladi-blö."

"Oh! Putschikna-permiäsitksan."

"Bidditi-babbeti-boop!"

So. Boring. Ellis was wrapped around the ceiling like a spider, enwoven in silky, white fabric held in place by her imagination. She twirled a long knife around her fingers; the plain black one, unfortunately, not the one she'd covered in diamond shards and rhinestones. She wasn't worried, mind you. She had this. She was *unnnntouchable*.

Underneath, in one of the Upside-Down Palace's secret meeting rooms, Lukacz pointlessly continued his pointless negotiations with the Count. Ellis could barely hear them, so she made up the words she thought they might be saying.

Well. The creepy guy wasn't really a Count. He just wore a dark top hat and coat that made him look like he had a bit of creepy royalty in him. He certainly acted that way, trafficking and selling children in his home-grown mansion somewhere in the underbelly of the Travelling City.

Usually, that kind of offence got you immediately chucked off the city walls by an Enforcer or a seaver. But the Count had managed to maintain a secret household, home-grown within the city's rock face, for the best part of four decades. Nobody had even known that his mansion lived down there, its walls and windows tightly pressed into the rock and maintained purely by his manifestations. It had disappeared with the Count's arrest, of course, all its inhabitants lost to the breathing stone.

But the Count might be useful for the city yet, Lukacz had decided. With the right sweet words, he might be convinced to return some of his victims to the surface. And anyway, you couldn't just chuck people like that out of the city. A talented manifester might be able to fly out of the cloud sea with an imaginary pair of wings or teleport right back to the Upper City.

So, Lukacz had set up this meeting with the Count and now attempted to have what sounded like a civilised conversation with him, flanked by a group of five seaver to keep the peace. Over breakfast, he had told Ellis that, best case scenario, he might convince the Count to spend a life sentence working in the Mineshafts that led deep into the underbelly of the rock face. To sit where the cloud sea could just about tickle his toes and manifest a list of items the city's inhabitants had requested from their Government.

All in exchange for being allowed to live out his natural lifespan, no freedom, no enhancements, *no sir*.

Not a great deal. Ellis wouldn't have taken it, she told Lukacz as she slid into her black catsuit and attached two knives to the side of her boots. Then again, Ellis didn't mess with kids. That was poor taste.

"Bli-bli-BLIIRI-BLI."

The talking below intensified, and Lukacz raised his hands. The Count bellowed, a sound that rang through the columns that raised the hall on hallowed, outstretched palms. The gallery didn't have any windows, but colourful stained glass had still been installed along a marble façade, interspersed with long, heavy carpets hung from the ceiling. Ellis had insisted on those. Nothing to break a manifester's concentration like interrupted eye contact when he's trying to tear your skin from your bones with nothing but a thought and a bit of desperation. It was good to have something heavy and real to disappear into.

Her heart tingled like a spell, and Ellis felt her limbs tense. She trusted her instincts more than anything else in this world. There'd be a fight breaking out, and soon. Her knuckles closed around her knife, and she threw her head back with a grin. *Finally, something to do.*

The Count shook his head in distaste at something Lukacz said and took a few steps back. Lukacz wasn't a member of the inner circle of Government, but he was still about as close to their rulers as you could be. Ellis forgot his exact position and title, but he was important enough to warrant sending a seaver in his stead. The Count's requests be damned, Lukacz *should* have sent a bloody seaver. One dies, you make a new one; who cares? And as much as Ellis was about to enjoy what would happen now, she didn't relish the idea of Lukacz being in danger. He was getting too old for this shit.

The seaver flanked to apprehend the Count, and she could see Lukacz's face tense up as he strengthened his mental shields. It would take a talented manifester to break through Lukacz's mantra, his idea of who he was that he held outwards like a shield.

The trouble was, the Count *was* a talented manifester. Realising he could not directly affect Lukacz or his seaver bodyguards, he raised stone walls around the seaver that kept them fixed in place. The banging of their fists against the newly arisen walls echoed in the hall like a drum, a pounding heart rhythm to the fight that had now officially begun.

Ellis glanced downwards and made the net disappear. She

fell, first quickly, then slower, as concentration broke her fall.

The Count summoned a set of knives between him and Lukacz, and Ellis could feel Lukacz's concentration split between protecting himself and keeping the weapons away.

"Cease this immediately", Lukacz demanded his voice its usual growling self. Without any hesitation. Lukacz never hesitated, never doubted. They had that much in common, at least.

The Count did not reply. His eyes narrowed, and he stepped towards his opponent, the knives moving in tandem with him, swimming through the thick-flowing air like silver-glowing fish.

Ellis tried to be as quiet as possible, slowing her breathing and the beating of her heart as she fell through the air at a snail's pace. She threw her knife from her right to her left hand, then hurled it towards the back of the Count's neck, intending to sever his head from his body with a single strike. She already imagined the blood sputtering from the remains of his body, hitting Lukacz straight in the face. He'd be so *displeased*, and it'd look hysterical, especially with how long it would stick to his clothes and skin if he didn't manifest it away, and Lukacz never manifested on himself, so –

The Count heard the whir of her weapon and turned around. The knives followed his widening eyes and surrounded her blade like a group of angry sharks. With a clang and a shatter, it fell to the ground. Then, the Count's weapons shot upwards and chased towards Ellis, cutting through the air with rage.

Most teachers at school will tell you only to attempt a manifestation when your mind is fixed on your goal and you're able to picture the outcome you are trying to achieve. That it is simply a game of input and output and that the harder you try at it, the more success you will have.

Ellis thought that was bullshit. When the knives flew towards her, she didn't have time to imagine a detailed plan of escape. She could have tried to summon a wall in front of her or a gust of winds to blow the weapons off course. But she didn't. Thoughts did not come close to penetrating the panic, excitement, and adrenaline inside her mind. The only thing she remembered was the carpets – *the carpets are safe* –

So, she vanished into thin air and found herself partially wrapped on the other side of her favourite carpet, the one that depicted the construction of the Amusement Park. It was heavy and velvety and, most importantly, enlaced with a steel net in which the Count's knives got stuck as they pursued her, wriggling like a silver catch outwitted by a fisherman.

She heard the Count curse on the other side and allowed herself a quick grin.

If she was quick, she could finish this in a single strike. She tried to picture Lukacz, his eyes narrowed in concentration, facing off against the ridiculous top hat and coat.

It was enough. A heartbeat later, she found herself just behind the Count, the memory becoming reality as his dark attire rose before her. She looked at her empty hands, expecting to find one of her sparkly knives in there, and moments later, felt the heaviness of steel and rhinestones sitting between her fingers.

The Count turned around, perhaps feeling a ripple in the air. His eyes widened, and steel started to manifest into a wall between them, skeletal fibre upon skeletal fibre. At the same time, she felt vicious thoughts pull on her skin as the Count imagined yet unshaped violence afflicting her.

"Too late", Ellis tooted triumphantly and let the knife shoot off from her hand straight into the Count's heart, passing through the steel wall that was slowly taking form. She had it twist around twice, three times for good measure. She wasn't worried now. The Count's face was torn by panic, pain, and rage, and he'd not manage a single coherent thought, let alone a manifestation.

So, he died, and that was that.

Disappointingly, Lukacz stood too far away from him to have blood splattered on his clothes.

"Thank you", he said, giving her a nod. She spat on the floor.

"Could'ave told you this wasn't gonna go well."

"Yes, well. You say that about all interactions with other people."

"And am I ever wrong?"

"It has been said, in legend, that such a sparkling scenario has indeed occurred. Once or twice", Lukacz said with a raised eyebrow. He prodded the Count's collapsed body with the tip of his shiny black shoes. No reaction.

"He's dead, boss man", Ellis said helpfully.

"Yes", Lukacz responded slowly, "A shame. I was hoping to at least get a list of victims' names out of him to inform the families."

"And here I thought you were after selling him into effective slavery for the Government."

"Two birds, one stone", her boss replied with a small sigh, "But alas, there was no reasoning with him. Well, this is perhaps the most satisfying solution, although it would have been nice to make the execution a little more public. You know, deterrence and all that."

"I'm not a big crowds girl, boss man", Ellis protested, "I get shy."

She grinned and twirled her bloodstained, sparkling knife around her fingers.

The corners of Lukacz's mouth twitched.

"Come on, trouble", he said instead of responding to her provocation, "We have something else to do today."

"What? I was planning on reading the masterworks of Professor Plutarch Erraldinius for the rest of the day to further my education on the history of the mechanical mouse."

"Very funny."

Lukacz rubbed his hands as if some blood had sprayed on him after all.

"Supposedly, we've had an escapee from the Asylum. I don't know the details yet, but it sounded urgent."

"A rogue seaver?" Ellis groaned. "Who cares?"

"That's the thing", Lukacz said, and for the first time today, there was a flicker of worry in his eyes.

"It's not a seaver that's escaped. It's one of the inhabitants. And, technically speaking, that's impossible."

THE TRAVELLING CITY

CHAPTER 6: REIHAN

It wasn't often that Reihan went to the Brothel of Transformative Curiosities. In fact, she had been only twice before. Once when she was thirty-two, she had been asked to cover a few shifts as oversight and administration after a batch of seaver in the Brothel malfunctioned. Reihan remembered first entering the gold-plated gates of the entrance hall, covered by dark-blue shawls that hung from a tree's crown. Perpetual nightfall coated the dome-like roof of the entrance hall, battling an onslaught of stars and planets that rushed across the darkness, coating each visitor in the most flattering starlight. The hall was always filled with dancers, bending their bodies into silver-glowing liquid metals, growing into the heights of the space above. Reihan had once asked one of the dancers if the transformations hurt, and they had just laughed.

The Brothel had different sections based on what a visitor was in the mood for. Conversations of intellectual stimulation with some of the resident philosophers; gilded cages that one might enter and where one might be transformed into any object of one's desire; explorations of endless empires and landscapes filled with unknown civilisations and fantastical animals. All were contained within the endless corridors the escorts imagined into existence, shifting the space around the Brothel in such unpredictable ways that air travel around the building was strictly forbidden. And, of course, there was the Wing of Romantic Fantasy, in which the escorts would transform their bodies at the drop of their visitors' feather-light desire. Phillippe's domain.

Back in the day, Reihan had been stationed in the Unknown Exploration Wing, logging visitors' requests to be immersed in a domed city filled with soft, warm water, swimming within its sugar-sweet embrace amidst a people so light and ethereal that a mere glance upon them dispelled their presence. She had watched the escorts create an endless sea of forests, filling the air with so much freshness that the visitors' skin lost all signs of age. She had heard visitors describe being drenched in a dimension filled with lava, coating their bodies to stone, only to be released an endless second later.

The second time, something like forty years ago, Reihan had been called to the Brothel as a juror in a trial. A client had forcefully altered their escort's mind and body beyond any of the requests that had been approved, twisting them into a hand-sized meat puppet before trying to smuggle them out in their coat pocket. It was by sheer luck that the perpetrator had been caught, losing concentration for a second when a dancer had brushed up against them, which caused him to release the escort back into their original body.

Reihan and the jury had been given a choice. Either they would convict the perpetrator to manifestation duty, lowering him deep into the bowels of the Travelling City's Mineshafts, where he would be condemned to an existence of manifesting items on the never-ending citizen requests list. Or they would simply kill him and throw his body over the city's edge into the sea of clouds. Reihan and the jurors had unanimously decided on the latter. About twenty years before, the city had been blessed with a boom of children born with strong powers, and many of the essential city functions were now being maintained by them. There was no need to take gambles on someone willing to abuse his manifestation abilities in so perverse a manner.

Rehabilitation was a rare gift, and the seaver considered few people worth the risk. Below the city and below the rock carving its way through time and space lurked the mind fog, created by the humans' subconscious desires, and below that ebbed and flowed the sea of clouds, a peach-yellow mass that no thought or traveller could penetrate. Unable to leave, they all had to live on that small rock that housed their city, some of them able to summon the contents of their deepest desires with nothing but a stray thought. Given all that, Reihan had never had much sympathy for humans who decided to screw up.

The Brothel hadn't changed much since the last time she visited. She still passed through a hall full of dancers, now dripped in a sea of colour that shifted with each change in the onlooker's perspective. The dancers transformed their limbs as they moved, growing feathers, scales, or tails in tandem with music soaring from invisible heights. They ignored Reihan. Seaver were not part of their clientele.

She hurried past the dancers and walked up to the central administration desk, occupied by a girl in the middle of childhood, wearing the tallest hat she had ever seen. Layers and layers of dark lace formed a tower full of nesting birds atop her head, and when Reihan got close enough, she thought she heard distant voices amidst their tweeting.

"Hello there", the girl said, looking wary when her eyes registered Reihan's white skin and thick, white braids. Seaver were immediately recognisable, and for most people in the Travelling City they were immediately bad news.

"Don't panic, I'm not here about a violation", Reihan pre-empted.

"Oh, good!", the girl replied, immediately lowering her voice by about two octaves and taking on a more business-like tone, "Then what can I do for you?"

"I'm looking for Phillippe."

The girl raised her eyebrows.

"You can't book him out."

"I am aware."

"No, I mean, even if you weren't a seaver, you couldn't get your foot in edgewise. Any slots he's made available are booked out all the way until Autumn. He's one of our most popular escorts."

Reihan suppressed a sigh.

"It's about an inquiry he made. He'll squeeze me in with his break time."

The girl opened her mouth, and Reihan got the feeling she was going to argue.

"I came all the way from the Asylum. It is a crime to waste seaver time."

It absolutely wasn't, but few people bothered finding out the rules until it was time to break them.

The girl rolled her eyes but nodded.

"Fine. He is in the Wing of Romantic Fantasy."

She pointed at a gate towards the far side of the entrance hall, which glowed in a soft, understated red.

"His room is the highest one in the tower. It's thirty-seven floors, so I hope you brought some time with you."

Reihan did her best not to flinch. She simply nodded as mechanically as she could, then made her way through the dancers. They moved out of the way like fluttering moths, and Reihan felt her heartbeat fasten. Phillippe had never mentioned how far up he lived.

The gate opened into a narrow spiral staircase, aglow in the same dark red light that had seeped out from the entranceway. Doors of various sizes and styles hung on the stone walls like paintings, and Reihan could hear the invariable moaning, laughing, screaming, and chatter from underneath the floorboards.

One floor, five floors, ten floors. She could feel her body

breaking out into a sweat and cursed under her breath. Her chest beat hard, and she took a quick break right next to a slightly ajar door behind which a horned man was being penetrated from five sides, creating a misshapen star.

Reihan lingered for ten or eleven breaths, then felt too awkward to stay and forced herself up further. Floor fifteen, seventeen, eighteen. She felt her heart on her tongue, and her limbs started to shake. She had not planned for this.

Damn you, Phillippe.

"Hey, sweetie, can't we extend the fun a little?", she heard a melodic female voice behind a nearby door, small like the gate of a birdcage.

"You're only timetabled for forty minutes."

"Oh, don't be like that. I thought we were having a good time?"

"Yeah, sure, but I've got other customers today. Sorry. Rules are rules."

"But I never get more than forty! It's not fair – I barely get off before it's all over again."

"You're entitled to as much time as the city owes you. I don't make the rules."

"Yes, but –"

Reihan groaned loudly, then hit her legs a few times as they threatened to cramp up. Once, twice, then she was up on floor twenty-five, thirty, then up at the top of the staircase, drowning in sweat and barely able to reach the final door of the tower. Just before she could knock, Reihan's legs gave up for good, and she collapsed on the last stair, her head smacking against the stone wall behind her. She screamed, then cursed as loudly as she could. For a moment, all she could hear was ringing in her ears, then footsteps moved closer to the door, and Phillippe's head peaked through.

He wore a simple white tunic but must have recently been with a client as blue-glistening scales still adorned his chest and fingers. A crown of thorns sat loosely on his long silver hair, and tiny pearls surrounded his eyes.

He looked down at her, then smirked.

"You really should exercise more if this tower is enough to knock you out."

Reihan opened her mouth to respond but found a small lake of blood underneath her tongue, sweet, warm, and disgusting. She spat it out in lieu of the witty retort she had been saving. Phillippe's eyes widened.

"R-reihan?", he asked, then quickly knelt beside her, "What's happening?"

"Seaver", Reihan simply responded, still pulling in breaths far too fast.

"I had noticed that", Phillippe said softly.

"Once we leave the Upside-Down Palace, seaver bodies are adjusted for a … for a very particular amount of exercise in a day", Reihan explained with effort, "depending on what role they were chosen for. Me in the Asylum – not so much."

"Ah", Phillippe made. He clicked his tongue, then helped

Reihan edge onto his doorstep. They sat next to each other there, letting their legs dangle over the staircase down to the lower floors of the tower. The moans and shouts melted into a strange sort of music, and Reihan wondered if it was Phillippe's doing or if, for once, she could trust her instincts.

"And you can't –", he started, but Reihan interrupted him.

"No."

"You didn't let me finish."

"I don't need to. I know what you're going to suggest, and I have tried it. You can't train, you can't eat more or drink more or drug yourself. You can't get a modification or a manifestation that lasts for any time at all. Nothing works. Nothing I'd have any say over anyway."

She took a deep breath.

"You should have told me you lived this high up."

"I'm sorry", Phillippe mouthed, "I didn't know."

"You didn't ask."

"Yeah, well."

His voice trailed off, and he scratched the back of his neck, underneath some of the scales that shimmered in the half-light.

"It's not like they teach us much about you seaver in school."

"Yeah, well", Reihan echoed, and they exchanged a brief, shy smile, "It's not like we want you guys to know all our secrets."

"See? My honour is unsmirched."

"Not sure I'd put it like that exactly."

Phillippe laughed, but less loudly than Reihan would have

expected. He quickly changed the subject.

"So? Any changes?"

He was talking about Alexander, who had been caught up in a visitor's despair manifestation. Although Reihan had tried to warn him, Phillippe had foolishly, predictably gotten his hopes up. As if the shock of the experience would be enough to rip Alexander out of his catatonic state.

It hadn't, and she told him as much.

"Oh", Phillippe made. He took a few deep breaths and wiped something out of the corner of his eyes. Reihan wondered for a second if it was tears, but it was flecks of glitter, shimmering in the half-light between old stones and underneath the hinges of the doorframe.

"Never mind then."

"Sorry."

"It's not your fault."

"Still."

"Do you think a stronger manifestation might shake him –", he started, and she interrupted him.

"Absolutely not."

"Why not? I'd be careful!"

"It's been tried before. It didn't work."

"Not by me. I might be stronger than the people who tried before. You should see what I'm able to do with clients every day."

He gesticulated at the scales across his chest, growing with his rage. Soon enough, they'd swallow him, she thought.

"Why wouldn't I be able to –"

"Phillippe."

Her tone cut through where she doubted reason would have. He sighed. For a horrifying second, she thought he would start crying for good, but he held onto himself, sitting stiffly on the cold stone floor. People often cried in front of her, often without expecting any reaction. It was as though she was furniture in the room, expected to wait out the storm that filled the air with unspoken lightning. She had borne witness to the most heart-rendering of sobs and the softest of squeals, warm like melted butter. But a century of anything will leave anyone cold, and emotions lose their sparkle once they become predictable.

Still, she placed her hand on Phillippe's arm and tried not to question the fact that he flinched too quickly, too hard at her touch.

"You know, seaver are born without genitals", she said randomly. Phillippe snorted involuntarily.

"I'm sorry, what?"

"We're in the Brothel. The thought came to mind", she explained, suddenly feeling sheepish.

"Right. I guess you wouldn't… need them? They do make you people in tubes, don't they?"

"It's called cloning."

"Right", Phillippe repeated, a wicked grin dancing around his lips, "Details, details."

Reihan rolled her eyes.

"So you don't have any – you know…", he continued.

"Any...?", she teased.

"Well, you know."

"What? You use them every day and can't even pronounce the words?"

"I just don't want to embarrass you, dear seaver."

Phillippe paused.

"Also, that's hardly all I do. Romantic Fantasy isn't all about bits connecting, you know."

"Isn't it?"

He rolled his eyes.

"You'd think that a being without genitals would know more about love."

"Is that the equation?"

Reihan shook her head before Phillippe could respond.

"I didn't say I didn't have them", she continued, "I just said that seaver are born without them."

Phillippe blinked.

"Wait. Do you grow them at a certain age, then? Like a plant?"

"Plants don't have geni – never mind." Reihan rolled her eyes.

"There's a guy who does alterations in the undercity. I'm not sure if it's a genuine procedure or a manifestation, but you shouldn't question it too much for obvious reasons. Especially given that manifestations aren't *supposed* to work on us."

She probably shouldn't tell him that. But a little trust gained you trust in return. And Phillippe needed someone he could trust.

"Right. I suppose that makes about as much sense as anything. And … you got that procedure done?"

"Yeah. Something like seventy years ago now", she said, a little proud and a little self-conscious. Phillippe grinned.

"Seventy years? So, it's all dust and cobwebs up in there now?"

"You know, just because your entire artificial species is forced into life-long servitude, that doesn't mean you can't have a regular and functioning sex life."

"Oh, regular and functional. Talk dirty to me, seaver", he laughed. Reihan rolled her eyes again but couldn't help herself from smiling. They let the laughter fizzle out, then sat in silence for a few moments. It didn't feel awkward, Reihan thought. It felt like nothing much at all, like sitting with her own thoughts. Which, in a way, was nice. Usually, humans made her feel nervous, like she was being observed inside a rotating glass or like she was supposed to do something. Phillippe made her feel at ease, despite most of the things that came out of his mouth.

Phillippe exhaled slowly.

"Thanks for trying to distract me", he said, as if it had only just occurred to him why she had chosen that topic of conversation.

"You're very welcome", she replied.

"I don't mean to sound ungrateful", he continued, slowly, measuring, "But part of me wants to talk about him sometimes."

He hesitated.

"But it's not your job to listen to me."

"It's not."

She looked up at him and was surprised to find apprehension in his eyes. Was he afraid to be rejected? By a seaver of all things? She smiled inadvertently. After a hundred years of service, she wasn't above feeling high on a little rush of power.

"So, make it worth my while, Phillippe. I shall offer you my ear for whatever you shall offer in return."

He barked out another surprised laugh.

"Bribery, seaver? Really?"

"Whatever else do I have left in this world? And anyway, didn't you tell me to branch out?"

He grinned.

"How does a round of drinks sound to you? I don't have another client until far later tonight. And I hardly need to be sober for that one."

"Difficult request?"

"Not particularly", he shook his head, "But that one truly is only after the colliding bits. Tedious."

Reihan wasn't sure how to respond. Phillippe saved the moment when he jumped up, shedding scales as he rose. The air around him stirred, and he turned back into the androgynous young man who had saved her and Alexander in the Asylum. Black hair hung down to his chin, cut razor-sharp at the edges, and glittery blue sparkles adorned his eyes, painted on in thick artistry. He smelled of wind and smoke and peonies.

Reihan nodded to his room, deliberate in her decision not to look impressed. Phillippe was incredibly powerful, which made any acknowledgement of that fact dangerous. She had seen enough humans consumed by foolish ambition and ever more foolish pride.

"You got anything in there?"

"No. They don't let you keep booze or weapons in your rooms. And they have daily checks. You know, like we're not all insanely talented manifesters and can do whatever we want."

He gave her a wicked grin.

"Well, then, couldn't you manifest us something all the same?", she asked.

"Sure. But I'm no master mixologist. The taste is never quite the same when I do it myself. Also, more importantly, being here is depressing. Let's go to a bar."

The Travelling City had an assortment of bars and small restaurants, some near the Amusement Park and the Menagerie, and some in the Undercity. Reihan had never been to most of them. Her privileges did not extend that far, so she depended on grateful family members or Enforcers to invite her out for a meal. Most of them never did, so Asylum fodder it was.

"I still can't walk anywhere", she protested, swallowing the longing that the suggestion stirred within her, "I would need hours to recharge, and I can't stay away from the Asylum that long without being noticed."

Phillippe frowned.

"They really keep such close tabs on you?"

"Don't they do that for you?", Reihan retorted.

"Fair enough."

He shook his head.

"Do not worry, dear seaver. Your gallant escort has the solution for all your problem."

Before she could protest, he leaned down and wrapped an arm around her. Unlike before, where her touch had surprised him, his posture betrayed no hint of uncertainty. He moved as if he owned the universe, striding like a long-forgotten god banished from the sky for his beauty.

Stop it, she told herself, the sharpness of her thoughts ripping her out of her trance.

"Let's go", Phillippe whispered, and his hair tickled the sides of her cheeks. Then, with a flutter of lashes, he was gone, stale air remaining where he had stood a heartbeat ago. She moved to the side of the room and leaned her back against the hard stone of the tower. Beneath, one of the brothel workers started moaning in tandem with her client. She couldn't tell if it was fake, but the enthusiasm on display was impressive either way.

Phillippe returned a few seconds later.

"Ah", he made, looking at her as she leaned against the wall, "Right."

"Seaver", she repeated, gesturing up and down her frame, "The fact that you can't manifest on me is literally the reason you people created me."

"Yes. That occurred to me about five seconds after I had

teleported."

"That soon?", she mocked.

"Yeah, well. I've never –"

"Are you going to tell me you didn't learn about this in school again?"

"No", Phillippe responded, a soft smile on his features where she would have expected annoyance, "I was going to say that I've never been friends with a seaver before."

Reihan felt the sincerity of the moment stretch between them. For a long, awful second, she felt tempted to snatch the bond that was slowly growing between them, just to keep things simple for once. She was getting too old to chastise herself for such a predictable impulse.

And yet. And yet.

"It seems I have a lot to teach you."

"I look forward to it."

His smile was sincere as the air between them seemed to vibrate, then he clapped his hands.

"Well, I suppose with you having to return to the Asylum, the bar idea may be a bust anyway, especially with the one I wanted to take you to."

"Which is?"

He winked.

"You know the quarter next to the Amusement Park? All the small houses and huts suspended on floating rocks?"

"That latest spout of madness? I've heard of it, but I haven't been."

"Well, it'll make you absolutely furious, and we must go at the earliest opportunity."

Reihan's eyebrows shot up to her hairline.

"Over my dead body. Which, no doubt, will crash into the cloud sea once whoever is responsible for manifesting the floating islands goes to take a nap or has a particularly distracting shit."

"Ah, don't fret. I'll be there the whole time."

"Which should comfort me how?"

She shook her head before he could respond.

"That's a discussion for another day. For the time being, you may have to cart me home."

Phillippe hesitated.

"What, in an actual cart?"

"What, am I a sack of potatoes?"

"Well, you said –"

"You're a master manifester, and the best thing you can come up with is a cart? How about the city's smoothest wheelchair, made of sugar-sweet clouds, with cushions so soft they put me to sleep?"

Phillippe grinned, relishing the challenge.

"Now, that I can do, dear seaver. That I can do."

The wheelchair held up surprisingly well to being carried through the air. Reihan had wisely insisted that Phillippe add straps to hold her arms and legs in place. With that, the air breezing around her face felt less terrifying than exhilarating, and the regular flapping of Phillippe's wings became an underlying drum to the sun's game of peaking in and out of the clouds.

"Do you do this often?", she asked. She had no idea if the winged creature Phillippe had manifested into had initially been created with a mouth, but after a few moments, she could hear his reply, always in that same voice of his.

"As often as I can. Sometimes I fly so far above the city that I can't see it anymore and just let myself fall."

"Aren't you scared that you'll crash into us?"

"On some days, I relish the thought", Phillippe admitted. Reihan laughed, not taking him seriously.

"Oh, I've had days like that."

"I thought you might understand. A century in this place, and you've been a servant all this time. I don't know how you're still sane."

"Who says I am? I'm here with you, aren't I?"

Phillippe laughed and turned his wings inward. The Brothel of Transformative Curiosities lay on the platform above the Asylum, which was also crowded by the Watchtower and the houses of particularly crafty and talented merchants. Curved golden roofs sparkled in flecks of sunlight, and small shimmering bridges appeared and disappeared between the houses at the whims of their inhabitants.

The platforms were too far apart to build a lift between the Brothel and the Asylum, especially with the Asylum so close to the Undercity, a district most liked to forget about. Instead, the platforms were connected by the Weeping Stairs, a natural rock formation that had, centuries ago, been converted into a gigantic sprawling stairway. If one had travelled all the way to the top of The Weeping Stairs, one could walk up to the Brothel, past the invisible Casino that floated sideways in the open air between the Undercity and the Amusement Park. It was easy to lose one's way in the Travelling City, and the geography of the place changed frequently.

Reihan had been adamant that she did not want Phillippe to push her down the Weeping Stairs, not with all the gravel underfoot and the threat of small avalanches if one of the travellers was having a particularly bad day. Some things did not change, not even in a hundred years.

Instead, she had asked him to push her out to the Watchtower and then to descend slowly down to the Asylum, using the wings he had so proudly manifested.

"Where are you going?", Reihan asked when she realised that Phillippe had stopped their flight from one platform to the next and held them suspended in the air.

"Do you fancy a tour of the city? It just occurred to me that you've probably never seen it from above", Phillippe asked, and before she could respond, he flapped his wings once, twice, three times, and they were level with the top of the Weeping Stairs, evading the stalactites hanging from the roof. There were few travellers below, but even so, they looked up with astonishment at the seaver in the wheelchair in the claws of a gigantic bird.

"You could have asked", Reihan responded half-heartedly.

"Better to ask forgiveness rather than permission", Phillippe responded, "Come on, seaver. What would you like to see?"

"The Amusement Park", Reihan said without hesitation, "I'd like to see that from above."

"The Amusement Park?", Phillippe echoed but still made way towards it, "You know it's really not all that impressive once you've been a few times."

"I've only been once", Reihan responded quietly. She was almost sure he wouldn't have heard her past the wind, and yet he did.

"Why?", he responded.

"Because seaver don't have access rights. Not unless they're with a human who is willing to take them."

"Why don't you have access rights?", Phillippe asked, his voice soft, as if that were the point of the story.

"Because why would we need any amusements or distractions?", Reihan responded ironically, "Those were hardly qualities we were programmed with inside great tube mother."

Phillippe did not take the bait. He stayed silent as they floated atop the Travelling City. A second later, sunlight broke through grey-rushing clouds and fell, soft as a feather, onto the bustle below. Reihan had never seen the rock that was her home in its entirety. In her mind, it had always been fragmented, a mosaic of different corners that people tried to turn into their own kingdom, hearth, utopia, pleasure trove. Now, she saw all these ants crawling up and down the mountain, a house in every crevice, flowing as the waves with its citizens' desires.

"Aren't they so small?", Phillippe whispered, "So inconsequential if you look at them from up here. And yet they decide upon all our lives. Mine. Yours most of all, seaver."

"Hmm", Reihan made, unsure what else to say. She didn't disagree. It was hard to disagree.

"All I've sacrificed for the power to float up here, and all I can do now is look down. What's even the point?"

His voice rose, frustration colouring its edges.

"In a way, I feel no more powerful now than before I went down to the *World's End*."

"Are you trying to tell me we're the same, Phillippe?", Reihan mocked, hoping to break through his gloom, "Because I'll struggle to believe that as soon as you're allowed to enter the Amusement Park and I'm turned away at the entrance."

Phillippe laughed.

"Are you calling me melodramatic, seaver?"

"Your words, not mine."

"Ha", he laughed, "Who took you there, Reihan? To the Amusement Park."

"That's none of your business."

"I know. But I still want to know. Was it a member of Government, grateful for fifty years of service? A family member of one of your charges at the Asylum? An anonymous beneficiary?"

"No."

"No?"

"No."

Phillippe flapped his wings impatiently. The sun disappeared again, and Reihan felt the cold winds claw on her skin.

"You know, I can keep you up here until you tell me. If I wanted to."

Phillippe's voice was suddenly as soft as spiked wine. *Intoxicating*, Reihan thought. She could see why his clients were obsessed with him. But she liked power more than he did, and she hated feeling helpless.

"Your patience will run out before mine", she said sharply.

Phillippe laughed.

"That's probably true. Shall we find out, nevertheless? I'm sure we can find ways to pass the time."

"You're not allowed to keep me up here. I could have you punished for even just suggesting it."

She could hear the grin in Phillippe's voice even though she did not turn around to his feathered face.

"Oh", he made, "Is that so? And how will you punish me up here, dear seaver?"

Reihan was tempted to meet the challenge in his tone. But duty was a stronger mistress than Phillippe.

"Phillippe. Stop this. I need to go back to work."

"All right, all right."

Phillippe sank lower, flapping his wings with the most frustratingly small motions.

"I suppose I shall never find out any more about you, even as I bare my very heart to you, Reihan."

"You haven't bared anything", Reihan responded as they descended further.

"Would you like me to?"

Phillippe's response came quickly, as if on instinct.

"Perhaps I would", Reihan said, then shook her head, "Perhaps I just want you to let me down. I suppose you'll have to find out."

There was a short pause, and they fell silent for a little while.

"Are seaver allowed to flirt with humans?", Phillippe finally asked, his voice a little unsteady.

"Since when do you care what's allowed?"

"I care when it pertains to you."

Reihan allowed herself a small, self-indulgent smile. The giant Ferris Wheel started to fill their vision, a blood-red instrument that had been imagined into being by a group of anonymous manifesters about a century ago. When Reihan had been on it, the one and only time, she had felt like she had gained her very own wings, reigning over stormy, thick clouds that shifted into stories and darkness. Her whole chest had threatened to burst with emotions she didn't often let herself feel.

"I went to the Amusement Park with my best friend. My lover, I suppose you could say."

It was still hard to say.

"It was a long time ago, but the rules have not changed", she explained, then added:

"Rather, nobody ever bothered to write any rules about this."

"Your human lover?", Phillippe asked quietly.

"Yes."

The winds roared above them now. A storm was brewing. The Enforcers would need to disentangle it before a dance of lightning crashed into the Travelling City.

"Didn't you resent them? Your lover?", Phillippe asked a frustrating while later. Where the silence had felt comfortable before, now she felt its edges digging into her skin.

"Whatever for?"

"Holding all the power. The manifestation, the privilege, the – being human. Giving crumbs and flecks away to buy your gratitude. It's crass and predictable."

"It wasn't like that."

"Wasn't it? Could it be any different?"

Phillippe's breathing went heavy as he slowed down to approach the platform on which the Asylum rose like a white stone flower. The grass flew up to greet them and became engulfed in Phillippe's gigantic wings, which disappeared as soon as the wheelchair hit the ground. Phillippe flicked his wrist, and a small path appeared through the grass, making it easier for him to push her towards the Asylum's front doors.

"Nice trick", Reihan commented drily. Phillippe scoffed.

"It's nothing special."

"Indeed? We'll spend months growing that grass back."

"I can change it again", Phillippe responded, sounding slightly exasperated.

"I'm sure you can."

Her voice took on a strained quality. Phillippe pushed the wheelchair a little slower, and somehow she felt more at his mercy now than she had done at the top of the Travelling City.

"What's the issue, Rei –"

"Reihan!"

One of the seaver from the Asylum ran towards them, her white uniform, white skin and white hair unmistakable. She had named herself Freeday after the last day of the week. Many seaver named themselves eventually, but Reihan remembered that Fee had taken longer than most to do so.

"Where have you been?", she demanded. Reihan cocked her head to the side.

"At the Brothel", she explained as though that was an explanation that ought to make sense to Fee. Her colleague shook her head.

"Well, you best have had important business there."

"Why? She's shouldn't have to stand to attention at all hours of the day", Phillippe snapped. Fee glared at him.

"This is seaver business. It does not concern you."

"She was visiting me, so I'd say it does", Phillippe retorted, "Is that illegal now?"

"It is when her charges go missing", Freeday responded with an accusatory glare at Reihan. Reihan frowned.

"What are you talking about?"

"Your patient down on floor two. Alexander."

"Alex is missing?"

Phillippe's eyes widened.

"You need to leave. This does not concern you", Freeday repeated, her voice rising with threat.

"The hell do I –"

"Freeday. When I left, Alexander was in his room, same as all my other charges. If he's not in there, I'm sure someone else took him out for observation."

Reihan couldn't imagine why someone would have bothered, but after a century at the Asylum, few things still surprised her.

"You misunderstand me, Reihan", Fee said, her voice thin and panicked, "I mean that he left the Asylum. Of his own accord. He just walked out the door."

Both Phillippe and Reihan stared at her.

"That's impossible", Reihan finally said. Fee nodded.

"I know. But there are witnesses. Several of the visiting families, and some seaver who didn't realise he was an inmate. I know how this sounds, but –"

"You're sure", Phillippe mused, "You're telling the truth. Or you think you are."

"I am", Fee snapped, "Now, you really must leave."

"Phillippe is Alexander's his brother, Fee", Reihan said, "He deserves to know what happened."

She stroked her chin, hunching over in her wheelchair.

"Was anyone working on a drug? A stimulant, maybe? Or did someone manifest a copy of Alexander to make everyone think they found a cure for the Submergence?"

"I don't know, Reihan", Fee responded with a nervous look towards Phillippe, "But there's a man from the Government who wants to talk to you. I stalled him for as long as I could, but he's getting impatient. And he's got this creepy woman with him, I think she's a shadow…."

"The Government. Amazing. Just my luck", Reihan muttered, then turned around to Phillippe.

"Are you okay with rolling me inside? I assume you'll want to be in the meeting."

Phillippe nodded, staring blankly ahead for a few moments. Then he frowned.

"Why didn't he come to me?"

"Phillippe. I know it might be hard, but try not to get your hopes up. We don't know what happened yet", Reihan cautioned, her heart beating hard against her pale skin.

Phillippe barked out a laugh.

"If you think I can do that, you truly are a machine."

Reihan did not respond, a sour feeling spreading through her chest and limbs. They did not speak another word until they reached the Asylum.

CHAPTER 7: PHILLIPPE

Their steps echoed in the white halls of the Asylum. Phillippe was surprised that the sound, cold and infuriatingly unmusical, didn't drive Reihan insane when she walked through the corridors. Through the open door of the staff room, Phillippe saw the Asylum's two visitors awkwardly hunched in between large shelves overfilled with threatening instruments that he would ask Reihan about once she was less mad at him. Neither of the visitors had sat down yet, which was just as well, given that most of the chairs were occupied with piles of white laundry that smelled like absolutely nothing.

Reihan straightened her back, then stood up from the wheelchair just outside the room. She entered without turning back around to Phillippe.

As he followed her, unasked and probably unwanted, he recognised one of the visitors. His breathing softened to a slog as he fought to stay in the moment, accepting reality as it reared its bright red head.

Now of all times, you show up?

"Finally", one of the visitors said, a young woman who stared at Reihan unblinkingly, "Aren't you seaver always supposed to be on time?"

"Of course", Reihan agreed, "Me being late is thus impossible."

The woman stared at her for a moment too long, and her companion began to speak.

"I am Lukacz the Fourteenth, from the Government's Overseeing Provision. Earlier today, we were informed by your colleagues that you seem to have misplaced one of your charges at the Asylum. The lady is my bodyguard and personal assistant Ellis."

"Charmed", Ellis added with a dangerous smile.

Reihan appeared unfazed by their introduction.

"I do not recall misplacing the patient in question", she responded, her voice neutral,

"Alexander was in his room when I left the Asylum earlier today. I did not put him anywhere else since."

"And did you lock the door, seaver?", Ellis asked. Reihan shook her head.

"That is not Asylum protocol. In the event of a fire, we may need to evacuate quickly, in which case it may take too long to track down the keys for each door."

"Very good", Lukacz said in a similarly calm tone to Reihan, "But does that not mean that your charges can leave their rooms whenever they please?"

Finally, Phillippe spotted a note of irritation on Reihan's blank features, a slight twitch in her left eyebrow.

"Overseer, have you ever visited the Asylum before?", she asked.

"What does that have to do with –?", Ellis began, but Lukacz raised his hand, and she fell silent as quickly as if she had been placed in a dome of glass.

"Once, many years ago. To survey the security standards of the building."

"Very good. And did you come into contact with many of our patients then?", Reihan continued. Lukacz shook his head, but Phillippe thought he saw a note of resignation on his face as if he could tell where this conversation was headed.

"In that case, you will not be aware that all our charges are catatonic, except for random and short-lived outbursts. It is a documented and unavoidable consequence of repeated exposure to the collective unconscious below the Travelling City, commonly known as the Submergence. Our patients generally do not move, eat, wash or react to their environment."

She raised an eyebrow.

"With all due respect, Alexander could not have left the Asylum without assistance. I have worked here for a century and have never seen any patients improve."

"Never?"

Phillippe couldn't help but ask, even though the seaver had never given him any hope of the contrary. Reihan turned around, and he could see her expression soften as she looked at him. It was strange. Her features hardly rearranged, and yet her usual mask of coldness warmed as quickly as a Spring afternoon. He thought he could hear birds and smell flowers and hoped she would stop being mad at him soon.

"Never", she repeated nonetheless.

"Very well. Thank you for your account, seaver", Lukacz said and finally sat down after removing a small pile of undershirts from a creaking chair, "Given all this, we must assume that Alexander was freed by someone interfering with the Asylum from the outside."

"Or the inside", Ellis added, sitting on the table surface to the right of Lukacz.

"Forgive me, but how exactly would that work? To have Alexander move of his own accord, one would surely need to use a manifestation", Reihan responded drily, "And there are only seaver employed at the Asylum."

Ellis shrugged.

"Just keepin' an open mind."

"Ellis", Lukacz cautioned her, then rubbed his temples.

"Do you have a log of visitors for Alexander that we could review?"

"I do", Reihan said, then hesitated, "Although that would be a fairly pointless endeavour."

"And why is that?", Lukacz asked.

"Because Phillippe here has been Alexander's only visitor since he was admitted."

For the first time, Lukacz and Ellis's eyes focused entirely on Phillippe as he stood behind Reihan, half concealed by the seaver and the straps and bonds overflowing on the shelves.

Phillippe opened his mouth to introduce himself as Alexander's brother.

He planned to do so with excruciating smugness, of course. He would be the one who had visited all this time, and now that Alex was well again – maybe, *maybe* he was well again – he would be remembered as the one who came even when it broke his heart. Who came even when he had to do battle with his memories every time, like a knight fighting windmills.

"I do believe I am still capable of recognising my own son. At least his eyes, which he has not yet altered", Lukacz said, stopping the sounds that were trying to arrange themselves in Phillippe's mouth. He felt his hands shake, with anger or surprise, he wasn't sure.

"You …"

Phillippe found no words to continue the sentence.

He hadn't forgotten Lukacz either, not his cold voice, nor the curve of his nose, nor the twinge at the corners of his mouth. His father was the one who had forgotten about them in the Undercity, in mom's little flat in which she had died all by herself when her sons had been out working.

Lukacz didn't get to recognise him.

"Really?", Ellis broke the silence, "You have kids?"

Reihan cleared her throat, then clearly regretted it as she drew the stares of everyone in the room.

"Well, as I was saying, unless Phillippe got Alexander to leave the Asylum, the logs will not be helpful. I can still fetch them, of course. I am here to serve."

"About that."

Lukacz focused on Phillippe, and he could feel the Overseer's eyes burning on his skin as he just about escaped meeting his gaze. He hadn't seen his father in long over ten years. His heart twisted, and it did not feel like enough time.

"You are, from what I understand, a very powerful manifester. I expect it might be in your power to free your brother from his state, and you would have a clear motivation to do so."

"So?"

The word rolled out, dropping to the ground where it lay, the letters slowly manifesting into existence. Thankfully, none of the others noticed, even after the word sprang apart after a few seconds of life.

"So, if you are the one to have caused this miracle, I would ask that you stop wasting our time and come forward. You are not in trouble. But knowing how you achieved this may help us release some of the other patients from their state."

Phillippe didn't believe him. But more than that, he couldn't respond. He was back at sea. The water surrounded the horizon, and he was alone. The waves got ready to submerge him, to drown out all the words, just like they always did. He would never escape this choice he'd made. All this ill-gotten power and he could do nothing with it that mattered.

"Phillippe."

He could hear Reihan's voice over the crashing waves and felt her cold fingers close around his wrist. He blinked, and the conference hall came back into view, with its inhabitants looking a little worse for wear, all damp and with dripping clothes and hair. Phillippe felt his cheeks burning, and Lukacz stared at him with an unreadable expression. Reihan stood next to him, her fingers still on his skin.

"Phillippe was with me when Alexander left the Asylum. He couldn't be responsible."

"Are there any witnesses for that?", Ellis pressed, looking like an angry, wet cat as she wrung out her black hair.

"Ellis, the word of a seaver is above suspicion. That is the law", Lukacz reminded her and nodded at Reihan, "Please forgive my associate. She means no disrespect."

Reihan simply nodded, neither following up on the insult nor downplaying it. Phillippe coughed, finding specks of seawater in his lungs.

"I'll admit that I tried. I tried to fix his mind whenever I visited. But no manifestation worked. He was like a white wall, and no colour would stick to it. The remnants of the mind fog were far too strong."

Reihan glared at him, but Phillippe merely sighed.

"Whoever freed Alex is more powerful than me."

"That is concerning", Lukacz noted, "As you have recently been registered as one of our city's more powerful manifesters."

"Registered?", Phillippe echoed.

Lukacz sighed.

"In your position at the Brothel of Transformative Curiosities, son. Do you not think we are aware of our citizens' abilities?"

Phillippe glared.

"Nice to know you've been keeping tabs, dad. Beats sending a name day card."

Ellis snorted.

"Why doesn't it surprise me that you're a deadbeat dad, boss man?"

Lukacz gave her a look, and she fell silent.

"Either way", Reihan began and let go of Phillippe's wrist, "This entire situation is concerning. I talked to Freeday on the way here, and no intruders were spotted in the Asylum. Whoever achieved this is not only more powerful than Phillippe but powerful enough to influence Alexander from afar."

"Well. They could have fixed the boy and, poof, teleported out of the place again. Or they made themselves look like one of you creepy seaver", Ellis added, "Or maybe they were nuts enough to make themselves invisible. Save us the trouble."

Phillippe grimaced. Turning invisible was equal to making yourself disappear entirely. Many had tried to hold onto a sense of self when their entire body had faded from existence, and all had failed.

"Indeed. Or it was Phillippe himself who influenced his

brother from afar", Lukacz added, and Phillippe glared at him.

"I told you, I didn't –"

"Very good, and I am keeping that statement in mind."

Lukacz crossed his fingers and fixated on his son. Not a hint of emotion lay in his expression, so estranged and in that so familiar.

"Nonetheless, as a matter of formality, consider yourself under investigation for the duration of this incident."

"Consider myself –", Phillippe echoed, but Reihan interrupted him.

"Very well. In that case, I propose that Phillippe, supervised by myself, takes an active part in the search for his brother. This will allow him to clear himself of suspicion if he is innocent and allow me to keep my eyes on him in case he is not", Reihan said.

Lukacz measured her, then nodded.

"That is acceptable."

"Oh, yay! New friends!", Ellis mouthed.

CHAPTER 8: REIHAN

It was hot. The entire city was boiling under the unrelenting rays of three suns, with not a single cloud providing recluse to its suffering citizens. A section of the Enforcers was looking for the unhappy soul who had, wittingly or not, caused this weather-borne torment while others were working on unravelling the manifestation itself. But until they figured it out, the heat was here to stay.

"So, they really don't give you any summer outfits? With cute skirts and little heeled sandals?"

Phillippe had draped her generously curved body over one of the chairs in the corner of her room, and the heat was making her positively miserable as she loudly and repeatedly stressed to Reihan.

"Why are you so obsessed with that? No!", Reihan responded short-lipped. She had grown more tolerant of Phillippe's intrusive questions, something the escort had noted with much glee.

"So, where did you get the trousers and that fancy cloak on the mantle?"

"Hand-made or donated."

Phillippe groaned.

"Boring. I was hoping you would say that you stole them from the group of badass Enforcers you seaver are modelled after."

"I told you this before, we aren't modelled after anyone in particular."

"Except for the wishes of your great tube mother."

"Except for that, of course. How silly of me to forget", Reihan said, a smile dancing around her lips. She decided on a dark green shirt and pulled it over her head, tucking the front pieces into her black velvet trousers. There were technically no rules on what seaver could wear or where they could go. Reihan nonetheless anticipated that she'd be drawing a few stares patrolling the street in non-white clothing, with Phillippe by her side currently in the shape of a two-meter-tall woman wearing a feather-light version of battle armour. Phillippe had a very strange way of taking the search for her brother seriously.

"Need anything else? Or can we finally get going?", Phillippe complained, still stretched out across Reihan's chair in a supremely uncomfortable-looking position. If her armour had been real, it would have dug into all manner of places on her skin. This way, it flickered when the light hit it, dancing in and out of existence.

"So impatient", Reihan replied, then waved Phillippe to follow. The people at the Asylum were no longer surprised to see Phillippe walk out of Reihan's room or for her to follow the seaver around the grounds and pathways of the compound. Some of them even greeted her in the reverent, shy way that was typical of Asylum workers.

"Then again", Reihan said, bemused at Phillippe's nervousness, "I suppose you people only have a hundred-odd years to work with. Must be awfully stressful getting everything done."

Phillippe laughed.

"Yes, the pressure is nigh-on unbearable. However will I manage to explore all the odds and ends of… one city."

She smirked.

"I'm sure with your cell regeneration features and vaguely competent tank-born construction, you can feel oh-so superior to a regular human, seaver."

"Vaguely competent construction? Thank you ever so much, Phillippe. Do people really pay for that level of charm at the Brothel?"

The escort's features darkened ever so slightly and Reihan cursed silently. Still, Phillippe smiled again a moment later, picking up a good mood as easily as a stray though.

"For me, it's all theoretical anyway, isn't it?", Phillippe asked, "For a powerful manifester, neither age nor death truly matter from what I can tell. Lottie, my boss, is four hundred years old but she looks like a child."

She grinned.

"It's not hard to imagine ever-lasting beauty and youth. You may take my expert opinion on that."

They left the Asylum and made their way through the small orchard that led to the edge of the compound, which would allow them to circumnavigate the Weeping Stairs and descend straight into the caverns that housed the Undercity. The apple trees were immobile in the heat, with not even a single cooling breeze gracing them with its presence. Reihan was starting to regret the black velvet that clung to her legs, but then again, she refused to wear her seaver uniform for anything that was not strictly part of her role.

"Of course. And you think you're the first to consider yourself above death itself?"

She spoke softly. Phillippe was still new to power. She didn't want to be cruel, but she shouldn't pretend with him.

"One memory that makes you realise how long you've lived for, and the whole façade of youth fades away until we're left with a steaming skeleton in the middle of the plaza. I've quite seen that happen one too many times already."

"But surely that's just because those people never fully internalised the manifestation", Phillippe countered, "Once you do, you can be young even if you've lived for a millennium."

"Indeed? And I assume your brain alone will be capable of such an impressive feat of self-deception?"

Reihan shook her head.

"Just be careful, Phillippe. The only things worth having exist in the present. Not a future that may never come."

Phillippe said nothing in response to that.

The orchard parted in front of them, and Reihan unlocked the white gates of the Asylum with a touch of her fingers. The Weeping Stairs rose to their left. The staircase was part natural formation, part artificial, a heap of white limestone hewn into the rock around which the Travelling City snaked like a sleeping dragon. Even this early in the day, the large platforms were crowded with travellers from both the higher and the lower regions, children playing catch underneath the black shadows of the stone overhang, and merchants manifesting their carts from one step to the next. Some of the more talented manifesters had taken the shape of winged creatures to soar above the rest, who either climbed the available ladders, pulled themselves up with homemade lifts or waited for someone willing to fly them onto the next level. There were always people left stuck on the stairs by the end of the night, and a troop of Enforcers had to get them back home safely. Reihan took a few steps towards the Weeping Stairs, then turned around.

Behind her, next to the landmass on which the Asylum lived, the rock face fell into nothingness, and only peach-coloured clouds stretched as far as the eye could see. Reihan's vision was framed by the walls of the large tunnel in which they stood, outlined by black rock sketched out in a god's unsteady hand. She took another step towards the edge and felt her feet grow heavy and a hint of adrenaline rise in her throat. Still, she could see nothing besides the sea of clouds beneath.

Phillippe did not comment on the delay when Reihan turned back to her and allowed her to lead them to the Undercity. Next to the Weeping Stairs hung a wall of woven ladders, all leading into the same system of caverns in which the Travelling City's weakest manifesters had made their home. Reihan sighed and motioned to take hold of one of the ropes, thinking of the exertion of climbing back up later. That alone would take her a significant portion of the day's energy.

"There's no need", Phillippe said, snatching her hand from reaching the ladder. She had grown a pair of translucent butterfly wings, shimmering in the daylight. Reihan shrugged.

"Well, I don't like to presume…."

Phillippe cocked her head to the side.

"Why not? It's easier for us both if I use my powers."

"True. But they're your powers, not mine. Plus, some people, or so I've heard, do not find it quite as ridiculously easy as you seem to."

Phillippe smiled at her, a layer of sincerity beneath feigned arrogance.

"Why, thank you ever so much for your consideration, seaver. But this? It takes barely a thought."

With that, she took Reihan into her arms, and they floated down by the wall of ladders, leaving behind those unhappy visitors, grim-faced and tired, who made their way down by climbing. Reihan squirmed in Phillippe's grip to turn around. Much of the Undercity was made up of tents, their fabrics sewn together from the elaborate curtains that often came loose from the windows of the mansions further on high. Purple tapestries with yellow stars were particularly common after a night sky masquerade that the Brothel of Transformative Curiosities had hosted the best part of a month ago. From the upper levels of the cavern, the tents below looked like a mountain range with a million peaks. Closer to the walls and on the sides of the stone roads that weaved their way through the Undercity, Reihan could see tiny houses that had been hewn into the stone, with small windows, ill-fitting wooden doors and drying clothes replacing curtains.

Phillippe's feet connected with the ground, and she gently placed the seaver back down.

"Very gallant", Reihan muttered.

"Always happy to please", Phillippe replied, but her tone was tense. Her eyes swept across the thick crowds that poured from the ladders into the cavern, and she made her butterfly wings disappear before they drew more attention. Reihan waited for a moment to give her the chance to suggest a way to proceed.

Coming here had been Phillippe's idea. She thought that Alexander might have fled here after leaving the Asylum, or someone here might have seen him pass through. For lack of better ideas, Reihan had not argued against the plan, but now it seemed that getting here was as far as Phillippe had thought ahead. She leaned against a nearby way post, once a stalactite that had crashed down from the ceiling above and which had since been used as a place to carve out way pointers to some local shops. Reihan did not recognise any of the names.

"It's been so long since I came here", she said. Phillippe turned around, her expression confused and her eyes far away.

"What?", she said, more a sound than a question.

"This place has changed a lot in sixty years", Reihan confessed with a weary smile.

"Sixty years?", Phillippe echoed, "I wasn't – I mean...."

"I know."

"What was it like back then? Was it as much of a shithole as it is now?"

Phillippe's grim smile came easy.

"It was worse", Reihan replied, "The crowds were larger, there were fewer tents and more people sleeping by the side of the road. The air was always sizzling with uncontrolled manifestations, drawing on the energies of the entire cavern. Thunder and lightning were pretty much daily occurrences in here, like a perpetual storm waiting to come into being."

Phillippe blinked.

"I've not – I mean, I never heard of that before."

"Well, for the last forty-three years, they have discretely stationed Enforcers down here to keep people's manifestations from acting out in such a tight space."

Reihan shrugged when she saw Phillippe's surprised expression.

"Remember, the people living here aren't just those with weak manifestation abilities. It's also the people who have disproportionate trouble controlling their powers."

"Right", Phillippe muttered, then shrugged and pointed in a seemingly random direction.

"Shall we then?"

Reihan followed her for a little through narrow streets and across small bridges that had been carved into the morose rocks of the Undercity, littered with small breathing holes and hidden walkways. Now and again, multi-coloured steam shot out from underneath their feet or around the next corner, and with the crowds of people passing by, it was impossible to maintain a sense of orientation. But Phillippe did, somehow. Although she didn't seem to have a clear idea of where they were going, they never passed by the same waypoints twice, not by the sizeable illegal menagerie, or the geyser puddles that left skin raw and red, or the small trade school where teachers desperately tried to improve the manifestation abilities of their exasperated pupils. As they walked by a small collection of food stalls on the side of the street, half-hidden under a precariously balanced stone overhang, Reihan stopped.

"I need to eat something, or my body is going to collapse", she said, hoping a break might help Phillippe refocus. The escort stopped, but she didn't turn around.

"Liar", Phillippe said, and Reihan could see the corners of her mouth lift ever-so-slightly.

"How would you know?"

"You usually don't have lunch until a little while after now. And you usually have that weird, cheesy soup. I can't imagine that makes that much of a difference, nutrition-wise."

Phillippe finally turned around but didn't quite look at Reihan, instead fixing the stalls with a look of pure disgust.

"Plus, I'm pretty sure they serve unstable food here. One time, I saw a guy eat a melon stick, and it turned back into a rat that ate its way back out of this stomach."

"Lovely", Reihan said, blinking slowly, "Perhaps somewhere else then."

Phillippe sighed.

"Look. If you want a break, that's fine. But don't lie to me."

Reihan rolled her eyes.

"Whatever."

Phillippe shook her head, then looked back at Reihan.

"Do I really make you feel like you have to? Like I wouldn't listen to you otherwise?"

Reihan raised her eyebrows.

"I'm not the one who started with the lying, Phillippe."

"I'm not lying to you!"

"Aren't you? You know this place. You know every nook and cranny, and I think you also know where we have to go. You're wasting our time procrastinating."

Phillippe stared at her, her eyes blazing and golden, and all the sparkling manifestations prevented Reihan from truly catching her expression.

"My, my, aren't you clever?", she finally responded, sounding as irritated as a snarling cat cleaning its own tail.

Reihan shrugged.

"They don't make dumb seaver."

"Uh-huh."

Phillippe ran her fingers through her hair, golden-spun and unrelenting, and it got stuck between her long nails. The aroma of the food stalls wafted over, and imagined or not, now Reihan thought she could definitely smell rat.

"I'm from here. You've probably figured that out, haven't you?"

Reihan sighed, then gingerly took Phillippe's wrist out of her hair and led her to one of the small tables underneath the stone overhang.

They sat down, squeezed between two kegs and a hot plate spitting oil in between heavy slices of undefined meat. The bodies of unsuspecting customers rubbed against them as they queued to exchange favours and small trinkets for melon sticks. Reihan ordered them two glasses of cold water, using Philippe's name and profession for credit.

"It had occurred to me", Reihan confessed. Phillippe's back was hunched, and her battle armour had all but disappeared in favour of a beige shirt and some high-wasted trousers.

"Why else risk it? Why else descend into the mind fog and risk becoming Submerged if the need wasn't real? Especially when you had your little brother in toe."

Reihan clicked her tongue when she saw Phillippe's face fall and saw that she was right.

"Granted", she added, "we always have some self-important idiots from the upper districts trying the same thing, but you don't strike me as so greedy that you'd risk going mad just for some additional manifestation powers."

"So, you get it?", Phillippe asked quietly, "Why we had to do it?"

Reihan sighed. She didn't, not really. She should tell her that rather than spare her feelings.

"Was it really that bad down here? Could you not have done anything else?", she asked instead.

Phillippe shrugged.

"Sure. Maybe. I guess there's always something, isn't there? But Alex and I could barely manifest, so we had no privileges. Our name didn't carry any assets, nothing. Any food we made for ourselves disappeared in a matter of minutes. We just couldn't make anything last."

Her eyes flared.

"It got really bad after mom died. And I, a full-grown adult, still couldn't take care of my brother, no matter what kind of work I tried. I was just so sick of being powerless. Of the fact that nothing I did seemed to matter. So, call it pride. Call it desperation. I don't care."

Phillippe looked at the food stall as if the sight reminded her of something unpleasant.

"Alex was talking about going down to the mines to use the fog there to manifest for the city. It's no different from Submerging yourself, I told him. If we went down to the *World's End*, we'd at least have a chance to make a difference for ourselves."

"The Enforcers control the doses in the mines", Reihan said, "It's a lot safer."

"Yeah, but most people still go mad eventually. You lose most of your manifestation abilities as soon as you come back out of the shafts, and then your brain can't deal with you being powerful one minute and back to normal the next. You've given yourself up for nothing."

Phillippe shook her head.

"I know it was the wrong choice, okay? If I truly lost my brother, it wasn't worth it. I – you don't need to remind me."

Reihan took a long sip from her water, then cocked her head to the side.

"We're going to your old home", she realised, "Because you think he might have gone there."

"Where else?" Phillippe's voice was very quiet. "If he's in his own mind, it would make sense for him to think he could meet me there."

Reihan blinked.

"And you didn't go there before? You waited until I could come with you?"

"Ah – maybe?"

"*Why?*"

Phillippe sputtered out a nervous laugh that hung between them, turning into a silver-glittering spider's net. Irritated, Reihan ripped it apart with slim fingers.

"Because I'm scared. What if he's there, but he's crazy? What if he's forgotten that mum died, and I have to tell him all over again? What if he's not there at all?"

Phillippe sighed and pushed all humour and sadness from her expression until there was a measure of calm that, to Reihan, felt both frightening and familiar.

"I'm worried about what I'm going to do if I lose my cool. What I'll – conjure up. This place is messed up enough, I don't need to make it any worse."

"Fuck."

Reihan felt her long sword on her side, just peeking out beneath her cloak. Had she remembered to take it this morning? Either way, it never truly left her.

"Am I out of line?", Phillippe asked, her voice still awful and quiet.

"No", Reihan sputtered, feeling her own control slip by an inch, "It is your duty to alert a seaver if you feel as though you might lose control of your manifestation abilities. I can supervise you until you're done with your search."

She rose, and the water on the table moved over the edge of the glasses, creating a small lake.

"Let's go. Enough waiting around."

"You're mad at me", Phillippe realised, her mouth slightly open, "Why?"

"I'm not mad. Seaver don't get mad. Let's go."

Phillippe's childhood home lived at the edge of the Undercity, a stone-clad tortoise shell rippled by the elements, encasing a tiny assortment of rooms and corridors. Most of the walls had collapsed over time, and the furniture had been carried off by the other inhabitants of the neighbourhood. Stone had grown over the tortoise's shell, out of the rock face that eventually stretched out and became the Undercity's very own sky.

The house was empty, but still, Phillippe and Reihan spent as much time there as they could, walking around every corner and checking under every broken ceiling.

"It doesn't look like anyone stayed here", Reihan finally said, "At least some of this rubble would have been cleared up."

"Doesn't, does it?", Phillippe replied, her voice very far away, "Then where could he have gone?"

Reihan shrugged, more attentive to Phillippe's mood than to the question. She had been right to ask for the seaver's help, and Reihan was annoyed to admit it. Everything around them had the feeling of weak and untamed manifestations. The scent of sulphur shooting out from beneath the earth, children with beaks and cloven feet running about, a mild explosion shaking the foundations of a house built on stilts. It would be a disaster if Phillippe lost control of her powers here. And yet –

"Maybe… maybe someone close by saw Alex? Wander around, I mean?"

Phillippe's voice ripped Reihan out of her thoughts.

"There was a neighbour I used to talk to; an old guy who worked on the Weeping Stairs. He used to hang out near his fence and talk to me every day when I came home from work. Maybe he would have spotted Alex."

Reihan nodded.

"Sure, we can ask around. I took the day off."

"You can do that?"

Reihan snorted.

"Well, I took off for the day, but it works to a similar effect."

Phillippe grinned, but there was a lingering hesitation between them. They found a few stragglers sitting on smooth bits of the rock face above and around Phillippe's house, having put up tents and blankets against the winds ripping at the edges of the tunnels. Phillippe claimed not to recognise any of them and said that people in the Undercity moved all the time, but Reihan felt as though she was lying. She subtly changed her eyes every time they came near any of the people who may have been her old neighbours, and she barely spoke, leaving the investigation to Reihan.

None of them had seen anyone who fit Alexander's description.

"What if he changed the way he looks?", Phillippe suggested as they started to head back to the centre of the Undercity, with crowds of people once more a constant ebb and flow around them.

"Well, he hadn't done that when he was spotted leaving the Asylum", Reihan cautioned, "And from there, it's not a far way to come here. It's possible that he put on a disguise in the meantime, of course. I guess it's hard to say."

"Right."

They were swept into a small plaza by a swarm of people, chit-chatting about storm sightings and the new gambles in the invisible Casino, when a fight exploded. Two people faced each other on the side of the plaza, and a tear-drop shape formed around them as people quickly stepped aside. One of them, a bald man with blazing black eyes and crutches, shouted violent abuse at an androgynous human with long-raining red hair, who hovered a few inches above ground and watched the display with an impatient snarl.

"Ah, just ignore it", Phillippe said when she followed Reihan's gaze, "That kind of thing happens down here all the time."

"Indrir, I swear to all that is holy, if you don't tell me where she is, I will end you right here and now!"

The bald man hurled the words at his opponent, who rose a few inches higher yet.

"I have no idea what you're talking about", they said, their lips both tight and quivering, "What you do with your wife is none of my concern."

"Bullshit!"

With the bald man's fury, the rock face surrounding the plaza began to shake, with bits and pieces of stone raining down from the porous ceiling.

"Do you think you can threaten me?", Indrir replied, raising their red, thin eyebrows. A snake appeared out of thin air and wrapped itself around the bald man's ankles. He spat out his surprise, then crushed it under his crutch.

"Bastard!"

The crutch grew longer until a blade peaked out of its end, chasing after Indrir.

"Reihan, let's go", Phillippe insisted, keen to follow the crowds who were dispersing quickly, keen not to get caught in the crossfire, "This is about to get ugly."

"Agreed", Reihan said blankly, then drew her sword. Indrir had, by now, manifested a fiery wall that hung between them and their assailant and still danced out of the way of the crutch-shaped sword. Reihan stepped closer to the fighters and raised her voice as much as possible.

"Cease this immediately."

She raised her sword and pointed it at the bald man.

"You there. Under the authority of the Thirteenth Travelling City, I demand that you curb all manifestations at once."

The walls around them were still shaking as the man's thoughts dripped out of his mind, unable to focus solely on the blade at the end of his crutch.

"You've got the wrong one, seaver", the man said between clenched teeth, "It's Indrir you want. They seduced my wife almost a fortnight ago. I've got no idea where she is."

"Neither do I, as I've told you many times", Indrir said, then extended the wall of fire even further so that it singed the bald man's skin, "She probably just went and left you. Wouldn't be the first time that happened."

The fire roared with indignation.

"Stop this", the seaver demanded, stepping through the wall of fire. As she had imagined, it did not affect her, the manifestation too weak to cut through her inborn immunity.

Indrir stared at her, their beautifully painted mouth falling open.

"Look, I didn't —"

"Come down and put out that pathetic fire, or I'll run you through myself", Reihan snarled. Indrir measured her for a moment, then nodded and gently flew down to the ground. The bald man saw his chance and raced towards them, blade outstretched. Reihan stepped to the side, then yanked up her sword so that it cut through the crutch. She felt the blow shatter through her arms, but she could fix that later.

Shocked by the resistance, the bald man fell on his back, but his manifestations did not stop. The walls shook harder still, and more rocks rained down from the ceiling, larger this time and far quicker.

"Fuck", Reihan murmured, then ran her sword through the bald man's heart. The shaking stopped.

Indrir blinked.

"Am I – are you going to arrest me?", they asked, their voice unsure. Reihan sighed.

"I'm not an Enforcer. I don't care about your petty human disagreements."

She fixated on them, her eyes white and harsh.

"If you can control your manifestations, you're free to leave."

"I ... can."

"Prove it. Conjure an apple in the palm of your hand. Just one, coloured red. Maintain the manifestation for ten seconds, then have it disperse."

Indrir stared at her.

"Are you serious?"

Reihan pulled her sword out of the bald man's body, his blood dripping onto the pale stone ground. She was so tired of this already.

"Entirely", she replied.

She felt Phillippe's stare in her back, a silent witness.

"All right, all right."

They shook their red hair and stretched out their hand. The apple flickered in and out of existence, Indrir's control waning with their fear.

"W-what happens if I can't hold it?", they asked quietly. Reihan sighed.

"Take a few deep breaths. Close your eyes."

"What happens if I can't –"

Reihan stepped close to them.

"Close your eyes, human. That's an order."

Indrir closed their eyes, their breath still shaky. Reihan sighed, then took the hilt of her sword and hit it against the back of their head. They collapsed immediately, as if their consciousness was eager to escape their hull. She turned around to Phillippe.

"Could you find me some Enforcers? This person needs to be put in containment until they've calmed down, at least for a few days."

Phillippe stared at her, at the blood running from her sword and the two bodies lying by her side.

"Phillippe. Now."

Phillippe blinked, then nodded.

"Of course. On it."

Reihan stayed on the square until the Enforcers had removed Indrir from the scene, carrying them up to the Containment Centre in a small winged cage. Reihan finished giving her report to a senior Enforcer, a gruff man named Hannes who never manifested for personal gain, looked every day of his sixty-five years, and whose moustache was the subject of several of the regular performances in the Brothel of Transformative Curiosities.

"Right. And the manifestation continued after Bertie fell on his back?"

"Yes", Reihan confirmed, for probably the fifth time. Phillippe was still waiting for her on the other side of the square, perched on an overhang like an oversized bird. Reihan knew she wanted to talk, so, for once, she did not mind Hannes's overlong interrogation.

"Are you sure it's finished now? We can't be doing with an earthquake ripping the city apart in the middle of the night."

"The manifestation wasn't picked up by anyone else, as far as I can tell. Most of the crowd had left, and anyone looking would have been too far away to understand where the tremors were coming from. Indrir, maybe, but I knocked them out."

"How about your friend over there?"

"Phillippe?"

Reihan shuddered for a moment.

"She's fine. I trust her."

"Really?"

Reihan narrowed her eyes. Her arms were still hurting from cutting through Bertie's crutch earlier.

"Since when are you allowed to question my judgement, human?"

"Just doing my job, Reihan."

Hannes looked tired. The Enforcers had been out when Phillippe had found them on the Weeping Stairs, already in the middle of an operation. Reihan hesitated for a moment, then pushed back her thick white braids.

"Sorry. Long day."

"Same", Hannes grumbled, "Fucking teens tried to summon some kind of sex demon up on the fifth stair. Paperwork for days with them being minors."

"What a nuisance."

"You're telling me."

He frowned.

"What're you out here for anyway? Are they having you do rounds again? I thought you said you were done with all that."

All seaver had to patrol the Travelling City to handle altercations. Reihan used to enjoy it as a way to get out and about the city, even if few people met her with anything but fear, discomfort, or outright annoyance. But she had managed to negotiate patrol out of her list of duties a long while ago. The city owed her. Still.

"I'm not on shift", Reihan explained, "But there should have been a seaver down here."

Hannes sighed melodramatically.

"Well, you're telling me", he repeated, "Whenever we need them, most of the seaver in this city seem to disappear magically. No offence."

"Can't tell you anything about that, I'm afraid."

Hannes sighed again.

"Well, up to the Amusement Park we go. I'm sure by the time I get there, someone will have managed to turn the Ferris wheel into a ball of pudding. Hell of a day, Reihan. Hell of a day."

"Stay safe, Hannes", she told him, and the rest of the Enforcers marched off.

With the blood cleared from the square, people trickled back into the open. Blue lights appeared somewhere above them, and Reihan realised how late it was and how much of the day they had lost.

Phillippe still sat perched on her overhang but jumped down once she saw Hannes had left. Reihan slowly moved towards her, still feeling her sword heavy at her side.

"Hey", she said.

"Hey", Phillippe echoed, her eyes large and cautious.

Reihan sighed.

"You're not in trouble. No need to look scared."

Phillippe forced a wry smile onto her features.

"Have I done something I should be worried about?"

"I don't know. Haven't you usually?"

Phillippe didn't laugh, not this time.

"So, this is what you do. When someone loses control."

Each word struck Reihan like a knife. But this was real, and there was no point in turning away from reality.

"I thought you knew that. I thought that's why you wanted me to come."

Phillippe blinked rapidly as if she had just realised something.

"This is why you were mad!"

Reihan rolled her eyes to conjure up a bit of levity even as she felt like a hypocrite.

"Well, yeah. It's a bit rude to ask."

"What? For you to run me through with that fancy sword of yours in case I temporarily lose control?"

"Yeah. Not exactly what I planned on doing with my day."

Phillippe snorted, but there was little humour in it.

"Believe me, the feeling is very much mutual."

Reihan felt irritation rise in her throat.

"Then what did you think you were asking? What did you think we seaver do when you humans lose control?"

"Well, I don't really know. You're immune, so I just thought –"

"What? That I'd give you a hug and a pat on the back and tell you that everything's going to be okay?"

Reihan scoffed.

"Grow up, Phillippe. This is a small place, and there's no room for errors, not for any of us."

Phillippe stared at her for a long while, and from the oceans that moved across her face, Reihan could tell that there were a million things she wanted to say. In the end, though, her features softened, and she took Reihan's hands in hers, still pained and clam from the sword strike earlier.

"I'd never ask you to do that to me. I'm sorry that I made you think I was."

Reihan's hands felt hot between Phillippe's long fingers, and a flash of guilt made her feel sick.

"I – that's all right. I know you misunderstood."

"But you were still mad."

"At… believe it or not, even I get mad at the way things are. At the fact that I have to be the one to do this. But I'm not mad at you. Never at you."

She cocked her head to the side and smiled.

"Hm. That last one's maybe promising a bit much."

Phillippe grinned and squeezed Reihan's hands before letting go.

"Well, yes. I do still have to take you back, and who knows what kind of trouble I can get up to on the way?"

She gestured at Reihan's sword.

"Did you take that with you earlier today? I feel like you didn't."

"Of course I did. I'd hardly have it now if I hadn't brought it."

"Yeah, no, I'm pretty sure you left it in your room."

"Then how do I have it here, Phillippe?"

Reihan smirked. Phillippe narrowed her eyes.

"You know, one of these days, you'll have to tell me more about –"

"About what now? I'm sure there's nothing to talk about", Reihan cut her off with a grin, "Now, shall we?"

CHAPTER 9: PHILLIPPE

Phillippe had started to realise that nothing really happened when he skipped out on his clients. Sure, there were complaints. But Lottie, the four-hundred-year-old girl at the front desk, took care of those. She told him off afterwards, but she didn't throw him out on the street. Nobody else was as good at what he did, and they both knew it.

It was a welcome change. In their past life, Phillippe and Alexander had worked at meat stalls in the Undercity, had helped with the construction of new bridges and public buildings, and had entertained and sang on the Weeping Stairs. And even their best had barely been enough to secure them a spot the next day. More often than not, they hadn't been able to keep up with the others, who were more graceful in shaping the boundaries of their fragile world.

When Phillippe had first started at the Brothel of Transformative Curiosities, he had felt so grateful to be chosen for the position that he had accepted every client. He had meticulously quizzed each one for their every desire and preference, and Phillippe had put his heart and soul into creating the most fulfilling experiences for them, delighting in his newfound ability to bring fantasy into reality. When they were children, he and Alex had sometimes walked past the Brothel, that impossible building with its translucent, glowing walls, its shifting high roofs and towers, its gold-plated double doors that looked so surreal in the moonlight, and its beautiful dancers and escorts who felt like beings from another world. They had dreamed of what it would be like to find themselves turned about its centre, drenched in colour and life and experiences that would have them live forever.

And, at first, things had been just that; exhilarating and impossible.

When Alexander had been at home after their descent, dazed but ultimately all right. When Submergence was just a word. When Phillippe had only been given the easy clients, the ones whose touch was soft, whose words were kind, and who only needed a fraction of the time allocated to them. He had felt like a prince in one of the tales his mother had whispered at night, draped in beauty and sin. And in the evening, he would return to his brother with sweet bread and wine, and Alex would reassure him with soft-slurred speech that surely he'd be feeling better the next day. Until his brother had stopped responding altogether and until Phillippe had been given the full range of clients the city had to offer, their touch hot and intrusive and as inescapable as night terrors.

But they weren't inescapable. He was escaping them right now. He hadn't opted for wings that day, simply levitating himself to further heights by the force of his desire. It was harder to do – without feathers, there was less to remind him that he should be able to fly – but he enjoyed the envious glares of the passers-by when they saw him soar above their heads, a vision in purple silks and gold-glittering dust. That only worked until he got to the upper districts, however. There, everyone's manifestation abilities were renowned for their flair and might. He didn't want to come across as though he was bragging, so he lowered himself onto the platform next to the elevator that led back down to the Marketplace and the Artisan's Quarters. He could spot the top of the Watchtower in the West, its exterior smooth, grey, and empty. In the East, part of the rock face rose higher than the floating islands, but the rocks' cliffs and peaks were so steep that only the bravest or most desperate amongst the citizens chose to live there. It was nothing like the luxury that was palpable in every inch of the Upper City.

He was greeted by the shade of dark green trees, with leaves as long and wide as sunrays, smelling of mild excitement and calm summer rain. The air was awash with manifestation, soft breezes contained within the patches of land the city had given to its most powerful inhabitants. There weren't any streets or town squares up here. No heat steaming up from cobblestones or rain-drenched alleys full of musty cold. White-stoned villas and sun-orange manors rose left and right, shifting from each vantage point and surrounded by shimmering blue waters occupied by fat, colourful fish and the occasional diver. This was the highest district of the Travelling City, the largest island suspended in the air by its inhabitants' conjoined manifestation abilities. It was heavenly, and Phillippe hated everything about it.

Many of the people here worked for the Government, had invented something unusually useful, or were senior Enforcers, just past the peak of surviving a long career. Phillippe spotted some of them in the front gardens of their homes, half-hidden by large flowering trees or a bedside of flowers. They wore whites, greys, and blacks and waved at him with friendly smiles when he met their gaze.

He'd only been here once before, so he wasn't too familiar with the layout of the place. When he had first been given the position in the Brothel, Lottie had taken him. She lived in a stone castle atop a hill, only visible if you followed a small gravel path right to the edge of the floating island. The geography of the place was even more unstable than in the city below, with the citizens up here feeling more grandiose and confident in ripping apart time and space for the benefit of their architectural design.

"Do five years in the Brothel, and you'll have your very own patch of land up here", Lottie had promised him, a big smile on her young face. Her hat twittering in the morning air, she and Phillippe had eaten iced cream on the battlement of her castle, sweet juice dripping on the ground below.

"Just like that?", Phillippe had asked, astonished at the riches he had previously allocated to the realm of fantasy. Maybe that had been the problem. That he had been content to dream and hadn't believed in miracles.

"Just like that. Once you've proven your abilities to the city, few doors will remain closed to you. You can participate in hidden soirees, gamble away your soul at the Casino, take up a post in Government – it's your choice, darling."

"But all I do is fulfil people's fantasies. It's – I mean, it's difficult, but I've worked far harder before."

Lottie shrugged.

"Sure. But nobody cares if your face stinks up from Undercity meat or if you break your arm lifting rocks. People care what you can do for them right now, especially if nobody else can. They don't care who built the bridge they're walking on, but if you can make it glow all pretty, they love you. It's just the way people are. Disappointing."

Lottie took a large lick from her iced cream, a layer of vanilla coating her upper lip. Some of the birds from her hat flew out to a nearby fountain and drank in the tranquillity of the day.

Phillippe had grown to hate the place then, even if he hadn't been able to explain it to Lottie in a way she had understood. He had never thought much about his promised mansion up in the sky except when he imagined how to make it fit his brother's whims and interests. It would have a high tower for Alexander to watch the clouds settle atop the Travelling City. It would have to be large and have extensive grounds for the thousands of animals his brother wanted to keep. And a pond for them all to go swimming during the Summer months. Beyond that, he'd never gotten very far. Especially after it became clear that Alexander had been Submerged.

Phillippe shook his head and tried to concentrate on the path ahead. He didn't want to ask any of the residents about the way to his father's home. He wasn't in the mood for pointless conversation, and he doubted many would know. Lukacz was an Overseer for the Government, which meant that he was forced to maintain a certain degree of solitude and secrecy. And anyway, Ellis had described the way to him the last time she had unexpectedly dropped by his room atop the Brothel, upside down like a spider lowering itself from the ceiling. Indeed, once he followed a small gravel road past the same self-same illusions of beauty, he found a small river leading into a collection of trees on his left-hand side, accompanied by a pathway of smooth, grey stones.

Phillippe stepped from one to the next, and after a few steps, the space had shifted. Gone were the vast meadows and tall hills on which obscenely large manors loomed. Instead, Phillippe smelled the fresh air of a forest and skipped from stone to stone atop a gurgling stream, whispering long-forgotten secrets.

This looked right – it felt right.

Private and unassuming, another secret hiding just behind the next bend in the forest. Ahead, he spotted a stone-faced cottage with a low-hanging roof and several outbuildings flanking the small clearing on which it stood. A recently used fire pit sat right by the spot where the river met the emerald-green meadow. His father was nowhere to be seen, but Phillippe knew it was Lukacz's house.

Phillippe skipped across the last few stones, then he felt solid ground beneath his feet once more. He wondered if his dad got home the same way or if he just walked over the forest ground, watching the water but never touching it. He shouldn't care so much.

Maybe he shouldn't have come here at all. Like all his recent ideas, this had been poorly thought out.

"Lukacz?", he called, before he could think better of it.

The forest answered with animal calls and the soft running of water. This was for the best. He should just go home – or he should teleport to Reihan's room and bother her once her shift was over.

"Phillippe? Is that you?"

His father's voice rang from deep within the house as if it had swallowed him whole. Phillippe stomach churned, and he suddenly felt as though he was breathing through a tube.

"Uh-huh", he made and immediately wished he'd said something more cutting. A pair of keys rattled, and the cottage's front door was unlocked from the inside. Lukacz slowly stepped out, wearing a pair of dark trousers and a flannel shirt. Phillippe resisted the urge to roll his eyes at how twee and mundane it all looked.

"Are there news – of your bother?", Lukacz asked, sounding slightly out of breath. Phillippe hesitated for a moment before he realised that, of course, his father had to think this was why he had come.

"No", he said brusquely, "No news."

He felt a squirrel run over some of the purple silks that made up his long-flowing trousers, and suddenly he felt very out of place, like a firework in the middle of Lukacz's calm oasis. *Good.*

Lukacz hesitated for a moment.

"Well, how can I help you, Phillippe?"

"What, you're not going to invite me in and make me a lovely little brew of forest herbs?"

His father frowned, not appreciating his tone.

"I'm fresh out of those, I'm afraid."

Phillippe clicked his tongue.

"Let me guess – Ellis smoked up all the funny herbs?"

"Ellis drinks hot chocolate, so dark and so thick that it barely moves in her cup. She calls it her moonshinesing. Also, she does not generally come here."

"Well, it is a little –"

He interrupted himself.

"You live out here by yourself?"

Lukacz nodded. Realising that his wayward son was not about to leave any time soon, he gestured towards the fire pit, where two wooden stools suddenly appeared.

"It's a requirement of my position", he explained once they both sat, the fire starting with a slow crackle, "But I quite like it. I remember you and Alexander had this story you thought up about a mystical forest and its immortal inhabitants. Wasn't one of them a grumpy old dragon? I've felt like that at times."

Phillippe felt embarrassed at the mention of his childhood fantasies and felt a sting of – what? Jealousy? Anger? He didn't want Lukacz to remember things like that about him and Alexander. He had given up that right when he left.

Lukacz left Phillippe's silence uncommented and continued with his explanation.

"Members of Government are supposed to live in secrecy and isolation. Otherwise, we are too vulnerable to hostile manifestations. Imagine the thoughts of a whole city directed against a small handful of people. That's why we usually send seaver in our stead for representative appointments and negotiations."

He frowned.

"Surely your mother told you all this."

"Mom never believed that you actually got hired into Government. She thought it was just a convenient excuse for you to leave."

Lukacz looked saddened, but Phillippe thought he saw more resignation than surprise.

"And you? You've always had your own mind, boy. What did you think?"

"I didn't care."

The words came fast, and he meant them now, even if they weren't true. Lukacz did not react to that. *He sits still like a tree*, Phillippe thought, *rooted into that damned forest floor*. He looked around, meeting the eyes of small birds sitting on branches, the rings of tree bark and his reflection in the glass of the cottage windows.

"I guess she was wrong, though. Hated your guts for the wrong reasons."

"You believe that I deserved your mother's ire."

It wasn't a question. Phillippe wished Lukacz would stop sounding so dispassionate.

"Well, you did leave her with two young children."

"For the call of duty. The call we all must answer."

Phillippe raised his eyebrows.

"What about the duty to do right by the ones you love? Your family?"

"You boys were provided for", Lukacz answered, "Your mother was more than capable, and the State Teachers would have stepped in had she died before you came of age. Beyond immediate need, love is the only thing that lives apart from duty. It is the only thing we give freely."

"Love is the only duty worth taking seriously."

Lukacz frowned.

"So says the man who loves amidst an inferno. None of us can live if we all do as we please. But love is given and taken freely. It can be no different. Thus, it must always relent to obligation and duty."

"That makes no sense", Phillippe argued, feeling bile sit on his throat, "If I love someone, I'll take care of them. I'd burn down this whole damned city if I had to. I –"

"And that makes you dangerous."

"It's what makes me a decent person."

He shook his head. Lukacz sat back on his chair as far as he could without falling backwards. The noises of the forest surrounded them with incessant chirping and rustling, and Phillippe suddenly felt very tired. Why had he even come here?

"I was sorry to hear what happened to your brother. And to you."

Lukacz's words were quiet, half-buried in the embers below. Phillippe kicked a foot of dirt into the fire to make it spark a little higher.

"You heard about it when it happened? When Alex was admitted?"

"Of course. My friend Emmett wrote to me. You might remember him. He was one of our neighbours in the Undercity."

Phillippe vaguely remembered picking up some of Alexander's old things from their house in the Undercity. Spare clothes and trinkets for him to take to the Asylum, as if he was moving house and not about to be locked away from the world. Had he talked to Emmett that day? He could remember so little about that time, fleeing from the seconds with fantasies and wishes.

"When you were written into the Brothel's pages, I had already guessed what you boys must have attempted. When Alexander was later admitted to the Asylum, I knew for certain."

"You didn't come to visit", Phillippe said, the words now so large they clogged up his tongue, "Didn't feel like shouting at me for what I'd done?"

Lukacz was silent for a little while. Phillippe was tempted to look up, to look for the disappointment and disgust in his father's features that he was sure he deserved. But he didn't.

"The rules of my post still applied, Phillippe. And I'm sure you would not have wanted me to add to your grief."

"I'm ... I just hoped... I –"

And the words, the feelings they were supposed to convey,

were too large to break free. Phillippe felt his eyes sting, and suddenly he wanted nothing more than to teleport out of this place, to fly above the city free and alone. Lukacz leant forwards and placed his hands on Phillippe's knees. They were as broad as an old friend's smile. Phillippe looked up in surprise and saw Lukacz's gaze, mild and kind.

Suddenly he remembered walking through the markets with his father when he'd been a child, holding onto those big, gruff hands. He had always wanted to walk with his dad, Alex and mum further back. Lukacz had always indulged him, had remembered his preference after a single instance, and had – he had bought Phillippe sweet cakes and carried him on his shoulders when it got dark.

"I am sorry for all the grief you suffered, son. If you'll take any words from me seriously, believe me when I say that it will get easier with time."

"Do you hate me? For what I did to Alex?"

Those were the words he didn't think he could summon into existence. And yet now they hung between them, loud and crass and inescapable.

"You're my son, Phillippe. I am sad that you saw no other way to live than to come by stolen power. I am sad that we are not more alike. But I care about you, and I always have."

"But you left… How could you care about me and still leave?"

Phillippe's face was hot and wet, and he didn't care. Lukacz's grip on his legs tightened.

"I know it makes no sense to you. But part of me left because I cared. Because I wanted to make this city a safer and better place for you to live. And because love can only ever be a boon, not a burden."

Phillippe closed his eyes, feeling the salt drip from his lashes.

"You don't make any sense, dad."

Lukacz finally laughed, a low rumbling sound that was so familiar. And slowly, Phillippe joined him, and they sat for a long while in the forest clearing filled with shy, slow laughter.

CHAPTER 10: ELLIS

Alrighty, here we go!

A jump, a push, and she soared through open skies, the diorama of the Travelling City rushing past. She should slow down, but she didn't. Her feet would find the ledge, and if not, her head would. She'd manifest herself back together just as her cranium split apart, blood and brains flying out. The cries of birds sounded as if they were egging her on, and she was deliriously happy, knowing that Lukacz would be worried seeing her like this.

She floundered her arms about, trying to turn back upright. It was early morning, rosy hues painting wide streaks onto the palladium and gold roofs of the Upper City houses. Some schoolchildren manifested rainbows and glittering rays into the skies, and fishermen hung out their wide, steel nets, hoping to catch exotic animals flying to their city from Elsewhere.

She didn't normally like to be awake this early in the day. It lowered the chances that a dream might come by, and she might lure it to push its tendrils into her head. She'd never dreamed before, but like everything else, Ellis considered it only a matter of practice.

She landed as perfectly as she had every other time she'd done the fall. The courtyard of the *World's End* had a landing platform originally intended for the city's inhabitants who wanted to jump down to view the cloud sea up close. By now, it was long overgrown by a strange amassment of mossy, talkative plants. They caressed Ellis's feet and shins and told her stories of the guests with fairy-thin voices that she half-ignored as she assessed the pub's exterior. Rough, large brickwork, made to last the ages even after it had been abandoned. No part of the *World's End* was made of perishable materials. Ellis wondered if whoever had built the pub had foreseen how high the cloud sea would rise and had somehow known that the pub would have to be abandoned. Then again, much drink still lay in its barrels, all of it of miraculously high quality, and the fire in its hearth had never gone out.

She threw the doors to the pub open and strolled in with the sunlight. In the unfamiliar glow, spider webs lit up, strand-by-stand, and most of the pub's visitors averted their eyes.

"'ello fellas!", Ellis said, "Time to rise and shine, yeah?"

She was met with incredulous stares, underlined with a rumbling murmur. Most people came here to forget their former lives or simply to die. Most of the figures she saw huddled alongside low tables and towards the bar's edge had probably never truly been human. Most likely, they were manifested copies of visitors from decades past. That was fine, in theory. Nothing wrong with it; they probably still had some of their human counterparts' memories. But Ellis didn't like interacting with other manifestations. She preferred to think of herself as unique.

"Have a drink and be quiet", a voice called from the back of the pub. All dark figures were huddled together, so Ellis couldn't tell precisely where the sound had come from.

"You be quiet!", Ellis shouted back, then brushed black strands away from her face, annoyed at the intrusion. She felt her expression slip, then dragged it up as though she had picked up the edges of her skin with a needle and was now pulling back the thread.

She jogged towards a table where a single figure sat, their face hidden in shadows. Ellis opened her mouth to speak to them, then felt the staleness of the air.

"Ugh", she made, "What's the point in you still sitting here?"

The figure groaned, and Ellis manifested a full glass of liqueur into her left hand.

"C'mon", she said, "Whoever left you here is probably dead by now. That, or they walked out into the cloud sea and are stinking, raving mad. You're not linking back to anything."

She took a sip of the strong, gold-coloured liquid and resisted a wince. She offered it to the shadow opposite herself.

"Take a drink for the road and then buzz off. No one's dreaming you up anymore, pal."

The figure groaned again, but Ellis saw its edges dissipating. Most people didn't think there was any point in talking to discarded, half-lost manifestations. They just sent the seaver to go and clean them up.

"Right!", she called, swinging herself back up, "Any other ghosties in here? Or are there actually any mad, stupid humans who'd have a drink with me?"

"Can you just be quiet?", a woman groaned whose upper body was slumped over the bar. A half-empty glass lay spilt beside her, coating her arms in sticky purple. She didn't seem to mind, her posture as liquid as the pale, thin hair that flowed across her arms and back.

Ellis strolled up to her, three more ghosts disappearing upon looking at her firm, confident stride, bright and real as the sun.

"Nope", she said, slamming her liqueur glass on the bar. It would have shattered if her mind hadn't held it together.

"Nope, I think I'll just annoy you until you perish."

"You won't have to wait long then", the woman muttered. Ellis could see the lines on her face, circling her soft features. They weren't deep, not quite yet.

"Nah, I reckon I won't. Still would be a shame to waste my time, wouldn't it? After I came all the way down here just to talk to ya?"

"To me specifically?"

The woman coughed.

"I doubt it. I have no idea who you are, and nobody in the world cares about me."

"Probably not", Ellis agreed readily, "But in this very particular moment, you have the unique chance to be moderately useful."

"Go away", the woman croaked.

"Come now. You'll die down here either way. Might as well go out not bein' a bitch", Ellis tried. The woman blinked up at her.

"I might still go outside. Immerse myself in the clouds and become all-powerful. Show them all...."

"Yeah, yeah, yeah, but you won't, will ya? We both know that if you had the guts to go outside, you would've done it already."

The woman shook her head but ended up just bobbing her upper body on the sticky table.

"What do you want?", she finally asked, resignation heavy in her voice.

"Right. You lot are all crazy for those manifestation powers, right? Follow the ascent of every new player on the board, yeah?"

"I wouldn't say crazy –"

"You're down here, sunshine. Crazy doesn't even begin to cover it", Ellis interrupted, "Anyway. I'm looking for a particular new player on the scene. Young, previously unknown. Enormous power. Will have appeared in the last few weeks or so. Anything like that ring a bell?"

The woman's eyes turned glossy.

"I don't really know", she said dreamily, "It's so hard to keep track. People lie about their powers. They buy things and say they've created them. Or they hide how strong they are to work an easier job. I –"

"Think, woman. Think, and I'll give you some advice that

might help you out there."

Ellis pointed back towards the landing platform. The woman's eyes turned upwards, although there was barely any hope behind all the glass that covered her pupils.

"Like what?"

"I want a name first."

"I don't have a name. Just a …"

She hesitated.

"I heard someone speaking of a place. A new realm inside the rock face. An unspeakably beautiful house that grows every day. A million different rooms, and nobody ever tires there."

She shook her head.

"That was a new story. I hadn't heard it before."

Ellis sighed. It was something, at least. Lukacz had told her about want-to-be emperors who carved out a place to reign deep inside the rock face of the Travelling City, creating their own little kingdoms surrounded by stone and secrecy. Could Alexander have fled there to catch his breath? Or was someone using his powers to create a fantasy dungeon? She could check for whispers in the Upper City. The rich and powerful always explored the new kingdoms before everyone else, before the Enforcers could shut down the worst atrocities that invariably took place in the dark. Most people didn't even realise that there were mansions and castles in the middle of the rock on which they all lived. Ellis found the idea depressing, to know so little about your own world, minuscule as it was.

"So? What do I do when I step outside?", the woman asked,

pulling on Ellis's shirt. Ellis's face twisted, but she kept her voice calm.

"There's a chant you can sing to protect yourself from the madness", Ellis said, "You sing it as you walk into the storm, and you stay safe."

"R-really", the woman asked, torn between suspicion and child-like hope, "How do you know it?"

"I've used it myself. How else do you think I became as powerful as I am?", Ellis lied. The woman swallowed.

"All right then. Teach me."

Ellis made up a quick little sing-song with false words that sounded as tempting as hot chocolate on an open, rained-on windowsill. The woman's eyes glazed over, wanting to believe in the esoteric wisdom of Ellis's hastily constructed lie. She stood up and walked out into the clouds.

Ellis sighed, then downed the remainder of her liqueur. Halfway through their conversation, she had realised that the woman wasn't real, just like the rest of the shades that had resumed their muttering. Her corpse lay not even five feet away from them, having slumped down on the side of the bar. At least it looked as though she had died recently, so the information obtained from her shadow could still be helpful to their investigation.

Still, Ellis shuddered. She knew the *World's End* had been built aeons ago when the Travelling City had been fresh with migrants from the continent below. The stones were of a different colour than could be found on the rock face above, large and slapped together with too much concrete. She could imagine the old migrants congregating here when the place hadn't been empty and creepy, huddling by the fire and toasting each other with foamy ales. She could imagine weddings being celebrated here, children chasing each other around the chairs and benches, and grandmothers indulging them with far too many helpings of sweet pie.

Ellis tried to imagine herself into the scenario, but, like always, she couldn't. She was a much better fit for the ghost-ridden death trap the place had become. Because, really, if she stopped pretending for a while, who was she, if not another ghost? The manifestation of a nightmare that had haunted a little girl dreamed up and conjured into reality, then forgotten and discarded. Ellis had barely known who she was until Lukacz found her a few years back when she had been an angry spectre haunting the Travelling City. As a nightmare come to life, she had no past, and if the philosophers were to be believed, she had no future either.

And she didn't care. Why should she care? Lukacz thought she was real, so she was. She didn't want to know who the girl had grown up to be, whether she'd had other nightmares just like her or whether she was stuck in some boring marriage somewhere, pumping out two children every five years. She didn't want to meet her and be disappointed. She didn't want to remember that without Lukacz she was a thought on the wind. Lukacz was real, and if she got really lost, he'd find her again.

She shook her head so viciously that the other ghosts disappeared for a moment. Then she closed her eyes and teleported back to the city.

CHAPTER 11: REIHAN

The day began with a storm warning. All upheaval, chaos, and everyday catastrophes aside, a storm warning forced everyone to cancel their plans, from the inhabitants of the Undercity to the members of Government, whoever they were. Every registered citizen of the Travelling City, whether they currently had a home or not, had a designated place on the city's bannisters, outcrops, hanging bridges, towers, outlooks, and cliff edges; on every platform of the Weeping Stairs, and at every window of every house with a view. Almost every person's manifestation ability, however insignificant and deficient, was called upon to counteract the storm's destructive force.

Reihan took a deep breath, then tied her thick braids behind her ears and strapped her sword onto her back, shifting under the familiar weight. She'd been through seven storms in her life. She would have been content never to see another, but such was life. A series of wishes that kept shifting with the seasons.

With a slight shift in the smell of the room, Phillippe appeared behind her, making an effort to sit on her bedside table nonchalantly.

"Did you hear –?", he began.

"Yes", she interrupted him, "And you should be reporting for duty."

"I still have some time", Phillippe protested, then narrowed his eyes.

"Where are you stationed?"

"Weeping Stairs", she said, "On the top, close to your district."

"Right, right", Phillippe said, sounding a little distracted, "They have me right outside the Brothel. Obviously."

"Of course", Reihan agreed, then her tone softened, "You haven't been through a storm before, have you?"

"I'll be just fine", Phillippe responded immediately, sounding just as haughty as she had expected him to, "I know what I need to do."

Every citizen had an area corresponding to their projected ability. They were supposed to keep that area safe from the storm's influence, creating a safe haven for those who may have had to flee their own districts. Unravelling manifestations had never been Phillippe's strong suit, at least not compared to his ability to create, but on this occasion, the city did not care how he got rid of the storm's madness. It just mattered that his streets stayed clear.

"Are you stationed by yourself?", she asked, even though she knew she should make him leave.

"Don't know."

"You never bothered checking?"

"What for?"

Phillippe threw back his long hair, hanging in an elaborately woven braid over his back. Tiny jewels sat inside the folds.

"I'll find out soon enough. If I have to do it alone, I will."

He let the words linger a little, then his gaze came to rest on her.

"Although – do you think you can switch your station with the seaver at the Brothel? I'd like to keep an eye on you."

"No."

The word fell out of Reihan before she could collect herself. Phillippe stared at her, and the awkwardness stretched between them like a canyon.

"I know they won't let me switch", the seaver finally added, long seconds too late. Phillippe looked hurt but tried to cover it up with nonchalant irreverence as he bid her goodbye and good luck in the storm. Reihan took a long, shaky breath.

Damned storms.

She was responsible for five humans on the highest Weeping Stair. It had been a pain to get up there to begin with, with her relying on Phillippe's wheelchair whenever she could convince one of her charges to push her over a flat part of the platforms. Her arms burned from pulling herself up ropes and ladders, and she knew she'd have to repair some tears and cuts in the morning. Her group consisted of two sisters, their seasoned faces a mirror of one another, an old man nursing a crooked back and a walking stick, a teenage boy with shaking hands, and a tall-faced man chasing the tail end of youth.

They could hear thunder crashing in the distance, the roar of the world's primordial thoughts coating the horizon in madness. The teenager let out a quiet whimper.

"It'll be all right, dear", one of the sisters said, raised a hand to put on his arm, then thought better of it at the last moment.

"We've been through a storm when we were about your age", the other sister added, "It was really scary, but we were all fine."

The teenager gave them a grateful look before he remembered that he was supposed to be unaffected by it all and turned back towards the sea of clouds that shifted endlessly amidst angry winds. Below, Reihan could see the other platforms winding down the length of the Travelling City. The other seaver asked people to try out different formations, just like Reihan had done in the past. This time around, though, she just asked her group to stay together.

"Why?", the young man demanded. He was tall, with hair that was so light that the colour had to be manifested, "Wouldn't it make sense to spread out across the platform so that we cover more ground?"

"No", Reihan simply responded, "It won't make a difference."

"It might", the man protested, "I always find that my manifestations come out better when there's nobody close-by to interfere."

"Don't overthink it", Reihan responded, and her tone was authoritative enough that the man did not argue with her any further, even though his expression told her he wanted to.

Thunder shattered through the sky, and the storm moved into view as suddenly as a nightmare. Purple waves splashed across the horizon in clouds that rose as fast and high as a thousand skies. Lightning broke apart the view, destroying any matter it touched and leaving only the madness of non-existence. They could hear the roar of animals within the storm, the cries of children, of loved ones, and the laugh of an uncaring god, mocking their feeble lives and miseries. Acid rain came down around them, breaking down the stone platform they stood on. The teenager started to scream.

"Concentrate", Reihan commanded, "The rain doesn't have to be real."

The old man narrowed his eyes, and the acid rain was blown out into the sea of clouds. The roaring quieted down a little, and the rest sighed in relief.

"What the hell is this?", the young man demanded, shouting into the void below. The two sisters flanked the teenager, each holding up their hands as if praying to the sun that had disappeared amidst the purple madness. The old man stepped closer to Reihan.

"Will we get through this one?", he asked quietly, understanding in his eyes. The storm had hit them on the side of the city where they were stationed. They would receive the full extent of its madness.

"Hold on to your thoughts", Reihan simply responded, "For the good of the city."

The old man lowered his head. The roaring flowed into musicality, taking on the appearance of soft notes, dropping to their feet in sweet surrender. Each sound looked so unassuming as it wriggled towards their feet, like a blanket made to smother them. They would look so pretty, all dancing together within the purple storm, forever singing the song of humanity as it became one. The smell of orange petals surrounded them as Reihan thought she saw a flying Enforcer disappearing between two soft bouts of cloud, washing onto the platform like bright purple foam. Her heart ached even as she shouted her commands to the humans around her.

"Hold onto your thoughts!", she repeated, "Don't fall for the illusions! Your view is the view, your world is the world!"

It was no use. The tall man stumbled ahead, humming a sugar-sweet melody as drool glistened on the sides of his mouth. His feet carried him towards the flocks of cloud that beckoned him, the roaring now a choir of young bodies calling him into their arms.

"Stop!", one of the sisters said and ran after him intending to grab his arm.

"You can't save him", Reihan protested, "Stay in your post!"

The sister hesitated – just long enough, as ten thick arms suddenly shot out from the clouds and pulled the tall man into the mist. He did not even have time to scream, then he was gone.

"You are not real", the old man mumbled beside Reihan. His eyes were large and wide.

"You are not real. None of this is real."

"Hold onto your thoughts", Reihan repeated, trying to make her tone soothing, "Stand your ground. It will only attack you if you let it."

"I-is that really true?", one of the sisters asked, the one still close to the mist. It swayed around her feet, a purple scarf waiting to wrap around her neck and smother her into eternal slumber while singing to her of faraway lands.

"It is", Reihan lied. The teenager was crying now, tears streaming out of eyes that he firmly held shut. Reihan was tempted to tell him to open them, to at least try and fight, but that might just panic the others. Either way, she reckoned they didn't stand much chance up here.

"Imagine a circle of light", she tried anyway, "a protective circle. The storm can't come in there. You'll be safe."

"A circle. Circle, circle, circle", the sister closest to her muttered, "Okay. I can do that."

The old man echoed her, and together they produced flecks of light, raining down from the cave overhang above.

"Good", Reihan encouraged them, "Keep looking at the light. That will strengthen the protection!"

It kept them distracted from the other sister, whose eyes had turned glassy as a bauble. She walked to the edge of the mist, then threw herself into its soft embrace, like a bird stepping out of the nest for the very first time. Only Reihan watched her die.

Pointless. And yet, what's the alternative?

Reihan stood outside the circle, trying to direct the storm's attention towards herself. Like every time before now, it did not seem too interested in the seaver, but still, it tried to lure her with the sweet smell of freshly baked bread that she remembered from the kitchens of the Upside-Down Palace. She saw Phillippe dancing around the clouds, glorious and laughing and utterly inhuman. And she saw herself just as she was, but free, floating at his side. She did not look away, but neither did she move.

"Keep chanting", she told her humans, "We're nearly at the end now."

She had no idea if that was true, but their chant intensified briefly. Even the teenager now opened his eyes, although his gaze was fixated on the freckles on the remaining sister's nose rather than the purple waves that held them surrounded. Reihan could no longer see the edge of the platform. She could not see the groups of people below or the ceiling above. If the storm wanted to, it could simply suck the oxygen from the air, and they would all die. They had let it come far too close. And the storm would not leave unless someone drove it away.

The old man's voice rose to a crescendo, and he started speaking in a language she did not recognise. Her heart clenched as she saw the familiar glass run across his eyes and saw his gaze turn towards the other two in the circle. Streaks of red started to form on the woman's face, and she cried out in pain.

Reihan drew her sword and sliced the old man's head clean from his body.

"Keep chanting", she told the teenager and the woman, but they stared at her as if they'd just seen a demon. Then the woman turned around, her body shaking.

"Where's my sister?", she asked.

"Keep chanting", Reihan repeated, although she knew she had lost this fight.

"Where is she? Eldred? Eldred!"

She ran into the clouds. The teenager stared at Reihan, his body limp.

"I'm going to die", he said pointlessly.

"I'm sorry", Reihan responded. It hurt just as much as it always had, "I wish I could do more."

"It's not fair! They said you seaver would help us. That you could save us from the manifestations if they became too much."

He gestured at the storm, filling the entire world.

"This is too much. I don't know what it is, but it's too much."

Reihan shook her head. The purple clouds engulfed them both, and it became hard to breathe, as if the air was coated in a rain of thick perfume.

"I can't save anyone", she said slowly, as long arms came out of the clouds and crawled towards the teenager's legs, "That's the only way I can help."

Reihan had lost against a storm before. Once, her entire team had wandered into the purple clouds near the highest peak of the Travelling City. She and the humans had clung to the mountain paths that overlooked the roofs below, and the winds alone had nearly carried them away into a bright and golden distance that looked much closer than it was. In the end, the voices within the storm, soft and calm and different for each listener, convinced Reihan's entire group to take just that one step further. Reihan had never seen their bodies on the side of the mountain, so part of her hoped, against all reason, that perhaps the storm had kept its word and transported them into a world of perfect fantasy.

People thought the seaver couldn't be affected by the storms. That because they were supposedly immune to manifestations, the storms couldn't do anything to them. Reihan knew they weren't immune, not really. Nothing was truly unaffected by the world, however much it acted as though it was. She was sure that the purple clouds' whispering pull on her was weaker than on the humans. She could hear them through the mist, crying, shouting, clawing at invisible spectres. But the pull was there, tugging at every cell in her body with promises she did not let herself listen to.

She had no fear of looking her desire in the eyes. But this wasn't the time.

So, she stumbled, half blind and swimming through half-familiar scents, until her body collided with a solid wall. The last wall of the Weeping Stairs. If she pulled herself up by one of the ladders – if a ladder still existed amidst all this madness – she could find Phillippe. She could…

Then she hesitated and pressed her back against the cold stone. If Phillippe gave into the song of the storm, if it drove him mad, she knew what duty demanded of her.

She believed in duty. She believed in it more than in herself and more than anyone else on this godforsaken rock.

But the thought of running her sword through Phillippe's body as his laughing, irreverent face looked down on her made her feel like she could not breathe. She took a deep breath, then another.

Phillippe would be fine. He was strong-willed, despite how he might appear. He had survived the fog beneath the city that was equally as maddening as the storm. He experimented with his manifestation abilities every day. And he had grown to understand what temptation looked like as he whisked along its borderline.

And if he wasn't fine, he might destroy the little world they lived on. And the seaver that had been stationed with him most likely had no idea of how powerful Phillippe truly was.

Another seaver might hesitate. Another seaver might fail.

Reihan sighed, drinking in the air, jelly-thick though it was. She still felt her legs, however much she wished she couldn't. She could manifest a ladder even if she couldn't find one. It would draw the storm's attention to her, but she could weather it. She could get up to the next level and perform her duty. But one of these days, she thought, it would be enough. Perhaps it was a blessing that the seaver did not live a day beyond two hundred years.

The streets around the Brothel were clear. After making her way by smell and touch through the fog-filled streets, Reihan's heart ached when she saw the clear air and the grey-dark skies lurking somewhere above the storm, with a deep, fat moon sitting amidst the stars. The Brothel's towers and roofs gleamed in the dim light of evening, and Phillippe sat perched on top of a soft-swinging gable, his gold-glowing head resting between his knees.

She was about to open her mouth to call to him, but no sound came out, stuck between relief and residue fear. Phillippe must have heard her regardless as he turned around and met her with a quick smile, too broad to match the day she'd had.

"Reihan! Finally!", he said, then swung himself down, only manifesting wings halfway through his fall. Reihan felt her legs shake but forced herself to walk up to him. She couldn't let her guard down, not yet.

"Where is Piotr?", she asked, looking around the empty square surrounding the Brothel, a league of white panels and small stones.

"Who?"

Phillippe sounded decidedly disinterested and instead circled Reihan, looking for signs that she might have been affected by purple air and thick fog.

"The seaver. Grumpy guy with a killer sense of humour. He should have been stationed here with you."

"Hm? Oh, right. He left a little while ago. Said that it seemed as though I had everything under control."

Reihan cocked her head to the side.

"That doesn't sound like Piotr."

"Well, he did."

Phillippe did not seem interested in continuing that line of conversation and instead asked her how things had gone at her station. He had clearly not left the Brothel, as he was shocked when she told him about the state of the Weeping Stairs, now most likely completely overtaken by the storm.

"So, what happens now?", Phillippe asked, spreading out his wings as if he ached to throw himself into the sky, "Should I go down there and disperse the clouds?"

"Then what happens up here?"

"Who cares? There's no one in the Brothel anymore; they all moved to their own posts across the city. I'm just guarding stone and windows up here, and on the Weeping Stairs I could help –"

"No one", Reihan said, "You can't help anyone down there."

Phillippe frowned.

"But there must have been dozens of people down. I saw some of them walk down when I was on the roof, I –"

"Phillippe!" Reihan couldn't help her voice getting louder. All the relief at how sane he was gave way to the despair that clung to her throat.

"They are gone, and you need to… I need you not to ask any more questions right now."

She felt her legs shake again, and this time she lowered herself onto the ground, leaning her back against the stone-cold walls of the Brothel. She took a few deep breaths, refusing to look up.

Phillippe was silent for a long time.

"The fog drove your friend mad", he finally said, "Just a little, and just for a moment. I wasn't paying attention, and the fog had snuck around a corner, then encircled him like a snake."

Reihan looked up at him, her eyes white and hopeless.

"He's fine", Phillippe hurriedly explained, then awkwardly crouched beside her, "The madness left him again. But I didn't know it could affect the seaver."

"We have minds like everyone else. Everyone can be led astray by fantasy. It just affects us less."

"But you walked through so much of it –"

Phillippe swallowed.

"Your friend ran away when a path cleared to the Palace. I don't know where he went, but he seemed pretty freaked out." He hesitated for a second.

"His mind seemed to be sound enough, though", he repeated, measuring the minute expressions on Reihan's face.

"I'll check in on him. It may have been his first time to realise…."

Her words trailed off, and she shook her head. Impulse struck, and as unstable as Phillippe looked as he perched next to her like a bird, she put her head on his shoulder.

"I'm glad you're okay either way", she whispered.

He hesitated as unspoken thoughts clumped together in his mouth. In the end, he relaxed and nodded.

"Me too. I was worried about you. I nearly came down about fifteen different times."

Reihan chuckled,

"That sounds like you."

"But in the end, it was you who came up. Because you were… worried about me?", he asked, and she wasn't entirely sure what the hesitation in his voice belied. But the easiest thing was always to be honest, even if you left out most of the truth.

"Yes", she said, allowing the word to trail off across the mountain into the grey, full sky. The clouds were vanishing now. Soon the clean-up would begin, and the count, and the time when all she could do was to be Reihan the seaver and to function so very perfectly for everyone else.

Her head on Phillippe's shoulder felt heavy and warm. Phillippe chuckled.

"Growing soft, seaver?"

"Never", Reihan laughed and closed her eyes for a moment, "Or, who knows? Maybe you inspire me to make foolish choices."

"Hmm", Phillippe made, "Happy to be of service, of course."

CHAPTER 12: REIHAN

There had been no news for a while. Ellis dropped by briefly to inform Reihan that she was chasing a lead in the Upper City, then just as quickly disappeared again. Reihan didn't try to make conversation, which she expected the nightmare would appreciate. Over the last hundred years, she had developed a keen eye for people who shared common prejudices against the seaver. That, or maybe Ellis just didn't like anyone. Which, Reihan thought, was fair enough.

"I can't just sit around", Phillippe complained, lounging on her bed. He flaunted chin-length autumn brown hair, uncharacteristically pale skin, eyes as black as the universe, and heavy purple robes to match his mood.

"So, you've decided to lie around instead?", Reihan asked drily. She was trying to read one of the many books Phillippe had procured at her request. Most of them she'd heard about via the reviews in years-old literary digest magazines. The current novel, disappointingly, did not offer the thrilling horror she had been promised. Even if it had, however, she wouldn't have been able to concentrate with Phillippe's constant chatter in her ear.

"Well, yes. I'm being dramatic, and I was rather hoping it might spur you into action."

"Me? What exactly do you expect me to do?"

Phillippe sighed.

"If I knew that I would have suggested it."

"But of course. Silly me."

Reihan pointedly returned to her book, turning over the next page even though she hadn't reached it yet. Phillippe rewarded her with a series of progressively lengthening sighs that made the corners of Reihan's mouth twitch. In all honesty, she was relieved to find that he hadn't completely lost his spirits. When she had seen his gloomy get-up earlier in the day, she had worried that the lack of news from Lukacz and Ellis had finally managed to drag even Phillippe's mood down to her level. And, silly as it was, she liked that he was happier and freer than she would ever be. It was like seeing a story unfold that she didn't have to partake in.

Phillippe sighed again, this time so melodramatic that he made himself cough.

"All right", she snapped, slamming the book shut with a loud bang, "We're going out."

"Where to?", Phillippe asked, trying and failing to sound petulant.

"Wherever. We could go for a walk."

"Exercise? How terribly tedious. Think bigger, seaver. Imagine anything's possible."

Reihan grinned.

"Alright then. We could rent out an airship. Or try some ridiculous new food creation cooked up in the Artisans' Quarters."

"Hmm. Both tempting", Phillippe replied, then his brows narrowed as an idea struck him.

"Or we could combine flying and eating with an even grander diversion."

"I'm listening", Reihan said, the book already forgotten.

"Well, dear seaver. You do remember that this fair city has an Amusement Park, do you not?"

Reihan hesitated for a moment, then broke out into a wide smile.

"Really? Can we go?"

Phillippe rolled his eyes and suddenly looked a little dejected.

"You could have asked me any time. You didn't need to wait until I offered."

"Well, they wouldn't let me–"

"No", Phillippe interrupted her and raised himself from her bed. His eyes were serious.

"But you can ask me for any privilege you like. I don't care. I have so much – too much, I –"

He caught his breath, then smiled an insincere smile.

"And I promise I'll never refuse you, no matter how things turn between us. That way, it won't feel like you're dependent on me, right?"

He winked.

"Because it would be a terrible idea for anyone to depend on me. We saw what happened to my brother."

"Phillippe…"

"So, it's settled then? Amusement Park?"

Reihan admitted the smile she was holding back and nodded.

Phillippe flew them to one of the highest outcrops of the Travelling City's rock face, a long stretch of land on the same level as the Upside-Down Palace and located underneath the Upper City islands. A gigantic Ferris wheel dominated the skyline while other rides fell seemingly into nothingness. There were the simple attractions, too, like hot air balloons rising into the sky, small teacups spinning around their axis, and the myriad of games where manifested pets and trinkets could be won. The more thrilling rides came with a tree of warning signs, 'enter at your own risk', as they catapulted the riders into the open skies and depended on talented attendants to teleport them back into the Amusement Park's safe zones. Reihan wasn't allowed to ride on any of them, despite Phillippe's insistence that he'd fly her back to solid ground even if she couldn't be teleported.

"I'm not about to get into trouble with the Enforcement Commission", a park manager told them with a gruff voice and an irritated stare at even having to explain what to him seemed perfectly obvious.

Phillippe seemed ready to argue for the remainder of the day, but Reihan managed to drag him away with the promise of sharing a portion of spicy tentacle balls with him as they rode the Ferris Wheel to the top.

"I could have absolutely caught you. It would have been no problem", he said, glumly watching the latest crowd be thrown out of a spinning cart, screeching and screaming in delight.

"I'm sure. But the attendants are just doing their job."

Reihan chewed on a particularly tough piece of tentacle meat. She liked it, she decided.

"Plus, I imagine you'd feel rather foolish if you didn't manage after all."

"I suppose I would, at that."

Phillippe laughed.

"Although it would finally solve the riddle of what you seaver are actually made of."

"There are no little wheels spinning inside my chest if that's what you're asking", Reihan replied, "We're flesh and blood, same as you. Just a bit more efficiently designed."

"What you're forgetting to add here is that you literally shut down in the middle of the day if you forget to eat breakfast."

"I never forget to eat breakfast."

"I bet you don't! Those would be high stakes to gamble with, dear seaver."

They chuckled over the last few pieces of tentacle meat. Reihan leaned her head against the window of the Ferris wheel cabin and watched the landscape draw by in a blur of disorderly colours. There were so many people below, playing games, watching the fire-eaters, and trading for tat at the various stalls. She liked watching them like a puzzle slowly coming together, even though she felt as detached as ever. She felt Phillippe tensing next to her but did not comment on it, nor did she move away.

Each inch of the park was littered with posters that promised ever more exclusive entertainments that the more talented among the Park's visitors could teleport to, using the painted depictions of living rooms, rooftops, and landing platforms as a guide. As soon as it turned dark, the attendants would clad the Amusement Park in a flurry of multicoloured lanterns. The smells would get even more intense as they rolled out more food stands for the night; hot chocolate desserts, chillies, sausages, roasted vegetables covered in cheese, and those honey-sugared fried fruits.

"So, does this beat your last time coming up here?", Phillippe asked, his voice almost a little too quiet to hear.

"Huh?", Reihan made.

"Didn't you say you came here on a date before? Please tell me this one is better. My ego is so fragile that I think I might perish if you don't tell me how amazing of a job I'm doing."

Reihan raised her eyebrows.

"Keep going like this, and you'll end up another story, just not for the reasons you think."

"Aw", Phillippe said, "And I even agreed to come on this infuriatingly slow machine for you."

"What, you're not enjoying it?"

Reihan looked outside once more, where they had just passed

the highest buildings of the Travelling City. Coated in pinks and gold, only the skies stretched into view like a lazy giant.

"It's fine, I suppose", Phillippe muttered into his robes, "If you can't fly, I imagine it's very impressive."

Reihan chuckled. She turned to face him, catching a glimpse of his moody expression. Phillippe sat as close to her as he had before, his dark eyes staring at her with a mixture of fear and uncertainty that gave her pause.

"You can see the courthouse from here", she said to distract him. She pointed to a tall, wide-columned building some way closer than the Upside-Down Palace.

"So you can", Phillippe said, moving closer to her still. He kept his hands in his lap, and Reihan noticed. Only their legs were pressed together as if they were children on a tight school bench.

"Did you ever go there? You seaver serve as jurors sometimes, don't you?"

"Yes", Reihan said slowly, "Although that's not a very pleasant story."

Phillippe motioned her to keep speaking regardless.

"I wanted your company, seaver. I didn't say it all had to be pleasant and lovely."

Reihan shrugged.

"Very well. But remember, I warned you."

She sighed.

"It was something like forty years ago, I think. The accused was an Enforcer famous for solving cold cases. He'd risen through the ranks quickly and was said to have an eye for details that other investigators, much his senior, had missed."

"Did he commit the murders himself?", Phillippe asked, ever keen to show off. Reihan chuckled.

"No. Cold cases, remember? Some of those murders had been committed before he was even alive."

"Ah, right. I knew that", Phillippe replied, colouring slightly.

"Once he had obtained a high status, however, our accused suddenly regressed to an average quality Enforcer. Most cases he was given remained unsolved, and he spent most of his time living in as much luxury as he could amass. Finally, some of his co-workers grew suspicious and looked into the cold cases he had solved at the beginning of his career."

Phillippe stared at her, and she could tell he was frantically trying to figure out the conclusion of the story before she told him.

"Well, what they found was rather shocking. Many of the supposed key witnesses in the cases no longer remembered ever having met the Enforcer. Nor could the killers, who had all confessed to the crimes back in the day."

"He... manifested thoughts into their mind?", Phillippe realised, "Is that even possible?"

"Unfortunately, it is", Reihan responded, her voice dark, "It is one of the most despicable practices there are. Freedom of thought is the only freedom that matters, the only freedom that allows us to choose what is right. Plus..."

She sighed.

"Plus, some of the victims had gone insane through his repeated intrusions. It wasn't a pretty sight."

"So, what did you rule?", Phillippe asked breathlessly. Reihan stared at him.

"We sentenced him to death, of course. What do you think?"

They stayed at the Amusement Park until it got dark, drinking their way through ever-more elaborate concoctions that tasted like fresh herbs in spring, lemon, and sugar, the first kiss on a lover's body, elation, and pointless heroics.

Reihan swayed slightly as they walked, arm in arm, under curtains of red-glowing lanterns, a myriad of lights forming a blanket of stars overhead, and their feet soft against the ground below. She was less drunk than overwhelmed by the sights and smells and tastes that whirred past her and the crowds of people smiling and waving at Phillippe, who was growing ever more elaborate in his movements. The moodiness had left him, and now he was manifesting tricks for captivated audiences; summoning small fireworks, pulling glowing flowers out of thin air, and amassing a small army of fireflies that followed him like a river flowing through the blackening air.

He is utterly gorgeous, Reihan thought as she watched him pull a small, glowing frog from behind a child's ears, who screamed with delight. *He is utterly gorgeous, and I'm a fucking idiot. This isn't the job. None of this is the job.*

But she was old enough to know that chastising herself for feeling this way would do nothing to quench her desire. A small concession to foolishness might calm the storm threatening to rage inside her chest. And anyway, perhaps it wasn't so foolish to live a little.

"Phillippe", Reihan muttered, almost hoping he wouldn't hear her. Phillippe turned around as if he had just waited for her to say something. The child ran off, and he hurried towards her, perhaps misinterpreting her slurred tone for drunkenness.

"Are you all right, dear seaver?", he asked, cocking his head to the side with amusement.

"I'm fine", she said, feeling her words come out with a little more enthusiasm than she had meant to. She felt the air sugar-sweet on her tongue, and the world was light, pulling her up into the free, open skies.

"Thank you for taking me here", she said, her tone carefree and musical. Phillippe grinned.

"Thank you for coming with me. My day isn't complete without you and your morbid stories!"

"Lucky for you, I have a century's worth of those."

Reihan laughed and spun around. Phillippe grinned and took her hand, directing her spin until she fell, laughing, into his arms, almost pulling him down with her.

"Careful there!", he said, "I may have the dead gods' given grace, but I've also been keeping up with you at the bar."

"Ha! You let me overtake you, I'm sure of it!"

"Is that a challenge, I hear?"

He smiled.

"The night is young, and so many more bad decisions are yet to be made."

"Indeed", Reihan said, slowly tugging on his robes until he looked down into her pale eyes.

Their gaze met, and her desire was unmistakable. She made it unmistakable. His breath quickened, and she felt him tense up again, although his grip around her back also tightened as if he wanted to hold on to her as much as he wanted to let go.

"Ah", he said slowly, his voice thick, "Perhaps it is time we went somewhere a little more private?"

"Are you sure that's what you want?", she asked. She hadn't expected that she would struggle to read Phillippe's mood. Frustration gnawed at the edges of her desire, making her wonder if it wasn't easier to retreat now that they could still laugh it off.

"Yes", he replied, half-closing his eyes. He lowered his head to hers, impossibly slowly, impossibly softly, lashes fluttering against his cheek.

"Sometimes that's all I want."

He hesitated as if he was waiting for a single word to tear him down. Instead, she closed her eyes and softly kissed the side of his mouth. Phillippe didn't tense and he didn't move. He held her back in perfect equilibrium, and Reihan waited, one moment, another, time passing them by like a stranger. Then Phillippe breathed in and moved his lips against hers in a painfully gentle descent. She felt longing, sharp and tangy, on her fingertips as they held onto Phillippe's arms and on her lips that Phillippe caressed with painful slowness. Desire cut her like a knife, and she needed to move, so she moved upwards and slung her arms around Phillippe's neck. Phillippe opened his mouth and sighed as his lips parted and he kissed her with the desperate desire of one who wishes to be known just as deeply as they were felt.

The crowd crashed into them, racing towards some newly opened attraction, and Reihan pulled Phillippe to the side with a laugh, hiding between two stalls that offered trinkets and food.

"Home, yes?", she breathed.

Phillippe looked a little uncertain but then responded to her laugh in kind.

"Yes, definitely", he said, and metal, whirring wings sprouted out of his back.

When Phillippe said home, Reihan hadn't expected him to mean the Asylum. Halfway around the bend down from the Artisan's Quarters, she realised where he was taking them and reminded him that the seavers' living quarters were the last place she wanted to be right now, especially given that if Reihan was present in the Asylum, she could be called upon at any time in case of a staff shortage.

So, Phillippe flew back to his tower in the Brothel, landing on the balcony. They stepped inside his room through an unlocked door. There were carpets beneath Reihan's feet that felt soft and velvety like a blanket of first snow and smelled of rosewood. A myriad of sparkling chains hung from the ceiling, catching the starlight from outside amidst dried flowers that peaked out from every uneven collection of books and elaborate clothes that hung across chairs and dressers. Reihan felt seduced by the feeling of the space itself.

After she took a few steps into his room, she felt Phillippe softly touch her back. She stopped, and he gently folded his hands across her chest and sank his head into her shoulders. He sighed; a painfully sad and sweet sound.

"Do you ever wonder if we imagine all this? All the knowing glances and brushes of hands and all the excitement of finding another person who understands you the way you want to be understood? Sometimes I'm so afraid all I see is what I want to see."

Phillippe's voice was quiet.

"Are you asking if I truly know you?", Reihan responded. She felt warm and like she might so easily sink into Phillippe's embrace, even though his words felt dangerous in a way she couldn't quite place.

"I'm asking if anyone could?", Phillippe answered, "Sometimes the thought of it seems too good to be true. Sometimes all of this feels too good to be true."

"No. Life is hard and long. But there is good that offsets all the misery. I believe that."

"Because you must, to get you through your days?"

"Because I do", Reihan responded, and there was not a hint of doubt in her mind. She was afraid that Phillippe might argue with her, but he didn't. Instead, he brushed his nose against the side of her throat and sighed again, deep into her skin.

"I wish I were more like you", he confessed, "Sure and true. Like a knight from an old story, one of the soldiers that roamed the continents below."

Reihan turned around, so they were facing each other. *He looks so lost in the dark*, she thought.

"I don't. Despite … Despite what you might think, I wouldn't change a thing about you", she confessed, whispering the words to make them less threatening.

"I –"

He gestured towards the bed instead of finishing his sentence.

"I know how to make you happy. I know how to make this a night to remember. I could do that for you if you want, I could –"

Reihan took his hand.

"But you don't want to?"

Phillippe shook his head.

"It's not that simple."

"Is it because of your clients?", Reihan asked, feeling foolish for asking something so obvious. Something that should have occurred to her a long time ago. Phillippe shrugged, uncomfortable.

"I want nothing about us to have anything to do with them. With their boring, irritating, disgusting desires. What I feel for you is so different, and I don't know what to do with it. I don't know how to touch you in a way that would be different from what I do with them."

He glanced across a speck of moonlight on her cheekbones and brushed across it with his fingertips. His voice trembled.

"It's not fair. I want to be able to —"

"Fair never has anything to do with it", Reihan replied, her voice soft.

"I don't want you to leave me because I can't give you what you want", Phillippe said, his voice so fragile she thought it might break upon hitting the air.

Reihan nodded and kissed the side of his lips once more. She opened her mouth but wasn't sure what to say. The moment hung between them, as gentle as a spider's web coated with water and light. Suddenly, she felt the air stir behind them and took a step back. Phillippe raised his hands, conjuring small flames in both his palms, revealing the figure who had manifested into the darkness of his tower. It was Ellis.

She glared at Phillippe, completely ignoring Reihan's presence.

"I might have found your brother, sunshine", she said, wasting no time on greetings or pleasantries, "It's possible he's holed up in a mansion in the rock face. I just found out they're hosting a party tonight, so we can sneak in pretending to be guests."

She took a step closer, then rolled her eyes.

"Dead gods. Sober up and get ready. We're leaving right now."

CHAPTER 13: PHILLIPPE

Ellis led them, barely any soberer, to Lukacz's cottage in the upper city woods, complaining at every step that they couldn't teleport because 'someone insisted on bringing his pet seaver'. Phillippe felt ready to wring the nightmare's skinny neck for that comment but knew that Reihan would be horrified if he intervened on her behalf. For her part, Reihan seemed as impassioned as always. Perhaps slightly unsure on her feet, maybe slightly red-cheeked after the drinks, but not at all shaken after their conversation. Phillippe envied her that, feeling his face glide into dreamy irreverence one moment, then into uncertain despair the next, his eyes ever returning to the back of the seaver's head.

His father's cottage gleamed with light, and shining steam snaked out of the chimney into the black trees, barely visible against the dark blue air that filled the forest paths and sat atop the whispering stream. Tiny fireflies fluttered close to the windowsills, little stars in this eternal, starless forest.

Ellis knocked on Lukacz's front door, a secret rhythm that Phillippe forgot as quickly as he heard it. Lukacz expected them with a tray of tea and oat cakes, welcoming them to a tiny living room that hardly fitted four chairs around a table. Most of the room was taken up by a gigantic stone fireplace, clearly hewn by hand and still, in parts, unfinished.

"Thank you for allowing us into your home, " Reihan said politely and sat on the chair closest to the fire. Phillippe was amazed at how she always seemed to know what to say. He stood close to the door, tongue-tied and embarrassed at the sway in his step. Ellis chose the chair furthest away from Reihan and took three oat cakes at once.

"Sorry about the delay, boss man. We couldn't —"

"You're right on time, Ellis", Lukacz interrupted her. He nodded at Phillippe.

"Are you well, son?"

Phillippe coughed, hoping that might improve his voice.

"I am", he replied, then sat next to Reihan, "What have you found out?"

"He can barely walk, but he's hopping straight to business! I can tell you lads are related!", Ellis laughed, then poured herself a cup of steaming black tea. It smelled like wood and fire, and Phillippe wondered if his father had mixed the leaves himself.

Lukacz shot her a pointed glare, and she fell silent immediately.

"Help yourselves", he invited Phillippe and Reihan, "This is going to be a long night."

"Thank you", Reihan said and nibbled on the side of an oatcake. Phillippe ignored his father's invitation, pointedly tapping his foot on the floor.

"Dad. Please. Don't make me wait any longer. I need to –"

Lukacz sighed, then drew a map from the shelf above the fireplace.

"You need to not get your hopes up, first and foremost", he cautioned, then unrolled the map on the table between them. It showed the Travelling City, with all its landmarks and details, even when it came to the ever-shifting geography of the Undercity. However, where maps normally showed the city's rock face as only a mass of ascending and descending cliffs, this map depicted various buildings encased amidst the stone, tightly embraced by immovable walls.

"What in the hell is this?"

Phillippe was the first to speak. Ellis gave him a condescending smile, evidently smug about the fact that she had known about this when he hadn't. Reihan traced the outline of a building that looked a little like a castle inside an underground cavern.

"I had my suspicions", she muttered, "But so many…."

"And these are only the ones we know of", Lukacz said, "There are likely more, perhaps layered on top of one another."

"Is that even possible?", Phillippe asked, slowly realising what he saw, "Although I suppose for someone powerful enough to sustain a mansion underneath the city, anything might be possible."

"True enough", Lukacz said. Reihan cleared her throat.

"If you know about these places, why haven't you intervened yet?"

All eyes met hers, and she shrugged, almost defensively.

"I'm not talking about you as an individual. But surely the Enforcers could storm the houses if their location is known."

"Why should they?", Ellis asked. Phillippe cocked his head to the side. He wasn't about to agree with the nightmare, but the same question had also occurred to him. Reihan glared at Ellis.

"Because there is a reason these places are hidden underground. If they were doing nothing untoward, their owners could simply live here in the Upper City."

She shook her head.

"I've heard stories of seaver who disappeared, only to reappear years and years later, broken by the time they spent in underground kingdoms, endless labyrinthine structures that led from one nightmarish fantasy to the next."

"Sounds fun", Ellis said, yawning, "Now, can we get to the point, boss man? Before our robot here goes on a crusade."

Lukacz ignored her, instead holding Reihan's withering glare.

"We monitor them with a series of spies and shut down the places where things go too far. But if we shut down one of the manors, another opens in its place, one whose location we have to determine over many months of reconnaissance."

"I understand the difficulties involved with enforcing justice", Reihan replied sharply. Phillippe shot her a questioning glance, and she met it with clear discontent. Lukacz cleared his throat.

"Ellis has determined the location of a newly manifested manor underneath the Amusement Park. It is already renowned among a certain clientele for its manifold diversions and its ever-shifting architecture. We're not sure who it belongs to, but it has only existed for just over a month."

Ellis proudly pointed at the mansion in question, recently added with fiery red ink, its outlines clumsily drawn as if by a child. Phillippe felt his heart skip a painful beat.

"The timing could work", he whispered. Lukacz lowered his eyes.

"Still your heart, son. You'll only run yourself down."

But Phillippe didn't listen. He could only see the drawing burn itself into his eyes and imagine his brother captured within.

"Only question is why your brother dearest hasn't left yet", Ellis said.

"We have no way of knowing that until we go there", Reihan responded, her voice level.

Ellis raised an eyebrow.

"We? And how exactly do you expect to be able to get down there, seaver? Not to mention that your white skin, white hair, and creepy white eyes would stick out like a sore thumb."

Reihan shrugged.

"I wasn't volunteering. Still, no point wasting our time with speculations if the objective remains to find Alexander."

"Which it does", Phillippe said sternly, "If he's in that house, I will find him."

Reihan hmm-ed quietly.

"I have no doubt. But be careful, yes?"

"Am I ever not?"

The seaver barked out a laugh.

"Is that a serious question?"

Phillippe grinned and felt some of his confidence return. She did not seem angry at him, at least. Disappointment he could deal with once he returned. Disappointment he was used to. But before any of that, they had to manifest into that mansion.

"Will you need me to come?", Lukacz asked Ellis, much to Phillippe's surprise. He hadn't expected his father to volunteer, not as one of the city's highest-ranking officials. Ellis seemed to think about it for a moment, then she shook her head.

"Nah. 'ppreciate the offer, boss man, but if your son's as much of a bigshot as people think he is, we'll be just fine."

"Very well. Please don't start any fights that are avoidable."

He pulled another sheet of paper from underneath the map. It was a small flyer depicting a half-dark corridor, a stark stone wall staring at them from underneath candlelight emanating from iron-black sconces. *Find yourself within the Labyrinth*, the flyer promised.

"I don't like this", Reihan muttered, "It seems as though they'll test you before they let you into the main entertainment halls."

"Well yeah, of course. Otherwise, any old Enforcer could march in and shut the whole thing down straight away", Ellis replied.

Phillippe just shrugged.

"It'll be drunks and socialites going. How hard could those

tests be?"

"Hopefully not very, given how tipsy you still are, sunshine", the nightmare said with curved lips. Phillippe shrugged again.

"Shall we then?", he asked, and before waiting for a response, he focused on the paper and teleported deep into the bowels of the city.

They found themselves within the image, cold stone surrounding them. Ellis's breath went fast, creating white nets of mist and condensation, and Phillippe thought he noticed the nightmare shaking.

"Which way?", she asked, glancing from one end of the corridor to the other. Both paths looked identical, so Phillippe decided that it did not matter. He started walking in a direction, and after a few moments' hesitation, Ellis followed him.

They walked for what felt like an hour, then two.

After another few hours, they had to take a break, sitting with their backs to the stone wall and edging towards the faint warmth the sconces let off. Phillippe manifested some food and drink for them, which they consumed silently.

After resting for some time, they got back up and continued. Their steps formed a brittle, irregular rhythm that threatened to slowly turn them to madness.

"Is this the test?", Ellis complained, "To see when our patience runs out, and we just teleport back into the city?"

Phillippe shrugged.

"Perhaps. It seems as though we could keep going endlessly."

"Ugh. Don't say that. You don't think they forget about their guests in here?"

"Maybe whoever's on duty is drunk, lying in a corner somewhere?"

Phillippe let the words ring inside the corridor, then shook his head.

"Or maybe we're missing the point."

"Speak for yourself, pretty boy", Ellis grumbled, "What're you thinking?"

"Well, what sorts of people would the owners of this labyrinth want to meet?"

"I dunno? High society bimbos and overly rich doo-das?"

"People with too much power", Phillippe said, "And people who don't play by the rules."

"Right", Ellis replied, drawing out the vowels. She touched the walls with sharp, long fingers, running her skin over the cold stone.

"So, we break some walls to break some rules? Make 'em pay attention to us?"

"I suppose so", Phillippe said, "Although, come to think of it, would it still count as breaking the rules if we only do so to conform to our host's expectations? Wouldn't there need to be some rebellious intent behind it?"

"Mate, you might be overthinking this."

"I'm not sure", Phillippe replied, then with a single thought, he crumbled the wall next to them. An identical corridor faced them, laying orthogonal to the one they'd been walking down.

"Told you", he said. The nightmare made a face.

"That's just because you drew attention to it. We would've been just fine if we'd crushed the wall before your philosophical pitter-patter."

"Says you."

"Yeah. Says I."

Ellis sighed and crushed a few more walls, all with the same intent. By now, the manor had become a true labyrinth, outstretching its arms around ever-repeating edges.

"So, this is clearly not intimidating anyone", she conceded, "Maybe we just need to wreck more of their shit to get our host's attention?"

"What a good idea", Phillippe replied with a slow-forming grin, "In fact, let's make them come to us."

He concentrated on the wall in front of him. He imagined that just beyond it lay the halls where their host held the night's entertainments, whatever they might be. He imagined intrigue, violence, and power just brimming behind the wall, turning about the eternal axis that was he, Phillippe. Everything held its breath, everything was waiting just for him to step into its midst. He imagined gold walls and gold-painted dancers, rivers of wine and air filled with opioids that made you think the heaviest thoughts. He imagined white silks caressing his skin, iridescent and tantalising, just feather-light enough for him to rip it apart if its touch frightened him.

Everyone stared at his beauty, and their love for him was unconditional. A widening circle of ever-willing friends wearing extravagant gowns and suits with beautiful thick fabrics and masks hiding their mouths and the rims around their eyes, and where smiles lay in every turn of the head. He pulled the scene towards him, closer and closer, feeling his heart ache with the effort of it. Ellis fidgeted.

Phillippe touched the wall, and it crumbled underneath his heavy-ringed fingers. He heard music and eerie laughter, and the ground beneath them fell apart.

"W-what is happening?", Ellis screamed, trying to reach for him. Phillippe felt someone else's powers surround them. The touch made the hairs on his arms stand up, and he felt indivertibly afraid, despite everything he wanted to feel. He thought he could probably have stopped the invasion, but perhaps their host would have considered it rude. Before he could think about it further, the corridor disappeared entirely, and he was alone, floating in a black night sky, with only the occasional star blinking at him with despair.

Alexander materialised before him, just like Phillippe would have expected him to.

Because why wouldn't his brother be here? All his thoughts cried out to him, as inevitable as gravity.

"Hello, you", his brother said, his voice dreamy, like he had just woken up.

"Hello, you", Phillippe echoed.

Alexander looked around, then laughed in that quiet way of his.

"What have you gotten yourself into now?"

"I'm looking for you", Phillippe said, "Remember? I told you that I'd come for you."

"I remember."

"You do?"

Phillippe stared at his brother. Alexander smiled, which made the moment break apart. Phillippe shook his head.

"I'm dreaming you up, aren't I?"

Alexander shook his head.

"I thought we'd agreed that we'd stop believing in fantasies."

"And only believe in each other", Phillippe added, even though the promise had always been a lie. Alexander nodded.

"You didn't forget."

Phillippe shook his head. Alexander looked so much like himself.

"Where are you, Alex?", he asked, his voice merely a whisper, "I want to save you, but I don't know where to start."

"Sorry, brother. Nothing has changed. I'm in the same place you left me."

Phillippe closed his eyes for a moment.

"Of course."

Of course it's a dream.

"Isn't there anything you can tell me?", he asked pointlessly.

Alexander smiled.

"That I'm okay. And that I love you."

"I love you too."

His brother's voice turned wistful.

"When we were children, there was a man on our street. Do you remember? He was weak like us. He could hardly control the few powers he had. He and you sometimes talked about how angry you were about the way things are. Do you remember?"

"I think I do", Phillippe replied. Alexander sounded as though he was suddenly far away. Was this still part of the test?

"He liked to collect things. Little children who followed him around, little figurines of hero Enforcers, seaver who chatted with him over their lunch breaks. He always stepped on the even stones, like he knew exactly what he was doing. He counted out all the steps."

"What about it, Alex? Who is this man?"

Perhaps this was just the rambling of the Submerged. Alexander and him both.

"You know who he is", Alexander replied, "I'm with him now, even though he's disappeared. But you know all of this. I was just wondering when he changed. If he changed at all. Or if he was always awful, just like the rest of the world."

His voice turned ever quieter and dream-like.

"Who is that man, Alex? Do you have his name?"

"I think… I think I hear…"

Alexander's voice rose, and then it fell as though he was half-speaking and half-listening to someone.

"It's strange. Everything is topsy-turvy. It's hard to focus."

He stopped. Then, within a blink of the dream, he became

something else. His jaw, a giant's jaw, unhinged to reveal a black hole that shot towards Phillippe, ready to swallow him whole. Phillippe felt his body twitch, but he commanded himself to stop, not to fall towards the stars that were sure to burn him alive.

"Stop it!", he snapped, "Is this any way to greet your guests?"

Alexander stopped, his jaw turning into a grin.

"How would you like to be greeted?"

The voice was neither male nor female. It was the air that shifted and convulsed in response to the idea of Phillippe that had disrupted its flow. Phillippe wondered if they were genuinely suspended in the cloud mountains above the Travelling City or if he was still trapped inside a cavern in its belly.

Alexander disappeared. Phillippe felt his heartbeat continue to gallop. He was still a little drunk. He was sure they hadn't actually walked for hours earlier, lest he would have sobered up. It must have been yet another illusion.

"How about a with a rich, heavy glass of red wine?", he suggested, trying to seem entirely unaffected. The air shifted and took on a deep crimson character. He opened his lips and tasted a smooth warmth that went to his head immediately. One time a client of his had bid him drink wine out of his mouth. Phillippe had done so, swirling his tongue around his teeth and feeling out a grape that somehow tasted identical to this one.

"Naughty, naughty, reading my memories like this", Phillippe said, trying to downplay how overwhelmed he felt at the realisation that their host was powerful enough to do so.

"How could I resist?", the voice whispered, "I want to know who comes knocking at my door so late at night."

"And? Will you let me in?"

The voice left him for a little, contemplating the question. Phillippe made himself float back and forth. Perhaps he could catch one of the stars in the air. Perhaps that would impress his host. Swirl it around his mouth and pay for entrance with a kiss. It wouldn't be like the one he had gifted Reihan, but it might be enough to buy a night's worth of debauched fun.

"You kissed a seaver?"

The voice sounded greedy.

"Did you fuck her too? I hear some of those robots are made so that you can."

"Let me in, and I might tell you about it", Phillippe replied, imagining a shield around his mind, "I'm not giving you any more until you do."

"Spoilsport", the voice replied in a heightened tone. The air parted, and Phillippe felt himself falling, rushing feet-first towards a bed of stars that waited to burn him up. He stopped breathing as his stomach fell into his chest. But the shield around his mind remained.

"Oh, very well", the voice purred, "Welcome to the party, Phillippe."

And with that, the air around him disappeared entirely, and he found himself elsewhere.

CHAPTER 14: REIHAN

Reihan left Lukacz's house shortly after Phillippe and Ellis had disappeared, having grown tired of the awkwardness of sitting with Phillippe's father over stale confections and bitter tea. She felt hot and restless and still a little drunk. She asked Lukacz to take her back down to the Artisan's Quarters, then walked slowly through the black-blue streets, filled only with the sound of her shoes echoing from the walls of sleepy houses. Even if Phillippe returned tonight, she knew he wouldn't be able to take the restlessness out of her step. She understood why it was difficult for him. But in the grand scheme of things, the seaver didn't have much life that belonged just to them, that they did not give up in service of the city. On days when she worked, she had two hours for herself. She had one day off for every ten that she worked. And at any point , she could be called upon to solve a crisis when she was out walking in the city.

Reihan was all right with that. She understood that humans needed the seaver, their eternal watchers, servants, and executioners.

But in a life like hers, she couldn't afford to try and manifest the same fantasies of love that Phillippe chased. She felt the same elusive thing between them. But sex was just sex. A few moments when she could lose control before she was expected to shoulder everyone's burdens again.

She shivered at how cold the night had turned, long past the time of celebrating, drinking, and dancing, and descended into the time when nothing was to be done but the things you'd later come to regret. She realised, finally, where her steps were carrying her. She needed to speak to Seamus. Needed to, even if part of her still did not want to. It had been two years since they'd last seen each other, their relationship weighted down by secrets that Reihan had only shared with him and all the expectations she had put on their friendship. Seamus had only five months and seven days left to live, and a little while ago, Reihan had decided that it would be easier never to see him again. Seamus never got in touch with her of his own accord, anxious not to bother her. But, as Phillippe had said, tonight was a night for foolish decisions.

Seaver weren't put in the same retirement homes that the privileged and powerful humans used if they decided to let their life run its natural course. In truth, few seaver made it to the end of their pre-determined lifespans, just as most of the powerful humans in the city either died at the hands of one another or themselves. If they reached their one hundredth and ninety-ninth year, however, seaver were given the privilege of not having to work while still being provided with access to food, drink, and housing. That law had been so archaic by the time Seamus reached his final year that he had needed to find precedence for it in some old legislation stored at the back of the city's Library. The Enforcers had given him a small apartment at the intersection between the Artisan's Quarters and the Weeping Stairs, overlooking the Mineshafts and the Upside-Down Palace. Reihan had only ever walked past with other seaver pointing out Seamus's darkened windows and asking her if she'd gone to visit him yet. Her answer had always been the same.

Now, she breathed against the painted wooden door that led into the building, imagining what she'd say after two years of angry silence. She pushed the door open, slowly and carefully, so as not to wake any inhabitants of the building that might be sleeping. Public entrances were always open in adherence to Enforcer legislation. You could only lock doors that belonged to you.

She guessed her way to the door she thought belonged to Seamus. Her heart beat faster, thinking of all the years she had spent believing herself to be his closest companion. The humiliation of finding it to be otherwise. And all the memories of laughter and warmth and longing she felt as though she couldn't hold onto now that the end was in sight.

Seamus opened the door before she had gathered up the courage to knock.

"How –", she began, and the other seaver laughed quietly.

"I saw you walking up the street. I doubt you'd come to this part of town at this time of night if you did not want to speak to me."

"Rather presumptuous of you."

Seamus gave her a sad smile.

"And yet, am I wrong?"

Reihan shook her head.

"Why are you still awake?", she asked instead.

"I don't sleep much these days. It seems like a silly waste of time."

"I understand that."

The night hung between them, strained and yet too familiar to truly feel cold. Reihan cocked her head to the side and gave him the half-smile she remembered he'd always liked.

"Aren't you going to invite me in?", she asked, every word carrying the leftover desire from earlier that night.

Seamus stared at her for a few moments, his white eyes perfectly matching hers. His hair hung down exactly to his chin, its edges razor-sharp, and the collar of his sleeping shirt ironed at a perfect angle. He looked every bit like the last time she had seen him. Then, he stepped back.

As soon as she walked through the door, Seamus leaned down to kiss her matter-of-factly. If he could smell the alcohol on her breath, if he could somehow feel her desire for another, he did not comment on it. He had been the one to show her, in actions rather than words, that jealousy and possessiveness were foolish emotions. At least for a seaver, at least when whomever you'd chosen as your lover could be as easily killed by a manufacturing error as a mob of angry humans. To his credit, Seamus had never tried to hurt her like she'd tried to hurt him. He had never fucked any of her friends or been particularly obvious about taking other lovers. Reihan had been less discrete.

Seamus moved his hands from her back to her chest, where the modders had installed erogenous zones to mimic the ones humans had. Seamus had been there when she'd had it done. He'd held her hand and promised her it would be worth it. And it had been. She had been glad of the changes and enjoyed trying them out with him over the course of many an empty hour at the end of a long day.

Seamus stroked over her chest with long, practised fingers, and she felt her breath quicken, just as it was supposed to, and for her body to heat up, just as it was supposed to. The desire from earlier returned, its edges still sharp and hard, even as it was feasting from memory. Soon enough, she could let go for a few moments and leave all this foolishness behind.

"Come", Seamus said and took her hand. He pulled her toward a half-open room, most likely his bedroom, but she resisted for a moment. She pointed at the window she'd seen from the street, a half-grin spreading on her features. Something to take the monotony out of the well-rehearsed steps between them. His gaze followed hers, and he raised his eyebrows.

"It'll be a memory worth making", she explained and kissed the side of his neck when she sensed his hesitation. Goosebumps formed on his white skin, and she felt his fingers tighten around her hand.

"We have to be sensible, Reihan", he said, although his voice hitched when she sucked on a particularly sensitive bit of skin just underneath his chin.

"You'll just have to be fast then", Reihan challenged him, trying to pull him toward the window, imagining Seamus pressing her naked back against the glass and taking her standing up until sharp release made her scream his name.

"No", Seamus decided. Reihan sighed but knew there was no point in arguing. She let him pull her towards his bedroom, where he removed his clothes, leaving her to do the same. She imagined for a second how Phillippe might have gone about it, how he'd try to cut out every mechanical, well-practised part of the act and turn it all into a representation of the bond that tied them together. She couldn't even start to imagine it, and yet the thought was senseless, frustrating, and utterly intoxicating. She felt Seamus's hands turning her back towards him.

"I missed you", he whispered, then moved a cold hand up her thigh, dipping into the wetness between them. Reihan didn't respond. He knew her better than anyone, and there was no need to explain to him how she felt.

His movements were the same they had always been, enough to make her head swim with heat, enough to make her collapse on his bed, open and desperate for the wait to be over. It was enough that she was drunk and wanted to feel. Every touch, every movement made her feel so sensitive she wanted to writhe in the sharp, open air. Almost anything was enough for her.

Seamus glanced down for a moment, taking in the sight of her. A shy smile played around his lips, and then he moved down, taking her the same way he always did, from the top, his eyes half-closed, with shallow breaths and his muscles far too tense. Reihan closed her eyes and thought about Phillippe. She imagined him dancing within the bowels of the forbidden manor, drunk on spiced wine and with the eyes of a million admirers caressing every curve of his body. She imagined the beautiful tilt of his mouth that she had kissed, and the heat built up within her as Seamus's lean body moved in precisely the right way at the right angle.

Before she realised it, she was screaming, locking her legs behind Seamus's back and throwing her throat up in the air. She lost control for just a few seconds, writhing around senselessly, and she loved every breath of air she greedily sucked up. Seamus was quieter, but he nonetheless collapsed when some of the tension left his body, embracing her with the presumptuousness of an old friend. Which, she supposed, he still was.

He made her sweet coffee with thick cream, sugar and liquid chocolate, just the way she liked it. They sat in the kitchen, looking out the window against the deep blue streets that would, in a few hours, be conquered by dawn. Seamus did not thank her for coming, nor did he ask why she had changed her mind. Instead, he asked about work and the other seaver in the Asylum. They caught up with the slow, mellow conversation that had always flown so easily between them. Finally, Seamus asked about Phillippe.

"Are you still observing him?", he asked, taking a sip of his black coffee.

"Hm", Reihan made. She was not embarrassed, but neither did

she meet Seamus's eyes.

The seaver clicked his tongue.

"I'm worried about him. You might have to intervene sooner or later."

"I know what my duties are."

"And you hesitated to perform them before."

It had happened a long time ago. Seamus had needed to step in. The fact that he had was the only reason Reihan hadn't been deactivated for her failure. Part of her still resented him for it.

"There are too many stressors coming together, and we can't afford for him to blow",

Seamus continued, purposefully oblivious to her reluctance to continue the conversation.

"He's not a bomb, Seamus", Reihan protested.

"They're all bombs, Reihan."

Reihan sighed.

"Am I going to be just as cynical after two hundred years of service?"

Seamus laughed quietly.

"Once upon a time, I thought the mindset I have was an inevitable outcome of our existence as seaver. But maybe you'll prove me wrong. I suppose I'll never know."

Reihan fell silent for a moment.

"I'm sorry for the reminder", she muttered. Seamus glanced at her, impatient.

"Don't apologise. I told you that before."

"You've told me a lot of things, Seamus. You can't expect me to listen to all of them."

Seamus's mouth turned upwards.

"I suppose I cannot. I suppose I should enjoy the laze of retirement and let you youngsters run the show."

"Youngsters!"

Reihan snorted just as she was about to put her coffee to her lips.

"Compared to me, anyhow."

"You don't feel a day older than when I first met you at the Asylum, Seamus."

"Trust me, I do."

Seamus gave her a wry smile.

"Is it very painful, love?", Reihan asked, gently taking his hands.

Seaver bodies were not built for more than two centuries. After a while, the repairs all failed. They weren't meant to live forever, weren't meant to rise above the humanity who had created them. Many seaver, close to the end, chose to take their own lives rather than endure the pain that came in those final days.

"Sometimes it is painful", Seamus admitted, and Reihan knew he was downplaying it.

"But I will see things through until my final day. I might yet be needed. And anyway, it seems silly to give up this close to the end."

"Well, we wouldn't want to be silly, now would we?"

Seamus smiled politely, not quite understanding her sarcasm.

But he let her hold his hand a little longer.

CHAPTER 15: ELLIS

Ellis walked along a gravel path, empty grass planes by her side. Ahead lay a lake slowly creeping onto the path as if it were scared to be left alone. The waters were suspiciously quiet, mirroring the grey skies overhead.

She had spent a long time alone before Lukacz had found her. She tried not to remember those years, all that time tethering between existence and nothingness. Perhaps she was already older than everyone else in the Travelling City. Perhaps she was older than the world itself, and the girl whose dream had birthed her was a god. She didn't think it really mattered now that her days were full rather than empty.

But she still didn't like being alone. The only sound in the world being her steps on the ground and the wide waters ahead reflecting only her eyes, a mirror to her loneliness. The host probably thought this was extremely funny.

When she reached the water, she looked down. The grey skies slowly gave way to a vision of interconnected rooms, a spider's web full of masked party guests, dancing and chatting over drinks or amusing themselves in dark corners. Some were reading in a library, and some were having an animated discussion in a stone bath, with violet mist steaming their faces. In another dark room, smoke gave way to red streaks being painted onto willing flesh, while in another, an empty stage loomed menacingly. Ellis took a step forward, half-expecting the water to give way and allow her to fall into the party's merriment. But the ground below her feet remained solid as the lake's cold wetness started seeping into her trousers.

"Yeah, yeah, I get it", Ellis murmured impatiently, "But where's the trick?"

She waited around for a while. The sounds of music quietly emerged from the projection below, children's songs played on a zither. Ellis jumped about within the lake, splashing the waters and trying to catch the descending droplets. When she got tired, she threw herself down, not caring that her clothes got soaked. She stared out into the lake and thought about nothing much at all.

Slowly, a severed head emerged from the waters. First, just its eyes, dark and brown and strangely far apart, then the rest of its enormous face came into view. Dark wrinkles structured the landscape of its skin, and Ellis thought she could see tiny specks of light glimmer amidst the darkness of its deepest folds. Its eyes stared past her, but she knew better than to turn around.

"Hello there", she said instead, not bothering to get up. Her arms rested comfortably on her knees, stretched out in anticipation.

"Can you take me to the party?"

The head kept floating towards her, but its mouth was stitched shut with bright red thread. Behind the stitches, she could see small creatures rummaging between its teeth. Tiny fingers poked out of its hairy ears.

"Pretty please?", Ellis asked just as it floated past, "You don't have to scare me or whatever your master sent you here to do. You can do whatever you want. Or whatever I want, if that's easier."

The head didn't slow down. It reached the gravel road, then bobbed along its winding path back the way Ellis had come.

"So, did I go the wrong way?", Ellis asked, jumping up.

The head still bobbed, not slowing down or looking back her way, but she chose to interpret its movements as a nod.

"Well, then it's high time you show me the right way", she decided and took a flying jump so that she came down on top of the head. She ran her hands over its ugly crown, barely featuring any strands of greasy black hair. The skin felt soft and melty, and her touch produced as many wrinkles as it smoothed out.

The head waited until she positioned herself comfortably, then floated along the path. Ellis held onto its ears and closed her eyes. The grasslands disappeared, and the music suddenly sounded like it was a lot closer. Ellis waited, then waited some more, feeling the head below her bob with gentle motion. Finally, she felt the air shift, and the bobbing stopped.

"Get off", a voice grunted below her, "We've arrived, 'mare."

Ellis opened her eyes to the library she'd seen in the lake and jumped off the head, who had by now grown a whole body. A small one, at least in proportion to its head, carrying a tray full of steaming black drinks, with tiny ice cubes and umbrellas floating atop the liquid.

"Thanks for the ride", she said to the goblin. She'd seen his like in books written and illustrated to frighten children. The creature shrugged and walked off, but Ellis couldn't help but smile as she saw that the bobbing continued just the same as it disappeared between two bookshelves. Personal grievances aside, living manifestations tended to stick together.

The library was dark and dusty, its shelves reaching the ceiling and forming a labyrinthine set of passages. Warm light emanated from hidden candles amidst the hard-shelved books, rendering only half the titles visible. A few partygoers were present, sat on the floor and were immersed in whichever book they were reading. Each turn of the page was quitted with a dreamy, almost lustful sigh.

Ellis dried her clothes with a thought, then started to look for an exit. She remembered that this part of the manor was interconnected with the livelier parts of the party. Maybe there she would find Phillippe before something happened to him. One powerful Submerged was bad enough to lose – she didn't want to make it two.

She picked a young woman whose mousy brown hair formed a curtain between her and her book and the rest of the world. Ellis knelt beside her, moving her face so close to the woman's that their breaths met uncomfortably.

"Hey", Ellis said, "Been to the main event yet?"

"Shhh", the young woman whispered, "This is a library."

"Sure. And the sooner you tell me how to get out, the sooner I'll get out of your hair."

"Shh", a few people close to her made, "Shh, shh, shh."

The sound seamlessly intertwined with the zither, whose sounds still floated through the passages. Ellis sighed and got back up. She wasn't about to get much out of these people. They wouldn't leave this place until they were thrown out, and then they'd probably dream of the books they'd read here for the rest of their lives.

Not her problem, though.

She wandered about the bookshelves for a little but found the path between the stories to be mercifully singular. Floating flecks of dust glowed within the candlelight, and she thought, just for a moment, that it would be funny to set the whole place alight.

The path led to a small red door, not made of wood but something altogether softer and pultruding, as if it was a living thing she had to push through to proceed. Outside the door stood a seaver. Ellis froze. The seaver noticed her approach and placed his pale white hand on the doorknob, glowing in a faint golden light beneath his touch.

"Would you like to enter, my lady?", he asked in a tone that sounded more unsure than she'd normally expect from their kind.

"Enter where?", Ellis asked, keeping her distance.

"The main", the seaver said, "Where most of the people are."

"The main what?"

"The main", the seaver repeated, visibly confused. Ellis took a few steps closer, and the seaver's posture did not shift, not like it did in the world above when they realised what she was.

"Were you born here, mate?", she asked.

"Weren't we all?", the seaver replied.

"Right", Ellis muttered, then nodded towards the door knob, "Let me enter that main of yours then."

Even though Ellis knew the seaver was harmless, the hairs on her neck stood up as she walked past him. He had most likely only been born a few days or weeks ago and would be used precisely as long as he did not realise that there was more to life than this manor. Perhaps he'd never realise it and live out his two-hundred-year lifespan down here in the half-dark. Or perhaps they'd made him longer-lived. The technology for creating seaver had long been sold on the city's various black markets, and robots like this were cropping up all over the strangest places, modified in various ways.

They always gave her the creeps. Their Palace-born counterparts were used to hunt manifestations like her when they stepped out of line. No human could oppose them once the seaver had decided on someone's fate, no matter how much they might want to protect their wayward thought creations.

That's what nobody else seemed to get.

Whether they worked shitty jobs day-in and day-out, or whether they served the highest-level Enforcers on top of the bloody Palace, the seaver were dangerous. Active duty seaver like Reihan were famous for how efficiently they disposed of rogue manifestations that had been as quickly forgotten as they had been created. For years and years, Ellis had heard of the seaver from the Asylum with the quiet voice who was called when her kind got out of hand. The pale ghost who killed both manifestations and humans with equal dispassion and then returned to scrub the dust from some poor Submerged bastard's skin as if nothing had happened. Reihan and her mentor, the seaver Seamus, who wore white suits, whose hair was razor-sharp, and who was even quicker to pick up the sword than his pupil. Their names were familiar whispers in the shadows of the Undercity.

Ellis found them terrifying, and for scaring her, she hated their guts.

On the other side of the door, she found herself in a wood-panelled corridor branching out into three pathways. She tried to remember the layout of the place from the reflection she'd seen in the water, but she could not recall a branch like this. The manor's interior had to be shifting, either in line with the designs of their host or a collaborative set of manifestations by their guests. Ellis hoped dearly that none of their thoughts would become strong enough to break through her sense of self and start to mess with her body. If she felt even an inkling of power nagging on her, she'd teleport out of this shit show that very second, the wonder brothers be damned.

She decided that she liked to be right, so she followed the path on the right-hand side. The corridor was adorned by vibrant landscape paintings, showing beautiful rolling meadows and forests that people claimed existed on the continent below. Groups of sheep and cattle grazed peacefully amidst shepherds creating clouds with pipe smoke while glimmering dragons floated overhead. She had the odd feeling that if she touched the pictures, she would find herself within the scene, so she stayed far away from the walls.

Finally, she reached a wooden door, with steam and chattering voices escaping through its small cracks. Ellis hesitated for a moment, then froze when she recognised one of the voices. It was Phillippe, speaking in husky tones, and met at every turn by adoring laughter. Ellis rolled her eyes, then entered.

She was met with a bout of lavender smoke, just at the right temperature, floating about her face with the softest caress.

"Oooh", a voice made to her left, and she just caught glimpse of a woman retreating into the clouds, her golden, intricate mask glittering amidst the half-dark of the room.

"Close the door", voices echoed left and right, "Close it, close it now."

Ellis could barely see further than a few feet ahead. Hawk-nosed and sparkle-eyed masks shifted back and fro, but Ellis could not make out the bodies they were attached to. She slowly moved on, one minuscule step at a time. She could still hear Phillippe's voice, the loudest amidst a mountain of whispers, coming from somewhere up ahead.

She kept going until she found a wall. It was white and shiny with wetness, gleaming between wafts of thick air. Ellis thought there might be something wrong with her eyes because the walls kept shifting even when she looked straight ahead. She stepped closer and squinted. Then, suddenly, she saw the creatures. Half-forming, half-formed snakes and dragons and ivy and flowers crawled over the walls, all white and only managing to protrude outwards by a few inches. Whenever Ellis blinked, the whole scenery changed, and where the dragons had previously razed flora and fauna from above, they were now being strangled by the might of the plant life.

She stepped back and went in another direction, now aware that she was wading through a bathhouse whose layout was currently shifting. *I'm me*, she reminded herself, *I'm Ellis, and nothing in the world is going to change that.* Finally, she heard a gurgle and almost stepped into a rock pool filled with steaming purple water. She looked down and saw various shapes beneath the cloudy mist.

Someone pulled on Ellis's pant leg. A beautiful naked woman, her blonde hair clinging to every curve of her body and with her silver mask half-slipped off her nose, blinked up at her.

"Come in", she demanded, her voice hoarse, "I'm bored. Entertain me."

Phillippe's voice was very close now. He was almost certainly just beyond the other side of the pool, floating in the heat and laughing into the ear of one of the guests.

Ellis cursed internally and started wading into the waters, removing not a single item of clothing.

The beautiful woman laughed.

"You're funny", she decided, "Do you want to kiss me?"

Her chest was entirely visible above the water, strands of hair caressing the gap between her breasts.

"Not really", Ellis responded. The woman shrugged, unbothered.

"Then tell me something."

"About what?"

Ellis was getting irritated. She should be the one to ask the questions. She should not be thrown by seaver and naked women. Had the years under Lukacz taught her nothing at all?

"About the outside world. I've not been in so very long. Is it still so terribly boring?"

Ellis, who had never found the Travelling City boring in any way, shrugged.

"What's so great in here?", she asked instead.

"I don't need to think", the woman replied, absent-mindedly stroking her chest with nails so long they curved at the tips. *She looks like she's been in here for longer than a month*, Ellis thought. Maybe their host was playing around with time, too. *Great.*

The woman's mask slid all the way off her face and fell into the water, coating the surface in fine silver sparkles. Ellis saw several scars around her full mouth, made by a whip or a thin knife.

"Outside, I need to think all the time. Life gets very dangerous if I make the wrong choice. In here, there's just pleasure after pleasure. I can be drunk from noon to night. I can sit in the warm, and it never gets cold. I can fuck whomever I want and never need to think about having done a good job."

She smiled half-drearily.

"I never want to leave. But I do wish to know that everything outside collapsed without me."

"Well, it didn't", Ellis said, although she felt a bit childish, "The outside world is the same it's always been."

"How would you know, shadow? Maybe I dreamed you up? Maybe you've never even left this place."

Ellis didn't want to, but she hesitated for a moment. She had to think about these things. Even if it was just to remind herself that it couldn't be true and that she had nothing to worry about.

"Who is Lukacz?", she asked.

"Huh?", the woman made. Her eyes were half closed, and her hair hung on the water like a net.

"No", Ellis said slowly, "You would know him if you made me up."

"Whatever, shadow", the woman said, sinking deeper into the water, "Leave me alone."

Her head dipped beneath the surface, then she was gone, her entire body disappearing as if it had never existed.

Ellis tried to calm her racing heart, then she waded further into the mist. After a while, she thought she felt something cold on her skin. She looked up and saw a dark blue sky amidst which snowflakes dripped out of tiny, chubby hands. They swirled around the mist, then disappeared when they hit the surface of the glowing purple water. Everything around Ellis was empty and still. But feeling alone didn't make her feel any better. There was no point in staying sane if no one was watching her.

"Phillippe, where are you?", she whispered, straining her mind. A few more snowflakes landed on her forehead, thick and white.

"Find him", she commanded, and the flakes peeled off her wet skin and started glowing in an eerie light. They floated a few inches ahead of her, held in suspense as if they were scanning the area. Then, seemingly content, they chose a direction. Ellis followed until the mists parted again to reveal a group of soft-glowing rock pools overlooking a sharp cliff's edge and a roaring ocean below. Winds were screaming overhead, but down here, they were kept warm by the steam emanating from the water, black and glimmering with starlight.

"Oh, look, she's naked!", a voice croaked from ahead.

One of the rock pools was occupied by a small group of animals, which Ellis recognised from the time Lukacz had taken her to visit the Menagerie.

A glorious peacock was at the centre of their conversation, its dark green feathers shimmering in the half-light as all the other animals hung onto its every word. The bird sat next to a kraken whose tendrils ensnared its lower body, a toad with a hanging gut, a cow with a wide, long beak, and a cat, rolled up on the dark rocks surrounding the water. Tiny fireflies whizzed between them, following the streams of conversation, alight with curiosity.

"Get dressed", the toad croaked again in her general direction. Ellis shook her head, feeling water drip from her pants and shirt.

"It's very rude, you know?", the kraken said, "We're having an important tête-à-tête. You can't show your face to something like that."

"Fuck off", Ellis said and felt the words across her entire body.

"I would argue that it's far more exciting for her to show her face", the peacock said, with a calm alluring voice, "Disguises are fun, but what's more thrilling than displaying the very core of who you are when you talk about things that truly matter?"

The rest of the animals fell silent and considered what the bird had said. Ellis sighed with relief.

The peacock was speaking with Phillippe's voice.

CHAPTER 16: PHILLIPPE

The conversation was slick and slow-moving. Phillippe found himself returning to the sound of the ocean rather than staying with the voices of the other guests. He knew he was expected to say little. He was there to look beautiful and say small words that could conveniently be turned this way or that. To be an idol whose attention was to be won without being taken away.

The topic turned from the politics of the day to the ideal direction of the city. Some thought the Travelling City flew on a pre-determined path, destined to reach a perfect utopia in the skies where life went on forever, and all uncertainties were assuaged. Others thought that the people who manned the Watchtower, led by immortal Cian'Erley, directed the city's path away from the continent's mountain ranges and flying constructs to allow the city to maintain its isolation and safety. The prevailing theory, however, was that the inhabitants' philosophical beliefs played a significant role in directing the city's path through the cloud sea as long as enough of them thought along the same lines.

Various societies had thus been founded around the different geographical directions, with each convinced its own values and ideas were the ones that should be followed. Generally, the different factions were so fundamentally at odds, and rather enjoyed screaming at one another over roasted poultry at the marketplace, that productive consensus became a conceptual impossibility.

In conversations such as this, North had been designated as the branching paths of freedom, wherein the city would be allowed to break apart into a hub of neighbourhoods, housing complexes, or even singular ships whose routes would be true and different for each one, to meet and depart as they pleased.

On the other hand, South represented more of the same, a steady path through the cloud sea with each of the districts assuming their ideal shapes, working coherently to weather the storms that the universe and its dead gods threw at them.

West had been determined to be the direction of progress, forcing innovations that would channel the people's manifestation abilities into their most powerful and potentially dangerous iterations.

At the same time, East represented the path of tradition, of better training humans to contain their powers so they could continue to live safe and predictable lives that minimised suffering.

Of course, this was all theoretical. The cloud sea looked the same in every direction, the occupants of the Watchtower were probably perpetually on lunch, and the city's inhabitants probably didn't have all that much influence over where it was going to fly next. Phillippe was convinced that he was talking to bored, high-ranking bureaucrats and lawmakers from Government who had decidedly too much time on their hands. People who had more power than they should but not enough to make a genuine difference.

"I am not convinced that people really know what's good for them", the cat murmured from the dry, warm rocks outside the pool, "They might think that they crave the choice and solitude of riding off into the sunset on their private airships, but when given the choice to do whatever they want, everyone fundamentally goes for the same things."

The cat nodded in the direction from where Ellis had appeared.

"Look at this place. Everyone wants sex, food, love, and diversion. We're not so different when it comes down to it. So why split up and make ourselves more vulnerable? I say we go South."

A small communal manifestation of the Travelling City moved in the stated direction. It hung between them, a marker of their unfinished conversation. Phillippe sighed internally. He knew he would only gain information about their elusive host after this debate had been settled. Until they reached a gap between one impossible conversation and the next.

"I think you underestimate people", he said. He did not elaborate further, but the city moved a tiny bit back North when everyone's eyes hung onto his shimmering feathers and contemplated that beauty equated to wisdom.

"It depends, does it not?", the toad cautioned, "If we run our communities and ships and whatnot sensibly, we can do whatever we like. Let people be free and separate from the Travelling City as long as we avoid needless suffering. So, have them establish their own communes, but not in a way that devolves into pirate towns or slave empires."

"And how would we do that exactly?", the kraken asked, twisting one of its arms that sat on Phillippe's lower body. Phillippe knew precisely how to make heat flow into the area he felt the arm was touching. And he did because the kraken might like that, because every small detail might make a difference, and because he was used to feeling disgusted.

"Send the seaver with them", the toad replied, "Have them keep a tight rein on what happens in the colonies. I know we don't like them, but it is undeniable how important they are. We wouldn't keep them otherwise."

"So, condemn them to another eternity of servitude", Phillippe muttered.

"What, the people?", the toad asked, misunderstanding him, "It's not servitude if the protection is for their own good. Nobody wants to return to the old days when everyone was ruled by star manifesters who'd subjugate everyone else to their whims."

"No, it's much better now that we pretend things have changed", the cat yawned.

"Oh, believe me, it's not the same it used to be", the kraken laughed, "People these days couldn't imagine the things we sacrificed to turn the city into what it is now. How many died so we can stew in our own filth in comfort."

"So, perhaps that is what we should concentrate on", the cow proposed, "Neither freedom nor safety is sustainable without progress. The world grows ever more dangerous and we have to adapt to survive."

The animal sighed with a decidedly female voice.

"I don't know if any of you were outside during the last storm, but it was a travesty. So few of our citizens knew what to do against hostile manifestations. Even some of the seaver were consumed by it. If we can't defeat the storms or whatever else lurks in the cloud sea, everything else is a moot point."

"But if we make ourselves too powerful, the seaver can't serve as a safety net anymore", the toad argued.

"There is already no safety net", Phillippe said gloomily, "Some of us already have to make our own decisions of which rules to follow."

"Yes, my love, but I believe all of us are quite happy with there being one rule set for us and one for the people outside. What is tenable for some is not tenable for all. There must be Overseers to ensure the masses don't go insane", the kraken said.

"Must there?", the cat asked, "If we can make everyone happy and contented, I don't think anyone would want to be a mere onlooker."

"But we can only do that once everyone is safe", the toad cautioned, "Why else do we hide away and almost never use our powers? Every move we make is a risk."

"So, we'll die fat and happy", the cow said, her eyes narrowing. Everyone turned around to the fervour in her voice. Even Ellis, who had been plucking fireflies out of the air, looked down.

"No one's at risk of dying quite yet, dear", the kraken said with an unpleasant, uncertain laugh.

"Aren't we?", the cow replied sharply, "Look around you. We pretend that we can choose our city's direction, but we've long since made our decision, contented and stupefied as we are down in these hidden manors and kingdoms. We are close to gods with these powers we've been given, and what do we do with them? We watch the people we love suffer and perish."

Phillippe remembered an old story in which it was the gods' deaths that gave humans their powers. He had found that idea hard to stomach. He wasn't sure he believed in gods, dead or alive.

The cow shook her head.

"We're so far East that we think we're back at the Centre. I'm proposing that we at least explore what lies beyond."

The manifested city glowed at the sound of her passion and moved firmly West, further and further, until it reached the edge of the rock pool. No one replied, feeling awkward at the way in which a passionate consideration of reality had consumed their thought experiment. And in the fragile context of a party, they would rather accept someone else's conclusion than challenge the cow in earnest.

Phillippe laughed, a beautiful, silvery sound and the tension melted as everyone's eyes turned back on him. He spread his glowing, purple and green feathers and draped them over the cow and the kraken's skins.

"What a shame our host couldn't be here to witness the historic moment whereupon we decided on the new path for our fair city."

Everyone smiled at his exaggerated, ironic tone. Even the cat rolled on its back and exposed its furry belly. The sea roared far below, but up in the warmth of the pools, the sound was almost inviting.

"They don't often show their face", the kraken confessed, "After what happened at their last place, I can't blame them."

"What happened?"

Phillippe had heard rumours, surely exaggerated as they passed through the many corners of the Undercity until they finally had reached his and Alexander's ears. Rumours of entire empires that spread across planes of reality somewhere deep beneath the Travelling City, lost in an instant when its host lost concentration.

Usually, the lapse of concentration was caused by something funny and inconsequential, like a talking insect or an unexpectedly sour confection or a chair whose leg broke at just the wrong moment. Good stories, although Phillippe had always guessed that they were mostly made up.

"They used to run *Five Bodies*", the kraken explained, "But then the Enforcers caught wind of what was going on down there. They burrowed tunnels into the earth and sent in hordes of seaver. Most of them didn't make it back, but *Five Bodies* shut down for good."

"Cost the city heaps of resources replacing those seaver", the toad murmured, "What a waste."

"*Five Bodies* was real?", Ellis asked, and for the first time, Phillippe caught a glimpse of what he guessed might be shock on the nightmare's face. He had never even heard of the place. It must have existed before he became privy to insights into how the city truly operated.

"But of course. Did you never go?", the kraken asked, visibly amused.

"I don't know", Ellis replied, and Phillippe guessed that she was telling the truth. Lukacz had implied that the nightmare did not remember much of her early years.

"You'd remember", the cat said with a snicker, "It was fantastic. A gigantic pit under the earth where fire spontaneously combusted everywhere. The drinks were so thick in the air that all you had to do was open your mouth, and you'd get drunk. And the music was loud enough that it shook the city above."

"But that was just for the regular guests", the kraken interjected with a superior grin, "At its core, *Five Bodies* was a never-ending labyrinth. Its corridors moved every five minutes, so you'd never find the exit."

His tendril tightened around Phillippe's lower body as if it was about to tear him in two. He could feel manifestations tugging at his outer shape, trying to turn him back into his human form. And he knew what would come next.

The kraken continued.

"But here's the real kicker. The corridors didn't just move. They teleported, shifting through space itself. And because of that, every five minutes, the place would split your body apart as it teleported you somewhere else. Just a little bit, at first, but towards the end, you were in a hundred places at once, feeling the entire structure twist and turn around you."

"It really was quite exquisite. That stretch, the knowledge that every next turn might be the time when your concentration rips and your body stays in pieces."

The toad wetted her lips. The cow looked away, but Phillippe thought he saw a glimpse of disgust in the turn of her brows.

"Of course, not everybody could handle it. That, and apparently quite a few people got thrown down there for a joke or as punishment."

The kraken rolled his eyes. Phillippe nodded, feeling his beak bob. He wondered if he could have handled that labyrinth. If he could have ripped it into a million pieces with a thought, then shook out all the dismembered corpses, having them softly glide into the cloud sea to be laid to rest. This entire city was built on blood. It needed to be - ... He wasn't sure. But he felt restless and hot, and all he wanted was to get out of this pool full of people whose arteries oozed with the dried knowledge of centuries.

"This is a decent replacement, I suppose", he said, "But it is a little tame, isn't it? I am still looking for somewhere that is really going to dazzle me. Something new."

The kraken looked at him, measuring in how far his words were a barely concealed invitation and in how far Phillippe was fishing for information. Phillippe knew his subtlety was losing its edge, but he struggled to concentrate. He threw Ellis a look he hoped she would understand. They had to leave soon.

"Then you probably want the Casino", the cow grumbled,

"Over the last few weeks, that's supposedly gotten rather good. If you're into that sort of thing."

"Some excellent illusions. And they change their gambits all the time", the cat added, licking the wet fur around its belly, "But I'm not sure it wouldn't still be a little tame for our peacock friend here."

"It's just gotten good over the last few weeks?", Ellis pushed.

"Yes", the kraken said, stretching out the vowels, "They must have hired some new manifesters to oversee the betting. It's really rather exciting."

He pressed his tentacle deeper still into Phillippe's flesh, tearing through feather and skin.

"I might look for you there, love", he murmured into his ear.

"I'll be the one in red", Phillippe whispered back, then disentangled himself from the embrace.

"Well, that gives me some inspiration at least", he said, his voice noticeably breathy, "I thank you all for your delectable company."

"Come back soon", the toad entreated, "We'll stay another while or two."

The kraken merely smiled, and the cat did not bother looking up. The cow shot Phillippe a long look that he couldn't quite read. He wondered if she had been as uncomfortable within their round as he had; and, if so, whether she was there for some untold purpose. But before he could think about it further, Ellis pulled on his arm, and they teleported away.

He remembered Ellis leaning him against one of the high tables and leaving him there with the promise of getting them something to drink. The room was crowded with masked dancers, and the light was too dim to glimpse anything except for specks of white falling onto the glimmering fabric of their dresses or the precious stones that adorned their masks. The music was oddly light, a wind of harp and flute that swept across his cheeks as quickly as it was forgotten.

The high tables were empty except for Phillippe and protected him from the inadvertent touch of the dancers as he huddled into the deepest parts of the darkness. His body could not forget the kraken's tendril pressed around his core and he felt his vision fade in and out, breath coming slowly. He was so angry, he wanted to peel off his skin and throw it back into the pool for the animals to fight over.

All this for what? Alexander was not here. Maybe he was somewhere else. Maybe he wasn't.

"There", Ellis said, slamming two glasses of clear liquid on the table. Phillippe took a greedy sip of the one closest to him, then shot Ellis a disappointed look. The cocktail was not nearly as strong as he had hoped.

"You've had quite enough tonight, wonder boy", Ellis snapped, "Might do you good to form a coherent thought for once."

"You wouldn't like it if I thought about all this rationally", Phillippe replied haughtily, "Who knows what conclusions I might reach?"

"What, that all these people are assholes and that we'd be better off without them? Don't frighten yourself with your originality."

"It sounds a lot less threatening when you can't enact it all with a thought", Phillippe replied, "When you never have to start to consider what getting rid of the assholes would actually mean."

"I reckon you'd still end up down here. But this time you'd be alone", Ellis replied, "And all that'd be left would be mirrors on a lake. Could you stand to look at yourself by the end, Phillippe? Could you?"

Phillippe sighed.

"I suppose not."

He groaned.

"But how can you stand it? You've seen the worst we're capable of. How do you block it out and go on with your day?"

"Have I? Lukacz told me that I was born out of a child's nightmare. And children don't know shit about the really scary stuff. I'm chicken shit as far as nightmares are concerned."

Phillippe glanced at her and started to laugh just as her face cracked with amusement.

"So, do you have regular nightmare meet-ups?", he teased, "Conventions where you come in your best dress and determine who gets the 'scariest boy' medal that year?"

"Oh, hell yeah. I'd go to that."

"We'll host it at the Brothel if you gather up all your friends."

"Friends", Ellis snorted, and Phillippe left it at that. He changed the topic.

"But didn't you live out on the streets for years? We probably ran into each other and just don't remember."

He sighed.

"Point is, you know what life is really like in this city."

"Yeah. And it sucked. And now I'm not there anymore."

"But other people still are. I was down there a year ago. It's hard to forget once you're up here with people who waste their time on silly disguises and pointless philosophising."

Ellis shrugged.

"So, do you care about other people so very much, you saint? Or are you just mad that you felt powerless and humiliated and want someone to pay for making you feel like that?"

Phillippe hesitated for a moment. It was less her insight that made him pause than the fact that he realised he *still* felt powerless and humiliated. He could still feel the kraken's touch on his body. He scoffed.

"Does it matter? The world is awful, whether or not I am equally awful."

"The world isn't awful", Ellis laughed, "You're on top of the food chain now. You get everything you want at the drop of a hat."

She shrugged.

"And if you hate your life that much, you can always change it. Find a new job or something. The world is what you make of it, wonder boy. Your personal, slimy box of oysters."

"I –"

Phillippe hesitated.

"Working at the Brothel was the dream for so long", he said, "And in a way, it's what I wanted. I get to spin up fantasies for people and make their day just a little bit better."

"So, it's just the touching?", Ellis asked, and he thought he read genuine sympathy in her eyes. In a way, that made it worse, and he scoffed.

"Whatever. I don't even have to feel it if I don't want to. I just —"

He frowned and took another sip of his drink. He desperately wanted to change the topic.

"Just because life is better for us now, that doesn't mean it is for everyone."

"And how will you fix that, pretty boy? How do we reshape the world to make it good for everyone? And how do we make sure we don't screw it up?"

She shrugged.

"You have to block out ninety percent of what happens here if you want to sleep at night. You know that. I know that. Hell, there's a reason the seaver pretend that they're robots. It's probably just easier for them that way."

"That's no reason not to try."

"It's the best reason not to try", the nightmare said, then finished her drink with a quick swig.

"Now, about the reason, we're actually here. Doesn't it sound to you —"

But by the time she looked up again, Phillippe had disappeared.

CHAPTER 17: REIHAN

Reihan was surprised that she managed to get to sleep before the sun rose. But as soon as she entered the familiarity of her Asylum room, she felt herself drifting off, her body suddenly as heavy as it was warm. She did not dream. Seaver did not tend to, although there were exceptions. Reihan had dreamed before, but that had been a long time ago.

She was startled awake by soft steps pacing at the foot of her bed. She was conditioned to wake at the quietest noises, the smallest signs of disturbance, so she felt her consciousness return with a flurry, like snow manifesting in winter air.

"Phillippe?", she asked, guessing who her visitor was. Phillippe's body was half-shadow, melting within the darkness that anticipated the oncoming sunrise. She didn't think he was aware of what he looked like, how much his edges were straying.

"Phillippe", she repeated, her voice firmer now. He turned around to face her, and a smile melted onto his face, sideways and loopy.

"Reihan", he responded, "You made it back."

"Of course. I was worried about you."

"Me? Oh no. Dangerous parties and dangerous people is what I do. It's what I am."

"Is it?"

A pause.

"Are you a dangerous person, Phillippe?"

The shadow shook as if Phillippe was laughing. But his mouth did not move, his teeth a set of shining rows in the dark.

"Am I?", he replied, "You tell me, Reihan. Aren't you seaver supposed to be the ones deciding this?"

"I only ever make a decision based on what humans tell me", she said, "A dangerous human makes themselves known. Whether it's their words, their body language, or their moods that give them away, part of them always wants to be heard. And once you have shouted at me enough times, I will start to take it seriously."

"And it's that easy? Really?"

"Really."

She sat up, tightening her blanket. She pulled her legs up against her body, a silent invitation for Phillippe to sit on the side of the bed, as he had done many times before. But Phillippe remained standing. She could feel the room shake with an unknown force, the shadows convulsing and twisting in the air that surrounded her friend. She felt his helplessness, could see it in his sterile grin.

She wanted to ask how she could help him, but she knew that would only make it worse. She wasn't the one who was supposed to ask questions. She and the other seaver were one of the last anchors for Phillippe, who had found all his limitations cut and fluttered in the air above the city like a wayward kite.

Was this the only reason he was drawn to her? That she reminded him of a life he had hated but wasn't quite willing to relinquish? The thought cut deep into her chest, and through the pain the realisation became reality. But this wasn't about her. These kinds of moments were never about her.

"Give me your hand", she asked softly, stretching out her own towards him, "It will be easier to control your powers when you are linked to me."

She had no idea if that was true. But humans needed guidance, and Phillippe let himself be guided, taking her white, cold fingers between his own. He sat on the bed and closed his eyes, breathing slowly.

Reihan did not feel the shadows come to rest, but their movements did not speed up either.

"What happened?", she asked quietly. She was supposed to ask that. She had to find out what Phillippe's triggers were.

Phillippe still smiled that unholy smile.

"Sometimes I want to make everyone disappear", he said quietly.

Reihan tried to level her breathing.

"Tell me", she asked. Phillippe did, even though she had hoped he wouldn't.

"When I lived in the Undercity, I never thought about the

people in Government. I thought life was unjust, but mostly I just thought about ways to get ahead."

Phillippe was whispering as if they were being listened to by someone he was afraid of.

"But now that I've met more and more of the people who run this city, I –"

He hesitated.

"I'm losing faith that any of our suffering was ever worth anything at all. The people who could have fixed everything for Alex and me are – they're just bored, Reihan. They do nothing, they hide away in the depths, and they're probably the same people who come to the Brothel to fuck me. Just one last fucking insult."

He stared at her.

"Why is there still an Undercity if we can create a world with a single thought? Why don't they change things? Why don't I –?"

His voice was quiet, soft, and brittle. His hands shook around hers. Strings of his kite were coming loose and colouring the skies for a brief, radiant moment before being ripped away by storm clouds.

"I don't know how to live in this place anymore. What I should do with all my power."

He pressed out the words.

"And still, I'm too weak. I can't do the one thing that matters. I can't cure my brother."

His voice broke.

"Not even when I focus all my thoughts on it. I have spent so much time wishing a version of me could do right by him. A version of myself that was better."

He sighed, soft and sweet and utterly resigned.

"Alex is my second self. There was no part of my day that I didn't tell him about. He knows all the characters and fantasies with which I fill my days. If he's gone, it's like none of them ever existed. It's like I'm dead."

Reihan nodded. The shadows had grown taller again, towering over Phillippe's head. She spotted horses amidst the shifting darkness, like the ones from the continent that you could find hand-painted in children's books. Windmills with arms like giants. A sea as blank as a mirror. A woman with branches for arms and eyes as dark and wise as time. They looked down on Phillippe silently, expectant. Reihan wondered how often he thought of them for their shapes to be so well defined, their edges as black as ink.

She could offer to listen to Phillippe's stories, and she was sure she would be enthralled. She could picture the tree woman conquering the world with the help of a gigantic snake, who had, perhaps, a penchant for wisecracks at the worst possible moments. She could imagine the tree woman's playful rivalry with one of the horses, the champion of some long-forgotten wind god. She imagined that the sea led down into the underworld, where the heroes found themselves to be villains, and the villains discovered truth.

But the stories would consume Phillippe if she did nothing but feed into his addiction. And then his lonely addled mind would eventually consume the rest of them. That is why you can't live in a manifested world. It convinces you that nothing matters besides fantasy.

She shouldn't give him false hope. None of the Submerged ever recovered. When they found Alexander, he would be as mute as the day he had been admitted to the Asylum, and now it would be worse because Phillippe had imagined him to be otherwise.

But still.

Phillippe's hands were pale and clamped around hers, and she felt such sympathy for the way he struggled to pull himself through his days and for the fact that he did so regardless.

"Did you find any hints about where your brother might be?", she asked.

Phillippe swayed his head back and forth, hinting at a nod.

"He wasn't there. But I saw him."

He opened his eyes, suddenly aware of how insane he sounded. He squeezed Reihan's hands and laughed self-consciously.

"It was a mirage. Or a vision. Or maybe someone was just screwing with my head. But if there is any truth to what I saw, I think Alex went to the Undercity to find me and was picked up by someone I used to know."

"Who?", Reihan asked, unsure how seriously she could take him with his army of fantasies still lurking over his shoulder.

"An old man I used to talk to when I came back from work on the Weeping Stairs. I think he lived alone, just a few houses down from ours. He'd lurk by the fence of his backyard in the early evenings. He'd rant about his job or about not having a job. I don't really remember…"

"And where do you think this man took your brother?",

Reihan asked slowly. Phillippe fixated on her.

"The Casino. Several people at the party mentioned that a new manifester might be employed there."

"Okay. That gives us a lead, doesn't it?", Reihan asked, even though the words felt heavy and menacing. She was just moving the problem ahead of herself. If the thought of losing his brother had pushed Phillippe this far already, what would happen if – *when* – they found him with a broken mind?

She disentangled her hand from his, and Phillippe looked up at her once more, his eyes large and bauble-like. This wasn't doing anything. She was no beacon that could safely contain manifestation powers. She couldn't save Phillippe if he decided to become dangerous. She couldn't save anyone except for that cold, theoretical mass of innocents she'd never met.

What was the point in deluding herself? If there was any way to maintain his equilibrium, Phillippe needed stability. He didn't need a seaver lover. And he didn't need someone who withheld the truth from him, however justified that deception might be.

The seaver were always watching humans. Everyone knew that, as soon as they were taught as children to avoid their strange white guardians. As the last bastion of humanity's virtue, the seaver would always interfere when someone lost control of their powers and would always protect those who could not protect themselves. How could Reihan not be proud of that duty, however difficult it might be to execute it?

It was harder when duty became personal. When an

experienced seaver was asked to shadow a specific human who might pose a risk because of the sheer amount of power they held. It wasn't an uncommon assignment, but it was important that you weren't caught. Once the humans felt like they were being personally targeted and no longer safe as part of an anonymous mass, they would surely riot against their protectors.

So, it was always better when the human initiated the relationship. And Phillippe had made that whole process so very easy. All Reihan had to do was request to process Alexander and then show a basic level of devotion to her charge.

And there was nothing wrong with growing attached to the object of your surveillance. It wasn't as though she had ever really lied to him or pretended to like him better than she did. And Phillippe knew she'd have to interfere if he ever went too far. Of course, he knew. They spent nearly every day together, and she'd told him, if not with her words then with her actions.

And she knew that while killing him would crush her, she could do it. Because she had to. And because she had done it before.

"Phillippe", she said softly, "If I asked you to stop all manifestations right now, could you do it?"

She shifted, so her arms were only an inch away from the sword that leaned against her bed. She didn't normally keep it there but it appeared, like every time she needed it. Phillippe slowly looked up. His gaze was still glossy and unfocused, but at that moment she felt that he understood her perfectly.

For a long, horrible while, she thought he would shake his head and force her hand. But then he threw back his head and laughed.

"You're always so damned serious, Reihan."

She blinked, and he continued to laugh until he had to wipe a few tears out of the corners of his eyes. She noticed the familiar sparkle on his eyelids and felt an irrational jolt of comfort.

"I am a seaver-machine that hath emerged from great tube mother", he imitated the wooden voice she used when she spoke with strangers, "I hath come to survey humanity and to see if they might meet my impossibly high standards. And whenever I am displeased, I will pull my big sword out of thin air and scare the living shit out of everyone."

He chuckled, and despite herself, she felt the corners of her mouth twitch.

"This is ... this isn't the time to –", she started, but Phillippe interrupted her.

"I will walk through a manifestation storm unprotected because I am very hardcore", he continued, still using the same voice, "But doth not ask me to climb stairs without whining about it for days and endless days. Also, doth not question my configurations, bestowed upon me by great tube mother. They are perfect, and I will eliminate you if you so much as suggest otherwise."

"Configurations?", Reihan repeated, feeling her eyebrows rise.

"The greatest configurations, from the greatest of tube mothers", Phillippe responded with far more confidence than the comment warranted. He grinned, and suddenly he looked every bit like himself. No inky shadows on his shoulders, no shifting edges. Just the friend who spent every evening sitting on her windowsill, talking about his day and wise-cracking about the people he had met that day. Who brought her books he thought she might like and who knew no greater pleasure than correctly guessing at her taste.

"What are you doing?', she asked, shaking her head. Phillippe sat up and cleared his throat, still grinning madly.

"Great tube mother hath bestowed upon me the ability to tell the most gruesome of stories to the humans. They feature a lot of blood, body horror, and death, which great tube mother assures me will make them more appealing to the masses. I believe there is a lesson in the stories for the humans, which is mostly to not do anything at any point ever. In the interests of communal safety, of course."

"You are the one who always asks me to tell you something", Reihan protested but couldn't keep the laughter from bubbling out of her words.

"And you never disappoint. I'm just saying it as I see it", Phillippe replied, finally resuming his normal voice. He smiled at her, and she smiled back hesitantly. Outside, the sun finally began to rise, reached through the window and caressed their faces. Everything felt so much more familiar, so much simpler in the light.

"Phillippe, you have to be careful", she whispered.

"I know how to be careful", he whispered back, then took her hand and squeezed it.

"Do you?", she wanted to respond, but she didn't want to hear his reply. Instead, she let him hold her hand, then leaned against the bedrest and closed her eyes. After a moment, she felt Phillippe lean back next to her, pressing his shoulder to her shoulder and his arm against her arm.

"What a fucking night", she grumbled and felt him laugh.

"You tell me. I got fondled by a kraken in a hot spring."

Reihan snorted.

"And you say that I have the worst stories."

"At least nobody died in this one. Although I felt the rather strong impulse to cook up some calamari. There was a cat at the party that I'm pretty sure would have eaten it, too."

"Why is there always a human-turned-cat when things get properly weird?", Reihan asked, her eyes still closed, "Hey, did I ever tell you about the time when a wing of the Asylum shifted into another time zone, and we had to walk around a version of the place from a hundred years ago, all while led by this ethereal white cat?"

"And let me guess: the cat had caused the time leap to isolate you seaver and was planning to consume your holy tube mother flesh to give himself the power to resurrect a dead god?"

"Close enough. It turned out to be a training exercise, and the cat was our district governor in disguise."

Phillippe laughed again, then leaned his head on her shoulder. She enjoyed his warmth as it settled into the heaviness of her limbs. She would have to request the day off to give her body time to recover. One of the many personal days she had taken over the recent months, perhaps too many already. She'd have to call in some very old favours soon.

Phillippe pulled the blanket over both their bodies, and Reihan felt her eyes slowly shut.

"So, did you enjoy our date?", he murmured before she fell asleep. Reihan chuckled.

"It was unique, I'll give it that. However will you top things next time?"

"Well, let's see. We've had the emotional meltdown, the oversharing, the sudden interruption by an unexpected guest, and a rather nice kiss."

"It was rather nice", Reihan murmured. She felt Phillippe smile. Or maybe she just knew that he would.

"So, next time, I thought we could go to the *World's End*, cut off the cliff's edge, fall straight down through the cloud sea on our make-shift airship, and then crash into the continent. Find somewhere that'll serve us dinner, and then we take it from there?"

"Excellent suggestion", Reihan said, "The near-death experience will help us bond. As you might imagine, I have much experience with these types of situations."

"Really? Do tell me about another time you walked into the remnants of an overly imaginative slaughterhouse."

"Hmm", Reihan made, now struggling to keep her eyes open altogether, "So very greedy for entertainment. Whatever would you do if I left you to sit with your own thoughts for a night?"

"Not even great tube mother would be so cruel."

"You don't know her as I do. Great tube mother's whims cannot be predicted."

She felt Phillippe nod in nonsensical agreement, then his

breath slowed and grew louder. Reihan sighed, content in giving into her wants and into that feeble, irrational hope that moments stretched out forever and that the past did not predict the future. And before long, she fell asleep, resting on Phillippe's soft, warm head.

CHAPTER 18: REIHAN

Lukacs's living room was as small as she remembered, and the table at its centre was just as wide and impractical. Pale light fell between dark curtains, and specks of dust fluttered about like fireflies. The hearth was cold, and Ellis perched inside it like a disgruntled cat roused from its mid-afternoon slumber. Lukacz hadn't bothered putting out chairs and confections for them this time. He leaned against the windowsill, sucking on a long pipe whose smoke glid out of the half-open window, with not a single cloud making its way towards the rest of the group. Reihan could smell the sage and tobacco in the air, and she suddenly remembered the time she and Freeday had smoked an entire bag of tobacco they'd found on the Weeping Stairs. It had screwed with their lungs for days, and the sensation had been more scratchy than death-defyingly glamorous, but still, it had been worth it.

Phillippe had flown her up to Lukacz's cabin. Since the only public elevator had fallen victim to the last storm, there was no way for seaver to reach the Upper City if not for the help of a winged manifester. Reihan had only been to the district twice before, each time with Hannes and each time to investigate a rather tedious set of murders. She had told Phillippe all the gory details on their way through the skies, enjoying the little shocked noises he made despite his best efforts.

In the distance, purple and blue fireworks marked the end of one season and the start of another. Nobody was sure how long one season was supposed to last, but once enough of the Travelling City's inhabitants agreed that it was time, they shot evening-coloured fireworks into the skies, followed by a festival of kites that would turn the airways into a colourful tapestry that lasted the best part of three days. Phillippe had promised that he would take her to = see the kites from above.

Things between them were good. Almost too good; their moods artificially elevated after their narrowly avoided argument. But Reihan didn't want to analyse every little cause of her happiness. She just wanted to feel the pull in her chest when he plucked a flower out of thin air and wove it into her braids, and brushed his hand against hers when they walked. She didn't want to talk about the fact that she had no idea where this was going. She wanted to feel mutually relieved about the fact that he had been calm and that she could look at him without watching.

"I have called you here because I believe we have cause enough to investigate the Casino", Lukacz began. He had tasked Ellis with summoning Reihan and Phillippe back to his home, and the nightmare had, of course, delighted in being as vague as possible as to the reason why. Before that, Reihan hadn't heard from Lukacz in over a fortnight, not since Phillippe and Ellis had reported their findings from the hidden manor. When Seamus visited her in the Asylum, she had asked him whether city officials had made inquiries about the Casino. Seamus had been dismissive, advising Reihan to forget about the whole thing for now and to focus on monitoring Phillippe's mood. As usual, being told what to do by Seamus carried the same level of sting as it did comfort. But she let him get away with just about anything these days.

"You do?", she asked, raising her eyebrows, "I have heard nothing about an official inquiry".

Phillippe shot her an uncertain look while Ellis's eyes remained fixated on Lukacz.

"That is because there isn't one", Lukacz replied calmly, "While it falls in my jurisdiction as Overseer to investigate the operations of individuals and organisations, this is a delicate matter. Which should tell you more than you need to know about who the Casino's owners are."

The invisible Casino had been an institution in the Travelling City for several hundred years, but it had always tethered on the edges of legality. For starters, upside-down or sideways-hanging buildings had been outlawed seventy years ago after a particularly disastrous lapse of concentration had led to a manifesters' academy crashing head-first into the Amusement Park. Needless to say, the school had not re-opened after that.

Secondly, invisible buildings had been illegal since that big collapse of two floating housing communes a hundred years ago, leaving much confusion amidst the citizens who suddenly found bed sheets, chairs, wash baskets, and musical instruments raining down from the skies.

The Palace was exempt from both these rules. And Reihan had long made up her mind about what it meant that the Casino had never been shut down either. Even though it floated sideways somewhere above the Artisan's Quarters, West of the upper Mineshafts. And even though its exterior was completely invisible, and thus frequently fell victim to collisions with stray fireworks, rogue airships, or swarms of migrating birds.

"Really? You'd think Government would have something better to do than run a gambling den", Phillippe said with a sigh. Reihan raised her eyebrows, amused at his naivety. Like Phillippe, she was sure that many of his clients were in some way involved with the Government if they could get an appointment with one of the city's most desired escorts. And Phillippe knew better than anyone else how much time repeat clients left at the Brothel of Transformative Curiosities. He met her eyes, then shrugged after a moment, silently agreeing with her.

"Like what? They can't interfere with most stuff anyway, not without messing up something else. Might as well have some fun while they're running the place", Ellis said, and Reihan wasn't sure whether she was kidding. She looked oddly comfortable hunched over in the fireplace, with some hand-stitched pillows nestled into the edges and straights of her body. It looked like Lukacz had built a little den for her.

"It's a little more complicated than that. As you might imagine, betting is not only a diversion for the citizens but also a useful way for us to keep track of their manifestation abilities", Lukacz said, then cleared his throat.

"Not that I am condoning the practice per se. I have long thought that standardised tests should be conducted in a more transparent manner. But that is neither here nor there."

He pointed at a sketch of the Casino, as well as several recent flyers detailing special events that had taken place there. They promised extravagances upon extravagances; flying animals from the Menagerie, woods of glowing crystal trees adorning the betting tables, and a night of hot steam baths during which all games would be done in the nude. The barely sketched background of the flyers was shorthand for shifting realities, adjusting to the visitors' whims throughout the night. Ellis whistled.

"Some pretty fun stuff, boss man", she said.

"And you'd need an advanced manifester to maintain those illusions", Phillippe added, looking up at Lukacz, "You believe me then?"

"This is not a matter of believing you. I am simply confirming the reports you gave me. And upon comparing these flyers with the events of previous years, I can certainly see that a marked change in the quality of the entertainment has occurred."

He sucked on his pipe and exhaled slowly.

"That alone is not confirmation of Alexander being there, of course. But there was something else that gave me pause."

"Well? What is it?", Phillippe asked, breathless. His eyes were bright, and pale sunlight hit the thick layer of sparkling eyeshadow that coated his lids and lashes. All his fingers were bejewelled with extravagantly designed rings, and they twitched behind his back as he focused on his father.

Lukacz hesitated for a moment and released a perfectly spherical bout of steam.

"It's you", he finally said. He stepped closer to the table and moved a piece of parchment to the top of the sketches, flyers, maps, and notes pile. On the page were drawings of perhaps twenty-odd faces, all named and dated. Reihan scanned them. Most did not look familiar, but towards the bottom was someone she recognised. She looked up to Phillippe, who was sucking in a breath of air. Their eyes met again, and she thought the shock in his eyes was genuine.

"That's you", she said pointlessly. The same yellow eyes, caramel-brown skin, and long hair that Phillippe had worn when he had admitted Alexander to the Asylum.

"It… used to be", he replied, his voice sounding very far away, "What is this?"

"It is a list of suspicious visitors compiled by the casino's security personnel", Lukacz replied, "I do not have more information than that."

The tone of his voice had not changed. Nonetheless, the mood in the room turned as quickly as good luck. Ellis whistled.

"Liar, liar, pants on fire."

"I did not lie", Phillippe replied, his eyes wide, "I've never even been to the Casino before."

"Really? Then why would you be on the list, son?", Lukacz replied, "Nobody else from the Brothel is on there."

Phillippe spread out his hands helplessly.

"I genuinely have no idea. I swear on my life, I never went there. I didn't – If I had woken up Alex, I would have told you. I don't see why I wouldn't have. I would have proven to you that –"

He hesitated, then fell silent. Lukacz looked surprised for a moment, but he did not respond. Reihan gave Phillippe a long look, tracing his half-open lips and wide eyes. She still didn't understand humans well enough, she decided with an internal sigh. Perhaps she needed another hundred years. But she wanted to believe him. Maybe that counted for something.

"There could be other reasons for Phillippe being on a watch list", she said slowly.

"Like what, seaver? Go on, enlighten us", Ellis snarled. Reihan ignored her tone.

"If Alexander did not want to be found, he could have put his brother's old image on the watch list as a precautionary measure. That, or someone knows that Phillippe might go looking for his brother and wants him detained when he's getting too close."

"Yes!", Phillippe said, his lids fluttering, "That makes sense. The guy Alex told me about in that vision – I think I know him. And he knows what I used to look like. If he doesn't want me to find Alex –"

"Speculation", Lukacz interrupted him, "We don't know enough about what you did or did not see in that underground mansion."

Phillippe fell silent. Lukacz took another long drag on his pipe, then sighed.

"But, regardless of what this means, we need to investigate what is going on in the Casino."

"Gotcha, boss man", Ellis said, then jumped out of the hearth, "I can keep an eye on wonder boy."

"Yes, I was going to suggest that. Phillippe, I will not try to prevent you from coming, as I doubt I could if I wanted to. But you and Ellis stay together at all times, and she has permission to detain you if you veer off-plan. Is that understood?"

Phillippe nodded quickly, then sent Ellis a shaky smile.

"Partners in crime again? Watch it, you'll grow fond of me."

Ellis chuckled.

"You'll have to work on your threats, pretty boy."

Reihan relaxed a little, then sat on the edge of Lukacz's table.

"I know the Casino employs seaver", she said, "Mostly through illegal channels. If you get me inside, I will blend in easily enough."

"And how exactly would you get up there?", Ellis snapped, "We can't manifest you in. And if we try to fly up, we'll just crash into the wall. The Casino's invisible if you remember."

Lukacz and Reihan exchanged a look. *He knows what I'm thinking*, she realised. He had probably planned for her involvement from the start, but he wanted her to be the one to suggest it. And it would be awful, but at least it would allow her to do her job.

"Easy", Reihan said, keeping her voice as level as she could, "You sell me to the Casino."

Phillippe barked out a shocked laugh.

"I'm sorry, what?"

Ellis raised her eyebrows but remained silent. Lukacz's face was hidden behind a cloud of smoke.

"The Casino buys seaver from a variety of sellers. People who steal new-born seaver from the Palace, or who manufacture them illegally and give them additional… functions."

She sighed.

"We're born into adult bodies. We don't age until we die. So, you can't really tell how old a seaver is unless you know exactly what you're looking for. Most humans don't."

"We're not selling you", Phillippe said loudly, "Out of the question."

"It's a bit of a rogue suggestion", Ellis muttered, her eyes shifting, "Funny as it would be."

"Just in case that needed clarification, I'm not suggesting you leave me there", Reihan replied drily, "But it's a failsafe way to get me into the Casino. Plus, newborn seaver misbehave all the time because nobody explains what they're supposed to do. So, I could get away with quite a lot before anyone gets suspicious."

"Yes, but we'd still be selling you", Phillippe repeated, "It doesn't feel right."

"Do you want my help with finding your brother or not?"

"Yes, but…"

He groaned.

"Is this one of those moments when someone claims they're okay with something and then ten years later, in the middle of dinner, they say, 'remember that time when you sold me to a Casino?' I could never win another argument without you bringing that up!"

"A secondary bonus for me", Reihan said with a smirk playing around her lips, "Are we agreed then?"

"Sure, whatever", Ellis muttered, "I suppose wonder boy, boss man, and I can just teleport inside then."

"I won't be doing that", Lukacz replied.

Eyes converged back on him.

"Really? Chickening out now, dad?", Phillippe asked, visibly irritated.

"There may be people in the Casino who would be alerted by my presence. And you two would be considered suspicious just because you are accompanying me."

"So? Change your appearance. Surely that's not too difficult for you", Phillippe said, frowning. Lukacz shook his head.

"Members of the Government are not allowed to do that outside of the context of an emergency. That, and to play in the Casino, I would have to use my real name to confirm the stakes I can gamble with. Unless I want to declare nothing, which carries its own risks. But –", he interrupted Phillippe, who had already opened his mouth, "more importantly, you two will not need my help scouting out the lower floors of the Casino. Reihan, on the other hand, will likely require my assistance."

He pushed the flyers aside to reveal a sketch of the Casino — or of what it might look like if it were visible from the outside. A large betting hall dominated the bottom of the building. A smaller floor sat atop it, nestled into the centre of the building. Above that, the structure became more complex, with several small towers and apartments growing atop one another.

"Down here, we have the two main betting halls", Lukacz outlined, pointing towards the lower floors.

"All flyers depict an entrance spot that you can teleport to. No images of any other part of the Casino are in circulation, so you'll need to start there. If my information is good, Enforcers are stationed across all the main gambling areas to keep the peace."

"Enforcers?", Reihan repeated, then bit on her lower lip. *Of course*. If the Casino were owned by the Government, they would have access to the forces. Lukacz nodded quietly, confirming her fears.

"That means that the seaver are probably used elsewhere so as not to distress the guests. Most likely, they're used to monitor the inhabitants of the higher blocks and to keep order there. That is where they'll take you, Reihan", he continued, pointing at the tower blocks above the Casino.

"Who lives up there?", Ellis asked. Phillippe snorted.

"Probably some rich fucks who can't be bothered to teleport back into the city after a night of excess."

"Maybe", Reihan mused, tracing the lines on the paper with her long white fingers, "More likely, it's serfs. People who lost all their belongings because they gambled with stakes that ended up too high. Who started to gamble with time."

Phillippe and Ellis stared at her. She kept her eyes level with theirs.

"It happens. If you've lost everything, you can still sell yourself. If they're playing at the Casino, they probably have at least some manifestation abilities. Making them a pretty useful resource for anyone in Government who wants manpower for a project but doesn't want to go through the official channels."

She shrugged.

"They won't be serfs forever, just the time they gambled with. There are worse fates."

Silence followed her words, awkwardly settling in the pale room. Lukacz pointed at the map and drew their attention back to the plan.

"There is a point of connection between the apartments in the towers and the Casino floors, but it'll likely be well-guarded. So, we'll need a distraction inside the main betting halls that will allow Reihan to open the door. Phillippe and Ellis, you'll wait for the Enforcers to leave their post, then sneak into the tower blocks. Once we have reunited there, we can track down Alexander."

He encircled the point where the upper floor met the tower block. Someone had sketched a door into the plan, but Reihan wasn't sure whether this was an actual door or merely representative of the hope that there might be a door somewhere.

"Cause a distraction? You've picked the right guys for the job, boss man", Ellis said with a grin to Phillippe, who winked. Reihan cleared her throat.

"I can try my best to help out on my end, but no guarantees. Should something go wrong, I can take out a human manifester, but if there's other seaver up there, I'll be outmatched. That, and I really can't be caught. If a seaver becomes aggressive for no reason, people tend to get nervous."

"That's why I'm joining you up there", Lukacz replied, "Between us, we'll have a better chance at reaching the door. Also, being with me gives you plausible deniability if you're found out. They won't deactivate you if I confirm you acted on my orders."

"Deactivate?", Phillippe mouthed in Reihan's direction. She shrugged. She knew the risks.

"Divide and conquer", Ellis muttered, "Sure, sure."

She glanced back at the map.

"But how d'you reckon you'll get into the apartments, boss man? It's not like you'll have a flyer of someone's kitchen lying around."

She grinned.

"Wait, wait, wait, I got it. You could disguise yourself as a seaver and go up with Reihan here. We could do a nice little two-for-the-price-of-one kinda deal."

"Again, I would prefer not to change my appearance", Lukacz replied with a sparkle in his eyes as he looked at the nightmare, "Plus, I'd have to be incredibly precise to match all the subtleties of seaver skin, hair, and eyes. Chances are that I'd make a mistake."

"That, and they might test whether manifestations affect you or not", Reihan noted, "You're hardly the first person to think of slipping in with the servant class."

"Okay, then we'll dye your skin and hair. Bleach it out, nice and clean", Ellis said, fixating on her initial idea at the expense of all sensible considerations. Reihan giggled, and the nightmare threw her an irritated look. Phillippe grinned.

"I'd pay to see that."

"Absolutely not", Lukacz said firmly, then took another long drag of his pipe.

"No, nothing quite so convoluted. It will be you, my dear, who helps me to get inside", Lukacz said to Reihan while bowing his head slightly.

"You'll need to open a window for me. I'll encircle the building from the outside, looking for an opening. Ordinarily, that would be rather conspicuous, but if we act now, during the Season End festival, the kites should give me sufficient cover. Then, once I'm inside, I'll take over."

"Oh, if it's just that", Reihan muttered and started massaging her temples.

"What? All you have to do is open a window", Ellis said with a mocking smile, "Can't be too difficult, even for a seaver."

Reihan glared at her.

"I know you have a brain up in that skull of yours, so I'd suggest you use it. Do you think absolutely everything in the Casino is going to be invisible? Including the roulette and blackjack tables, the card dealers, the competition grounds?"

"No, of course not, that'd be daft", the nightmare muttered, glaring up at the seaver. *She is strangely deferential when challenged*, Reihan thought, *almost like she's scared of me.*

"So", she continued, softer this time, "If windows frequently opened just like that, the Casino would be at least partially visible as we look inside. Given that this is not the case, I presume that there are rules against opening windows by more than a specific angle or outside of particular weather conditions, such as strong fog."

She shook her head.

"Or maybe there aren't any windows altogether. This is quite a leap of faith we are taking here."

"There have to be windows", Lukacz replied, "How else would you maintain airflow in the buildings?"

"Manifestations?", Phillippe replied. His father shook his head.

"There are already so many manifestations at play in the Casino, it wouldn't be worth the risk. What if the thought of maintaining breathable air conflicts with the creation of an underwater display or some drugged-up cloud castle? No, I'm sure the air gets recycled somewhere in the building."

"That's a big if", Phillippe cautioned, "What is Reihan supposed to do if you're wrong?"

"Make a window", Ellis suggested. Reihan raised her eyebrows.

"How exactly?"

"Don't act like you couldn't. Seaver are actually fuckin' strong, even if you guys pretend like you're not. I've seen your friend cleave through a solid wall just to get to a shadow."

"My friend?", Reihan repeated. Ellis paled but did not lower her gaze.

"The butcher. Looks exactly like standard seaver manufacture, but he's well old."

Reihan narrowed her eyes.

"Are you talking about Seamus?"

"Who is Seamus?", Phillippe asked.

Lukacz sighed.

"Don't get distracted", he cautioned, then rubbed his chin, "But Ellis's point stands. I am aware that it goes against protocol to ask you, Reihan, but would you be able to use some of your reserves to create an opening to the apartment tower block if the situation required it?"

Reihan sighed, trying very hard not to look at Phillippe. *He shouldn't know any of this*, she thought, *and Lukacz should bloody well know better than to reveal all our secrets, especially to a person under investigation.*

"We cannot just choose to access our reserves", she replied, short-lipped, "That authorisation has to come from a human or a senior seaver."

"Could I authorise you?", Lukacz asked, and Reihan had to

smile.

"If you have to ask, you can't."

"Do you know anyone who could?"

Reihan sighed again.

"Maybe. I can try to sort something out before we get there. But I can't tell you any more, and I can't make any promises."

Seamus could authorise her, tear down that mental wall that had been forced on her through years of physical and psychological conditioning. He'd always turned her requests down before; every time she had begged him to limit the restrictions that gave her only so many steps in a day, and that meant her arms hung limp and heavy at night. But now Seamus was half-dead, and this job was important for the city. Perhaps he'd grown soft with his old age. Lukacz nodded briskly.

"That is fair enough. If you cannot let me in, I will try to find another way. Worst comes to worst, I will simply purchase you back from the Casino owners."

"Grand. I wonder if my market value will have increased, " Reihan said drily.

"Wait. Potentially dumb question", Phillippe said, then pointed towards the edges of the tower block again, "If Reihan opens or makes a window, why don't we all fly in through that? No need to gamble our way through the Casino and possibly draw attention to ourselves."

"Well, if there are windows, there'll probably be a tight schedule for when and where they are opened", Reihan replied, "I can't just stroll into a room and push open the first one I find without there being a whole host of questions I can't answer. I'll need the any guards in that tower block to be elsewhere."

"So, Reihan, you're using the distraction to open the window for me", Lukacz said, "And then we'll open the door for Phillippe and Ellis together. Which you two have to locate first and foremost before doing anything else."

"Yes", Reihan said slowly, "I suppose, for me everything hinges on you guys drawing the Enforcers and seaver downstairs. For me to do anything, you will have to cause a good deal of havoc."

Ellis groaned.

"Yeah, yeah, havoc, chaos, destruction, the bloody plague, whatever you want. I'll get it done."

Lukacz rubbed his short, coarse beard.

"She makes a fair point, Ellis. I don't know how long you may have to keep the Enforcers busy in the betting halls. The distraction will have to be something major. One of you may have to stay behind."

"Oh, we'll think of something grandiose and spectacular. Don't you worry, dad. We won't miss the show", Phillippe replied haughtily.

They concluded the meeting soon after, planning more minute details that relied more on guesswork and faint hope than reliable information. At the end of the day, they would simply have to try. And if they failed, they would have to try and make it out in one piece.

But, Reihan thought, understanding what exactly was going on at the Casino would be worth the risk. That, and someone had to keep an eye on Phillippe once he finally reunited with his brother. She might be able to talk him down from a ledge when no one else could.

She felt Phillippe's eyes burning into her skin. He didn't ask any more questions, not about Seamus and not about her reserves, not then and not later. He flew her home via the Menagerie, where they walked around the enclosures and watched the animals sleep. Perhaps to spite his own impulses, he talked to her about everything but not the things he wanted to.

CHAPTER 19: REIHAN

Reihan knew that seaver-imitations were created across the Travelling City. It made sense. A seaver's words were equivalent to the law, so if you had a seaver who confirmed that you are 'definitely allowed to set up bombs here', you probably got away with whatever you were doing. A good Enforcer could tell the difference between a real seaver and a fake by manifesting on them, exerting just enough power not to break something vital but enough to confirm whether the seaver carried its people's tell-tale immunity. But most regular folks were intimidated enough by white skin, white hair, and white eyes and stayed well out of the way of any seaver operations.

A few years ago, Reihan had been involved in shutting down an illegal cloning facility in the factory complexes that lay East of the Mineshafts. The complexes were made up of empty storage halls into which the manifesters in the mines summoned the wares they were supposed to produce for the city. After manifesters – usually former criminals and Undercity drifters – were given a list of requests, they were doused in a controlled dose of the mind fog. Then they materialised the desired items into a spot that was outlined on daily sketches of the warehouses. The factory halls were usually empty of personnel for fear of being merged with a suddenly manifesting object.

Someone, Reihan still wasn't sure who, had sniffed out an opportunity and set up a cloning facility in one of the decommissioned halls linked to a Mineshaft that was currently too flooded to use. When she and the Enforcers had entered, hundreds of half-grown seaver had hung down the ceiling in glowing tubes. Their empty eyes stared at them from every corner of the factory. Some of them had almost been finished, looking every bit like Reihan had when she had first awoken. Hannes had tried manifesting on them and had encountered some primitive resistance to his abilities. But none of the seaver had been conscious. That had been the saving grace of burning the facility to the ground.

On the way back to the Asylum, Reihan had been unusually chatty. Even though that was forbidden, she had spoken about her childhood in the Upside-down Palace, where she and her fellow seaver had been trained by the founders until they were deemed ready to perform their duties. She had gone on and on about the thorough processes of physical and mental conditioning that every Palace seaver had to undergo before they were accepted as peacekeepers in the Travelling City. None of the Enforcers had said very much while she talked herself hoarse, but occasionally they had shot her long looks and nodded profoundly in a way that felt oddly patronising. By the end of their walk, Reihan had felt so foolish that she had requested to work with another troop for a while.

It was with some relief that Reihan learned they were not going to the Mining District today. Lukacz led them through the Undercity's labyrinthine streets in search of a hidden passage through which they could access an old landing pad underneath the main rock formation of the city. The further down the district they tread, the more the streets looked like they had been hewn into the stone by hand, unaided by manifestations or advanced building tools. The shadows from protruding rock formations cast their path into a deep blue hue, and Lukacz frequently cursed when a half-covered tunnel turned out to be a breathing hole for the stone, opening by no more than an arm's length and releasing a bit of stale air.

Catching Reihan's stern silence, he assured her that the tunnels did exist and that, as a young man, he had, on occasion, gone down there to look at the illegal markets. Somewhat wistfully, he said that even then the landing pads had risen a mere inch above the shifting cloud sea, and the market's many floating lights looked like lanterns that would guide lost travellers home. There were many stories of other Travelling Cities roaming the clouds and lone ships carrying wayward wanderers who had left the continent behind. But Reihan had not taken Lukacz for a romantic.

The landing pads were a popular spot for illicit activities and less than savoury business transactions. Seaver were discouraged from going there, as their presence might cause a panic amidst the sellers. The Enforcers tolerated the markets for now, fearing that they might simply move elsewhere if they were shut down on the landing pads. In exchange for their tolerance, the markets had stopped offering

Submergence procedures, wherein brave and desperate souls were lowered into the cloud sea in rusty open-top cages and pulled back up after several minutes had passed. The Asylum had been far emptier since that deal had been struck.

Reihan wore her white uniform with the red symbol for seaver stitched on the front, and Lukacz had collared her with an iron ring and a chain he was holding in his left hand. She hated the feeling of the ring on her neck and the uniform scratching against her skin, but she also knew better than to discard an advantage for the sake of coddling her feelings. The uniform gave her a sense of legitimacy and increased the likelihood of her being accepted into the Casino. And the ring showed that she was there to be sold; a newly born seaver stolen from the Upside-down Palace, a reject that didn't pass the training but somehow escaped deactivation, or a home-grown specimen that looked real enough to fool the public. She had taken out her braids and had removed the rings with which she usually adorned her fingers and ears. The tattoos she had stitched onto her skin half a century ago were faded enough that she had been able to hide them beneath a thick layer of makeup.

"Would they expect you to know where you're from?", Lukacz asked Reihan.

"What do you mean?", she replied.

"Would newborn seaver be aware enough to remember the rooms they were born in? Ellis said that this is a question the sellers usually ask."

Reihan understood what he was getting at.

"I was born in the Palace. I can describe the place well enough, even now. But it's your own story you're worried about, isn't it?"

Lukacz cleared his throat. Reihan laughed.

"If you need to reveal the existence of a secret entrance to the Palace or secret corridor somewhere inside, by all means, do so. The founders can always change the Palace's structure if there are too many break-ins."

She shrugged.

"And if you have a deal with the founders to smuggle out seaver in secret, I won't be the one to tell the Enforcers."

"I would not wish to put you in an uncomfortable position", Lukacz replied softly, "I understand the difficulty of having secrets from those you are close with."

"I am no more obligated to the Enforcers than anyone else in this city", Reihan replied, "Our objective is for the Travelling City to survive and to maximise happiness and safety for its inhabitants. If the Enforcers help to achieve this goal, the seaver work with the Enforcers. If a criminal tyrant is the better option, following them would be our prerogative."

Lukacz shot her a long look that she found difficult to read.

"I did not know that", he said finally. Reihan shrugged.

"Our conditioning is thorough, but it leaves room for interpretation. One hundred years of experiences and reflection can turn the tightest cage into a watchtower."

Lukacz nodded.

"Then forgive me for my ignorance, Reihan. We do indeed

have a deal with the founders, whereby they provide us with newborn seaver for special operations."

Reihan nodded. It wouldn't do to be mad at Lukacz for that. He most likely hadn't set the deal up himself, and she couldn't expect him to know what happened to those seaver after they were returned to the Upside-down Palace.

Instead, she smiled at Lukacz, fighting to keep hold of her mischievous mood.

"They're creepy, aren't they?"

"Hm? What?", he made, his eyes still gliding from shadow to shadow as they circumnavigated a set of houses whose upper floors had merged with the cavern walls. As they walked underneath creaking floorboards and bridges, they could hear voices and animal sounds echo from above.

"The founders. Come now, you can say it. They are creepy bastards."

Lukacz barked out a laugh.

"Positively terrifying. If I never have to interact with one of them again, it will have been too soon. Why don't they speak? What's with the messages and the sounds?"

"And the teeth! Why do they need that many teeth? It's just excessive."

"Do they look like that all the time? I was wondering if their exterior might be a disguise."

"Maybe, but I've only ever seen them like that. Even when we'd sneak around the corridors of the Palace after dark to go and spy on them, we only ever saw the teeth, the eight legs, and the claws."

Lukacz laughed again.

"You did that?"

"Sure. The training and playrooms were boring. Our teachers were far more interesting."

Reihan laughed at her naivety. That had been before she had realised what the founders were capable of and what happened to seaver who were immune to the conditioning. Who asked too many questions or who under-performed in their studies.

"And did you ever find out anything illicit about them?"

Reihan smiled, although there was a hint of sadness underlying the emotion.

"Nothing, really. Not even after all the time I spent there. But maybe after this is all over, we can compare notes? Combine our knowledge and finally crack the founder mystery?"

"That is a sound bargain", Lukacz said seriously.

They eventually found the way to the market, past a half-collapsed colony of tents and through a dark tunnel lined with fake, glowing stars. The sun was just on the cusp of setting, so many sellers were still putting up their stalls when Lukacz and Reihan entered the platform. Most marketplace visitors hid behind elaborate illusions, taking on the form of ancient and long-dead gods, horned and winged beauties, half-plant half-stone constructs, or duo-chromatic spheres.

She felt everyone's eyes on her as they exited the tunnel and made her gaze perfectly neutral, banning every emotion that could have unsettled the humans. Ellis had spent the last few days stalking the market platforms, hiding within crevices and hanging upside down from overhangs, to find out which sellers supplied wares for the Casino. She had given Lukacz and Reihan the description of a silver-chested man with the legs of a bull, the horns of a deer, and who adorned himself with see-through, shimmering wings as light as the wind and fragile as the air. His eyes were black, and he had painted his pale features with barely visible white lines that emphasised his eyes and brow bone. They spotted him immediately. He had set up close to the platform's edge, accompanied by two assistants who had taken the shape of iridescent spheres, mirroring his every move. A small group of airships were docked just behind him, their puffy white sails fluttering in the breeze as the golden clouds chased one another in the distance.

"I hear you buy seaver", Lukacz said without bothering with pleasantries.

"And who told you that?", the bull-man replied. His soft voice stayed perfectly level, and Reihan could see nothing in his eyes. Only a tiny twitch deep within the black told her that it took him effort to maintain the illusion.

"Does it matter? I need to get rid of this seaver. Take it or leave it."

They had agreed that it would be best to pretend that they needed to shift Reihan quickly, taking a lower price for her than a fully functioning seaver would typically fetch.

"Desperate, are we? And who did you piss off to get a

specimen like that?"

The bull-man smirked, and the two spheres whirred around his head with visible excitement.

"My idiot son broke into the Palace", Lukacz hissed, "Tried to get a whole litter of seaver out. Things went bad, and now we've got to get rid of this one quickly."

"The Palace? Really? You're an original, sweetheart?"

The bull-man focused on Reihan.

"Look up."

Reihan did as she was asked, lifting her chin to expose her neck.

"Where did you grow up?", the bull-man asked.

"I stepped out of the tube", Reihan said in a dull voice, "then I was in a white room. There were the founders who said they were my instructors."

"What did you see when you looked out of the windows?", the seller asked further.

"The city, but it was upside-down. The founders said that was normal", she replied. She wondered if she was hamming it up a bit too much. New-born seaver certainly did not speak like that. But she knew what people expected.

Next, the bull-man quizzed Lukacz on how in the hell his son had managed to get into the Palace to begin with. Lukacz started to describe a hidden tunnel inside one of the buried districts on the platforms West of the Mineshafts, but Reihan found it impossible to concentrate.

The bull-man's manifestations clawed at her skin with unexpected forcefulness; looking for disguises and trying to mould her to his will. *Very rude*, Reihan thought, half-deliriously. He was supposed to ask first. But she said nothing, as this was certainly not information a newborn seaver would be expected to have.

After a few moments, the bull-man whistled and looked back to Lukacz.

"You've got the genuine article there, good sir", he said with a strained smile,

"Unfortunately for you, that'll make her hard to sell."

"I'll give her to you cheap", Lukacz replied, having his voice shake just a little, "I just want this whole thing to be over."

The bull-man snorted.

"Bloody amateurs. All ambition and no planning. You better put your son in line after this. If his stupid stunt got seaver killed, that'll cost all of us. Where do you think the materials to make them come from?"

"Yeah, yeah", Lukacz muttered, painting silent defiance on his features, "Just make me an offer."

The bull-man wrote down an offer on a piece of paper, then slid it over to Lukacz. He read it, then frowned.

"That's absurd."

He couldn't accept immediately, of course. A single favour or item would be a suspiciously low price to accept and might make the bull-man think twice about the merchandise he was taking on. They haggled for a little while. Reihan felt the hairs on the back of her neck rise and wondered if Ellis was watching the exchange from somewhere in the overhang, perched between stalactites like a spider. She couldn't shake the feeling that she had seen the nightmare before, perhaps as much as a lifetime ago. But she couldn't place it, no matter how long she lingered on the feeling.

Finally, Lukacz and the bull-man reached an agreement, and Lukacz handed her chain over in exchange for a small patch of land near the top of the Undercity, beneath a noodle shop and close to the ladders that led up to the Weeping Stairs. Overall, still a poor offer for a Palace seaver and especially for the information on the tunnel, but accepting it fit with Lukacz's role as desperate father trying to undo his son's mistake. The bull-man pulled on Reihan's collar, once, twice, to ensure it held. Lukacz left without another word, and she stayed behind, feeling an unsettling emptiness in her chest. She stood silently by the bull-man's side as he wrote out and sent various messages by simply having them vanish from his hands. Whoever he was selling her to was keen, as answers quickly appeared on a designated golden plate on his stall. Eventually, she was commanded to board one of the smaller airships.

"Take her to help Ka'a with their operation, then ship her straight up to the Casino servant elevator entrance", the bull-man told one of the spheres by his side, "I've let Ka'a know already, and I'll write to the Casino after you left."

The sphere bobbed up and down, then floated in front of Reihan. The bull-man sighed.

"Stop fretting. Nobody will know when she got sold to us.

Might as well get our money's worth before she gets sucked into that invisible den."

The sphere flittered.

"We'll split it three ways as usual", the bull-man replied, "Ka'a are good for it. Always have been. Then she goes straight to our friends at the Casino. Nobody's any the wiser. Easy."

The bull-man handed Reihan her own chains, and she took them with clam hands. She hadn't expected the seller to try and make double on his investment by selling her to two places in one night. But she couldn't protest if she wanted to stay undetected. She'd have to complete whatever job this Ka'a had for her and hope she'd still be taken to the Casino with enough time to help her friends up there.

"Follow the glowing orb", the bull-man commanded, "Don't wander off."

She nodded.

"Did they name you yet?"

Seaver were named right after they first exited the tube. It was possible that the bull-man did not know that, but it wasn't worth taking the risk.

"Reihan", she said. A lot of seaver were called Reihan.

"Reihan. My associate is going to take you to a tunnel. There will be other humans. Stay with them and do what they say. There are shadows you'll need to kill. The humans will show you how to tell the difference between friend and foe, all right? Afterwards, follow the orb back to the airship."

She nodded again.

"You can fight, right? They make you robots with inborn combat abilities?"

Reihan almost snorted. *Inborn. Sure.* It wasn't as though the founders had drilled them for hours upon hours in the Palace courtyard, pitching them against one another until their hands bled against the hilts of their swords.

"I have never fought before, but I know how to", she replied. He shrugged.

"That'll do. But if the fight against the shadows is going badly, I want you to run, okay? Just run back to the airship and leave everyone else behind. They're more expendable than you."

She nodded a third time. The orb bobbed ahead, and she followed him into the skies.

CHAPTER 20: ELLIS

"Nice digs."

Ellis's strolled through Phillippe's room atop the Brothel, running her fingers through hanging rows of precious stones that caught the light at every turn and dropped it at a whim. Every part of the tower room was filled with Phillippe's things; clothes hanging from antique chairs, jewels adorning naked mannequins, paintings he had been sent after lingering near the artists' stalls at the marketplace. Three full-size mirrors, framed with silken scarves, coats, and leather straps. Beautiful wooden instruments Phillippe had picked up, then discarded once he realised that he could simply manifest the melodies he was imagining. A small black and white cat lay on the windowsill, trying to catch flecks of sunlight. Phillippe had made it so that she could toss it up in flickers with her paws, and occasionally she yelped in delight when she managed a particularly good throw.

"Why, thank you. It doesn't scream 'lunatic in the woods' as much as old Lukacz's haunt, but I suppose we all work with what we have", Phillippe replied. Ellis smirked and sat on the windowsill, the cat entirely unperturbed by her presence. She liked it here, she decided. The place felt like Phillippe, unapologetically so. He might not fully know who he was, but he didn't try to hide his shifting moods. She could respect that.

"You should be nice to boss man", she said, "He's a good egg once you get to know him. Much better than most people."

"I'll believe that when I see it", Phillippe muttered, twisting a flower crown he had been stitching together.

"When you see it? He's helping you with this, isn't he? Isn't really his job. Big investigation work is more Enforcer stuff."

"Well, Alex is his son. It's really the least you would expect —"

"Yeah, but no. Government people don't have families, remember? They're supposed to give that shit up when they take up the post. And Lukacz is one of those geezers who's gonna take that seriously."

Phillippe scoffed.

"But he has a family. Trying to forget about us didn't make us go away."

"What, you'd have him rot in the Undercity until the end of the world when he could do stuff up here that actually matters? He banged your mum, she banged out you two, and that's that. No need to feel eternally obligated to your creations."

Ellis narrowed her eyes.

"Helping you out with this rather than palming it off on the scary Enforcement brigade goes against his whole big ethos, sunshine. Might want to think about appreciating that for a minute."

Phillippe sighed.

"You have a funny way of looking at things."

Ellis grinned and hopped off the windowsill, taking his words as a peace offering. They had better things to do than bicker anyway.

"I've been told as much. Now, you said you'd have stuff for me to wear to this fancy place?"

Phillippe nodded, and his enthusiasm seemed to return as he gestured around the room.

"But of course. Help yourself to anything you want. And if something doesn't fit, feel free to alter it."

"Oooh, fun, fun, fun!", Ellis called, then started rummaging through piles of clothes with the eagerness of a child who had just discovered it could grow wings. She tried on a sparkling red dress with a long slit down the side, which allowed the trail to dramatically follow her around the room, occasionally releasing bouts of black, luxurious smoke.

"Not sure about wearing red. Remember the kraken?", Phillippe called from the bed, where he was lounging with some sweet confections and a book he was half glancing at.

"Ew. Right", Ellis made, then picked up a lilac two-piece whose fabric was thin enough to leave very little to the imagination.

"Do you have anything with trousers? Like a pantsuit or something? Might need to kick someone in the face later."

"Who do you imagine you'd kick?", Phillippe laughed, "The Casino attendants? The cashiers? I'm pretty sure that's a good way of getting yourself escorted out of the front door and dropped back into the city."

Nonetheless, he picked out a sparkling black pantsuit from behind his bed and threw it over to her.

"I was thinking more of a nice, crisp seaver", Ellis muttered as she pulled on the rhinestones on the garment. It looked sharp and dangerous. She liked it.

"Okay, if I have a weird thing about dad, you have a weird thing about the seaver. You know they're here to help us, right?"

He turned around as Ellis changed into the pantsuit, something she found irrationally funny.

"Are they?", she asked, just as her mouth grazed the lining of the fabric, "Who's us, wonder boy? Us manifesters? Step out of line, and they'll hack our heads off."

She pulled the rest of the suit over her head and glanced at herself in the mirror. *Yes.*

"Or did you mean us nightmares, shades, and other creepy crawly things? Didn't know you spoke for us, now", she continued, "But let me tell you this, the seaver are not our friends. They run this show, and once we piss them off enough, they'll start cutting down the cast to the guys that'll fall in line."

"Reihan has been incredibly patient with all of us", Phillippe replied, now visibly annoyed. Ellis twirled in front of the three mirrors. The pantsuit fit her top half like a glove and flared out around her legs.

"Reihan is one of the most dangerous ones", Ellis said, shooting him an impatient glare, "Because she seems really, really nice and really, really human, so you let your guard down 'round her. And then you put one foot wrong, and she'll remind you that she's really not on your side at all."

"You don't know her."

"No. And if I want to live a long, fat nightmare life, I won't get to know her either."

She threw her hands up and twirled around again.

"So? How do I look, wonder boy?"

"Terrific", Phillippe said and summoned a smile, "Now, pick something for me. Make it extravagant!"

"Any preferences?"

"Surprise me", Phillippe said. He had chosen an androgynous body, with long curls of silver hair falling onto his flat chest, which he'd asked one of his friends at the Brothel to paint. Angra had used shining dark blue paint to draw concentric circles interrupted by irregular dots. As Phillippe explained to Ellis, the symbols were supposedly the sacred language of a god Angra and her friends were trying to resurrect. They were pretty, Ellis decided, whether or not they served as an interdimensional portal for a snake-headed deity to poke its head through.

She picked out a long, midnight blue skirt bejewelled with diamonds. Phillippe matched it with diamond rings on every finger and a row of diamond studs on his pointed ears. He left his chest bare but added a small silver-rimmed mask, dark as the night and shifting with each one of his thoughts. Finally, he changed his eyes to a dark blue, modelled after the sky's reflection in the depth of night.

Ellis raised her eyebrows and played with the only ring she

wore on her hands, a plain silver band on her index finger.

"What?", Phillippe asked, guessing at what she'd say, "It's a subterfuge mission."

"Yeah, yeah", Ellis said, "As if anyone'd recognise you with everything you've already changed."

"And who cares if I break this last arbitrary rule? It's not like anyone is really paying attention to my eyes."

"Nobody, I guess", the nightmare muttered, "I just don't like the idea of everyone always changing. How'd you ever recognise anyone?"

"Most people aren't able to change this much", Phillippe said, his voice soothing. Then he grinned.

"How about I tell you a code word every time I see you? Doesn't matter if we're on this mission or not. This will be a promise for life."

Ellis snorted.

"Really? And I'm just supposed to take your word for it?"

"Why not? Most of life is just hoping that other people aren't trying to screw you over."

"Fair."

Ellis chewed on her upper lip, then nodded and whispered the code word into his ear. Phillippe nodded solemnly.

"Very well. And so it shall be."

Ellis grinned.

"Ready?", she asked. She held out a flyer that had been dropped into the markets just that morning. It depicted a square, sun-drenched and covered with bleached sand. A blue-glistening fountain sat at its centre, water splashing out of the confines of its stone layers. The square was surrounded by houses half-sunken into the ground, and a gigantic blue sphere loomed in the distance, dark shapes dancing in its interior. 'Find the sunken treasure of a lifetime', the advertisement promised.

"Ready", Phillippe said, and they vanished.

It was hot. The kind of dry heat that stuck to Ellis's chest and pressed the air out of her lungs before leaving her teary-eyed and coughing. Her pupils struggled to adjust to the bright light, and she heard Phillippe groan. Then, a moment later, an ice-cold wave splashed into her face, and she instinctively stumbled backwards and raised her fists.

"Ha!", Phillippe shouted, and while Ellis blinked the liquid out of her eyes, he started dancing around the fountain as its waters continued to splash over its rim and soaked some of the other visitors that had hurried closer.

Ellis's gaze wandered further. The square was encircled by dusty terracotta houses, covered over and over with pipes that released white-sparkling steam. Same as on the flyer, they were half-sunken into the ground, their windows cracking near the bottom where the glass met the hot, sandy ground. The further on she looked, the lower the houses sank until her sight failed and they melted into the horizon. Ellis was sure that the later rows of houses were an illusion, but it was impossible to tell how far she'd be able to walk before falling off the edges of someone else's manifestation.

Behind the fountain, staring her down with singular intensity, was a gigantic dome filled with water and iridescent fish. It was so large that it seemed to hang above her even as she craned her neck just a little further than ordinary humans could. It held the same blue water as the fountain, forming a perfect half-circle that swallowed the sky. Inside, amidst the schools of fish, she saw the remnants of a concrete tower block, half-opened by old bombs and crumbling with disrepair. Amidst the towers, humanoid shapes fell through the waters, but from this angle it was impossible to tell how fast they were going.

The dome was accessible by a small, gold-rimmed gate, flanked on both sides by a group of Enforcers. No seaver, just as Lukacz had predicted. Phillippe approached her, shaking some drops out of his hair.

"I'm pretty sure that isn't water", Ellis commented with a sly grin. Phillippe shrugged.

"Whatever it is, it's refreshing."

He frowned.

"You'd think they'd adjust the temperature in here. It's far too hot. Almost like they want to drive their customers away."

"Not almost like", Ellis replied with a distasteful look at the other visitors who were busy splashing fountain water over their clothes and arms before it disappeared.

"Look at them. These are normal people who've pulled out their one and only Freeday dress and meditated for three nights before summoning up the power necessary to teleport here."

Phillippe followed her gaze to clumsy white lace dresses, damp and sad under the water that now clung to them. Many visitors sat in the shadows cast by the nearby houses, their faces dejected and bored.

"So, this isn't the main Casino yet?"

"This is the entrance, and most of it's just an illusion to impress the masses", Ellis said, then gestured at the dome, "In there is where the real fun begins."

"Great. What are we waiting for?"

They walked up to the golden gate, the sand fluttering underneath their feet, floating by their side for a moment before falling back into its slumber. Four Enforcers guarded the entrance, each brandishing a faintly glowing bastard sword and a look of curious politeness with which they appraised Ellis and Phillippe.

"Hello, boys", Phillippe purred, "Mind letting us through?"

Most of the Enforcers met his disarming smile with a soft chuckle, but one of the men stepped in their way.

"Why hello, esteemed guests, and welcome to the Casino. I'm afraid before you progress into the dome, you'll need a win in the Beginner area."

"Whyever so?", Phillippe asked, adjusting his skirt just a little, "We'll gamble plenty once we're inside."

"Yes, but once you're inside, there are only high-stakes games", said one of the other Enforcers, "We have to make sure you can handle the basics. That, and you need to register your name and assets over there. While those are being checked, you may as well pass the time with a gamble or two."

He pointed to a small stall to the side of the square where a teenager with a colossal scowl and even bigger heart-shaped sunglasses flicked through a magazine.

"And you couldn't just take our word for it? I promise we're very resourceful", Phillippe said with a charming smile.

"C'mon, beautiful", the first Enforcer said, smiling pleasantly, "The sooner you start, the sooner you'll get inside."

"Ugh", Ellis made, feeling impatience rise in her throat, "But —"

"Sure thing, no problem", Phillippe interrupted, dragging her away by the arm. Ellis huffed but did not protest when the escort led them to the registration stall. No more than a few slats of wood sat between the teenager's freckled skin and the brutal sun that hung low in the sky. The magazine displayed various airship constructions, showing which parts had to be manually built and which were generally reliant on manifestations.

"Hey, dwarf", Ellis snapped, "Eyes up."

The teenager refused to look at her, but he did push a page of paper toward them that listed a series of names, occupations, and assets.

"These will be checked before you can progress, so please don't try and be cute", he murmured just as Phillippe started writing, "You can only gamble with assets you have declared here. If you want to declare anything else, you'll have to come back here and go through this whole fun process again. Once you enter a designated game, you agree to play by the house rules, which may extend to the stakes you gamble for."

Ellis raised her eyebrows.

"What if I'm a manifest nightmare, and I don't want to declare anything?"

The teenager raised his eyebrows but still stared down at his magazine. It was clear that he didn't believe her.

"If you don't want to declare any assets, you can gamble with your time and labour. Put down how much you're willing to play for in increments of days, months, or years."

Aside from helping Reihan, this must be the other reason Lukacz hadn't wanted to gamble his way through the betting rooms, Ellis thought, even under a fake name. It was fair enough. His time was more valuable than hers.

"Can she gamble with some of my things?", Phillippe asked, brushing his long silver hair over his shoulders.

"Nope. That's against Casino policy."

"It's fine", Ellis snapped when she caught Phillippe's pitying glance, "I just won't lose."

"Are you —"

Phillippe interrupted himself, then smiled.

"Okay. You know what you're doing."

Ellis smirked.

"Glad you're across things, wonder boy."

While one of the Enforcers teleported to the Brothel and checked Phillippe's assets, they walked over to the sunken houses. The

Casino attendants had set up card and roulette tables inside, simple games of chance that were easy enough to predict and manipulate. Tables covered with white wine stood unattended in the corners of the room, half-melted ice cubes swimming amidst the liquid. At least it was somewhat cooler inside, as the walls steamed with dry ice that rushed through the pipes. Phillippe and Ellis sat on a plush, red bench beside the first roulette table they saw. Outside, they had agreed to bet on the same number and thereby pool their manifestations. That should speed things up.

Ellis squeezed between Phillippe and a bald, skinny man who had scratched his head so many times that small lines of blood had formed on his scalp. On the other side of the table sat a small group of middle-aged women holding talismans made from rose quartz and moonstone. Phillippe pulled on Ellis's sleeve and moved his lips to her ear.

"I can't feel any manifestations", he murmured, "Am I missing something?"

Ellis tried to feel out for strands of power. Of course, the whole place was teeming with the residue energy that upheld the illusions of the desert settlement surrounding the blue water dome. In their immediate vicinity, however – on the roulette table or the pearls used to determine the game's winning numbers – Ellis felt nothing.

She shook her head, then shrugged. *Let's still go for it.* Phillippe nodded imperceptibly.

"Welcome newcomers", a bored-looking attendant said, a long-haired blonde with a sunburn stretching across her shoulders and chest.

"Would you like to place a bet? The bank offers four pieces of ruby jewellery, fifteen meals at Jeremiah's Delicacies, or a horned labour pig in exchange for a correct guess of which number the pearl will fall on. Player's choice."

"But of course", Phillippe said with a disarming smile. His assets had not been confirmed yet, so all he could bet for now was time spent in serfdom, "I will bet a week's worth of my time."

"So will I", Ellis said.

"High stakes", the bald man next to her muttered. Ellis raised her eyebrows. She had assumed this to be a relatively low bet.

"Very good", the blonde attendant said with a fake smile, "And what number shall it be?"

"Forty-nine, red", Phillippe said, fixating on the spot towards their end of the table. Ellis followed his gaze, then looked at the pearl the attendant had taken between her long, false nails.

"Anyone else?", she asked into the round. The bald man shook his head and looked down at brittle, chewed-up fingertips. One of the ladies from the other side of the table bet on thirty-two black and offered her wide-brimmed hat that smelled of freshly brewed coffee and lemons. Another woman from that group, tall, grey-haired and slender, shot Ellis and Phillippe a long look, then bet on the same number they had chosen.

Once the attendant released the pearl into the wheel and it clattered through the number boxes, Ellis and Phillippe focused on tracing its path towards the number reading forty-nine. Normally two people were not supposed to manifest on the same thing, as their powers could interfere with one another and have unforeseen effects. Children were taught that at school, in those General Behaviour lessons everyone hated. But given that they expected resistance from the other players – at least from the woman with the hat, if not from the Casino attendant – Ellis and Phillippe nonetheless pooled their powers. It wasn't as though anyone could check.

Getting the pearl to move into the designated box was so easy that it almost teleported there, leaving a path of flashing lights behind. The woman with the hat sighed loudly, and the bald man beside them muttered something incomprehensible.

"You should know better than to bet against people who show up looking like that, Marian", the tall, grey-haired woman said as she put her new horned labour pig on a lead, "It's obvious they're big shots just passing through."

Ellis collected two ruby rings for their victory and gave the bracelet and necklace to Phillippe.

"A pleasure to play with you", Phillippe said smoothly, although his voice was slightly strained.

"Yeah, yeah", Marian muttered, "Great fun was had by all. Twat."

Once they were back outside the building, hiding from the sun in the shadows of an overhanging roof, Phillippe pulled on Ellis's sleeve once more.

"Did those people –", he started, and Ellis nodded.

"Jup. Tried the count on good old lady luck. Idiots."

"But I thought the whole point of these games is manifesting the outcome. You're never going to win if you don't do that."

"I know", Ellis replied, "That's why the Enforcers aren't letting them progress. You know, to games where they might actually gamble away their house or the rest of their working life."

Phillippe shook his head, then sighed.

"This is pointless. Why don't they just go home?"

"Maybe they can't? Maybe they didn't think this through? Or maybe they're thinking that sometimes they can win by playing their cards right. Look at granny-hair and her pig. You just gotta be smart."

Phillippe shook his head again but said nothing else. By the time they returned to the Enforcers, his assets had been checked, and they were cleared to proceed.

"Have a most wonderful time", the Enforcers said and stepped aside to let them pass through the gate. As they approached the dome, only a hairsbreadth away from their eyes and hands, it somehow seemed even more gigantic, even more impossible than before.

"Here goes nothing", Ellis muttered, and Phillippe grinned.

"Right behind you."

Ellis stuck out her tongue, then pressed her body into the dome before she could think better of it. The water was cold, viscous, and stubborn, and she worried that she wouldn't be able to breathe. But that was nonsense. Of course, she'd be able to breathe. She could breathe, the water had just the right temperature, and she'd soar through the waves until she reached the concrete towers. Phillippe grinned brilliantly as he swam in pirouettes around her, his long skirt floating like a dream. Below, long-fingered plants were dancing in rhythm with an inaudible tune, and a swarm of green-glimmering fish moved past them.

When they got closer, Ellis could see that the concrete towers were overgrown with ivy, and light-fluttering flags hung out of bombed-out windows, swaying within the depth of the tides. She let herself fall through the water, and felt her fingers, nose, and legs brush through a cold resistance that strengthened the closer she got to the tower walls. *Another test, another barrier.* She pushed ahead, imagining a breeze that carried her onwards while a big hand pulled her towards the biggest opening she could see. It yawned like the black mouth, perhaps belonging to a beast that had slept for too long. And, being a nightmare, she made herself fall into it head-first.

CHAPTER 21: REIHAN

Air travel was an unregulated nightmare in the Travelling City. With many citizens able to sprout wings or summon a flying vessel at a moment's notice, it was unreasonable to expect everyone to fill out permits for every journey they wanted. So, it was only if you wanted to use the giant airships – those you needed to move a family from one district or another or to transport building materials – that you had to get written permission from Government. This gap in legislation had the somewhat predictable outcome that most people simply stayed below the size restrictions and used five little ships rather than going through the trouble of registering a large one. Collisions were now frequent enough that a winged division of Enforcers regularly encircled the city, ready to catch anyone who accidentally fell out of their vessel.

Reihan loved being on airships. In fact, she loved it so much that in her youth, she had spent a few years building a small air glider. She had read up on how to assemble a motor from scrap and had bargained incessantly to gather the relevant materials. The glider had been a rickety amalgamation of half-rusted metals, curtain sails, and vegetable oil, and it had never taken off. One night, frustrated beyond measure, she had tossed the whole construction over the back edge of the Asylum platform, much to Seamus's bemusement, who had not been able to resist saying, 'I told you so'.

The fact that she had just been sold into effective slavery dampened her spirits somewhat, but Reihan still enjoyed the view of the city in the gold-glowing dusk as its citizens started raising the sea of blue-purple kites that heralded the change of the season. She spotted three gigantic paper dragons that pushed themselves through the waves of smaller planes. Someone had manifested the illusion of flames coming from one of the dragon's open mouths, ricocheting off the golden-glowing rooftops of the Artisan's Quarters.

The sphere wasn't great company. It flittered up and down, seemingly happy to maintain its artificial shape until it had dropped Reihan at the rendezvous spot. Its instructions must have been very strict as it could surely not expect a newborn seaver to escape and reveal its identity to the Enforcers. Technically, she shouldn't even know what an Enforcer was. A newborn seaver knew precisely one thing, and that was to obey the founders.

The airship slowed its descent where the rock fell sharply enough that not even the most optimistic citizens had settled there. Flocks of red-feathered birds nested inside breathing holes in the stone, and Reihan could feel used-up, acid air sputtering out in irregular intervals. She guessed that they were somewhere on the city's Eastern cliff's edge.

The sphere flittered, and the ship turned onto its side, sliding as close to the rock as it could. Reihan could have stretched out her hand and stroked the birds' beaks if she had wanted to. She remained stock still, of course, trying to remember if she had ever been briefed about this area. She came up blank.

The ship sputtered out some black fog, then stopped, suspended in the air. She couldn't hear a motor running, so Reihan guessed they were relying on a reasonably strained manifestation. She looked to her right and saw that one of the stone's breathing holes was larger than the others and conspicuously empty of birds or other nesting animals. It must surely have been used as a hiding ground at some point, ripe for smuggling or storing illegal wares. She looked at the sphere, but still, all she could see was a ball of iridescent colour, releasing no words or expressions to guide her. She sighed internally, then moved to leave the raft, pushing the chain from her neck into her uniform belt so it wouldn't get caught anywhere. The sphere did not protest, so after a moment's breath, she gathered her courage and jumped into the hole.

Despite her suspicions that she was entering an old smuggler's tunnel, she could have gotten unlucky. The stone on which they had built their city was alive in a way that neither humans nor seaver fully understood. And whichever beast they lived on, its breath came with irregular force, frequency, and frenzy, and many of the city's underground passages became make-shift airways at some point or other. But no blast of air came blowing out of this particular gap, and her feet connected safely with solid ground. She took a moment to catch her breath, then turned around. The airship was still waiting at the outset of the tunnel, and the sphere stared at her unblinkingly.

Ahead, the breathing hole widened as she proceeded. Her steps echoed amidst walls filled with hundreds of tiny holes that looked like steel-teethed insects had gnawed on their edges. Ahead, past a few bends in the tunnel, Reihan heard hushed human voices. One of the things the seaver had silently but univocally agreed on was that they didn't tell humans about their superior hearing. The element of surprise did tend to come in useful.

"What if it reports us?", she heard a female voice caution, "I can't go to the containment centres."

"The message said that they got a newborn one. It probably doesn't even know what an Enforcer is", said a male voice, older and more abrasive.

"That, and nobody knows we have it. We can do whatever we want with it", said another female voice, soft and round like a warm smell.

"Well, we were supposed to return it, remember? It'll be used in the Casino afterwards", cautioned the first woman.

"Accidents happen. Either way, we've decided on this now", said the man, "Are you committed or not?"

"Yeah, yeah", murmured the first voice. Reihan sighed internally. It was time to ham up her 'dumb seaver' act if she wanted to get out of this alive.

She walked around the last corner that separated her from the humans, then forced her face into a blank mask.

"Hello", she said in her best dull voice, "Are you the people I was supposed to meet?"

Five faces turned around to her.

"Yes, sweetheart. That's us."

It was the man who had spoken twice before. He was short and broad, with shoulder-length black hair in need of a wash. His eyes were pure black – either a manifestation or a body modification – and two swords adorned his belt. A tall, thin woman turned to him, her blonde hair falling over her shoulder.

"Dead gods, they look so weird when they're new. I always forget how much seaver mod when they get older."

That was the first woman Reihan had heard. She noted the stiletto rapier on her side and the bombs strapped to her back. She sighed internally.

"Come here, lovely", an elderly woman said – the third speaker – and stretched her hands towards Reihan, "now don't be shy."

She was short, with a hunched back and tight grey curls. Her blue dress hung down to her ankles. Nothing about her looked dangerous, and she did not carry any weapons. Reihan accepted her invitation and approached until the woman could touch her.

The remaining two group members were men. Brothers, Reihan guessed, from how similar they looked. Both carried bows on their back, although the younger brother's weapon hung at a precarious angle, and he had stuffed too many arrows into his quiver.

"Now, dear, we're going to go on a walk through this tunnel, all right? You are going to follow us. Do you think you can do that?", the old woman said, touching Reihan's white hands with her own. They were wrinkled and warm but had no callouses or scars, Reihan noticed.

Reihan nodded.

"Very good", the old woman said, then frowned.

"Now, this is a very old tunnel. There might be evil things in here, things that want to hurt us. You don't want that because we're your friends."

Reihan felt very tempted to ask what 'evil' or a 'friend' might be, but this wasn't the time to cause a philosophical debate for the sake of her own amusement. So, she merely nodded.

"If the evil things appear, I want you to kill them", the black-haired man said, then handed her one of his swords, "Just poke them with the pointy end. But make sure you don't hit any of us."

"Of course not. You are friends", Reihan replied, trying hard to keep a straight face.

"Good! Good. You learn fast."

"How will I recognise the evil things?", Reihan asked because she figured she should.

"Ah. They'll have frayed edges, and they might shift from one place to another", the blond woman responded, "They'll – well, basically attack anything that jumps out at you that isn't one of us, okay?"

"Okay", Reihan responded, cursing internally. *Shadows.* Of

course. Why else would they need a seaver?

With the group sufficiently reassured that Reihan would follow basic instructions, they started moving through the tunnel, which continued to widen at every step. Soft breaths rushed through the stone, getting stuck in the holes in the walls after they caressed Reihan's skin with a gentle touch. She could smell faint notes of orange and sulphur. The path shifted up, then down again, and the lack of any reference points made it impossible for her to guess their current altitude. Underneath her feet and shuffling around her legs were small grey mice, their whiskers flittering with the faint sounds of children screaming. Reihan wondered which one amidst their party had inadvertently manifested the sounds into existence. But no one commented on it.

She was tempted to ask the humans where they were going, but she knew that showing curiosity would be considered suspicious. Given that they had started on the furthest Eastern point, which housed parts of the Undercity, the Upside-Down Palace, and the factory district next to the Mineshafts, they had to be going West. Which meant that, at their current trajectory and current pace, they could be just about anywhere that wasn't one of the floating islands. *Great.*

She was ripped out of her thoughts when a clattering noise shook through the hallway. Reihan's eyes flew wide open, and she raised her sword before she had fully grasped the situation. The rest of the group jumped and drew their weapons, except for the old woman, who took a few hurried steps back.

The younger brother released a quiet whimper. The strap with which he had secured his quiver had ripped, and his arrows slowly rolled on the ground. A few tapped against Reihan's shoes, shaking with barely concealed fear.

"Oh Mikhail", his older brother sighed, "I told you –"

The black-haired man interrupted him when he shoved Mikhail against the tunnel wall.

"Are you fucking kidding me?", he snarled, "Do you think this is a bloody game?"

"I –"

"If you'd pulled this kind of crap during the last Invasion, I would have been well within my rights to rip you limb from limb. Is that what you fucking want?"

The louder his voice rang amidst the tunnel walls, the darker the corridor became. It felt like a hole had opened that was sucking out the light, the sound, the warmth – everything. Reihan forced her eyes from Mikhail's squirming and the black-haired man's poorly disguised panic. The mice climbed on top of each other, forming a distorted tower that squeaked with terror as it swayed. Teeth, claws, and ears melted together, and soon enough, a shadow would emerge from its core, a fear manifestation come to life.

"Let it go, Ernst", the blonde woman said sharply, "You said you wouldn't do this anymore."

Ernst took a few deep breaths, staring at Mikhail's horrified face. Then he sighed and released him. The tower's edges became less clearly defined, less inky-black, and the mice seemed to take a long breath. The old woman turned around to it and waved her hands until it disappeared.

"Sorry", Ernst muttered, "And sorry, Kadie."

Mikhail rubbed his arms and said nothing in turn. The old woman pulled her soft fabric belt from her dress and slung it around the broken quiver, allowing Mikhail to put it back around his back.

"Thanks, Angel", he said with a shy smile, "And sorry, Amber. You were right."

"It's okay", his brother said, "At least I get bragging rights now."

Reihan tried to cast her mind back to the history textbooks the founders had given her during her time at the Upside-Down Palace. Some of them had referenced Invasions of the Thirteenth Travelling City by other cities or ship-like constructions that roamed the cloud sea. Who, like their own ancestors, had emancipated from the Continent below for reasons none of them rightly remembered.

She had read eyewitness accounts of a gigantic, winged whale that carried houses on its back and shook off small buildings and bridges at each monstrous flap with which it roamed the skies. The inhabitants of the whale had envied the Travelling City its relative stability and had rained down flaming arrows and bombs in an attempt to take it over. When they found the districts protected by a collectively manifested shield, they had thrown their own bodies into its streets and islands, armed with scythes and spears, ready to butcher anyone who crossed their path. Most of them had been fought off in a months-long guerrilla war in which every house turned militia, shelter, and shield. But some of the invaders had disguised themselves as those inhabitants of the Travelling City whom they had assassinated, and their descendants still lived amongst them. Or so the story went.

Another account described drawn-out battles of attrition where one Travelling City tried to assimilate the landmass of another, usually as part of a collective manifestation effort. As far as Reihan had read, those battles always ended in an exhausted stalemate, both sides run dry of their powers.

No one knew how many Invasions there had been across the Travelling City's storied history, mainly because it was impossible to know which invasions were real and which resulted from manifest collective anxiety. But Reihan knew there hadn't been an Invasion in her or Seamus's lifetime. According to the textbooks, if Ernst claimed that he had fought in one, he had to be at least four hundred years old.

Further down the tunnel, they ran into shades that attacked them on sight; half-conscious nightmare manifestations, Reihan guessed. She moved to the front and raised her sword against their half-formed bodies, against strange long claws, wings dripping with inky black wetness, and roaring beaks. She stood side by side with Kadie, whose face was just as impassioned as her own. Angel moved to the side, fixating the nightmares with an unblinking stare. Her concentration seemed to slow down their movements and rendered their exteriors less solid.

Ernst was everywhere at once, making sure that the two archers in the back were covered, then jumped in front of Kadie and Reihan, raining down his sword like an angry god. Once the shadows lay slithering on the ground, he breathed far heavier than all the others, and Reihan noticed a slight tremble in his fingers. Angel murmured something Reihan didn't quite hear, then the old woman turned around with a smile and asked if she was doing all right.

Reihan guessed that the old woman had been an Enforcer in her heyday, part of the Deconstruction Provision that untangled other people's manifestation powers when they had grown too strong. Weak at producing their own but deft at manipulating the manifestations of others, Enforcers in that provision were usually owed quite a few perks by the city after they retired. Reihan wondered why she was here.

They continued until they reached the end of the tunnel. Cobblestones underfoot made the walking easier, and the sulphur fumes had been replaced by the smell of fresh grass. Half-realised streetlamps illuminated the darkness with blue-flickering light. Reihan wondered if they were maybe Mikhail's manifestations or whether the group's desires for comfort had merged in that strange way in which human intentions often did.

Ahead loomed a staircase that encircled a tower-shaped building made entirely of concrete. No new buildings in the Travelling City were allowed to use or manifest materials that looked like this. The concrete was from the Continent, and it had come to indicate that a building was an 'original' that had been hand-crafted by the original crew of the city. And only one original building this far West had this shape.

"Ladies and Gentlemen, welcome to the Watchtower", Kadie said with a grim smile.

"Now, let's blow it up."

CHAPTER 22: PHILLIPPE

The Casino was a defiant show of luxury amidst the concrete destruction. In front of every bombed-out hole posed a group of young visitors with impossibly light, shimmering gowns, immortalised by one of the Casino's own manifesters who faithfully captured their image onto paper and canvas. The fashion of the guests was so extravagant that even Phillippe felt under-dressed. Long, curved staves encircled with glowing dandelions, blue-dyed horns, scaled trains as long as an entire room, faces covered over and over in rose petals, dripping with honey; he could not stop staring at the creativity that surrounded him, his heart aching with a strange joy. Weaving the webs of everyone's fantasies, he had forgotten that other people were capable of the same. That the heavens were so much higher than they looked from his balcony.

The steel-grey, cold floors had been covered with luscious white carpets, inviting the guests to take off their shoes. Two bars adorned each side of the gambling hall, which stretched across the entire tower floor, aluminium-grey and shining surfaces hosting a myriad of bottles that glowed from within. Ancient, half-destroyed human statues stood abandoned within the hall as if they had been met by fate's gaze midway through a dance and preserved there for an unknown future. The young and beautiful guests had their image taken in front of them as if to defy the passage of their own time. In the corner of the hall, in front of another large hole, a band played ethereal, dark music that sounded like it was coming from underwater.

In a sense, they were still underwater. Occasionally, a school of shimmering green fish would swim through one opening of the hall, then out through another. When he turned his head a little too fast, Phillippe could see the light bouncing off what looked like soft waves, and his movements felt just a little more sluggish than usual. But most of the other guests seemed to have agreed that there would be air rather than water inside the gambling halls, so those hints remained hints rather than growing into reality. Whether the air was real, filtered in through vents that connected to windows on the upper floors, or whether it was all a manifestation, Phillippe wasn't sure.

Ellis sipped on a blood-red cocktail with tomatoes so large they barely let the liquid pass. She had acquired a large-brimmed black hat to accompany her pantsuit while Phillippe had fetched drinks from the closest bar. He had not given her the satisfaction of asking her how she got it.

"At some point, we might just have to go for one of those", Ellis said, not for the first time.

"Which one?", Phillippe asked. The nightmare shrugged.

"Any of them. Just as long as we stop standing around."

She was pointing at the portals spread all over the hall, rimmed by gold arches and glowing with fast-changing light. If you squeezed your eyes tightly enough, you could catch a glimpse of where they led; a maze spanning the width of an entire continent, a mausoleum filled with walking corpses, a vision of blackness and nothing else. According to the barkeeper, a man wearing the face of a seal and proudly displaying a rippling six-pack, you could enter the portals to take part in the more unusual gambles held at the Casino. He had warned Phillippe that inside the house chose the stakes, however, and that the rules were not forgiving.

In between the portals stood extravagant, wide-swinging tables where guests could play card games, baccarat, or roulette. And towards the other end of the hall were small, inconspicuous doors that, according to the barkeeper, led to private rooms where the guests could design their own gambits. That, he warned Phillippe, would have to be done under the supervision of the Enforcers, who were surveying the hall from the vantage point of a brutalist concrete staircase that suddenly stopped in mid-air.

Ellis sighed.

"It's so annoying that none of these portals is a door. I mean, that none of them show a door that your girlfriend could open from her side", the nightmare said, pouting. Phillippe took a long sip from his cocktail, a concoction that tasted like balcony herbs and dusty sunshine.

"Well, we're not quite there yet, are we?", he replied with a playful smirk.

"Huh? This is the main betting hall of the Casino, isn't it?"

"It's one of two", Phillippe replied, "Remember the sketch dad gave us? That had two floors. And it was the upper one that led into the apartment complex."

"Yeah, but that sketch looked completely different to whatever *this* is. I reckon boss man just got it wrong."

Phillippe snorted.

"I'll readily admit that he does have a propensity for making bad decisions, but his information has been good so far. And he said that he got it from people on the inside, didn't he?"

He gestured around himself.

"Think about it. What if it isn't just the special events that keep being updated? What if the entire place shifts on a daily basis according to the visitors' whims and desires? We do something similar at the Brothel."

Ellis nodded slowly.

"But certain features have to stay the same", Phillippe continued, "Otherwise, you'd never get anywhere, right? You'd look for the Wing of Intellectual Stimulation and end up in the Wing of Romantic Fantasy. Rather a different form of stimulation if I can propose any expertise on the topic."

He sighed.

"Anyway. To prevent everyone from getting lost in a building where both the customers and the employees are encouraged to manifest, you employ manifesters whose sole job is to keep certain key features of a building in place. I didn't realise that was a thing until I met some of them at our delightfully awkward all-staff get-togethers."

Ellis nodded again.

"Riiight. So, you're saying they'd have those peeps keep the two-floor structure for the betting halls. But why keep 'em separate?"

Phillippe frowned.

"I reckon they have the really high-stakes games upstairs."

He gestured to the card and roulette tables positioned across the hall, at the jewels, trinkets, small machinery, and scrolls of parchment spread around the corners of the tables. The guests, half-distracted by conversation and drink, exchanged them as easily as tat. None of them seemed to take the betting particularly seriously, and many small groups just stood around tables near the bar, waiting for a spectacle to emerge from one of the portals.

"People here are still betting with their possessions. But if that's all it is, how does anyone sell themselves into serfdom? I reckon the *really* high-stakes games where people sell their occupation, their home, the rest of their life – those are somewhere else. Upstairs, I reckon."

"And that brings us back to the question of how we get there. Great job, wonder boy. Led us right round in a circle."

Phillippe shook his head.

"No, think about it. What if this is another test, just like in the entrance hall? Before letting people up to the second floor, they want to check that they would be up for the games being played there. So, they need to be separated from us here on the first floor."

"So, do you reckon the Enforcers are hiding another portal on the stairs back there? Do we just go up to them and tell them we're bored of poker or something?"

Ellis gestured at the staircase that stopped midway through the air. Phillippe shook his head again.

"Possible, but it doesn't look that way, does it? The only obvious way to get anywhere else from here is via these portals."

Ellis made a face, then blinked.

"Wait. What if the second floor is behind those portals, then?"

"Hm? No, that's just where the more unusual gambits are held."

Ellis's eyes shone with sudden excitement.

"No, listen. If we enter the portal, aren't we saying that we're up for high stakes and whatnot? Your bartender man told you as much. So, maybe *all of them* lead to the second floor. Like, the second floor is just a series of fucked up illusion rooms in which they host their weird gambits. Question is just which portal gets us to the room with the door to the apartments."

Phillippe clicked his tongue appreciatively.

"Well, well, well, look at you, nightmare lady. Deadly, scary and a certified genius", he said.

Ellis grinned.

"So, do you reckon we can just ask someone which one the right portal is? Or would that be too suspicious?"

"Definitely too suspicious", Phillippe replied, "Why would we need to know where the door to the apartments is if we're just here to gamble? Most people won't even know that the apartments exist at all. We'll have to do this the old-fashioned way, I'm afraid. Enter the portals and play one gambit after another until we stumble across the place with the door."

"Ugh", Ellis made, "That'll take bloody ages. I have other things to do today."

"Really? Like what?"

"Well, I… screw you, Phillippe."

The nightmare made a face, then started to twirl. She pointed her arm straight ahead, and when she stopped moving, her finger landed close to a portal in which they could see nothing except blackness.

"How about that one?"

Phillippe took another look at the other portals. There were thirty-three in total, spread in irregular patterns across the hall. It was impossible to tell what exactly awaited them on the other end. They might have to play thirty-two gambits before getting to the correct room on the second floor. But they weren't getting any closer to Alexander by just standing around.

"Okay", he said with a soft sigh, "Let's try it."

On the other side of the portal, they fell into space. A vast expanse of dark nothing amidst stars that glimmered at an impossible distance. A slowly increasing number of moons moved across the horizon, pursuing each other in eternal warfare. As far as Phillippe could see, there was nothing above or underfoot, and if he closed his eyes, he expected that he might disappear, convinced that nothing had ever existed or would ever exist again.

But when he took another, longer look around, he spotted several planets, most of them far away but some close enough that Phillippe thought he could probably teleport onto their surface if he genuinely wanted to test the boundary of the illusion. There was no gravity, so he and Ellis floated aimlessly next to the gleaming portal they had exited from, accompanied by five other guests who had already gathered there.

Phillippe had always guessed that it would be cold in space, and it was, but nowhere near the freezing temperatures he had expected. When he felt goosebumps on his arms, he reprimanded himself. *No. This temperature is what space* should *have.* There was no reason for it to be colder.

They all floated for a few moments and exchanged awkward smiles.

"Does anyone know where the game master is? Surely seven should be enough to play now", asked a middle-aged woman, strikingly beautiful and clothed almost entirely in her thick, woodland-brown hair. Her eyes were pure lilac sparkle, and Phillippe caught a few disdainful glances flying towards her as it was obvious she had manifested on them.

"H-have you played this game before?"

The voice was so quiet that it almost got lost in the empty space between them. A young man had spoken, short and with intelligent, kind eyes. His clothes were not nearly as exuberant as everyone else's.

"They change the game every time", the first woman responded, her voice a tad bored, "Otherwise, what's the fun in playing?"

"Hmmm", made a third within their circle. A white-haired pale-faced man, who almost looked like he had modelled his appearance after a seaver. He swayed in the open ocean of blackness, and Phillippe could tell that he was utterly, roaringly drunk.

"Whatever – I'm sure there's a good reason for the wait. Let's stay here a little longer", said a middle-aged bald man with a beaming smile and a gold brocade suit that seemed to move on its own, constantly shifting to catch the best light. As he turned his head and smiled, Phillippe saw several gold plate inlays installed in the back of his head. Those had been popular a few years ago, supposedly able to strengthen your manifestation abilities. Phillippe and Alexander had never had enough money to try them out.

The last amidst their round did not respond. They had turned into a long, shimmering snake with wings, twisting their body around itself in a way that looked oddly comfortable.

They waited for a little while, then another. Nobody appeared.

"Ugh, this is ridiculous", the beautiful woman said, "What a waste of my time."

Ellis scratched her head.

"Do we even need a game master?", she asked.

"What?", the woman snapped in a way that prevented it from being a question.

"What do you mean?", the kind-eyed man asked, floating a

little closer to the nightmare.

"Well, what I said. Do we need a game master?"

"Well, someone needs to take our bets, don't they?", the man with the inlays replied.

"What if the bet is something we've already committed? We were told, in a pretty ominous way, that it can be the house's choice what we gamble with in these games", Ellis said, narrowing her eyes. Phillippe felt his fingers tingle as he realised what she was implying.

"You can't mean –", he started, but Ellis shrugged.

"At the entrance, the Enforcers excluded anyone too weak to play. That should make it technically possible for everyone to win."

She frowned.

"But why would that be important? Why would they care if some poor addicts get lost in here and die?"

"Because that would be horrible, and we're better than that", the kind-eyed man replied. The man with the inlays laughed a quiet, bitter laugh.

The nightmare snorted.

"As if, sunshine. They exclude the properly weak ones because there is no game master to rescue everyone who gets cold feet or who can't maintain a sense of self inside an illusion. So. I reckon they'll leave us out here until we figure out this game. The stakes are our freedom. Pretty high, I'll give them that."

"Wh –"

The white-haired man's eyes flew open, as if for the first time, and he shot towards the portal. Arms first, he tried to move through it but was repelled by so strong a force that his body was thrown back, tumbling into darkness. Only Phillippe's quick reactions slowed his fall and allowed him to return to their circle.

"No", the beautiful woman said firmly, "There is no force field. The portal is still open."

She tried to exit, but her manifestation was clearly insufficient to counter whatever imagined lock had been placed on the portal from outside.

"What. The. Fuck", the man with the gold inlays snarled, "I didn't sign up for this. What are we even supposed to do now?"

The snake slowly untangled its body, fixating him with an unblinking stare. He flew a few paces backwards, his face turning white. The woman pushed herself between them, raising her hands.

"Oh really?", she said, "You think we're supposed to fight? Well, you better pick on someone your own size –"

"That can't be it. The Casino rules explicitly forbid player-on-player violence", the kind-eyed man interrupted, twisting his hands and cracking his knuckles.

"Yeah, I'm not fighting any of you", the white-haired man snapped. He looked like he might throw up at any second, and Phillippe thought he could see strands of red peeking out from near the top of his head.

"Ah, wait, wait, wait. I think this might be a riddle", Ellis said. She had been looking around, floating to the back of the portal to see if there was anything to indicate what they were supposed to do.

"I hate riddles", the brunette woman said, then sighed.

"But I expect you might be right. Very well. What is there to interact with?"

"The portal itself. Which I tried", the white-haired man pouted.

"Nothing", the kind-eyed man said, his voice shaking, "That's what's so terrifying about this. There is nothing here."

"Calm down", the first woman said, and her tone softened, "They wouldn't have left us with nothing. We just have to figure out what to do."

"And there isn't nothing", Phillippe said slowly. His eyes fixated on the closest planet next to them, a giant made up of intersecting green and red land masses visible under a heap of storm clouds. Several eyes had opened within the storm's hearts, and unfocused pupils blinked at them.

"Really? Can you move them?", the kind-eyed man asked, floating a little closer to Phillippe. He smelled like lemon and raindrops.

Phillippe concentrated. Couldn't he do anything he wanted? What challenge was a little game when it came to the immeasurable power he had stolen? He had lost everything, so now he was owed everything. That was how the world worked.

"It's moving", Ellis breathed, then whistled quietly, "Go, wonder boy!"

"Gods alive", the man with the inlays whispered, "How is that even possible…?"

Slowly the planet came closer, taking up more of the horizon by the second.

"So, what now? Where do you want it?", Phillippe asked. His breath went a little heavy, although he knew that was irrational.

"Crash it into the portal?", the white-haired man suggested, a vindictive glow in his eyes.

"Uh-uh. Does anyone have an idea that isn't a glorified game of pool?", Ellis snapped. The beautiful woman laughed, then hesitated.

"Okay, don't mock, but what if we are supposed to play pool?", she asked.

"Serious suggestions only", Phillippe said between clenched teeth, trying to slow down the planet's movement.

"I am being serious! Maybe we're supposed to cause some sort of chain reaction. Make one planet hit another, which then hits another, which hits a target."

"All right", the kind-eyed man said, "Would that be feasible?"

He floated a little upwards, trying to see whether the planets lined up in a way that led towards a goal. But when he came back down, he shook his head.

"There is no obvious order to their constellation. Plus, I don't see anything that could be a target."

"Right. And there's no reason we could only move one of the planets at a time, right? We're all manifesters; we could all technically do this", Ellis suggested. The kind-eyed man gave her a doubtful look, but no one protested.

Phillippe blinked, then turned around.

"Did the planets move while we were here?", he asked, his

voice strained. The beautiful woman hesitated, then raised her eyebrows.

"Dead gods, you're right. There are exactly seven planets closest to us."

"And I swear some of them were further away before", the white-haired man said, turning to Phillippe, "Are you moving more than one?"

"Are you kidding me? One's hard enough", the escort snapped. Ellis chewed on her fingertips, then grinned at the white-haired man.

"You might have to find out for yourself, sunshine. Seven planets, seven manifesters, right? That's riddle stuff."

"But what are we supposed to do with them?", the kind-eyed man mused, then turned to Phillippe.

"You look like you're struggling."

"So sweet of you to notice", Phillippe snapped, "I am ever-so-busy trying to prevent the planet from crashing into us."

Despite his best efforts to slow it down, the force of the red giant was strong, as if it ached to come ever closer to their little group.

"But why would it be so compelled to move here? From what I saw, the initial push you gave it was relatively weak, and it's not like the planet is rolling downhill. There is no flow or resistance here. So, why is it urging towards…?"

He followed the planet's trajectory, which led straight towards their little circle. To the portal which they surrounded.

Ellis blinked.

"Maybe that's the riddle."

The snake hissed.

"Ha!", the white-haired man said, "I told you we had to crash the planet into the portal."

"Not quite", the brunette woman clarified, "We move all seven planets here. One hit might break the portal, but if we get all seven of them to move towards it at exactly the same speed and the same distance, the portal will be safe between the forces they all expend."

"And the combined gravitational force between them might break whatever lock they've placed on the portal and open the way back?", the kind-eyed man concluded, giving the rest of them a hopeful look. The man with the inlays nodded slowly. He gave the snake a long look and slowly floated back into the circle.

"It's the best suggestion I've heard", Phillippe said. He waved towards the other planets.

"All right, beautiful people! Let's get pushing."

They aligned in a circle around the portal, four on one side, three on the other. Phillippe felt pearls of sweat run down his temples as he slowed down his planet to a crawl to give the others a chance to catch up. Ellis, next to him, pulled a purple planet towards her, and the beautiful woman had taken on a white gas giant with a grim smile and a twist of her fingers. The man with the gold inlays struggled visibly, and the plates on his head started to glow. But, through whichever means his abilities were amplified, he was finally able to move his planet towards them.

On the other side, Phillippe heard more laboured breaths and cursing. He turned around and saw the snake steadily moving an ice planet towards the portal. The drunk white-haired man was visibly straining, but his planet was stuttering and spurting in the right direction at least, pausing every few seconds as he was gasping for air. But the planet they had allocated to the kind-eyed man – a small inferno-laden globe whose fires seemed to drip into the depths of space – had not moved at all.

"Any time now, pal."

Ellis turned around as well and shot him an irritated look.

"I ... I can't do it. I imagine it moving towards me, but nothing is happening."

"Come now, it's only an illusion. You're not actually moving an entire planet", the beautiful woman said.

"I know, but... it looks so real. I can't –"

The snake hissed, and suddenly the inferno planet jumped into motion. Ellis whistled.

"You can do two at once? Holy –"

"Get ready."

Phillippe pressed the words out. He didn't know how long he could keep his thoughts fixated on just his planet, to keep them from spreading outwards like a disease.

"We might have to be very precise with the distances."

The group floated closer to the portal until they all touched it with at least one of their appendages. This time, it did not repel them, which Phillippe decided to take as a good sign.

"Slow them down."

The voice appeared between them, seemingly without an

originator, although the hiss within its inflexion implied that it might be the snake that had spoken. They did as they were asked, and suddenly felt a resistance in the air dissipate.

"Ah! Much fun was had by all! See you losers never!", Ellis said, then jumped through the portal head-first. Phillippe laughed with the rest of them, then followed her back to the first floor of the Casino.

CHAPTER 23: REIHAN

Their homes were a point of pride for the inhabitants of the Travelling City. Adorning their houses with colour-drenched balconies, wide-swinging porches, sparkling fountains, glowing decorations, luscious plants, sweet-smelling flowers, and high-flying flags was a sign that the residents could afford luxury and, because of that, were at least competent manifesters. Impossible-looking structures were particularly in-vogue, whereby a small part of the manifester's consciousness always stayed behind to untangle the gravitational mess their creation was causing. Reihan couldn't remember a time when extravagance and opulence hadn't been in fashion for any district that could afford them.

The Watchtower was a functional building. It was one of the original constructs raised within the city, carved from liquid concrete and created not by manifestations but by old machines. The Watchtower, parts of the Casino, the Upside-Down Palace, and even some parts of the Undercity had been built in this material before the Travelling City had ever taken flight. Mostly, like in the Palace or the

Casino, the concrete structures were encased with illusions, soft as silk and malleable like the wind. But destroying any original part of the city was an offence, so the foundations were left standing, monuments of a time none truly remembered. Other than the founders, maybe.

"What are we waiting for? Let's go inside", Angel said with surprising eagerness.

At the bottom of the concrete tower sat a small staircase. At its end, a small door, barely large enough to fit any of them. Mikhail shifted uncomfortably from side to side.

"Something feels off", he muttered.

Ernst sighed. For a moment, he looked like he wanted to say something sharp, but he restrained himself.

"Do you want to stay here, boy?", he asked, "There's no shame in it. With the seaver actually working, we should be fine."

"No!", the young man replied quickly, "That's not what I mean. Just – this place feels abandoned. Like, there hasn't been anyone here for years."

"That's what I've been saying", Kadie said. Her composure had been level for the entirety of their trek through the tunnels, but now her eyes widened just a little, and Reihan felt as though her voice had become more intense without growing louder.

"The founders left this dump years ago if they were ever here to begin with. And who else is supposed to keep watch?"

Ernst nodded grimly.

"Cian'Erley?", Mikhail asked.

"Mikhail", Amber whispered sadly. Kadie shook her head.

"Cian'Erley isn't real. He's just a myth the founders made up to have people think that someone is watching over us. While they steer the city towards a collision with the continent."

"The founders", Angel snorted, "We don't even know if those are real either. They might just be stories mums tell their children to get them to go to bed."

She sighed.

"When I served with the Enforcers we were taught that the unconscious thoughts of the masses steer the city. Not some made-up monsters."

She stood a little apart from the group, and Reihan wondered how much she truly cared about all this. Maybe she had just joined Ka'a to feel connected to something again.

"Why would the founders lie to us?", Mikhail asked, ignoring the old woman.

"Honestly, who cares about the founders?", Kadie replied, "What I want to know is why we have a Watchtower to begin with? If this place is truly empty, why is the Government having us think that someone's steering this city? Have you ever asked yourself that?"

Ernst sighed.

"Look, we just need to make sure that someone is keeping a lookout for other Travelling Cities. If there is no nest of founders, Cian'Erley, or some other poor sod stationed here, people need to get wise to that."

He shook his head.

"We can't be surprised by another Invasion. We've grown too

weak. We wouldn't survive it."

"And we won't have to. Come on, let's go", Amber said, taking the first step onto the staircase. The rest of the group slowly followed, with Mikhail all the way at the back. Reihan stayed in front of him. She was trying to figure out how much of this she needed to report. It somewhat depended on whether Ka'a was just a group of conspiracy theorists or whether there was something legitimate to their worries.

Truth be told, she had no idea if there were any founders in the Watchtower. It wasn't like they let the seaver in on their secrets. If she hadn't been raised by them in the Upside-Down Palace, she probably wouldn't believe that they were real either.

But she had been told about mythical Cian'Erley, an old man with skin as thick as leather, water-blue eyes, and a single-minded determination to stay alive so he could warn the city of the things that loomed on the horizon. Who did not eat, who did not sleep, and who did not love. Foolishly, perhaps, she had believed in that single-minded symbol of duty.

The door opened and revealed a dusty spiral staircase. Only one person fit on it at a time, with concrete walls encasing them tightly. After a few minutes of climbing, there was a door to their left.

"Right. Let's see if this place is truly abandoned", Amber said. But Ernst pushed himself between the young man and the door.

"Sorry, lad. You'll have to leave the glory of being impaled by traps or decapitated by an angry founder to this old veteran."

He winked at Amber, and Reihan thought the young man

looked a little relieved.

Ernst pushed the door open to an entirely dark room. No windows, candles, or sconces produced the slightest bit of light, but the oppressive blackness held the kind of tight feeling Reihan was familiar with.

"Shades", she hissed, "Get ready."

Ernst did not question her instincts. He raised his sword immediately – and not a moment too soon, as a faceless, humanoid figure ran into the tip of his blade with so much force that it threw the veteran a few steps backwards.

"You're dead", Angel hissed, and the shade obeyed, fading into thin air. But there were more inside; Reihan could see them move in the dark.

"Duck", Kadie shouted. Amber and Mikhail shot arrows over their heads, which burst into flames halfway on their path. The light briefly illuminated the twisted, interconnected bodies of the shades. It was as if they were melting into one another, winding horn, growing into grimaces with far too many teeth, twisted into towers of repulsion. Nothing humanoid remained as Reihan, Ernst, and Kadie rushed into the room's centre, their blades singing a silver song.

"You're dead! You're dead, you're dead, you're dead!", Angel roared in a brittle voice above the silent battle.

A bulging heap struck a tentacle against Kadie's side, throwing her on her back. Reihan hacked it off before it could cause further damage, but the shadows clung to the woman's core like a thick film of oil.

"Make it go away!", she shrieked, "Please! I can't leave my babies, I can't."

"It's already gone", Reihan lied. She gently placed her hand on the darkness and applied pressure to Kadie's chest, "Don't you see? Shadows don't stick to you."

"They... no, they don't", Kadie said slowly, her eyes glossing over just a little, then she shook her head. Around them, the sounds of battle were abating.

"Help me up", she demanded, grabbing Reihan's hand that still rested on her chest.

"Of course, master", Reihan responded, trying to keep the slyness out of her tone.

Ernst, Mikhail, and Amber had ensured that the rest of the shadows lay in twitching heaps on the floor. Angel hovered between them, whispering sweet lies into their ears, that they were dead and had never actually existed.

"What a nasty collection of shades", Amber muttered, patting Mikhail on his back, "You did well, kid."

"Not a kid. We talked about that", Mikhail snarled, but some pride shone in his eyes nonetheless.

"Well, there's many floors left", Ernst said with a sigh and another look around the room, "Just because this place is infested, it doesn't mean that there can't be watchers, founders, or even Cian'Erley further up."

Reihan blinked. *Are none of them going to mention it?* How could she make them talk about it in a way that wasn't suspicious? She took a step, then forced her legs to stutter as if she was malfunctioning. She released an uncanny croaking noise from her throat. The humans turned around and stared at her.

"Are all shades like this?", she asked, staring at them with fear in her eyes, "These aren't like the ones the founders showed us in the Upside-Down Palace."

"The founders...?", Angel started, but Ernst interrupted her, rubbing the back of his head with an indulgent smile.

"Don't worry, seaver. They're not. In fact, these are some of the scarier ones I've seen, and I've been alive for four hundred and seventy-eight years."

Reihan sighed internally. *Missing the point...*

"This is strange, though", Kadie said after another moment had passed, "I've seen some pretty messed up shades even as far up as the Artisan's Quarters, where the kids' dad lives, but they're all still recognisable. Like, they're malformed pets, stumm nightmares, or half-realised wishes — crap like that. These are different."

"They're amalgamated fear manifestations", Angel explained, "They usually congregate in the mind fog below the city. It's rare that they even take such solid shape, let alone wander around."

"Then... why are they here?", Mikhail asked.

He was met with silence. Reihan kept her face deliberately level. Had the Watchtower become a nexus of fear for enough people in the Travelling City that they inadvertently directed the focus of their subconscious here? Was there some hidden connection between this place and the mind fog below the city? Or had the cloud sea itself seeped up through the tunnel network without any of them noticing? But that would mean the entire Undercity would already be drenched in the stuff. And that couldn't be right because she and Lukacz had walked through it just earlier that day.

Maybe the shades had been summoned by someone. Someone who wanted them to stay far away from this place.

"Either way, we keep going. Nothing we can do about it now", Ernst decided.

The upper floors were as infested as the ones below. Each viewing room and platform was submerged in half-defined shades whose bodies convulsed in the light and whose minds focused solely on destroying whatever entered their lair. Thick-lidded, red eyes blinked up at them, drenched in hatred or confusion. Stumps made up entirely of long, thick scissors scratched their way towards them until they were met by Reihan and Ernst's long swords. A headless shadow woman singing without a throat was hacked to pieces by Kadie. Flying through the air and leaving a strange wetness behind, dozens of barely visible spiders found their end with Mikhail and Amber's arrows. They hacked until their arms were sore, and their breath was raw with the black dust that emerged from the shadows whenever their bodies were destroyed. It lingered even after Angel told the shadows that their existence was an affront to the dead gods and that they should never have been born at all.

Finally, they reached the end of the staircase and climbed through a trapdoor into the top of the tower. A wide, white hall greeted them with reverent silence, encased by high windows and long-fluttering white curtains. No furniture bore witness to the passing time, nor were there any signs that this space had ever been inhabited. That is, apart from a few scratches they found near the trapdoor that looked as though they had been left by human fingernails. Although all the windows were closed, the white curtains moved in an eerie breeze.

Reihan stepped closer to the edge of the round hall. She could see the sun setting in the distance, blood-red rays sprawled out across the horizon. An eternity of clouds lay before her, the sole seaver at the helm of an impossible ship, made to some unknowable end.

"There's nobody here", Mikhail said pointlessly.

"I knew it", Kadie whispered, "I knew it. Everyone said I was crazy, but I was right."

"Gods alive", Ernst muttered. An archaic saying these days when all signs pointed to the gods being long dead.

Unlike Reihan, he didn't look at the clouds but down at the city, at the myriad of tiny walkways, bridges, and alleys that looked so small and so dark from their vantage point.

"The founders truly left us to our own devices", he said slowly, "But why?"

"Nobody's ever led us, boy", Angel said sharply, "The city has always steered itself."

"Then what is keeping us from crashing into the continent?", Amber asked, "Or from getting too close to the ground where the cannibals and murderers will get us?"

"Cannibals and murderers", Reihan echoed with barely

concealed scepticism. She couldn't help herself. Amber shrugged.

"There's got to be a reason we left, right? Nobody builds a flying city if they're not trying to fly away from something."

"How do we even know the continent is real now?", Kadie snapped, "Everything outside this city might well be a manifestation. That might be the reason why no one who sails off by themselves ever returns."

Mikhail did not say anything. His face was pale as he watched the people on the streets below. It was impossible to know what he was thinking.

"It doesn't matter, K. People like us only ever guess at the truth. We fight through the dark, hoping that at some point there'll be someone to remember us", Ernst said slowly, then turned around.

"All we can do is our part. And our part is to make others aware of what is happening here."

He gestured at the bombs on Kadie's back.

"If we set them off here, the debris should fall over the uninhabited side. Government will be able to repair most of the Watchtower, but..."

He sighed.

"Hopefully, it'll make people look. Hopefully, it'll make somebody think about what's happening to our city."

Kadie nodded and lined the bombs up so the debris would fly Westward and roll safely down the cliffs into the cloud sea.

Reihan knew she had to make a decision now.

Destroying any part of the Travelling City was an act of

domestic terrorism punishable by imprisonment or immediate execution. As a seaver, it was her right to effect this punishment. Ernst was a formidable fighter, and the rest of Ka'a weren't weak, but they were not expecting her to turn against them. In her estimation, she still stood a decent chance to take them on, which would allow her to protect the Watchtower.

If, on the other hand, she decided that she did not want to take that risk, she should still report the identity and goals of the terrorists to the Enforcers. At least that way the Government would find out who to punish for the Watchtower's destruction.

But if she was being honest with herself, she wasn't entirely sure she disagreed with what Ka'a were doing. To whatever end the Watchtower had originally been built, it was no longer fulfilling that purpose. They were floating aimlessly through the cloud sea, that much was undeniable.

And what if that was dangerous?

Who would warn them of future Invasions or an impending collision?

If there had once been a plan – a location the city was supposed to reach – who made sure they were still on the right course?

In a city so enraptured with its own fantasies and illusions, maybe it took a shock to make everyone pay attention.

What would Seamus do? *No.* She knew what Seamus would do.

The other seaver – ... they didn't speak much and agreed on less.

And she had never spoken to the founders, had only ever been instructed by them.

No. It was her decision. There was power in that.

So, she stayed silent. She followed the others down the Watchtower and stood by as Kadie manifested the bombs' triggers to disappear. They heard a rumble deep within the earth, like the roar of an angry giant, as the stones rolled down the Cliffside to the West. Ernst gave Kadie's shoulders a few hard squeezes, and she smiled her thin smile at him. Angel did not speak much, clearly deep in thought about something. Mikhail and Amber walked near the front, eager to leave the tunnels behind. Reihan stayed right behind them.

"You should come by for food sometimes. The kids miss you", she caught Kadie saying, "I thought you said that you liked my cooking."

"Hah", Ernst made, "Am I that good a liar?"

"Shut up", Kadie laughed, "Come by anyway."

"I'll try. I don't want to see them until I'm better. Don't want them to remember me shouting or … you know."

Kadie didn't respond. Ernst sighed.

At the end of the tunnel, the aircraft still waited for Reihan, with the sphere whirring in the fading rays of sunlight.

"Thanks for the seaver", Ernst said, then tossed his remaining sword over the railing, "As promised, you and your master may have my services for one job in return."

The sphere bobbed up and down, then motioned to the side so Reihan could jump back onto the ship.

"Are you sure she won't tell on us?", Kadie hissed, "Maybe it would be better to –"

"This one's going to the Casino, K", Ernst said, "It'll never come back."

CHAPTER 24: ELLIS

"You and your megalomania!", Ellis laughed as she and Phillippe returned from the bar, laughing and sipping their second round of cocktails.

"'Oh yeah, I can't see anything else, so I'll just try to move that planet over there like it's a billiard ball'", she imitated him. Phillippe gave her a little bow and licked the sweet cream from the top of his drink.

"Manipulating impossible scenarios is what I do, dearest nightmare", he said with a wide grin, "And it's always nice when I can use all this power to do something that's actually useful."

An attendant informed Phillippe and Ellis that they had won a free holiday in an Upper City manor, each during a different Season. Phillippe would have it in the height of Summer when the outer walls turned into cool blue springs, and Ellis had it when the surrounding woods were coloured red for Autumn, and the wide porch smelled like hot chocolate and cinnamon.

They spotted some people from their group after the game

had finished. The beautiful woman threw Phillippe an appreciative glance from the other end of the bar, and Ellis spotted the man with the gold-plated implants at the edge of a large group of people who loudly discussed setting up a game of their own.

As they made their way back to their table, they spotted the kind-eyed man being escorted by a pair of Enforcers, his expression grim and downcast and his hands shaking as he tried to smooth out his plain shirt. Without causing much of a stir, the three of them walked through a portal towards the end of the hall. They promptly disappeared when they reached its edges.

"We-eird", Ellis made, "Usually, Enforcers make such a big hu-ha when you're in trouble. It's how you know they're not actually that scary; cause they give you like a million warnings before they ever take out their shiny little weapons. It's the seaver you gotta watch – those bastards will kill you just because."

"Why would he be in trouble?", Phillippe asked, "He made it out, same as the rest of us."

"Yeaaah, but the big snake had to help him out, remember? I'm pretty sure you've got to complete the challenges yourself to win."

"So, he lost the gambit. And now the house is taking … what, his time?", Phillippe said slowly, recalling the man's plain clothes. He might have minimal manifestation abilities and might have only made it up here by using mind games and luck, hoping to turn his life around with some big win.

"Jup. Might be it's time to pay up. Poor kid", Ellis replied, stirring her blood-red drink that smelled like vanilla and sugar. She pouted.

"I don't like this place. So much of it feels desperate."

"Agreed."

Phillippe crinkled his forehead.

"If think about it for long enough, being here doesn't make sense, does it? At least for most people. If you're powerful enough to make it up to this floor, you probably have access to most of the things that you want anyway. So, why gamble?"

"Why not? Humans make no sense. If they have too much, their next trick becomes losing themselves in the most devastating way possible."

Ellis took a deep sip of her drink. The vanilla tasted so strong that it almost felt unreal. She didn't like it. She liked things that didn't pretend to be something else. She liked Lukacz because he never changed. She liked herself for the same reason. But this place, which should be a monument to some long-past war, felt nothing like itself. All it did was put up fancy things to distract everyone from the destruction and –

"You know, wonder boy, we're kind of dumb", she suddenly said. Phillippe laughed.

"Never a good start. Have we missed something obvious?"

"Well, where do you think the Enforcers are taking sad boy?"

"If he did indeed gamble with his time, he will have been taken as a serf. And Reihan said she thought the serfs were kept in the apartments above the …."

Phillippe interrupted himself and smiled sardonically.

"Dead gods, you're right. We are dumb. We just need to follow the Enforcers whenever they escort someone away."

Ellis grinned.

"It's okay. We'll just pretend we thought of that wayyy earlier."

"Deal."

After stepping through the portal, Phillippe and Ellis found themselves inside a coffee shop. Purple leather couches sat back to back with low tables, burdened with the weight of cappuccinos, tea, and lavish displays of cakes, slow-roasting beans, and incense. All windows were curtained off. A man with six arms was playing the piano in the corner of the room, next to a contrabass seemingly plucking its own strings and a litter of ginger kittens asleep on a large white pillow.

People sat in pairs, facing each other in silent contests while others looked on, eating cake, clinking their teaspoons against delicate china cups, and clicking their teeth together.

"Welcome", said a masked game attendant in purple robes that perfectly fit the colour of the couches, "Welcome to Identity, a gambit for a month of change. The house offers several prizes of your choice, which you may peruse on the far side of our café."

They pointed towards a chalkboard behind them, half-concealed behind a big-leaved plant. The plant itself was covered over and over with little eyes that looked greedily towards the visitors.

"Please help yourselves to refreshments before partaking in the gamble. Just be aware that before playing, you will need to –"

"Thank you", Phillippe said in his high, polite voice that Ellis found irrationally funny, "We are actually just passing through."

"Passing through?", the attendant replied, and their confusion was visible even behind their silver mask, "This is a game room. If you enter a game room, you have agreed to participate in the associated gamble and bet the required stakes. Besides –"

They gestured around the small café, its dark walls, and closed windows.

"There is nowhere else to go from here."

That wasn't entirely true, Ellis thought. On the other side of the piano, behind a particularly tall cake stand, was a subtle oak door, barely visible as it matched the rest of the café walls. So, this really was the second floor on the graphic Lukacz had shown them.

Phillippe did not argue, and Ellis wasn't in the mood to talk to the attendant either, so they strolled over to the closest cake stand and piled up confections on two white porcelain plates. Together with two cups of dark, cream-thick coffee, they carried their towers of blue icing and fluffy pink batter over to an unoccupied couch before picking a close-by pair of players to observe.

"Identity, huh?", Ellis said, then tried a piece of cake. Like her cocktail, it tasted a little too much. She washed it down with some coffee that was just as bitter as the one Lukacz made during long nights.

"Looks like a pretty boring game", she said after they'd watched the pair silently stare at each other for a little while. Phillippe raised one perfectly arched silver eyebrow.

"Really? Aren't you noticing anything?"

Ellis threw him a sceptical look, then fixated more closely on the minute movements on the pair's faces. The two women stared at each other unblinkingly. One was middle-aged, with dull blue eyes and unusual red hair that clung to her shoulders in thin strands. The other woman had barely left childhood, with dewy skin and short, blonde hair caressing red cheeks. Neither wore any visible makeup, and their clothes were surprisingly plain for this part of the Casino. In fact, as Ellis's eyes wandered to the other café visitors, she noticed the same lack of finery and extravagance with many of them. Only Phillippe still donned the shining, sparkling fashion that had dominated the lower betting hall. Phillippe followed her gaze and nodded imperceptibly.

"The attendant did mention that we had to do something before we started playing, right? I think we need to strip ourselves of all exterior manifestations."

"Why?", Ellis asked, honestly puzzled, "I mean, I don't really care, but why make everyone go bare-faced? Is this some weird power thing?"

Before Phillippe could respond, the staring contest they had been observing finally reached its conclusion. The young blonde woman's nose morphed into a long black beak, and her eyes turned into stitched-on grey buttons. More thread started to snake around her lips, beginning to tie them together, but the young woman raised her hands before it could finish the job.

"I yield", she said breathlessly, "I yield, I yield."

The red-haired woman smiled thinly and waved over the attendant.

"You've got to stop putting me with newbies", she complained insincerely, "I'm going to feel bad."

"We match people based on our internal manifestation ranking", the attendant explained, then offered their hand to the beaked and button-eyed visitor. She was shaking on her feet and seemed unable to see.

"Is there… any way that I could pay to have this removed before the month is up?", she asked, her voice shaky, "I need to work, you know."

"Of course", the attendant replied, "You may exchange the immediate removal of the identity manifestation for ownership of your home. I believe you work as a jewellery manufacturer in the Artisan's Quarters, yes? And you declared one of those nice flats that overlook the Brothel?"

The young woman remained silent. Her face was locked into a frown, as if she was already trying to remove the manifestation that had been stitched onto her. Ahead of the game, she had probably been told that it was impossible and, foolishly, hadn't questioned it at the time. Now, her acceptance of that fact created a mental barrier that would make it nigh on impossible for her to manifest on herself.

Phillippe and Ellis exchanged a look. Phillippe had been right about the structure of the place. No more gambling for sparkles and tat – this was the real deal. Ellis felt her heart start to race.

"If there were no stakes, what would be the point of the gamble, dear?", the attendant asked the young woman, but their voice was just as emotionless as before, "Now, will you require escorting out?"

The woman nodded weakly, and the attendant took her arm. Before leading her through the portal, they turned around to Ellis and Phillippe.

"Once you have finished your refreshments, please drop all existing manifestations affecting your bodies. I will then pair you with an appropriate opponent. Maybe… yes, the lady nightmare can go with Emma here. And we'll have to find something special for Phillippe, of course."

'Emma' gave Ellis a sardonic smile as she looked her up and down.

"Playing with a manifestation incarnate? Oh, that'll be novel, at least. Do take care not to let me rip you apart", she said, then got up for a slice of cake.

Ellis turned away. She was suddenly very aware of her surroundings. The fine film of sugary icing coating the roof of her mouth, the clanking of spoons against porcelain, the rust on the bass's strings that came off as the instrument was plucked. She slowly walked to an empty area of the café, carrying her slowly depreciating stock of sweets that suddenly felt as heavy as steel.

"All right, so this seems to be a pretty straightforward

exercise", Phillippe mused. He perched on the edge of the couch and sipped from his coffee cup with his little finger extended.

"Break through the other manifester's sense of self, then change their appearance until they yield."

He winked.

"Well, in the Brothel I always change my clients' appearances. And with them, I often have to break through rather many layers of shame, incredulity, and inertia. Even when they requested the service, mind you. People are absurd, but that is working in our favour for once."

He grinned, twirling the cup around his long fingers.

"Once they are told about the game, everyone will focus on their appearance changing, even if they are actively trying to prevent that very thing from happening. That will be an angle worth exploiting, I bet, and –"

Ellis found it hard to listen to him. She felt a ringing sound settling in her ears. Her legs wouldn't stop shaking, and she sunk deeper into the couch's backrest, trying to hide inside the leather.

"What is it?", Phillippe asked, his voice suddenly very soft.

"I can't do this", Ellis said. Pressing the words out was agonising when all her instincts screamed at her to stay still.

"Why not?", Phillippe asked, and Ellis was grateful that he wasn't trying to argue with her like Lukacz would have done. Lukacz who believed that she could do anything in the world.

"Because she's right", Ellis replied, her voice falling, "She'll rip me apart. There won't be anything left of me."

"What do you mean? I don't think they're allowed to kill –"

"You don't get it", the nightmare snapped, "You humans are just a collection of genes and DNA and bullshit, all whirled together random-like. Nobody really cares what you look like. Most parents will still love an ugly kid."

"And you were created", Phillippe said very slowly, "You were created to look exactly the way you do."

"Yes."

Ellis pressed out the word. She hated talking about this stuff. Why did it always have to matter what she was? She didn't want to remember how fragile her hold on the world truly was. She just wanted to exist.

"Hey."

Phillippe carefully poked her arm.

"Hey, gobbledygook. Don't fade on me now. Tell me what's going on."

Phillippe was here. He knew she existed. And he was boss man's kid, and boss man also knew she existed.

She took a deep breath.

"I was made to be me. I don't really think there was a point to it all, but if I stop being who I am, who knows if I won't just disappear? And even if I don't fade, if I change too much, I'll exist for no reason at all. Not even for the chance of there being a reason."

The words sounded as foolish out in the open as they felt inside her head. And still, the fear they brought was real. The sweat on her brows, the heaving chest, the lead legs, all of that was real.

Phillippe sat beside her and put his arm around her shoulders with a feather-light touch, so the heat from his body didn't make things worse.

"Okay, so you won't play. That's fine. We can work around that."

"Can we?", Ellis asked, her voice so shaky that it sounded like she was crying, "The attendant said we couldn't leave."

"Since when do people like us play by the rules, El?", Phillippe asked, squeezing her shoulders just a little, "You're a nightmare. I'm pretty sure that disrupting things is one of your many, many purposes in this life."

Ellis blinked up at him.

"Yeah?", she asked. His smile was as bright as the sun.

"Yeah! In fact, I have no doubt!"

She sniffled, then tried to match his smile. It was easier than she thought it would be.

"Okay. Okay! I guess we already found the door to the apartments. So, you just need one massive commotion-disruption-nightmare thingie to make sure you can sneak through, right?"

She brushed some stray black hairs out of her face.

"Let's just hope Reihan's on the other side already", Phillippe said, and his eyes wandered to the inconspicuous wooden door at the back of the room. Ellis knew what he was thinking. They couldn't see any Enforcers in the café, but that didn't mean they weren't there. They could be disguised as some of the guests, they could be sitting right behind the door, or they could have turned into parts of the furniture. They could be sitting on one right now. Creepy buggers.

"Well, I'll cause one big fucking hu-ha, you better believe it. If anything will give Reihan a chance to do her part, that'll be it", she promised, even though she had no idea what she would do just yet. But she'd think of something. She always thought of something.

"So, let's hope your pet seaver is as reliable as you all think she is because it'll be the best chance we have."

"And what are you going to do?", Phillippe asked, and she thought the worry in his voice was real.

"Not get caught."

The nightmare laughed at the uncharacteristically stern expression on Phillippe's face.

"I can always teleport out once I've caused enough havoc."

"Okay, but … be careful. We have to…."

He was visibly straining to come up with something, and Ellis had to laugh.

"We still have to become best friends, wonder boy. I know. We'll think of something to do after this."

She flicked his nose.

"Now you go and find your brother. Don't let the seaver kill you. And watch over boss man for me."

With that, she got up and, before anyone could stop her, raced back through the portal. She was Ellis. Nobody would change that. And she was about to show this place the biggest fucking nightmare it would ever have the privilege of witnessing.

THETRAVELLING CITY

CHAPTER 25: REIHAN

The airship delivered Reihan to a landing platform next to the bottom of the Mineshafts. At first glance, it was just an empty outcrop of land, but after a few moments, a young man teleported onto the platform, clad in purple silks and with his face hidden behind a silver mask.

"We got your message", he said, "We're more than happy to take a palace seaver if she's the real deal."

The sphere whirred in a way that Reihan thought looked decidedly irritated.

"Yes, yes, I'm sure you've done your own tests. Nothing wrong with a bit of caution, is there? You and your associates will receive your boon once she's been thoroughly checked."

Reihan felt the manifestations tear at her skin. The test was much more aggressive than whatever the bull-man had done. Even though she felt her inborn resistance kick in, the strain would start affecting her sooner or later. The sphere moved up and down; then, suddenly, the young man was engulfed in a case of lightning. Just for a flash, but it left the ground steaming, and Reihan blinked against the light that remained stuck to her pupils, clouding her vision. The young man took a few seconds to steady his breath, then narrowed his eyes.

"Now, was that display truly necessary?", he asked, "I'm just following protocol to ensure that you aren't selling me a fake. You will get paid as soon as I have seen the seaver in action to confirm her legitimacy."

Despite the man's calm façade, Reihan could feel the tension building behind his eyes. Once humans started using their fancy manifestation powers on one another, a fight almost always broke out. She took a tumbling step forward.

"What is happening?", she asked in a way that she hoped sounded anxious and robotic at the same time, "The bull-man said I was going to a Casino. Can I go there now? I need to work. It is important that I work."

She forced her hands to twitch just a little. The young man's eyes followed the motion, and he cleared his throat.

"Yes, we should take care of you, shouldn't we? Seaver have been known to get violent when you leave them dormant for long enough."

He took a step back and pressed his right hand into thin air. With a small 'ding', a door opened out of nowhere, revealing a small elevator cabin. There was nothing inside except blank steel walls, caving inwards near the top, and a thin metal railing.

"In you go", the young man said to Reihan and followed her

into the elevator. The sphere bobbed up and down as it watched them leave.

They did not speak on the long ascent to the Casino. The young man took out a pocketbook with a frayed, hand-painted bookmark sticking out the top, then nestled into one of the metal corners and began to read. Reihan stood stock-still even though her arms and legs were aching. Why in the world had her fellow seaver established a reputation for robotic behaviour and not for perpetual hunger or sloth? She could really do with a break.

The elevator rattled, and Reihan thought she could hear screams of joy echo from far away. As night closed in, more people were sure to raise their kites for the festival, and many had to be aglow in blues and purples by now. An optimistic part of her still hoped that Phillippe would be able to take her up there at the end of the night so they could watch the festival together, looking down on a glowing paper blanket as the new bedrock of their little world.

Finally, the elevator stopped, and the Casino attendant got back on his feet and smoothed out his robes. The doors opened into a wood-clad corridor, with small, panelled doors on one side and wide-sweeping windows on the other, looking out onto the Weeping Stairs and the Artisan's Quarters. Small, glowing kites rose in the caverns while giant paper dragons roamed the skies, releasing fires made of sparkles and glitter. And there were just as many outside the Casino windows, racing one another through the air and proudly displaying the intricate designs on the backs of their wings, their long-fluttering tails, and the beautifully layered colours that crowned their undersides.

Everything outside the windows lay on the side, and it took a little while until Reihan had re-oriented herself. She remembered this from when she had first left the Upside-Down Palace, but that did not make it any more pleasant on a repeat. The masked man shifted while watching her bend her head this way and that, then he finally cleared his throat.

"Why is this bothering you? Aren't you seaver built to sustain perspective changes?"

Reihan ignored him, closing one eye, then another. She could hear no footsteps down the corridor. None in any of the rooms immediately adjacent to their location either. Did that mean that Phillippe and Ellis had already caused a distraction, drawing the Enforcers and seaver down into the betting halls? It was impossible to know, but this might be her best chance.

The elevator door was still open, and she could see a small button to close it.

"Are you actually a Palace seaver?", the young man sighed, "Bah, I knew this was a scam. That's exactly why I don't —"

Before he could finish his sentence, Reihan opened her eyes again and, with a quick strike, hit the pressure points on the young man's throat and the side of his head. He slumped down, immediately unconscious. Reihan carried him into the elevator, then pulled a small key from a hidden pocket in her uniform. She unlocked the metal ring that was still clasped around her neck and attached it to the attendant, tying the chain around the metal railing. That should give her some time, at least, even though he could probably manifest the chain away with a bit of effort. But it was amazing how much humans forgot they were capable of when they were locked up and panicking.

She exited the elevator and closed its doors by pressing the button. Then she took a deep breath, re-oriented herself fully, and listened. Still no footsteps close by. *No time like the present,* she told herself, then walked up to one of the windows. As she had suspected, there was no obvious mechanism for opening them, and the glass looked firm enough to withstand a kick or a punch. It made sense. Surely the Casino owners would not risk the serfs escaping through the windows if they happened to get out of their apartments. But she was a seaver. A seaver who had used a dear old friend's declining mental state to convince him to release her restraints even though he had spent much of the last century telling her that she was not ready.

Ready or not, here I go, Reihan thought with a mad internal chuckle. She took a deep breath, then felt power well up inside her as she concentrated on tapping into her reserves. The aches in her arms and legs disappeared, and she could feel her head clear up like she'd just awoken after a long night's rest. There would be hell to pay for this later. There always was. But this rush – she could get addicted to it.

She checked for footsteps one last time, then kicked the window with the tops of her boots, connecting the steel inlays she had fitted there with the glass. It shattered, and shards of glass fell into the sky like rain. Reihan held onto the wooden beams to either side of the opening to prevent herself from falling behind them.

Still no footsteps. So far, so good. She brushed the broken glass from the windowsill, sat down and watched the sea of kites for a little while, waiting for Lukacz to emerge. One heartbeat passed, then another. She felt strangely calm as she imagined herself, in some strange way, to be the hidden centre of the festival. She watched it every year but had never much felt like a part of it. It wasn't her manifestations that caused the Seasons to change. And people always got nervous when they saw her walking through the crowds. But now she was close enough to touch the kites if she wanted to, run her white fingers over their soft paperbacks, and feel the paint strokes on their wings.

She heard a flap to her right and looked up to see Lukacz weave between the kites and their stringed anchors, sporting almost imperceptible wings. She waved at him, then jumped back into the corridor to make room for him to land.

"Very nicely done", he said once he had squeezed his wings through the window, then made them disappear, "I assume your friend removed your restrictions?"

"No", Reihan lied, although she suspected it may be a pointless deception, "I found a weak point in the glass."

"Hm", Lukacz made with a nod, then looked around, "I don't suppose you heard anything from Ellis and Phillippe?"

"No, although nobody reacted to me breaking the window, so I'm assuming they did something to draw people's attention downstairs."

"I never had any doubts that they were capable of that", Lukacz replied drily, "Let's just hope there will be a Casino left once they're done with whatever they were planning."

Reihan laughed quietly.

They followed the corridor past the broken window, the path cast in the deep shadows of the wood panelling and the almost vanished sun. No decorations adorned the walls, no gold or carpets or paintings of mysterious locations from far away. A purely functional space meant to contain those with nothing left to sell except for their time. Reihan concentrated on the rhythm of their steps to distract herself from the uncomfortable thoughts that wrapped themselves around her throat.

They seemed to have chosen the correct direction as the path snaked downward, presumably toward the betting halls. Eventually, they reached an open door on the right, revealing a plain room. In its centre hung a glowing gold sphere, its light dimming and brightening in a breathing rhythm. A vague humanoid shape hung suspended in its centre, although Reihan could not make out any identifying features. The sphere was inspected by two seaver, their long white hair unkempt and their uniform crumpled. They turned around once they heard Reihan and Lukacz at the door, and Reihan saw that their white eyes had red rims around the edges where the fluids had been poorly maintained.

"W-what –", one of them started, clearly unused to speaking. Reihan cursed internally.

She took a step forward and narrowed her eyes.

"Did I tell you to stop the inspection? The human could have died in the time you took to allow yourselves to be distracted."

The seaver sucked in a sharp breath and quickly turned back to the glowing sphere, counting breaths and measuring the temperature of its exterior. Reihan pointedly closed the door and motioned Lukacz to follow her.

"I'm sorry you had to see that", Lukacz said after a long silence.

"Do you think I don't know what happens to the other seaver in this city?", she snapped, the words escaping her hot-burning throat, "All those illegal clones that humans build but don't know how to maintain, and who can't maintain themselves because they're never taught how to, and who aren't given the right kit, and –"

She interrupted herself. She took two deep breaths, then shook her head.

"They expect to be talked to like that. So, that's what they respond to. I think that's the part that gets to me."

Lukacz nodded silently.

A little while later, they heard footsteps from further down the corridor. Reihan thought about hiding in one of the serf's rooms but worried about wasting time. If there were just newborn seaver left up here, she could deal with those.

Once they turned the corner, however, she knew she had miscalculated. It was a seaver, but this specimen had perfectly groomed skin and braided hair, wore a blue silk shirt underneath his open uniform, and his tightly lined eyes narrowed in suspicion when he saw Reihan and Lukacz.

"Halt", he said, "What is the human doing outside of containment?"

Reihan groaned internally.

"His services were being required. Alexander wanted help with maintaining one of the illusions."

The other seaver raised his eyebrows.

"Did he now? That'd be a first. And with the world's biggest commotion going on downstairs, too. What fortuitous timing."

Reihan shrugged, although she felt her chest tighten just a little. Alexander was really here. This confirmed it.

"And with Alexander's room being in the opposite direction. How curious", the seaver continued.

"I don't know what you want me to tell you", Reihan replied, cursing internally, "Orders are orders."

"Yes, yes, very good", the seaver replied, brushing a strand of long hair out of his forehead, "And now, why don't you tell me what Palace-born Reihan, protégé of Seamus the Long-Lived, is doing pretending to be a new-born idiot."

A pause.

"You know who I am", she said pointlessly. The seaver laughed.

"Obviously. I used to work with the Enforcers, too, you know. Saw you and Seamus go on missions back in his heyday. And I don't think I'll ever forget that tone of yours, even when you're playing dumb."

"So, what are you doing here?", Reihan asked, playing for time.

The other seaver shrugged.

"Got sick of us always being the first ones to be sent into the death traps. Watching all your friends die gets old after a while. So, I took the first gig that got me out of there."

He shrugged.

"Transferring is possible, just as long as you keep it off the books. And the Casino gives you quite a few privileges if you're willing to train the new-borns."

"Right."

"So. Reihan. The far more interesting question is why you are here."

His smile grew wider.

"Come on, it's just us and some serf still waking up from containment. And listen, I'm in half a mind to let you walk out with him if you just let me know what's going on. Did they take in someone important by accident or something?"

"Something like that", Reihan said.

She had to give it to Lukacz; he knew how to stay calm in a crisis. He was willing to play the part of the disoriented serf who barely recalled how to walk, let alone speak. But she could feel him close his fists behind his back. If she did not de-escalate the situation soon, he would attack. She sighed.

"Look. What's your chosen name?"

It was a sign of respect to ask a seaver for their chosen and not their designated name. And she had guessed correctly that the seaver before her had chosen for himself.

"Freeday", he replied. Reihan had to fight against a fond smile as she remembered frantic Fee from the Asylum. She hadn't spent enough time with her since this whole thing had begun.

"Freeday", she replied, "I'm going to need you to trust me. This is important for all of us."

"A big ask", Freeday replied sharply. Reihan sighed again.

"Seaver Sivel", she said quietly. Freeday gave her a long look.

"Seaver Sivel", he replied, "Don't make me regret this."

He allowed them to pass, continuing his lonely patrol through the corridors. Lukacz and Reihan continued until they could no longer hear his footsteps, then he stopped.

"Explain", he demanded, his voice low.

"You don't need to know about this", Reihan replied.

"Yes, I do. You work for the Government, and I am one of its acting members. You will tell me all about Seaver Sivel."

"Don't order me around. You don't outrank me", Reihan snapped.

"In this instance, I do. As an acting member of Government, I can give you commands that you must obey."

He scowled.

"Obey."

Reihan scoffed.

"We seaver were made to protect you. That doesn't mean we recognise your authority in all things."

The air around Lukacz's arm whirred. Reihan knew he was about to summon a weapon. She felt her fingers tense. She could summon her sword to meet his attack. But that would already reveal more to him than she should. Instead, she used her reserves to push Lukacz away from her, slamming him into the closet wall.

"Don't even think about it, human", she hissed. Lukacz did not respond, and after she blinked, she realised he wasn't there anymore. Before Reihan had the chance to realise what was happening, he already stood behind her, his arm tight around her stomach and his other hand holding a blade against her neck.

"I regret having to do this", he said calmly, "But I cannot work with you if I do not trust your intentions. Speak honestly, and I will release you."

"Is this really worth risking this entire operation for? One seaver secret?"

Reihan squirmed, but Lukacz's grasp was too firm, even against her newfound power. She imagined that he was manifesting his strength to be tenfold of what it normally was.

"A seaver conspiracy is more dangerous than any destruction my sons could bring. I have heard stories amongst the Enforcers of seaver disappearing at conspicuous times. I've never put much stock in it, but –"

"You will regret this", Reihan spat and felt the bile run down her neck like spit. She couldn't remember the last time she had been so angry. And she could do nothing. She was helpless, like a child.

"Speak, seaver", Lukacz said again, then pressed the blade into her skin. She could feel it cut through layer after layer, as slowly as a ticking clock, "I will not ask a third time."

Reihan breathed frantically. At this moment, she hated him and all the other ungrateful, greedy, cruel humans. But this wasn't worth dying for.

"Some seaver are planning a rebellion", she said, "They don't want to serve you people anymore. They don't think the city's stability is worth their lives."

"How many?", Lukacz asked. He did not sound surprised.

"Maybe a hundred. Maybe less. They don't represent most of us."

She coughed.

"Seaver Sivel are opposed to violence. They don't want to kill you, they –"

"Of course they don't", Lukacz responded, his voice entirely level, "No rebellion ever turns violent. How concrete are their plans?"

"I don't know."

"Stop lying", he said dispassionately and buried the knife deeper into her neck. Reihan cried out.

"I'm not lying! I'm not a part of them. I went to a few meetings, but I'm not – I didn't think…."

She struggled to concentrate with the blood running down her throat.

"*I hate you*. I hate the way you treat us. But if we don't watch you, you'll destroy the world. And, unlike you humans, I can live for something other than myself."

Lukacz hesitated for a moment, then released her. She pressed her hand against her bleeding skin and stared up at him with tears running down her cheeks.

"Very well. Thank you, Reihan", the Overseer said, "You've been very helpful."

CHAPTER 26: PHILLIPPE

After Ellis flew through the portal and the game attendant chased after her, Phillippe sat down opposite Emma, who accepted his invitation to play. Now that all Casino personnel had left the café, he felt more comfortable shedding the manifestations with which he disguised himself and to re-assume the shape into which he had been born. He and Emma fixated each other unblinkingly, and Phillippe's gaze wandered across the fine wrinkles around her eyes, the red lipstick that matched her hair perfectly, and the small pearl earrings that looked dull in the stale café light.

Suddenly, Phillippe felt a relentless pull on his skin, ready to rip it straight from his bones and tie it around the bass's rusty strings. He realised the staring was in some ways a ruse – while focusing on her appearance, he lost track of his own, and now he needed to spend valuable seconds refocusing on what he thought he looked like without his manifestations. It was more difficult than he had imagined, seeing as he hadn't worn this skin in months. He would have had an easier time maintaining an illusion he used more often, like the androgynous black-haired man or the woman in ethereal armour.

When Phillippe had been young, other children had sometimes manifested on him as a prank, changing his hands to claws or having him grow a tail beneath his trousers. He had never been able to stop them. He had run to his father crying and asked Lukacz to turn him back to normal. Until his father had left, and he hadn't felt like asking anyone else for help. Then, he had just waited for the thoughts to disappear with time and had endured the bull's horns, the feathered ears, and the cloven feet. He wondered how Lukacz would feel if he told him that story. If it would change anything, or if it would just reinforce his view that his son was a pathetic weakling and had never been worth returning for.

"Hey, are you paying attention?", Emma asked with a sly grin. Phillippe looked down and realised she had elongated his nose to the point where it dangled between his legs. Red, soupy liquid dripped from his pores, and his eyes started to itch. He sighed at her cruel lack of imagination, then changed the illusion by creating a subtly different version of his appearance. Manipulating someone else's fantasy was fine. It was his own that he struggled to control. Emma raised her eyebrows.

"Impressive. Most people panic once I manage to break through their shield."

"Shield?", Phillippe echoed.

"You know. Your conception of self."

"Ah. Right."

He opened his mouth, then closed it again. Instead, he concentrated on her and imagined her eyebrows growing outwards like bridges suspended by invisible hands. Nothing too strange, nothing that could inadvertently hurt her. Emma blinked, and her eyes narrowed in renewed concentration. But after another second, her eyebrows started to grow in exactly the way Phillippe had imagined.

"How are you —?", she started but was interrupted by a noise ringing out of the portal.

Whatever Ellis did, it was loud. A mountain of glass shattered, explosions chased one another, and Phillippe was pretty certain that he heard various animals roar alongside shouts of 'oh dead gods' and 'what the fuck is this?' The other café visitors perked up and interrupted their games, with some in the stages of a rather gruesome transformation. Then, the door at the end of the café flew open, and a small troop of Enforcers came racing out. Without so much as a glance in the direction of the guests, they jumped through the portal back to the first betting hall.

A moment of silence settled between them, fragile like a spider's web.

"What —?", an elderly man started from halfway across the room. Then, another louder explosion rang out of the portal, and a small flame shot out of its golden exterior.

"Dead gods, we have to get out of here!", Phillippe shouted and tried to make his voice sound as panicked as possible, "We're all going to die!"

"Yeah, screw this", Emma said, then with the blink of an eye, she was gone. The other visitors followed suit as they teleported out of the café, leaving only clattering cups and plates that shattered on the ground. Phillippe allowed himself a slight grin, then moved towards the half-hidden door on the other side of the room. Sometimes people were just so easy to manipulate. He wished it surprised him more, but he felt like he was getting towards the end of people surprising him.

But there was no Reihan opening the door from her side. Perhaps she was still further up in the apartments, creating a window for Lukacz. Perhaps she was racing down the corridors at this very moment to come and find him. Perhaps something had happened to her, and she was fighting the other seaver with her bare hands. Phillippe tried to move the door handle, forcing his heart to still. But the door handle did not budge.

Of course, Phillippe thought, the Enforcers would have locked it with a manifestation lest any unsuspecting guests wander into areas where they were not allowed. But that wouldn't be enough to stop him. He imagined the handle gliding smoothly down, allowing the door to swing open. He just had to –

"Stop! What are you doing?"

The game attendant had returned through the portal. Their mask was half-burnt off, and they wore the foulest scowl Phillippe had seen in quite some time. They raised their hands, and glowing, roped bonds appeared in their palms, ready to shoot towards Phillippe and contain him.

"I heard a noise behind the door. I just thought I'd —"

Despite his choosing an appropriately whiny voice, the game attendant's face told him with excruciating clarity that they weren't buying his story.

"Step away from the door. I don't know what you and that nightmare are playing at, but it ends now."

The ropes twitched in their hands, and Phillippe felt his stomach twist. He could forcefully teleport the attendant away from here, but they could just as quickly return, and this time with help from others. And he really, really didn't want this to escalate into a fight. He knew he couldn't trust himself enough not to kill someone accidentally. And he already struggled to live with himself as it was.

He remembered the story Reihan had told him during their ill-fated date at the Amusement Park. About the man who had forced his way into his victims' minds and made them believe in his version of reality.

Surely that would be better than death? Thoughts disappeared with time, like leaves on the wind. Soon enough, Phillippe would be the only one to remember what happened here. And although he felt like he was tying himself in knots, he made the decision. He imagined the attendant looking at him and told him to see nothing. No Phillippe, no door, then turn back through the portal because there is no reason for you to be here right now. Leave and forget all about us, and nothing else will need to change.

Phillippe met no resistance to his manifestation, and after a few moments, the attendant's eyes turned as glossy as a bauble, and he stumbled back through the portal. Phillippe couldn't help but close his eyes for a moment, feeling fear and guilt rise in his throat. He remembered the disgust in Reihan's voice when she had told him about the rogue Enforcer. He was no better than that. He had never claimed to be any better than that. But he hated the thought of disappointing Reihan more than he feared her realising that she really didn't know what she was dealing with.

He forced the door open and raised his hands. But just as they had predicted, he was faced with an empty corridor snaking upwards. The Enforcers were doubtlessly chasing Ellis through the betting halls and the underwater dome, and the Casino seaver were most likely stationed further up in the apartment complexes where they guarded the serfs. He closed the door behind him and changed his appearance to match Reihan's as closely as he could, mirroring her sex, her long white hair, her skin, her eyes, and the seaver uniform she always wore at the Asylum. He knew it wasn't a particularly good illusion, but it might fool someone at first glance. And anyway, it was better than looking like the Phillippe whose face was painted onto the Casino's 'Wanted' posters.

Phillippe followed the corridor, feeling like a flash of light gliding across the dark-panelled wood. On her left, through large windows, she could see that the sun had just set and purple-glowing kites now fully conquered the sky.

As she walked up the corridor, she heard a pair of quarrelling voices. After a few more steps, she realised they were Reihan and Lukacz. The seaver sounded uncharacteristically angry, and his father's voice grew louder by the second.

"Your paranoia doesn't give you the right –", Reihan snapped. She sounded short of breath.

"This has nothing to do with paranoia. It's time to accept that you seaver don't have as much power as you think you do", Lukacz replied, "We all need to accept our place in this city. The sooner you understand yours, the better."

"And why do we need to be the ones to obey you, human?"

"Because we made you."

Reihan scoffed.

"So, you think a child should always obey its parents, then?"

Phillippe would have loved to hear the answer, but the seaver and his father must have heard her as they abruptly stopped their conversation.

"It's just me. Phillippe", she called around a bend in the corridor, then stepped into view. Lukacz was standing in the middle of the corridor, his arms raised in a defensive pose. Reihan leaned against one of the windows, hunched over and holding her throat with her right hand. Blood stained the top of her uniform and the skin around her neck.

Phillippe forgot about everything else and ran over to her.

"Let me see", she demanded, pressing her head as close to the seaver as Reihan would allow. Reihan moaned but obeyed, taking her hand from her throat where a blade had cut a thin line into her white skin. Blood was still dripping from the wound, although Phillippe guessed it wasn't deep enough to be fatal.

Still.

"Let me take care of that", she whispered and pressed a kiss against Reihan's temple before she focused on the wound with single-minded intent. She softly touched the edges of the cut until it closed, particle by particle, her powers wiping away the pain and the blood. Reihan sighed in relief, and Phillippe's mouth curved ever so slightly upwards.

"Bah", Lukacz made, "I knew it. You people are not even truly immune. What exactly do you think puts you above us now, seaver?"

Reihan did not reply, but Phillippe felt her face burn underneath her touch.

"Shut up", she told her father, even though she wasn't sure what his and Reihan's argument had been about. Reihan's grateful look was enough.

Lukacz looked around, then cleared his throat.

"Where is Ellis?", he asked.

"Causing the world's biggest distraction, from the sounds of it. You know, the one that was supposed to let you guys open the door out of the betting halls. Thanks for that, by the way."

Lukacz looked at her derisively.

"You seem to have managed just fine", he said, "If you want a gold star, I'm afraid that will have to wait."

He shook his head.

"I worry about her being caught. A sha – a nightmare attacking the Casino … they won't give her a chance to explain."

Phillippe shook her head. Jealousy sat heavy on her chest, but with Reihan leaning against her side and her brother now so very close, she could stem its weight.

"If you want to find her, then go", she said, "But I'm not waiting around. We've already wasted too much time."

Her father gave her a long look.

"You're right", he said, "And if you get to Alexander before me, I expect I will never find him again."

Phillippe scoffed.

"You don't trust me. You really don't trust me."

Lukacz's eyes flared.

"Well, who am I supposed to trust? The seaver, who plots conspiracies right under my nose? Who tells me outright that she will dissent from her conditioning if she deems it necessary? Or should I trust you? Still the most likely candidate for whoever freed your brother. Who is wanted by the Enforcers in this very Casino? Who broke the city's most important rule just to –"

His voice had risen, but he forced it back down. He turned around and started walking up the corridor back the way he and Reihan had come from.

"I don't trust any of you."

As they searched the apartment blocks, they found one door guarded where the others were not. At the very top of the tower stood a soft-glowing double door, flanked on one side by a seaver and on the other by an Enforcer.

Both shot around as soon as they saw the three intruders, and the seaver raced towards them without asking questions. Phillippe felt the Enforcer's manifestation powers settle atop them like a cage, trying to contain them.

Reihan, immune to that level of manifestation, met the other seaver head-on and countered his grapple attack with a swift pirouette that saw her behind her attacker. She grabbed the back of his head and pressed her arm around his neck to restrict his airflow.

Phillippe felt the cage crawl deeper into her skin, like a cantankerous spider burying its fangs into flesh and blood. She inhaled, then exhaled, imagining the cage lifting with her release of breath.

It ripped apart in the pale air, and then, just as the Enforcer's eyes widened in surprise, she went on the offensive. She imagined the Enforcer slamming into the closest wall, then convinced his ailing thoughts to go to sleep. The Enforcer's head slumped down, and his body slid to the floor at the exact moment as the seaver fell into Reihan's arms. Lukacz stepped over to make sure they were truly unconscious. Then he commanded a sword to appear in his hand and bent down to the Enforcer.

"Dad, what are you doing?", Phillippe asked, pressing the words out of her throat, past the shock and the exhaustion.

"They have seen me, Phillippe. I cannot be associated with a heist."

"Why? I thought this operation was legitimate?", Reihan asked.

"There are many factions in Government, more than you can imagine. If my enemies find out that I was involved in this, they'll use it to their advantage, legitimate or not."

"You having a slightly harder time in your job isn't worth two people's lives", Reihan snapped. Phillippe met her gaze, and, for once, the seaver's frustration was clear as day. This was important to her. Phillippe raised her hands, staring Lukacz straight in the eyes. Her father sighed.

"Do you really want to argue about this? Now that we're so close to our goal?"

Phillippe narrowed her eyes.

"I won't need to argue with you. Now put the sword away."

Lukacz obeyed without another word. Phillippe thought she saw the hint of a smile across Reihan's features, but by the time she turned to the seaver, she wore her neutral expression once more.

"Can you get rid of the shield?", Reihan asked, pointing towards the soft golden glow that engulfed the door.

Phillippe nodded and imagined the light sliding away from the wood like crumbling dirt washing off with a gentle swell of rain. The glow scurried away, hiding in the cracks of the wall panelling, making a quiet, chittering sound as it moved. Reihan touched her arm with her cold, white fingers.

"You'll be fine", she said quietly.

"Are you just saying that?", Phillippe replied with a wry smile, "I know what you have to do if I'm not."

Reihan held her gaze for a long moment, then shook her

head.

"It won't come to that."

"Won't it? Why?"

"Because I know you. And I say so."

CHAPTER 27: REIHAN

Lukacz opened the door into a spacious apartment. Its walls flared outwards, then grew into a narrow spire. Sheets of paper on strings hung from the spire's height, slowly turning in a breeze that Reihan couldn't quite perceive. Below, every single wall was covered with windows, all in the same monotonous size and shape. None of them had handles with which they could be opened. In the darkness of the night, the glowing kites looked like blue and purple stars that had fallen from another galaxy, their beauty inescapable from this solitary viewing platform. On the side of the apartment was a small kitchen island that looked like it had never been used. On the other side, an unmade bed with a pile of sheets toppled over and collapsed on the floor. The fabric had curled around itself, and for a moment, it looked like the shape of a dead body.

In the centre of the apartment, a black fabric sofa stared back at them, wide-spread and fat, with enough seats to fit a dozen people. Untouched silver plates of chocolates and fruits sat on the seats, carved and arranged into the most intricate designs.

The sofa's only occupant, stiff and wide-eyed, was a young man. His eyes were large and golden, just like Phillippe's, and he wore an iron collar around his neck, heavy with a chain whose end disappeared into thin air. Reihan recognised his slender hands, his thick head of caramel-brown hair, and his tired, downward eyes surrounded by worry lines carved deep beyond his years. It was Alexander.

"Who are you?", he called. It was strange to hear his voice after only ever facing silence to her questions before. She realised she'd never imagined what he might sound like.

He narrowed his eyes, then jumped up.

"D-dad? Dad, is that you?"

Lukacz took a few steps towards his son, although he stayed just out of reach.

"It is. What are you –?"

He took another look at his son's frightened face and interrupted himself. His features softened, and he reached out to touch the young man's arm.

"Are you all right, son?"

"I – I think so", Alexander said, then his eyes flickered towards Reihan and Phillippe, the latter still looking like a poor copy of a seaver.

"What is going on, dad? Are you working for the Casino now?"

Reihan heard Phillippe inhale sharply, then she shifted out of her seaver form and back into her original body. Alexander jumped up.

"Is it –?", he started, his voice more breath than word. Phillippe nodded, the motion shaky, hectic, and altogether unsure, then he stumbled towards his brother, stopping only an inch before touching him.

"You're okay", Phillippe said slowly, "You're okay."

Alexander nodded, glancing up at him with uncertain joy. Slowly he buried his face into his brother's chest, then locked his arms around Phillippe's back and squeezed tightly. A moment, then another, and Phillippe buried his head into his little brother's hair and started to sob. Alexander moved his hands across his back.

"Hey now", he said with a small laugh in his voice, "I'm fine. You worry too much."

"You were gone", Phillippe said quietly, "I was so sure you were gone."

A minute, then two passed, with the brothers softly crying into one another's embrace. Lukacz said nothing but let go of Alexander's arm and stood patiently to one side.

Finally, Alexander disentangled himself and blinked up at his brother.

"Where did you think I went? I was here the whole time, I thought you knew that."

"I –"

Phillippe shook his head.

"I remember the vision you sent me, but how was I supposed to know where you were from that?"

"I wasn't trying to tell you where I was", Alexander replied, cocking his head to the side, "Reaching you was so hard – all I could do was show you that I was okay."

"Why wouldn't you try to tell me where you were?", Phillippe echoed, taking a small step back, "And how would I know where you were if you didn't tell me? Alex, I don't understand –"

Reihan felt a sigh rising in her throat.

Alexander blinked again.

"Well, they kept me here, together with all the other Casino serfs. When they threw you out, you said you'd come back for me. I knew … I knew you'd come back."

Lukacz cleared his throat.

"So, you are saying that Phillippe is the one who freed you from the Asylum?"

Alexander smiled an uncertain smile.

"Well, yes, of course."

He looked back at his brother.

"When I woke up from the Submergence, you told me we had to leave before the seaver found us. Don't you remember?"

"Godsdamnit, Phillippe! I knew it!", Lukacz snapped, then grabbed his oldest son by the shoulder, "Why do you always have to lie to me? *Why?*"

"I didn't lie to you!", Phillippe protested, squirming in his father's grasp. His eyes fluttered towards Reihan.

"Reihan! You believe me, right? I didn't lie; I didn't – I was with you when Alex disappeared, remember?"

She sighed, fighting off the disappointment already settling in her chest. She had to think. Make the rational choice, even if nobody else would.

"You were. I remember."

She turned to Alexander.

"Alexander. I was your caretaker at the St. Leopold's Asylum for the Mentally Incapacitated. Do you consent to answer questions that will help us determine how you were cured from the Submergence?"

The young man slowly nodded.

"I – of course. I'll answer all your question. But I don't see how I can be of much help."

He shrugged.

"It was Phillippe who rescued me. There isn't anything wrong with that, is there? He was the first person I saw when I woke up, and – I mean, I should say, thank you for taking care of me, seaver."

Reihan shook her head but couldn't help the small smile that snuck onto her features.

"There is surely no need to thank me."

Alexander took a deep breath as if to prepare himself for an onslaught of questions, but Lukacz shook his head.

"Not now. We need to get Alexander out of here, then we can determine who is responsible for his release from the Asylum."

Reihan nodded, but the worry lines around Alexander's eyes grew deeper. He tugged on the chain around his neck.

"About that. I can't leave. They tricked me into manifesting this collar on myself, then said it's now a permanent part of me. That I can never take it off again, and because of that, I can never leave this room, and I can never –"

He took a deep breath.

"All I can do is make those stupid game rooms for them. They said if I make enough, maybe they'd take the collar off —"

"Don't be a fool, boy. Just imagine the collar disappearing", Lukacz said. Alexander glared at him, and Reihan thought she saw a bit of steel behind his eyes.

"Do you think that hadn't occurred to me? I can't. Whenever I try, there's a mental block."

"What —?", Phillippe started, but Reihan nodded slowly.

"It makes sense. Haven't you ever found it harder to manifest when someone has told you it's impossible to achieve the thing you're trying to do?"

Phillippe shrugged but Lukacz nodded. The seaver continued.

"It's possible that the Casino attendants used a containment technique on Alexander."

Containment techniques had been in fashion with Enforcers a few decades ago. They had been used to limit the abilities of manifesters who struggled to control their powers but had otherwise shown no criminal tendencies.

"Containment techniques", Phillippe echoed, "I've never heard of those before."

"As I said, they're not really in use anymore. They're based on the conditioning we seaver receive before we leave the Upside-Down Palace; basically, a lot of hypnotherapy and drugs."

"More seaver secrets?", Lukacz snarled.

"No. It was a Government initiative. But it was

decommissioned when people realised that, over time, this kind of conditioning erodes *all* manifestation abilities, not just the outbursts they were supposed to contain. So, in the end, nobody wanted to undergo the program voluntarily."

She hesitated and shot pale-faced Alexander an apologetic look.

"Sorry."

"Ah", he simply made.

"But even if Alex can't, surely we should be able to destroy the collar, right?", Phillippe said, "If I just imagine it opening like that –"

Nothing happened. Alexander bit on the inside of his cheek.

"The same happened before, don't you remember? No matter how hard you tried, even your powers couldn't affect the thing."

"Of course not", Lukacz said slowly, "Now that you told us that the collar is a part of you, that knowledge has created a mental barrier for us also. We'll need to be very careful to break it so as not to accidentally hurt you when we deconstruct the manifestation."

"Oh dead gods, I'm terrible at deconstruction", Phillippe groaned, and Alexander raised his hands.

"Wait, please, don't do anything reckless", he stammered, and Reihan guessed that he was now inadvertently strengthening his mental resolves against his father and brother's attempts at removing the collar. A clever bit of conditioning indeed, even if it could only work on someone who hadn't thought much about the intricacies of his manifestation abilities and who allowed himself to be taken in by authoritarian claims of inevitability. A perfect trap for Alexander, newly powerful and frightened out of his mind.

She sighed and stepped next to Alexander, then raised her hands.

"Wait, what are you –", he started, but before he could finish his sentence, the seaver grabbed the collar and pulled it apart with her newfound strength. It broke, then fell on the floor with a loud clatter.

Silence sat between them for a moment.

"I suppose we could just do that", Lukacz said drily.

"Let's just get out of here", Reihan said, trying and failing not to sound smug.

Phillippe held her in his arms as they glided down from the top of the invisible Casino, safely covered by the kites whose light soaked up their skin and hair. Reihan had broken another window, more eager to show off her new abilities than she cared to admit. Lukacz led their little group to his cabin, where he hoped Ellis could rejoin them. He turned around every few seconds to keep a close eye on Phillippe and Reihan, leading him to, on occasion, nearly crashing into one of the loudly tooting paper dragons.

"Do you –", Phillippe started.

"I don't know yet", Reihan replied. His body had already started to shift again. He was clearly uncomfortable with wearing the skin with which he had been born, but at the same time, she suspected he wanted to look like someone his brother recognised.

"But you remember that I was with you. I couldn't have rescued Alexander at the same time."

"I know. But there are still a lot of unanswered questions, Phillippe."

"Believe me, dear seaver, I am as confused as you are."

"That line is wearing thin."

"… I know it is."

They flew in silence for a little while, then suddenly, Phillippe flapped his wings a few times, and they were hovering above the kites. They stretched like a night-lit carpet, a shifting sea of glowing paper. Each kite had been hand-painted, as using manifestations for the festival was considered taboo. Bold, colourful lines, intricate depictions of fairy tales and myths, of flowers, of sunrise, of the beloved departed, and of newborn children covered the wide backs of the paper planes. Reihan couldn't quite grasp the sight. It felt too beautiful and too fragile to be real.

"I promised, didn't I?", Phillippe whispered. She loved that about him. That he remembered the little, inconsequential things even if he might fail her in every other way.

"You did", Reihan said, "I suppose that's the one truth I can count on tonight."

"I haven't lied to you, Reihan. Not really."

His voice was soft, and she wanted to believe him. But she had been here before. Seventy years ago, she had loved another powerful manifester she had been told to observe. A beautiful and loud and reckless human who, like Phillippe, changed his appearance with the wind of his whims. He had taken life less seriously, though. Somehow, and Reihan didn't know how, he had always sounded like he was starting to laugh or had just finished smiling.

He hadn't seen most of the destruction he had caused. Most of it had been his subconscious, inescapable repressions and fears taking shape just a few houses or corridors down. It had taken Reihan and Seamus a long time to put the pieces together. But eventually, they had. And even at the end, he hadn't lost the smile in his voice because he hadn't seen it coming. Not from Reihan, not from the best friend he had loved, and not from the seaver he had spent the best years of his life trying to impress.

Afterwards, Reihan had refused to act on her duties for a long time. Seamus took over most of her responsibilities at the Asylum. Strangely, the mixture of guilt and gratitude made their friendship stronger for a while, although Reihan suspected that, in other ways, it had never fully recovered.

And Reihan knew that even if she said 'never again' a million times more when facing the abyss she saw looming in the clouds, she would choose duty every single time. Even if it killed her. And one of these times, it would. She turned to face Phillippe and, for once, allowed him to see her afraid.

"Please, Phillippe", she simply said. He closed his eyes for a moment. Lukacz had caught up with them and gestured angrily for them to follow. Alexander flew closely behind his father and threw Phillippe an unsure smile.

Phillippe lowered his head to her ear, and his lips brushed against the edge of her skin.

"I told you what I am. You know I am not coping with this

power. I don't know what that means or what it will mean. But you think you do."

"I know, Phillippe."

He lowered his head to hers.

"Can you help me, love?"

"I think you know the only way I can help you."

He sighed.

"I know. I think that's why I never asked you before."

Their faces were still so close that she could feel his smile.

"I care about you", he said, "Whatever you decide to do tonight, I want you to know that. I would do just about anything to keep you in my life."

"Are you just saying that so I won't kill you?"

"Would it work?"

His voice fell to a purr.

"Aren't you sick of doing the Government's bidding? Of living your life to protect people who treat you like shit? Live for yourself, Reihan. Live for those you love and live *with* us."

"And in what world am I supposed to do that? In the one that you and people like you destroy with your recklessness? I wouldn't follow orders that made no sense to me, Phillippe. It's just that they always do."

"Maybe you just need to trust us more", he said, flippant like he always was when he ran out of arguments, "Maybe we'd surprise you."

"Ah. Maybe."

She laughed at the absurdity of her response, and he joined her a few moments later. The Upper City slowly came into view, and the carpet of kites became smaller.

"Look", he said, "I didn't free Alexander. I wouldn't have lied about that. And I think deep inside you know that."

"Do I?", she asked, "Maybe you realised that curing the Submergence would put you on every dissection board available to Government."

"It would?"

"Phillippe. I thought we were past pretending with each other."

"Fine. Maybe it would have made sense to lie. If I didn't so desperately want to show everyone that I didn't effectively kill my brother with the Submergence. But I wouldn't have just left him at the Casino. I want Alex back. I would do anything to –"

He lowered his eyes.

"Anything again?", she echoed, "So, where does duty fall when it is torn in two?"

She wasn't mad at what he had said. She wasn't even truly surprised. Hers was the ghost of a life, a shadow hunting shadows so the humans could live in the sun. And, in the end, humans always chose each other.

Phillippe slowly shook his head.

"I don't know."

CHAPTER 28: REIHAN

Lukacz's living room was bursting at the seams. Phillippe and Alexander sat beside each other on the windowsill, slightly hunched over, slightly closer together than they needed to be, and looking slightly guilty, like children who had stolen a bag of sweets. Ellis, slightly worse for wear but otherwise unharmed, sat perched in Lukacz's cold fireplace, licking a spot on her wrist where some skin had been torn off. Lukacz stood in front of the closed door to the hallway as if he could somehow prevent everyone from leaving before they had cleared all this up. And Reihan sat on the edge of Lukacz's empty table in a pose that she hoped suggested nonchalance.

"So, you're the other one of boss man's kids. Jeez. Honestly never took him for a family man. 'Specially when he's so fond of doling out suicide commandos", Ellis said in Alexander's general direction, although the comment was aimed at Lukacz. The Overseer sighed.

"I asked you if you were all right, and you said you were."

"Yeah. Just peachy. Love being shot at from not one, not two, not three, not four, but sixteen different directions. Really gets the blood pumping. Or whatever nightmare juice us lot run on."

"It's a mixture of rum and flour", Reihan said drily. Ellis glared up at her.

"What?"

"It's … it was a joke", the seaver replied. The nightmare stared at her for a few moments, then wordlessly went back to licking her skin. Lukacz sighed.

"Very well. Alexander. Describe exactly what happened from the moment you awoke from Submergence. Leave nothing out."

Alexander nodded and opened his mouth, but Reihan interrupted him.

"Please be aware that this is an official Enforcement investigation into the cure of your Submergence and your illegal removal from the St. Leopold's Asylum for the Mentally Incapacitated. Anything you say here will be used to find and apprehend the culprit."

She glanced over at Phillippe, who shot her a mildly defiant glance.

"And Phillippe, please be aware that you are now officially accused of the illegal removal of your brother from the St. Leopold's Asylum – "

"Very good, Reihan, I'm sure everyone knows why they are here", Lukacz said sharply, "Now, please, Alexander. Begin."

Alexander nodded. For a moment, he looked like he was

unsure whether he should get up from the windowsill, but with a look at his brother, he remained seated.

"I woke up", he muttered. His voice was drowsy.

"Do you remember what exactly caused you to wake?", Reihan asked.

Alexander hesitated for a long while, then he shook his head. They waited in tense silence until he finally spoke again, clearly obliged by their patience.

"I felt like I was chasing one dream after another. Then a bit of the dream started falling apart until all that was left was reality. I suppose."

He frowned, resentment clouding his expression.

"It was awful. Like a blanket being ripped from you at the same time as you're drenched in ice-cold water."

"So, you didn't want to wake up?", Reihan pressed.

Alexander hesitated.

"I guess in the moment, I didn't. Not really. But I didn't really think about what that meant for everyone else. Knowing how worried people were – I would want to wake up. Of course."

"It's okay, Alex. You weren't yourself", Phillippe said. Alexander turned around to him and opened his mouth as if to argue but then closed it again.

"Yeah. I guess not", he finally muttered.

Lukacz motioned him to continue.

"Well, I woke up in a white room. Everything was white, I mean; the chair in which I sat, the bed in the corner, the walls, the door. Even the window was tinted white. I thought I had gone mad or something."

"You were in the Asylum", Reihan said, then added a little sheepishly, "The white is supposed to create a soothing atmosphere."

Ellis cackled.

"Well, I mean, I guess I can see that", Alexander replied quickly.

"And you say I was in the room with you?", Phillippe asked, his voice perfectly neutral.

"You were", Alexander replied immediately, "You stood by the window, smiling at me. The first thing you said was 'good morning'."

"I would never be that smooth", Phillippe muttered. Ellis laughed again.

"Got a point there, wonder boy."

"We are not rendering a verdict just yet", Lukacz reminded them with raised eyebrows, "Alexander, please continue."

"Well, you – Phillippe said we needed to leave before the seaver realised I'd woken up. I asked him why. Because I hadn't done anything wrong, and the seaver don't hurt you unless you've done something wrong."

"Ideally, we don't – ah, point taken", Reihan sighed.

Alexander stared at her. Ellis bounced back and forth, distracted enough by the interaction that she forgot to lick her skin.

"Well", he continued, "Phillippe said they'd keep him there by force to ask how he cured the Submergence. He said that what he'd done would only work on me, but he didn't explain why."

"Did you even bother to ask him?", Lukacz interrupted him. Alexander shrugged.

"I did, a few times. But eventually, he made me promise not to ask again. He said that it was too hard to explain. It clearly made him upset, so I didn't push it."

"Why would I – listen, this was obviously an imposter wearing my face", Phillippe said, "If I could, I would have tried to cure everyone else in the Asylum. Reihan, I've offered to help them before. You remember, right?"

"I do", Reihan said, thinking back to Phillippe's insistence on helping to unravel the effects of the despair manifestation.

"That certainly doesn't sound like you", she added. Alexander threw her an unsure look, then he continued.

"We left the Asylum not long after. Phillippe turned himself into a seaver, and we walked straight out. Then I told him that I wanted to go home, and we went to the Undercity."

"I knew it! I knew you'd go there", Phillippe said.

"Weird thing about that, actually", Alexander interjected, "When I told you that I wanted to go home, you didn't know where I meant. Or rather, you wanted to take me to the Brothel."

"I wouldn't think of that as home", Phillippe said with a frown.

"Again, I can attest to that", Reihan said, rubbing her temples.

"So, if you went to the Undercity, how did you end up in the

Casino?", Lukacz asked. Alexander's face fell.

"I was being an idiot", he muttered, "It was my fault, really."

Lukacz waited for a few moments, then exchanged a glance with Ellis, who motioned him to approach his son. Lukacz put a hand on Alexander's arm and said quietly:

"We have all made mistakes, son. Few of those are irreversible. You are here now, and you are safe. All I need from you is a list of people who were involved in keeping you at the Casino."

Alexander glanced up at him with evident gratitude. Phillippe looked over and scoffed quietly.

"It was old Emmett", Alexander explained, "You remember, the guy who lived just down the road from us in the Undercity."

He looked at Phillippe and Lukacz, who both nodded. Phillippe groaned.

"That's who you were talking about in the vision."

"Gods, that vision", Alexander said slowly, "My head was so muddled from trying to reach you like that. I felt like me was melting into you."

"And that's exactly why that type of mental linking is forbidden", Reihan said, "You're not on trial here, Alexander, so I'll let it slide, but please make sure you never do it again."

"Oh", Alexander made, his cheeks colouring, "Sorry, seaver. I didn't – I didn't know."

"I know you didn't", Reihan said, trying to soften her tone, "Please continue."

Alexander nodded.

"Well, Emmett spotted me when we were walking home and asked how I got better. After I explained what had happened, he offered us to stay with him. He said it would be better for us to stay hidden because the seaver and the Enforcers might come looking for us in our old house. He said they'd run tests on us to see how Phillippe managed to cure me. You – Phillippe really freaked out."

He started cracking his knuckles, a quiet melody to accompany his words.

"I don't know why I agreed to it. But Phillippe was acting weird, and I didn't see anyone else I recognised. Dad, you were still gone, and – I guess I didn't see a reason not to trust him. So, we stayed with him, just trying to lay low."

He gulped.

"During that time, I figured out that my manifestation powers got pretty powerful. Like, whatever the Submergence did to me, it stuck. Suddenly, I could conjure up food, clothes, jewels, everything. Emmett got really excited, and he asked me to manifest more and more stuff. He said he could move us into a better district if we got together enough high-quality wares to bribe an Enforcer. Then he disappeared for a few days."

He sighed.

"Phillippe said we should leave. He didn't trust Emmett, said he was just using me. But I've known Emmett since I was a kid, you know. You were friends with him, weren't you, dad?"

"I was", Lukacz said slowly, "But that was a long time ago."

"Let me guess, let me guess", Ellis said, perking up from the fireplace, "He sold you to the people running the Casino. Then got himself a swanky little position and a nice little mansion in the Upper City."

"How do you –?"

"Because it's predictable, sweet cheeks. Humans are all predictable."

Alexander sighed and nodded.

"Initially, it seemed like a good idea. We had to live somewhere, and Emmett's hut was pretty small. Up here in the Casino, they had this whole big apartment where we could stay, and all I'd have to do was create the game rooms. It sounded fun. I always liked the idea of creating these big fantastical worlds, and Phillippe and I –. Well, anyway, Emmett said the people in the Casino would keep us safe from the Enforcers until they'd forgotten about us."

"Until you realised they weren't letting you leave", Reihan said, frowning. Alexander nodded.

"Yeah. Emmett stopped visiting pretty soon. The last time I saw him was weeks ago. I asked him why I couldn't leave the apartments even if I were disguised as someone else, and he tricked me into putting on this damned collar, saying that it was insurance to make sure I wouldn't run away."

"How in the world were you dumb enough to –?", Ellis started, but Lukacz interrupted her.

"Ellis. We all make mistakes, don't we?"

The nightmare stared at him defiantly, but eventually she

nodded. Lukacz turned back to his son.

"You mentioned that they forced Phillippe to leave at some point, correct?"

Alexander nodded.

"That was the seaver. Once Phillippe figured out what the collar did, he tried to remove it. And he wouldn't stop trying – once, he nearly ripped my head off. After that, this whole troop of seaver burst into the room and threw Phillippe out of the window. He kept trying to teleport back into the room, but then an Enforcer came inside and changed the room so much that Phillippe's teleportation didn't connect anymore."

He looked up at his brother, whose eyes were torn between pity and confusion.

"That was the last time I saw you. Until today."

He elongated his smile until it melted into regret.

"I'm sorry if I was supposed to pretend you hadn't rescued me. I was just so happy to see you that I wasn't thinking. I'm sorry."

"No! No, it's fine, Alex", Phillippe said immediately and moved his arm across his little brother's shoulders, "You didn't do anything wrong. I'm just happy you're okay. That's all that matters."

"I wish I could agree", Lukacz said with a sigh, "But we still need to determine the identity of Alexander's rescuer. Whoever that is has knowledge on how to cure the Submergence, and that is knowledge we need access to."

He glared at Phillippe.

"And you are still the most likely candidate, son."

"Look, boss man, I hate to say it, but I don't see how it could have been wonder boy", Ellis said and stood up. She paced around the room until she stood beside Reihan, keeping a cautious eye on the seaver.

"If he stayed with Alex in the Casino all this time, he couldn't have been running round the city like a headless chicken looking for that same lost boy. He couldn't have done his shifts at the Brothel either, and in the Casino they said nothin' about him being fired or anything."

"But there were many clients that you did not show up for", Lukacz replied, "I checked in with your boss regarding your attendance."

"Look, you wouldn't want to see those people either", Phillippe replied haughtily.

Reihan shook her head.

"During the time when we were looking for Alexander, Phillippe visited me at the Asylum almost every day. Many of the seaver that work there can confirm that they saw him, too."

"So, look. It was obviously someone who took on my appearance so that Alex would trust them", Phillippe said, still pressing his brother into his side.

Lukacz nodded.

"Say I buy this explanation. This mysterious person modelled their appearance after a body you have very seldom worn since you came into any prominence and, importantly, since you left Alexander at the Asylum. Leaving the question of how they would have known what you truly looked like if they hadn't selected you as a target before the Submergence occurred."

"And before that, there would have been no motive to abduct Alexander", Reihan said slowly. Lukacz nodded.

"Exactly. That, and this mysterious rescuer seems to have operated without a clear plan. They were not trying to exploit Alexander's powers in the way Emmett did. And they were unable to foresee or, at least, prevent the deception that took place and allowed Alexander to be captured by the Casino owners. This doesn't sound like the handiwork of someone playing a long enough game to have learned of Phillippe's original appearance."

"Alexander", Reihan said, "Can you tell us anything of note about this Phillippe who rescued you? Anything you found strange, anything at all?"

Alexander hesitated, then shook his head.

"I … it's hard to say. He didn't know where we lived in the Undercity. And I guess he – I mean, he knew everything about me. Everything there is to know, every stupid little story we'd ever made up together. But whenever I reminded him about something from his own past, he seemed a little lost. He said he lost many memories from when he Submerged himself in the mind fog."

He exhaled slowly.

"I didn't really question it. I mean, it made sense – I remember how disoriented I felt in the months before I became fully Submerged. I guess I was a little scared that the same thing that happened to me was happening to him. But he still refused to tell me how he cured the Submergence whenever I asked."

"And you didn't find that suspicious?", Lukacz pressed. Alexander shook his head.

"Well, no! Because he knew all this other stuff. He knew about Lady Marian and the walking tree trunks. He knew about the wind horses and … well. How would he know about all that? Phillippe and I have been making up these stories since we were children. We never told anyone else about them."

He turned back around to his brother.

"I just don't understand", he said, now with clear hurt in his voice, "What is happening, Phillippe? Did you really not rescue me?"

Phillippe's face fell like a house of cards. Tears glimmered in the corners of his eyes, and Reihan felt her chest clench with sympathy. Suddenly, she believed him. She unreservedly understood that he would have done anything in the world to be able to tell his brother that he'd been the one who saved him.

He despised himself for being unable to fight his brother's condition even when he had been stranded with all that stolen power.

"And still, I'm too weak. I can't do the one thing that matters. I can't cure my brother."

He had told her everything she needed to know. He had never truly lied about who he was. She just needed to listen.

"I have spent so much time wishing a version of me could do right by him. A version of myself that was better."

She closed her eyes. Dead gods, was this even possible? But then, why wouldn't it be? The Travelling City was a paradise of euphoria. With enough power and a strong enough wish, you could do anything.

"I know what happened", she said. All eyes turned on her. Ellis moved so that she stood closer to Phillippe. As if she could protect him from her.

"Phillippe. When did you start wishing for a version of yourself that could cure your brother? Please be very specific."

Phillippe froze. Lukacz stared at Reihan, then groaned.

"Fuck", he muttered, "Of course."

"Of course…?", Ellis echoed, "Of course, what? Is there a copy of wonder boy running around the place?"

"A copy…", Alexander mouthed. Phillippe stared at Reihan.

"I … It was a few months after I left him at the Asylum. I told you that I tried to fix him every time I visited, but my powers had no effect on him. One evening I came home and drank myself through the night, wishing I wasn't such a damned failure. Wishing that there was a version of me powerful enough to help Alex. Who could be there for him when I couldn't."

"That's why he could only cure your brother's Submergence", the seaver explained, "Why he knew everything about Alexander but so little about himself — or rather, about you."

Phillippe slowly turned until he faced his father.

"I didn't know that was possible, dad. I swear, I didn't know."

Lukacz nodded slowly.

"I know, Phillippe. I know."

He groaned again, then walked up and down the table, cracking his knuckles in the same way Alexander had done.

"There are theorems of this being possible. Not of creating a shade copy of yourself – that has happened before, albeit rarely enough. But of manifesting a version of yourself that is stronger and more capable than you are. Power becoming more than it was through the sheer might of a wish."

He shook his head.

"I don't even want to start to think about the implications of this."

Reihan nodded.

"If humans learned that this was a way to artificially create more power... this is extremely dangerous knowledge, Lukacz."

"Yes", he replied, with a long look at everyone else in the room, "I know."

Ellis stared at him, wide-eyed.

"So, what's that other Phillippe's deal then? Is he a shadow, like me? Or is he ... human?"

"He seemed human to me. I mean, but I'm not good at telling humans apart from shades", Alexander said with an apologetic look towards Ellis.

"I don't think we'll be able to fully decide this until we find the other Phillippe", Reihan said, "Which we must do, even just to contain the knowledge of what happened here."

Lukacz nodded.

"I will curtail this Investigation immediately. Reihan, you tell the other seaver to stop all communications on the subject. And you three —"

He glared at his two children and Ellis.

"Not a word of this to anyone. I mean it."

"You got it, boss man", Ellis said, quieter than before.

Phillippe shrugged.

"Fine by me. I'm just happy this is all cleared up and that —"

He glanced towards his brother, but Alexander did not meet his gaze. He looked down at his hands, wide-eyed and stiff.

"Please don't hurt him", he muttered, "He saved me. That has to count for something."

"We can't promise anything just —", Lukacz began, but Reihan silenced him with a glare.

"We will do our best, Alexander. The other Phillippe has not done anything wrong, so there is no reason to cause him any harm."

She spoke soothingly as if to a child.

"But we need to find him to make sure he tells no one else about the way he came into existence. We do not want to encourage anyone going down the same path to cure a family member's Submergence or to amass more power. This city is overflowing with chaos as it is. This would make things so much worse."

"But if this is a way to cure the Submergence, wouldn't that be a risk worth taking?", Phillippe asked slowly. Alexander tensed even further.

"Absolutely not", Lukacz replied, "Think about how many people would be encouraged to Submerge themselves if they heard about your story. And how many copies they might try to produce of themselves. The Enforcers and seaver already have to hunt enough violent, mindless shades as it is."

"And the city is already too full", Reihan muttered, "At some point, we'll tip over into the cloud sea."

"Fine, fine. I don't really care either way", Phillippe said quickly. Silence fell across the room until Ellis finally stretched far and wide like a cat. She yawned.

"Well, that was a fun mystery. Is anyone else hungry?"

CHAPTER 29: REIHAN

"Respond", Reihan said. The young woman opposite her stared blankly ahead, her eyes as glossy as a marble. Her dirty blonde hair had not been brushed in many days, and her clothes were dusty and ripped at the edges. Hannes had brought her in that morning when he and his Enforcer troop had found her sitting on the Weeping Stairs. Nobody knew when she had wandered there and how many days and nights she had stared up at the rock face ceiling without anyone stopping to help. Reihan would nail an inquiry about her family members to one of the notice boards on the Marketplace later that day. But she doubted anyone would respond, if not out of apathy, then out of shame. And anyway, the woman would have a decent life here. From what Alexander had said, she was dreaming dreams seductive enough to captivate her until her dying days. And wasn't that what everyone in the Travelling City wanted?

"It is your duty to respond if you are able to. You are now part of St. Leopold's Asylum for the Mentally Incapacitated, funded by the taxpayer", the seaver continued. Next to her, similar interviews were taking place. One was led by Ember, who had recently cut her hair high above her shoulders, revealing a small neck tattoo displaying a bird mid-flight. She and Freeday had been spending a lot of time together after Reihan had begun to observe Phillippe. It clearly did her good.

"It is your duty to respond if you are able to, lest you waste valuable researcher time and the resources of the facility."

No response. There never was, not once. It was easy to think that things would never change in the Travelling City, right until change stood tall and loud outside her door. For three days out of the week, she had moved into Seamus's apartment to help him with the cooking and cleaning and to help maintain his bodily functions until they would shut down entirely. It was hard to see him like this, impossible that this was the man who had taught her everything she knew about being a seaver. She expected it would take years for her to accept his death when it finally settled into the empty corners of her life.

"Under the Thirteenth Government of the Travelling City, you are hereby committed to St. Leopold's Asylum for the Mentally Incapacitated", Reihan concluded, then got up to lead the newcomer to her cell. This was her last interview for the day. The sun had already turned golden, and she didn't know where the time had gone.

Reihan remembered that they had an empty cell on the first floor underground. The ground floor was reserved for the Submerged with regular visitors, although there was frequent rotation as family members lost interest and unreciprocated friendships died. She walked down a dirty white staircase, with wallpaper peeling off the ceiling and lying in crumbles on the floor. Someone would have to renovate this place properly, but only some people still knew how to do that. Most houses in the Travelling City were a mixture of barebones foundations and manifested additions, kept in place by communal memory. But they couldn't have manifestations in the Asylum. Being close to so many seaver meant they unravelled almost as quickly as they were spun up.

Halfway down the corridor, leading the Submerged ahead of her, she felt the air shift and heard a quiet intake of breath.

"Hello, Phillippe", she said without turning around.

"You know, I could have been someone else. What would you do then?"

"I don't get many visitors", Reihan replied. She reached the cell and pulled the door open. It was clean enough. She'd send Ember down for a more thorough job later. Or maybe she'd just do it herself. No point in discouraging the girl just as she was finding her feet.

"Whyever is that, for someone with your sparkling personality?", Phillippe purred. He teleported right next to her and leaned against the open door. Reihan carefully led the mystery woman inside and lay her on the bed. She had had a long day. Her body would be tired, and they could do a more thorough physical exam after she'd had a few hours of rest. Things did not move quickly at the Asylum, and if Reihan was honest with herself, she liked that.

Phillippe wore one of his favourite shapes; an androgynous

body with large eyes adorned with sparkles and long lashes, slender nervous fingers, sharply cut black hair and small-heeled boots. Once Reihan closed the cell behind her, he reached for her hand and found it waiting.

"Reihan", he whispered, then kissed her slowly. He held her face between his hands and Reihan felt a sting of longing that she could never quite get enough of. He parted her lips with his tongue, slowly, as if he was at risk of promising too much, then broke their embrace to rain down small kisses on her temples, nose, and cheeks.

"Tell me you have time for a break."

She had tried to be stricter with the time she allowed him. Between making up for the days she'd missed and taking care of Seamus, she had not been able to join him on many of his escapades. He did, however, fly her up to Seamus's house or back down to the Asylum a few times a week. He had not asked many questions about the old seaver, but he had wanted assurances in other small ways. She had folded dried flowers into his jackets and traded some of her home-sewn clothes for a plain gold ring that Phillippe wore on whichever finger he chose that day.

"I can make time", she said, squeezing his hands between hers. His smile brightened, and they walked hand in hand up to Reihan's favourite courtyard. Phillippe manifested a pitcher full of lemonade, together with two glasses filled with ice cubes. The sun had settled between the courtyard walls, and it was still warm enough that Reihan felt her limbs melting into the chair. Phillippe poured a glass for them and smiled an easy smile.

"Ellis and I went racing again today", he said, pointing towards the skies. All throughout Summer, the city's inhabitants held races from the top of the Upper City down to the outset of the cloud sea. The race was an exclusive affair, as it was difficult to watch if you couldn't fly – although more and more ship captains had cottoned on to the popularity of the event and had started to sell tickets to watch the races from the comfort of plush airship seats. Phillippe and Ellis were still completing the qualifying rounds, and competition was fierce. But it had been a good way for him to take his mind off his work at the Brothel, and the nightmare had jumped at every opportunity to spend time with Phillippe.

"And?", she asked, raising her eyebrows. She wasn't sure racing was a particularly safe idea for Phillippe, given that he still struggled with his powers spilling over in wild and unpredictable ways. Then again, it kept him happy and preoccupied, and she loved seeing him like that. She had told Seamus and Lukacz that she was done with observing him, to give the job to someone else for all she cared. They had replied that it wasn't up to her and that she knew better than to pretend that, when it came down to it, she wouldn't do what she had to. But for now, she thought they could stick their opinions where the sun didn't shine.

"Five", he gestured at himself, "And second for little miss nightmare. Boy, was she pleased with that."

"Did she practice a lot?"

"Yeah, for sure", Phillippe replied, craning his neck back to catch even more golden sunlight, "Apparently, things with Lukacz have been pretty quiet, so she's had more time on her hands than she knows what to do with."

"Really?", Reihan asked. She and Lukacz had met several times over the last few weeks to update each other on their progress on the search for Phillippe's double. She thought the Overseer had more than enough to do between that and helping Alexander get set up in his new home. But, then again, she wasn't too surprised that he didn't want to involve Ellis in this particular search.

"Hmm?", Phillippe asked, his eyes closed.

"Oh, nothing. I was just surprised at the idea of Lukacz taking things easy for once."

No way in hell would she remind Phillippe about the search for his double. He had not broached the topic, and while he had to know that she was inquiring about his whereabouts, there was no need to discuss problems that had no solutions.

"How is your brother?", she asked to distract him. Phillippe slowly blinked as he opened his eyes and sighed. He took a big sip of lemonade as if to strengthen himself.

"He seems better, I think", he said. At his own request, they had moved Alexander into one of the abandoned houses on the side of the upper rock face. It was a long and dangerous trek on a winding path up the cliffs, and few people voluntarily lived there. However, Alexander had insisted on the location even though – or perhaps because – his powers were steadily decreasing, just as Reihan had predicted. As far as she knew, the conditioning that ate up his manifestation abilities was irreversible. Phillippe didn't accept that.

They had said that curing the Submergence was impossible, too, he reminded her, and she didn't argue. *Let him try*.

Alexander had commissioned his brother's help to turn his home into a puzzle box of traps and locked doors. Initially, Phillippe had just been happy to be asked for help after enduring days and weeks of awkward conversations. Until he had realised that he was helping Alexander create another cage for himself.

Alexander said that it wasn't like that. That he could leave whenever he wanted. He sometimes went to the markets with Lukacz, disguised with his father's manifestations, and he had once visited Phillippe in the Brothel. Apparently, Ellis dropped in on him sometimes, and they played increasingly complicated board games.

"That's good", Reihan replied, then quickly squeezed his hand again, "It's normal that he'd need time."

"Yeah, I guess."

In a long and overdue conversation, Alexander had tearfully accused Phillippe of not being his 'real' brother. Phillippe had teleported out of the house before he could cause any real damage and had lingered above the city for half a day, a dark storm cloud with poorly defined edges. Afterwards, he had crawled into Reihan's bed and had refused to leave it for two days. The seaver had read him stories she thought he might like and fed him tea and soup over pillows and damp blankets.

She knew he was finally feeling better when he climbed through her window late at night and stared at the sky. For hours, they watched the constellations move without saying a word. Alexander apologised profoundly, both by letter and in person, but Reihan knew that things between them weren't the same as they had been. Maybe they never would be again. But she could tell that Phillippe was learning to live with it. Maybe she really had underestimated him.

His newfound closeness with Ellis and Lukacz surely helped. His father dropped by Phillippe's tower once every fortnight to take him out for a meal. For days after those visits, Phillippe struggled to find things his father had tidied away while shifting through mountains of newspaper articles and flyers Lukacz had left him for art exhibitions, wandering library collections, and writers' workshops.

"How are things at the Asylum anyway?", Phillippe asked, just like he did every time, like anything ever changed here.

"Nothing new to report", Reihan replied. They hadn't seen an increase in their intake of Submerged patients, nor had there been more attempts than usual to cure their condition by concerned family members or friends. Wherever Phillippe's double was, he had kept his secrets. Reihan sometimes wondered how similar he was to her lover. Whether they shared the same smile, the same irreverence, the same sadness in which they draped themselves.

"And you still don't want to transfer to the Brothel? I'm sure you could ask your friend."

That had been a frequent topic of conversation. Reihan raised her eyebrows.

"I've worked here for a hundred and twelve years, Phillippe."

"Exactly! You must be dead bored of the place by now."

"By which you mean that I'm good at my job."

"By which I mean that you should ask for a transfer. Come work with me."

Reihan stared at him, then Phillippe coughed out a laugh.

"Not like that. Near me. Downstairs."

"Oh, *downstairs*! Why, thank you ever so much, master Phillippe, how could I ever –"

Phillippe stopped for a moment, looking horrified, then he caught the smirk around Reihan's lips and rolled his eyes.

"We could go out for lunch together. We're closer to the city centre, so we could make it to a café and back before our shifts start back up."

"I should leave a job I've worked for a century just so we can have lunch together."

"Why yes? Is there any reason more true, nay, more honourable than the pleasures of lunch?"

"You make a strong case", Reihan said, her smile widening.

"So, you'll think about it?"

"Phillippe…"

Her voice softened.

"Are you even sure you want to stay working there?"

That had been another common topic of conversation. Phillippe sighed and shrugged.

"Yes. No? What else should I do?"

He had applied for a role with the Enforcers, but after an initial aptitude test, they had turned him down. He couldn't deconstruct manifestations at all, which was an essential requirement for joining the forces. Lukacz had organised a tutor for him to work with, but after a few sessions with no improvements, Phillippe had stopped going.

"There's still a ton of things you could do. You could make things. Jewellery, clothes, things like that. Or, take some time to write. You've earned —"

"And give up everything I've worked for?"

Phillippe shook his head slowly.

"If it was just me, I might – maybe… I don't know. But Alex's powers are disappearing. If I give up my job, it'll be just like before. We won't be admitted anywhere. Won't be able to buy so much as a drink or a meal. This way, I can give him the life he always wanted."

Reihan thought of the last time she had seen Alexander when Phillippe had flown her all the way up to his house. Her lover had spent a good twenty minutes deactivating various traps and solving the rotating puzzles to even so much as be admitted to the front door. Alexander had stared at her, pale and wide-eyed, and his hands had shaken when he'd served her tea.

"You know what I'm going to say to that", she replied. Phillippe smiled sardonically.

"Yes, yes. *All you people can manifest at least to a degree. You'll never truly go hungry, and you'll never truly go cold. Hells, if you get sick, you can make yourselves healthy, and when you get old, you can make yourselves young, at least for a little while. Everything else is a choice.*"

"How gratifying to know that you listen to me occasionally."

"I always listen to you."

"Good. In that case, I think you should leave the Brothel. I don't understand how you can do all that with strangers when —"

She interrupted herself when she saw the sadness creep into Phillippe's face. She sighed and continued in a softer tone.

"The work makes you feel talented and appreciated even when you don't like a client. Believe it or not, I understand that. But you can find that feeling in other things. You just have to get over that craving for instant gratification. Some deeds won't be appreciated for many, many years. That's life."

Phillippe sighed.

"If I find something, I'll let you know. It'll be easier to consider my options when things aren't so up in the air."

Reihan knew that concluded their discussion of the topic. Maybe she should transfer, just to keep an eye on him. She could ask Seamus to make it happen if she caught him on a good day. But part of her didn't want to change just for Phillippe's benefit. She was an Asylum seaver, always had been. It was a draining, frustrating job, but it was hers. Most of the work was easier now that her restrictions had been lifted, particularly the parts where she had to lift the patients to wash them or where they had to be transported from one floor to another. Sure, her limbs took longer to recover now, and she had to spend more time in her wheelchair to make up for the excessive strain she put herself under to take work off her junior colleagues. But she'd find a good balance one of these days.

Phillippe smiled at her, and it chased away the sour taste of uncertainty.

"Do you want to go for a quick flight before you get back to work?"

"Of course I do", she replied with a grin.

"Where to? Your choice."

He always made it her choice.

"Top of the Upside-Down Palace."

She liked seeing the place from above. It helped to make all the memories and fears appear as small as they should. On the way there, they passed by the invisible Casino. Nothing had really happened to it after they had freed Alexander. Lukacz assured them he was working on arresting Emmett and the people he had collaborated with to contain Alexander in his apartment. It took time, as it was proving hard to pin down who was responsible. But with the entertainments shifting less frequently and the game room illusions losing their sharp edges, custom to the Casino had died down.

West, Reihan could see the walls of the Watchtower that the Enforcers and some citizen volunteers were slowly rebuilding. People had been restless and nervous after the explosion, and many questions had arisen as to why there were no bodies amongst the rubble. The Government had issued a statement that Cian'Erley and his fellow watchers had managed to teleport out of the tower before it was destroyed and had produced a relatively convincing copy of the childhood myth for a public speech. Reihan hadn't told anyone other than Phillippe about her adventure with Ka'a and had sworn him to secrecy. She hoped the Government would post a group of Enforcers in the Watchtower once it had been rebuilt. Or maybe this would be the one time the Founders would choose to become involved. Reihan doubted it, but stranger things had happened in the Travelling City.

They reached the Upside-Down Palace. Reihan had always thought that it looked less like a Palace and more like a factory, although many thin, elegant towers had been added to its grey walls over the years.

"Do you sometimes wish you grew up somewhere else?", Phillippe asked, his voice barely audible over the wind blowing over the city.

"Do you mean, do I wish I was human?", Reihan responded. By the hitch in her lover's breath, she could tell that she was right.

"No. But do you?"

She paid him the courtesy of thinking about the question in earnest.

"No."

She sighed, then smiled.

"But the Palace is a terrible place to grow up in."

She closed her eyes. Just for a little while.

"Tell me something about it I don't already know", she said, even though she knew Phillippe had never been inside, "Tell me one of your stories."

The End.

Thanks for reading! If you enjoyed *The Travelling City*, why not review it on Amazon?

ABOUT THE AUTHOR

Adrienne Miller (pen name) lives in the UK with her dog, her cat, and her fish. She has loved Fantasy literature ever since her dad read her Tolkien's *Hobbit* when she was five years old. *The Travelling City* is inspired by her love for old-school role-playing games like *Planescape Torment* and *Baldur's Gate*, and the work of urban fantasy authors like Holly Black. *The Travelling City* is her debut novel.

For up-to-date information on other releases, or to sign up to the mailing list, visit:

www.adriennemillerauth.wixsite.com/adrienne-miller-book

Printed in Great Britain
by Amazon